BY NANCY HORAN

Under the Wide and Starry Sky

Loving Frank

Under the Wide and Starry Sky

NANCY HORAN

Under the Wide and Starry Sky

A NOVEL

BALLANTINE BOOKS · NEW YORK

Copyright © 2013 by Nancy Drew Horan

Published in the United States by Ballantine Books, an imprint of
Random House, a division of Random House LLC,
a Penguin Random House Company, New York.

BALLANTINE and the HOUSE colophon are registered trademarks of Random House LLC

Library of Congress Cataloging-in-Publication Data
Horan, Nancy.
Under the wide and starry sky : a novel / Nancy Horan.
pages   cm.
ISBN 978-0-345-51653-4 (hardback)—ISBN 978-0-345-53882-6 (ebook)
1. Stevenson, Robert Louis, 1850–1894.—Fiction.   2. Stevenson,
Fanny Van de Grift, 1840–1914.—Fiction.   3. Authors—Fiction.
I. Title.
PS3608.O725U53 2014
813'.6—dc23   2013021057

Printed in the United States of America on acid-free paper

www.ballantinebooks.com

2 4 6 8 9 7 5 3 1

First Edition

Frontispiece and part-title images: © iStockphoto.com

For my sons,
Ben and Harry

Out of my country and myself I go.

—Robert Louis Stevenson

Part One

CHAPTER 1

⌒

1875

"Where are the dogs?" Sammy asked, staring up at her.

Fanny Osbourne stood at the boat's rail, holding an umbrella against the August drizzle. Her feet were planted apart, and each of her boys leaned against a leg. Around them, a forest of masts creaked in the dark harbor. She searched the distance for the shape of a city. Here and there smudges of light promised Antwerp was waiting, just beyond the pier.

"We'll see the dogs tomorrow," she told him.

"Are they sleeping now?" the boy asked.

"Yes, they're surely sleeping."

Lanterns illuminated the other passengers, whose weary faces reflected her own fatigue. After a ten-day Atlantic crossing, she and the children had transferred to this paddleboat for the tail end of their journey, across the English Channel to Antwerp. Now they huddled on deck among the others—mostly American and English businessmen—waiting for some sign that they could disembark.

Fanny had begun spinning stories about the famous cart-pulling dogs of Antwerp soon after they boarded the ship in New York. As her sons' patience waned during the long trip, the dogs' feats became increasingly more fantastic. They swam out to sea to rescue the drowning, dug through the mud to unearth gold, gripped trousers in their teeth and pulled old men out of burning buildings. When they weren't busy delivering milk around town, the dogs carried children through the cobblestone streets, calling upon bakers who handed out sugar-dusted cakes and apple fritters. Now, moored a few yards away from the great port city, Fanny hoped that the dogcart was not a thing of the past in Antwerp these days.

"Eleven o'clock," said Mr. Hendricks, the baby-faced surgeon from

New York who stood nearby, eyeing his pocket watch. "I suspect we won't be getting off this boat tonight." They watched a cluster of customs officials exchange heated Flemish with the captain of their channel steamer.

"Do you understand what's happening?" Fanny asked.

"The Belgians are refusing to inspect anyone's trunks until tomorrow."

"That's impossible! There aren't enough beds on this little boat for all of us."

The surgeon shrugged. "What can one do? I am philosophical about these things."

"And I am not," she muttered. "The children are exhausted."

"Shall I try to secure sleeping cabins for you?" Mr. Hendricks asked, his pretty features wreathed in concern.

The man had been kind to Fanny from the moment she'd met him at dinner the first evening of the voyage. "Why, art!" she responded when he asked what had prompted her journey. "Culture. Isn't that the reason Americans travel to Europe?" The surgeon had stared intently at her across the table, as if deciding whether she was mad or heroic for bringing her three children abroad for an entire year.

"My daughter and I will study figure drawing and painting," she'd explained. "I want her to have classical training with the best."

"Ah," he said knowingly, "you, too, then, are a voluntary exile. I come for the same reason—the best of everything Europe has to offer. This year it's Paris in the autumn, then Italy for the winter."

She had watched him maneuver a forkful of peas into his mouth and wondered when he had time to work. He was a bachelor and quite rich, judging from his itinerary and impeccable clothes. His soft black ringlets framed an unlined forehead, round pink cheeks, and the lips of a *putto*. She had glanced at Sammy next to her, pushing his peas onto a spoon with his left thumb. "Watch how Mr. Hendricks does it," she whispered in the boy's ear.

"I can see you have mettle, Mrs. Osbourne," the surgeon said. "Do you have any French?"

"I don't, but Belle knows a little."

Hendricks emitted a worried hum. "If the Old World is to work its magic you'll need to learn the language. Flemish is spoken in Belgium, but French is a close second. If you plan to travel at all, that's the better language."

"Then we all must learn it."

Having determined the fastest route to the mother's affections, the surgeon smilingly made his offer. "I would be happy to teach you a few phrases." Every afternoon for the remainder of the journey, he had conducted language lessons for her and the children in the ship's library.

Now SHE TOLD Hendricks, "Don't ask about the sleeping accommodations quite yet. Give me a few moments."

Fanny glanced over at her daughter, Belle, who shared an umbrella with the nanny. She beckoned the girl, then bent down to her older boy. "Go to Miss Kate, Sammy," she said. "You, too, Hervey." She lifted the four-year-old and carried him to the governess. "Do keep in the background with the children, Kate," Fanny told the young woman, who took Hervey into her arms. "It's best the officials don't see our whole entourage. Belle, you come with me."

The girl's eyes pleaded as she ducked under her mother's umbrella. "Do I have to?"

"You needn't say a word." Looking distraught would be no challenge for Belle right now. The wind had whipped the girl's dark hair into a bird's nest. Brown crescents hung below her eyes. "We're almost there, darlin'." Fanny Osbourne grabbed her daughter's hand and pushed through a sea of shoulders to reach the circle of officials. Of the Belgians, only one—a lanky gray-headed man—had a promising aspect. He started with surprise when Fanny rested a gloved hand on his forearm. "Do you understand English, sir?" she asked him.

He nodded.

"We are ladies traveling alone."

The official, a foot taller than she, stared down at her, rubbing his forehead. Beneath the hand cupped over his brow, his eyes traveled artlessly from her mouth to her waist.

"We have come all the way from New York and have experienced nothing but chivalry from the English officers on our ship. Surely there must be some way . . ."

The Belgian shifted from foot to foot while he looked off to the side of her head.

"Sir," Fanny said, engaging his eyes. "Sir, we entrust ourselves to your courtesy."

In a matter of minutes, the plump little surgeon was trundling their luggage onto the pier. On deck, the other passengers fumed as a customs man lifted the lids of Fanny's trunks, gave the contents a perfunctory glance, and motioned for her party to move through the gate.

"Bastards!" someone shouted at the officials as Fanny and her family, along with Mr. Hendricks, followed a porter who loaded their trunks on a cart and led them toward an open horse-drawn wagon with enormous wheels.

Near the terminal, masses of people waited beneath a metal canopy. Women in head scarves sat on stuffed grain sacks clutching their earthly valuables: babies, food baskets, rosaries, satchels. One woman clasped a violin case to her chest.

"They come from all over," said the surgeon as he helped the children into the wagon. "They're running from some war or potato field. This is their last stop before America. You can be sure the pickpockets are working tonight."

Fanny shuddered. Her hand went to her breast to make certain the pouch of bills sewn into her corset was secure, and then to her skirt pocket, where she felt the smooth curve of her derringer.

"Take them to the Hôtel St. Antoine," Hendricks ordered the driver as the last trunk was hoisted into the back of the vehicle. He turned to Fanny. "When you know where you will be staying permanently, leave a forwarding address at the desk. I will write to you from Paris." He squeezed her hand, then lifted her into the wagon. "Take care of yourself, dear lady."

LESS THAN AN hour later, ensconced in the only available room of the hotel, she stepped behind a screen, untied her corset, and groaned with relief as it dropped to the floor, money pouch and all. She threw a nightgown over her head and climbed into bed between her slumbering boys. In the narrow bed an arm's length away, Belle's head protruded from one end of the sheet, while Miss Kate's open mouth sent up a snore from the other.

Fanny leaned against the headboard, eyes open. It had been a harrowing monthlong journey to get to this bed. Twelve days' travel on one rock-hard train seat after another from California to Indianapolis. A few days' respite at her parents' house, followed by a mad dash by wagon across flooded rivers to catch the train to New York before their tickets expired.

Six thousand miles lay between Fanny and her husband. Whether he would send her money, as he had promised, was uncertain. Tomorrow she would think about that. Tomorrow she would enroll herself and Belle at the art academy and wangle a ride on a dogcart for the boys. Tomorrow she would find a cheap apartment and begin a new life.

She got out of bed and went to the window. Across the square, Notre Dame Cathedral soared above the other night shapes of Antwerp. The rain had stopped, and the unclouded moon poured white light through the lacy stone cutwork of the church spire. When the cathedral bells rang out midnight, she caught her breath. She had believed in signs since she was a girl. The clanging, loud and joyful as Christmas matins, hit her marrow and set loose a month's worth of tears.

If that isn't a good omen, she thought, *I don't know what is.*

She climbed back into bed, slid down between her boys, and slept at last.

CHAPTER 2

In the morning, dressed in a blue jacket and a plaid skirt, Fanny tied a red scarf around her throat. *Wrong,* she thought, peering at the mirror. With her olive skin and wavy black hair, the effect was too much the *contadina,* not enough the artist. She tied on a sober white cravat, then ferreted around in her trunk, collecting the things she'd brought to present to the school: the letter of recommendation from Virgil Williams, her friend and teacher at the San Francisco School of Design; her silver art school medal; the charcoal sketch of the *Venus de Milo* that had earned her the first-place prize; and a collection of Belle's best drawings.

"You will need to exchange this downstairs." Fanny gave some bills to Kate Miller, who was dressed and getting the children organized. "Take them to have baths first, then to a bakery for breakfast. After that, you should go over to the cathedral and walk them all through it." She handed crayons to Hervey and two drawing pencils to Sammy. "Make a nice picture of the church for Mama," she said.

Out on the slippery cobblestones, Fanny took in the morning foreignness of Antwerp. She let go a relieved sigh when she spotted a wagon filled with shiny brass milk cans being drawn by a large harnessed dog. Two army grenadiers wearing high black bear-fur hats passed in front of her, followed by women in winged white headdresses bound for the flower market with baskets of roses balanced on their round hips. A few doors down from the hotel, old women lit candles in front of a shrine to the Virgin. The damp air at the Place Verte was heady with the mingled odors of flowers, horse manure, and bacon wafting from the hotel's restaurant. Except for the dogs, all of it—the flower market, the preposterous headgear, the religious statues on street corners—surprised her, for she hadn't read much about Belgium before she'd set off.

Fanny had chosen to come to Antwerp, rather than London or Paris, for reasons she knew to be vague, reasons issuing from her gut rather than from a thorough study of tourist guides or school brochures. Virgil Williams had told her about the Antwerp academy, but there were a number of good art schools in Europe. She'd never met a Belgian, but she'd heard they spoke a kind of Dutch. Her father's people were Dutch and decent folks, mostly. There was a trove of paintings in churches and museums to be copied in the practice of landscape and figure study, though Paris would have served even better. She'd heard that it was cheap for Americans to live in Antwerp. That was the sum of it.

"Go study art in Europe," said her friend Dora Williams, Virgil's wife, when Fanny confided her situation. "It's one of the few respectable ways a woman can leave a rotten husband."

During one of Sam Osbourne's contrite moments, after Fanny discovered he was supporting yet another whore in an apartment in San Francisco, she saw her opening. She extracted a thousand dollars from her husband along with a promise of monthly checks, bought train tickets, and darted for freedom.

Now, with a penciled map from a porter at the hotel, Fanny found her way through a maze of narrow, winding streets to the old convent that currently housed the Royal Academy of Fine Art. A young man at the gate directed her to a stone building blackened with age. When she approached the carved wooden door, she noticed above it a frieze depicting a draped male figure in the Greek style, holding a chisel above a block of stone. Beside him sat a goddess clutching a handful of sticks—no, they were *paintbrushes*. She felt goose bumps rise on her arms as she turned the heavy doorknob and stepped inside.

"I do not have an appointment," she said in English to a man at a desk. "But you may tell the gentleman in charge that I was sent here by the director of the San Francisco art academy."

Monsieur de Keyser, his chest puffed like a pigeon's in his morning coat, examined the items the American woman had spread out on top of his desk. In the pregnant silence, Fanny sat opposite him on a chair so high that her feet barely touched the ground. Behind the director, from floor to soaring ceiling, important-looking oil paintings proclaimed the school's stature. Her eyes took in green landscapes, portraits of powdered aristocrats, still-life oranges on shadowed cloth. Was the looming wall of art intended to make prospective students feel small? That was precisely the effect it was having on her.

"Why, why were you not born a boy?" the director cried out suddenly, throwing his arms heavenward. "You could learn more here in one year than in five at your San Francisco school." The man was saying "it's a pity" and "on your own . . . six months of hard work on anatomy, then a year in Paris and another in Rome" when it came fully clear to Fanny that none of her work or Belle's would ever hang in this room. There wasn't a prayer that she could talk her way into this school.

Her cheeks went hot. She stood up abruptly to take her leave, gathering her things before he could see the tremble in her hands.

In front of a café across the street, a woman in an apron was sweeping. Fanny pictured what awaited her back at the hotel—Belle's eager face, Kate Miller and the children asking, "What are we going to do next?" Fanny went into the café to collect her wits. At a table in a corner, she lit a cigarette and ordered coffee, all the while looking up at the tin ceiling to keep tears from spilling. *What a fine mess.*

The scene she'd glimpsed this morning at the St. Antoine came into her head: women in pastel dresses breakfasting beside pretty pyramids of buns and fruits in the marble-floored palm court. She closed her eyes and heard her husband's voice bellowing in her brain. *What fool notion made you haul the kids over to Europe on such poor information?* How on earth had she imagined she could make it all work?

She reached into her bag and took out a piece of stationery to write a letter.

> *My dear Mr. Rearden,*
>   *We enjoyed a comfortable voyage over on a ship that was only half full. On the second day at sea, who should appear on board but our nanny, Miss Kate! I had told her that I could not afford to take her to Europe, and we all said our goodbyes in New York. But the girl is a loyal soul. She quietly bought her own steerage ticket, and when she showed up on deck, she cried and said she would not cost me much, only meals. And so we are a party of five . . . Belle had her first proposal on the boat. A wealthy cotton man from*

Kentucky asked me for her hand. Of course, I told him no. She is far too young. I had similar interest from a New York doctor, who declared his devotion every time he saw me. Quite a bother.

The art and pastry of Antwerp are divine, and you will be pleased to hear that the charming old wooden shoe has not disappeared from the streets. Alas, the art academy is just as old-fashioned and not nearly as charming. Can you believe they do not accept women students? The director was distressed to have to refuse us. He offered to personally oversee our private instruction. I am thinking on it.

We are having the time of our lives . . .

Fanny sealed the letter, addressed it to Timothy Rearden, Director, Mercantile Library, and imagined her friend opening it. She pictured him going over to the Bohemian Club after a long day and having a drink with her husband. Rearden had remained friendly with both her and Sam during all their marriage troubles, though Fanny's relationship with him was much closer. For a while she and Rearden were a tiny bit romantic, holding hands and sharing a kiss during one of her covert visits to his rooms. But they had both backed away from that kind of intimacy. She was still married to Sam Osbourne, in name, anyway. Even now she and Tim Rearden flirted some in letters. He was a confidant, a scold, an adviser, a brainy playmate of some stature among their fashionable friends back in San Francisco. Best of all, he encouraged her writing, which was her first love, far more than painting. And he was a great gossip. He could be counted on to mention to Sam the details of her letter. Better that Rearden, rather than she, break the news about her failure at the painting school. Sam would be in full-blown fury when he found out.

THE NEXT ITEM of business was clear: *Get out of that blessed hotel.* What they would do, after that, she hadn't a notion. Of one thing she was certain: She would not go back to the humiliating role of betrayed wife.

Walking to the hotel, she noticed a fine old three-story brick building with a facade that zigzagged in steps up to a peak. At the entrance hung a sign that read BOARDERS in Dutch, English, and French. Above it, etched in stone, was HÔTEL DU BIEN ETRE. She consulted her French dictionary. The Hotel of Well-being.

Dear God, let it be.

Fanny reached to turn the doorbell ringer, but her fingers missed it by an inch. She was accustomed to such frustrations as a petite woman. While other people might view each other eye to eye, she found herself confronted by vest buttons, tie pins, and bosoms if she didn't tilt her head back.

She opened the door unannounced and found herself in a front hallway, where she nearly bumped into a white apron stretched across the belly of a bald man who introduced himself as the owner.

"I am wondering if you have rooms for a family of four," she said. "Five, actually. We have a governess who can sleep in a room with my daughter. You see . . ." In a spurt, Fanny poured out her predicament— unhappy marriage, surprise nanny on board, rejection by the art school—after which she appended the fact that she couldn't pay the hotel's asking prices. The bald man's expression shifted from confusion to alarm to sympathy. Soon enough he was patting her back and showing her to a suite of rooms two doors down from his own family's quarters.

Elated, she stopped at a shop on the way back to the hotel and spent too much on a box of chocolates. She would surprise them with it after dinner. The children deserved a special treat. Didn't they all? It had been a long and wearing journey.

At the St. Antoine, she found Sammy and Hervey cutting capers on one side of the room, trying to make themselves dizzy. On the other side, Miss Kate sat on a chair, drilling Belle. "Pencil of the barber," the governess droned.

"*Crayon du coiffeur,*" Belle replied lazily.

"The academy doesn't take women," Fanny announced, dropping her satchel on the bed.

"They don't?" Belle sat up. "What are we going to *do*?"

"We will go on living. We will have breakfast tomorrow morning, one way or another. We will go to the American embassy and get help finding a teacher. What is *your* suggestion? And why are you still in your robe? We have to check out."

Kate Miller leaned forward in her chair. The young woman's eyes darted from mother to daughter to mother. Sammy and Hervey, who were on the floor, looked up cautiously.

"Don't blame *me*, Mama," Belle said, pulling the dressing gown close around her neck.

Fanny saw the concern on their faces and knew she was taking the wrong tack. "I'm sorry, Belle. It has been a frustrating morning, but a little bit funny. You should have seen the man who ran the school. He was so puffed up." Fanny thrust out her chest in imitation of Monsieur de Keyser and pranced around the room like a prig. When she came to the part where he bemoaned that she and her daughter were not boys, she tugged at her hair and waved her arms dramatically. The children giggled, even Belle.

"And what did you say to the director?"

"Why, I told him I didn't care one whit for his stuffy old painting school."

"Oh, well . . ." Belle sighed. "It was too good to be true, anyway."

"We'll have none of that talk. This is your *chance*, Belle. This is *our time*."

The girl looked at her warily.

"Virgil Williams says you have a real artistic gift," Fanny said.

"Virgil says this, Virgil says that. It turns out Virgil isn't right about everything, is he?"

"Go get yourself dressed!" Fanny ordered. "We will simply hire our own teacher." She lifted Hervey off the rug and settled him on her hip. "Did I mention I've found a different hotel? Pack your things lickety-split, my pigeons," she said gaily. "We have a new home."

CHAPTER 3

"Papa" Gerhardt—for that was what everyone seemed to call the man, including his wife—took Fanny and her party into the family's sitting room. There she met the matriarch, a shapely woman whose round flat face resembled one of the painted plates depicting the Virgin that Fanny had seen in a shopwindow. Surrounding her was a gaggle of offspring.

"There are eleven," Belle said to her mother.

"I think that's excessive," Fanny muttered under her breath.

The oldest boy, their translator, who hovered nearby, looked puzzled. "Excessive?" he asked.

"Expensive." Fanny smiled. "It's expensive these days to have a big family."

All of the Gerhardts spoke some English, though it wasn't necessary. Alliances formed instantly. The middle girl took possession of Belle, who was her age. Sammy claimed a pretty daughter about his size, and Hervey was adopted by the older boys and girls, who promptly began stuffing him with sweets. Fanny's family had arrived at a moment when everyone in the household was engaged in preparing surprises for the wedding anniversary of the parents. Soon the Osbourne clan was elbow-deep in the planning, too.

Fanny and Miss Kate settled the rooms. In the evening, with the children and nanny out of earshot, Fanny told the Gerhardts about the long and arduous journey. "There was terrible flooding around Indianapolis. The oats and corn were thriving when we arrived, but by the end of the week, when we were to depart, the crops were underwater. There was no train service out of that town, of course. I waited for a couple of extra days but couldn't postpone any longer. I decided to try to get to the next station by wagon. At least eight times, the horses plunged over embankments into raging streams. It's a miracle we didn't all perish. At one point, we went across a bridge. Just minutes later we turned back to see it collapse."

The Gerhardts registered the proper horror, but there were more details to the story than Fanny chose to share. She had talked to several drivers before she found one willing to push past the blockades and chance his old omnibus. Daring as he was, even he had to be ordered on. When they came to a shaky bridge that had not been demolished by the roaring river below it, there were men waiting nearby to alert people to the peril. The driver had not wanted to cross the frail span, yet she had insisted on it.

"As we continued our journey, word went with us from one driver to the next that I was bent on getting our train to New York and was not to be trifled with," Fanny said. "I'm actually a little frightened now to reflect on how desperate the whole enterprise was. I risked not only my life but my children's as well." As she heard herself tell the story, though, she was as awed by her daredevil journey as the Gerhardts were. The mother sat next to her on the divan in the parlor, catching her breath from time to time. The father wrung his hands, got up, and poured Fanny a beer. "Brave girl," he said when they all retired at the end of the evening. He and his wife embraced her.

The family was so familiar in its simple warmth, Fanny felt as if her Indiana childhood were playing out in front of her. The children practiced dances and piano and violin pieces and wrote little dramas for the upcoming party. Fanny's boys played in the parlor while the smell of frying onions drifted in from the kitchen.

It half-grieved her to see the tenderness between the parents, for it showed how poor her own marriage was in comparison. Yet she wanted her children to know what real family happiness looked like. They should know what to want. Belle had been a honeymoon baby; she'd seen plenty of happy times growing up. But the boys had come along later, after sieges of hard feelings. Both were conceived during fragile reconciliations. In his seven years, Sammy hadn't seen nearly enough of his father.

THE DAYS IN Antwerp filled up. Miss Kate, whom Belle called "the governor" for her large size, brusque manners, and the dark down across her upper lip, worked at tutoring Sammy while Fanny and her daughter went out for hours to view the most important pictures and often to try to sketch them. The Osbourne women were an oddity in Antwerp, which turned out to be a rather small town. When Tim Rearden sent a package in care of the American consul, it was delivered directly to their little hotel rather than to the consulate. "I believe," Papa Gerhardt told her, "you and Belle and your governess are the only American women in town besides the consul's wife."

Belle was right. Virgil and Dora Williams were not as worldly as Fanny had given them credit for being. "Europeans are accustomed to women taking grand tours on their own," Dora had insisted. "You will find plenty of other female students like yourself. Women have been traveling without their husbands for years—to re*invigorate* their lives."

Fanny had laughed. "Ah, to be reinvigorated."

"I don't believe they take their children along, though," Dora added.

Fanny had looked at her friend in wonderment. "That's out of the question. My children are coming with me."

During the second week in Antwerp, when she went to the cathedral with Belle and Sammy in tow, they positioned themselves in front of Rubens's *Descent from the Cross* and sketched furiously. Off to the side, she noticed a cluster of curious locals staring at the peculiar little American family.

FANNY INTERVIEWED A drawing teacher who told them to go to Paris, where they would find the Julian Academy, which admitted women, but she dismissed the idea. They would stay here for a while, pursuing their own course of study with a tutor. Many of the things she wanted for her children—for herself—could be had in this place. The Gerhardts had taken them to their bosoms. On the boulevards, the men in baggy pants and funny little jackets began to look ordinary. In her letters to friends back home, she changed her signature, abandoning the family spelling of Vandegrift for the Dutch spelling. Fanny Van de Grift Osbourne. She liked the look of it. Much more authentic.

One evening she noticed Hervey was listless. Earlier in the day, the boy had been under Kate's wing while Fanny was out.

"Who are you today?" she asked her son. Hervey was wearing a coat she'd sewn for him that was like those worn by the San Francisco firefighters he so admired. The costume was one of two she had packed for him. The other was a soldier costume. Sometimes he dressed half as a soldier, half as a fireman, wearing his firefighter hat and carrying a sword so he could quickly switch roles if the spirit moved him.

The boy looked down to check what he was wearing. "All fireman," he said.

Fanny noticed his yellow ringlets were wet underneath his paper helmet. She put the back of her hand to his forehead. "He's got a fever," she said to Kate.

"He didn't have it this morning." The nanny's tone was defensive.

"Draw some water, cool but not cold."

Fanny bathed Hervey, then put him into bed with her. After three days, when he continued to be feverish, she called for the Gerhardts' doctor.

The man poked and prodded. "In truth," he admitted, "I'm a little baffled." He wrote down a name—Johnston. "You need to take the boy to Paris to this man. He's an American. Very competent."

Within two days, Fanny, Kate, and the children were on a train.

CHAPTER 4

In the seat opposite Fanny, Belle cuddled Hervey under her arm, while across the aisle, Miss Kate read a book to Sammy. Fanny felt the tension in her body ebb some as she leaned back in her seat. Hervey was sleeping, his curls falling over his forehead. She smiled as she noticed for the hundredth time how different her children were; a stranger wouldn't know they were related. Hervey was a tintype of his father, blond and blue-eyed, with a gentle nature that was all his own. Belle's beauty was earthier: She had Fanny's complexion, the same wavy hair that went where it wanted, the same dark brown irises shot through with streaks of gold like cat's-eye marbles. Belle's looks were an exaggeration of her mother's, though; her eyes were bigger and bolder, her figure more voluptuous.

The girl peered out the window, lost in what thoughts, Fanny didn't know. She was so close to womanhood. Fanny believed their emotional landscapes were similar: Both were tenderhearted, headstrong, tough and vulnerable all at once. Belle was saucier, far more impertinent than Fanny had ever been to her own mother. But studying her in the fading afternoon light, Fanny found herself thinking, *I was that girl. I was that girl.*

She was Belle's age when she met Sam Osbourne, and she was standing on stilts in her mother's garden. Fanny was the oldest of the Vandegrift children, the ringleader of the pack, lively as a cricket and still playing at a child's game when the handsome young man showed up at the house. Sam was almost nineteen, far more mature and sophisticated than the boys in the neighborhood. He was bright, with a degree from Asbury University and an impressive job as the private secretary to the governor of Indiana. He was charming, and he shared her sympathies against slavery.

Did any of that matter to her back then? What do a man's prospects mean to a girl of sixteen? No, it was his handsome face, his pale hair, the slender cut of his jacket, the little Vandyke beard he stroked. It was the sunny way he could tease her out of a snit, the way he looked at her so hungrily. It was the romantic notion that he counted Daniel Boone as one of his ancestors. It was his shiny boots, for God's sake.

She had married him when she was seventeen, and within nine months they had Belle. They were all children together, really. Maybe that accounted for why Belle sometimes seemed less like a child than a sibling; often enough these days, she was taken for Fanny's sister.

Those first three years of marriage in Indiana, Fanny had sewn tiny dresses for Belle and made a cozy nest of the house her father had built for her as a wedding gift with materials from his lumber company. In the evenings, Sam made love to her in every corner of that house. He was full of ideas and excitement, though she noticed that he fell from time to time into slumps of dark rumination. To Fanny, the melancholy only made him more attractive. In those days, she'd believed such brooding revealed a deep soul. When Sam went too deep, though, she had to pull him up out of the mental holes he dug.

"Was he a soldier in Lincoln's war?" Mr. Gerhardt had asked one evening.

"Yes." She understood why he asked it. Sam had gone off with the Indiana Regiment to fight in 1861 and had come back a different man. Probably just as all the soldiers in Belgium and China and Greece, in every war since the beginning of time, returned home: changed. The small faults in Sam's personality became enlarged. He was bent on getting rich quick. He drank more. He was still loving and sweet to her, but he was restless in a new way. With the gallant intent of getting her sister's consumptive husband to better weather, Sam left her and the baby and headed out to California. George, their brother-in-law, died on the journey. Sam hadn't turned back. He'd buried George and kept going, on to the gold fields.

Fanny reached across the space between seats and felt Hervey's head, nestled in the crook of Belle's arm. His cheek was warm, but so was her own hand. She couldn't tell anything by feel just now.

"Don't look so worried all the time, Mama," Belle said. "It puts creases in your forehead. Go to sleep, why don't you?"

Fanny closed her eyes and returned to musing. *How trusting I was in those days.*

When Sam sent for her, she didn't hesitate. She sold their house and sent him the money so he could buy a claim in a Nevada silver mine. His letters were full of stories about gold and silver miners turned to millionaires in the space of a month. Once he sent her a chunk of ordinary-looking rock that had a seam of silver in it. Excitement ricocheted around inside her when she held it in her hands. She and Belle would have to take the same route Sam had, by train to New York and then a ship down to Panama, where they would cross the isthmus by land, then sail up the Pacific coast to San Francisco. It would take twenty-nine days. People worried aloud to her parents about malaria and bandits, about a comely twenty-four-year-old woman traveling alone with a child. Jacob Vandegrift gave his daughter a derringer pistol to put in her pocket. "Carrying all that cash," he told her, "you'll feel safer with a gun on you." Her father didn't know she'd already sent most of her money to California. She was short on funds from the moment she set out.

Despite Jacob Vandegrift's sober countenance and his occasional outbursts of temper, a sentimental heart beat beneath his barrel-hard chest. That day at the train station in Indianapolis, he looked bereft when he handed over the free tickets he'd secured as a stockholder of the railroad.

"What will we do without you, Frances Mathilda?" he said. "You are the *glue.*" Her mother had shown characteristic calm. "You're a sensible girl, Fan. You will be just fine. The world has a way of taking care of you."

Even then Fanny had looked much younger than her age. At the beginning of the journey, when she walked down the train aisle comforting five-year-old Belle, someone said to her, "Where is the child's mother?"

Fanny shook her head as she remembered it. That whole trip had been full of mishaps. She'd run out of money at one point, and a sympathetic passenger passed a hat to help her. Somehow she and Belle survived the journey. When the ship from Panama spat them out onto San Francisco soil, penniless, Sam had been waiting, and a few days later, they'd charged off to Nevada in a stagecoach, dreaming of glory. During that first year in Nevada, they'd lived in a miner's shack in Austin, where they watched their savings disappear down one barren shaft and then another before Sam gave up chasing silver. Discouraged, they moved on to Virginia City, where he took a job as a clerk of the court. Fanny sewed for the wives of luckier miners, and for a while, it looked as if they might get themselves upright. Then Sam began keeping company with the local prostitutes who populated the bars. It was a habit he repented of, only to take it up in grander fashion in San Francisco.

Why didn't I leave him sooner? After all the discoveries of his betrayals during their eighteen years of marriage—the love notes stuffed in pockets, the gifts that weren't for her—every time he swore he would change, she eventually reconciled with him. The last time was different, though. Fanny had been sitting with Belle in the Oakland cottage's parlor with the door open. It was a warm day, full of April smells. The young woman had come up the walk to the porch—how she balanced a hat on that preposterous chignon was a mystery—and announced she was there for "a friendly visit." Fanny knew from the clownlike rouge on the strumpet's face what she was dealing with. "Don't come a step closer," she warned. When the woman put her foot on the threshold, Fanny shouted "Get out!" and the brazen creature turned tail, revealing a bustle the size of a wheelbarrow on her ruffled behind. Fanny glanced around to find Belle, who had witnessed the whole thing, shaking.

Fanny walked out into the yard that day and paced frantically. She looked with new eyes at the ivy-covered house and her beloved garden, just breaking into bloom. The papery orange poppies that had delighted her the day before seemed pure mockery. For so long she'd tried to make a happy household for her children, despite the rancor when Sam was home. She'd been putting a pretty face on this life of lies, telling the neighbors that her husband had to keep an apartment in San Francisco for the sake of his city job, that he regretted spending only weekends with his family. When she was among their artistic friends in San Francisco, Fanny held her head high, pretending her husband's philandering no longer hurt. Sometimes she flirted defiantly with Sam's friends; other times she affected a worldly hardness. In fact, every betrayal she discovered was a humiliating wound.

Staring at the cottage that day, she knew she had to leave, for in staying, she felt as tawdry as the whore at the front door. The strain of Sam's unfaithfulness brought low the whole tenor of life inside the walls of the cottage, even when he was gone. Fanny carried his dishonor like a sign on her back. How long would it be before the children, too, bore the shame that was rightfully their father's?

From their earliest years, Fanny had read to the children, put clay and paintbrushes into their small hands, taken them to music and dancing classes with high hopes that they would acquire a sense of beauty. She wanted Belle to have the advantage of fine-art training. She wanted Sammy and Hervey to become educated gentlemen. She wanted a creative life for herself. But in the oppressive atmosphere of the house, where was the air for dreams to breathe?

It was with these thoughts filling her mind that Fanny had packed their trunks, announced to the children they were going to Europe, and made a dash.

Their time in Antwerp had been too short, only a few weeks. When she announced they were moving to Paris, Sammy protested, "But we just got here." He looked out the window of their flat and asked fretfully, "Will there be dogs?"

Gazing at her little brood as they rattled in the train coach toward France, she felt a streak of optimism. *Hervey will be back to himself in a few days. We probably should have gone to Paris from the outset.* She shook her daughter's knee. "Are you awake?" The girl opened her eyes, nodded. "You know," Fanny said, "I have the best feeling, Belle. I just know something good is about to happen."

CHAPTER 5

Fanny and Belle sat side by side at the atelier, sketching. On an elevated platform, a nude model rested her elbow on a fluted column. Rodolphe Julian, the proprietor of the academy, circulated among the aproned students who had positioned their chairs at different vantage points around the model.

"Pas mal," Fanny heard Monsieur Julian say as he examined a Russian artist's drawing. The teacher frequently said it while observing her work, too. She believed she fell roughly in the middle of these women: not even close to the best, though certainly better than the wealthy dilettantes passing the year in Paris.

She and Belle had hurried over to the studio early this morning. On Mondays a new model began posing, which meant vying with other early birds for the week's best positions. Fanny attended the classes spottily at first. But Hervey had improved so quickly under the care of the American doctor that she was free to come with Belle. In the morning, the students worked on studies of the head; in the afternoon, the nude figure. One week it would be a man, whose private parts would be covered, just. The next, it would be a fully nude woman.

This afternoon a soft light from the studio's overhead windows fell on the model's voluptuous body. The woman had bright red hair, but her face and breasts were not visible from Fanny's vantage point. So she made a study of the woman's round buttocks and full thighs, narrow ankles, sharp scapulas, and slender waist, where the impression of a skirt band remained. An elderly French student rose with a tape measure in hand and, without touching the model's flesh, measured her legs. "Don't torment the woman, Marie," someone remarked in a dry tone.

The others in the room were all women. Monsieur Julian was progressive on that point. He accepted female students but kept them separated from his male students. Someone had told Fanny that the women students were charged twice the tuition. She simply shrugged. Monsieur Julian had clearly seen a business opportunity—the squeamishness of other art schools regarding the propriety of women drawing from the nude—and seized it. Female students barred from entering the École des Beaux-Arts flocked to this place for training in academic figure studies, and they paid whatever fee was demanded. That was how things worked, and she wasn't going to complain.

The atelier was especially crowded on Mondays. The women shared stories of shoes bought cheap over the weekend, of romantic interests, of difficult roommates. They laughed about a previous model who had been forced to hold the pose of the Dying Gladiator for a full hour. He had patiently arranged his body as if it were collapsing but kept himself upright with one arm. He curled his lips and wrinkled his forehead as the expiring soldier did in the famous statue. One of the American girls shaped the model's hair into clumps to appear sweaty from battle. When the poor man was due his break time, the old Frenchwoman, Marie, had handed him a robe and sent him to the basement for coals for the stove. He never came back. The mention of his name, and the image of the fuming gladiator stumbling out onto the snowy streets of Paris in a robe, sent them into bouts of wicked laughter.

The artists settled into quiet concentration. Fanny's nose detected two or three perfumes, and coffee, and an unfinished salami sandwich buried in a lunch tin. She felt joyous to be working in this airy room alongside these gifted women. *This is what I love,* she thought. *The beginning . . . the possibilities.* At the School of Design in San Francisco she had accompanied Belle to classes and, in the process, discovered her own knack for drawing, as well as a thrilling new social circle. She had thought herself rather sophisticated in her painter's coat and white cravat. Virgil Williams's school attracted some fine California artists. But Paris drew pupils from around the world.

The schools here—the École des Beaux-Arts, Académie Julian, and Carolus-Duran's atelier—were of a different caliber entirely. Brilliance was common in these hungry painters who'd found their way from Russia, Sweden, Spain, England, Belgium, Poland, and a half dozen other countries.

One of Fanny's fellow students, Margaret Wright, was an American journalist with a wry sense of humor. Twice widowed, she was living abroad with her daughter, an artistic girl who was Belle's age, and a son just a bit younger than Sammy. Margaret had come over to Europe a year earlier and was supporting herself by sending articles to newspapers back home about life in England and France. Fanny admired her spunk and they forged a quick friendship. This morning she was sitting on Fanny's left.

"Did you go to the Louvre?" she asked.

"We did," Fanny whispered. "Saw the actual *Venus de Milo*. It took my breath away."

"I know. It just causes people to fall silent."

Fanny began to laugh.

"What is so funny?" Margaret asked.

"I was just thinking about when San Francisco got a copy of the statue as a gift from the French government. When the crate was opened, they discovered the statue had no arms, and there was a huge outcry. The Art Association sued the shipping company for damages. And do you know, they won."

Margaret rolled her eyes. "Americans can be such boors," she said.

Fanny scanned the room to see where Monsieur Julian stood among the easels. He came in every morning and spoke to no one as he rolled up the cuffs of his white shirt. To spare it from charcoal, he said once, though of course it was to enter his role as master, and to show off his arms, muscled as a barbell lifter's. Monsieur Julian cultivated a mystery about himself, but everyone knew he was once a wrestler. His drawings were tacked up around the walls, along with the work of his students. The master was bent over an American girl's drawing. *"Proportion!"* he exhorted as he slashed heavy charcoal lines on her composition. The girl, eighteen at best, with brown hair cut in a flat fringe across her forehead, blinked at the ruined sketch.

"Hang it all," she muttered, crumpling the paper and starting over.

The room held its fair share of Americans. Fanny suspected they were, as she was, positively gleeful to be out of their old element. When Belle learned one of them was the sister of Louisa May Alcott, she nearly fell off her chair. "It's Amy!" she had whispered.

For every *pas mal* Fanny garnered from the instructor, her daughter received a more enthusiastic appraisal. It was slowly dawning on Fanny that it was too late for her to be an accomplished painter. When she first arrived at Académie Julian a month ago, she harbored fantasies of becoming good enough to make a little money with her art. She worked hard to improve, as she had done with her writing. Now she saw her talent with a brush was rather ordinary. Oh, she may have won a silver medal for her work at Virgil's studio in San Francisco, but here, she saw she was outclassed. Belle had a chance, though. More than once, Monsieur Julian had put up her drawing as the best of the day. If only she opened her eyes to it, Belle could experience a finer kind of beauty in Paris than Fanny had encountered in Indianapolis or San Francisco. With enough study, she could actually be a professional artist—a portraitist rather than a painter of pottery. That was what many of these women would do: return home and make a reputation by doing portraiture or pursuing teaching.

Fanny glanced at the clock and saw their time was nearly up. She worked faster, adding shadow to her study. But the model was breaking her pose. The woman stepped off the platform and slipped a camisole over her head. The sight of her red pubic hair caused Fanny to feel awkward. An underskirt came next, then a dress. *This is no place for modesty,* she reasoned. And yet it seemed somehow unprofessional for the model to be so abrupt as she slipped out of her classic pose and climbed into her clothes right there in front of all the students. The models should go behind a screen to avoid creating the reaction Fanny was feeling now—as if a lovely dream had been interrupted.

THE APARTMENT ON Rue de Naples was in Montmartre, the highest point in the city. Fanny was pleased to get a whole floor for fifteen dollars a month, plus two dollars for the concierge. It had a formal dining room with tall mirrors, and a kitchen with a porcelain stove and a hydrant that brought artesian water up to the apartment at no extra charge. Her building was full of artists and poets who had formed a tight little community.

Once Hervey's health was improving, Fanny went out with the surgeon she'd met on the ship from New York. He would show up with a liveried attendant whose sole purpose was to remove the surgeon's elegant cape when he arrived and put it back on him when it was time to leave. Fanny didn't doubt Hendricks's interest and delight in her, but she suspected he was only pretending to be a serious suitor, and that his annual trips were personal dramas in which he acted the dashing American abroad. He needed a ladylove on his arm, and she found it amusing to play the part as he gadded about Paris looking romantic, with his shirt collar turned up and his cravat tied in a bow à la Byron.

Mr. Hendricks would help Fanny into his perfect carriage and ride through Paris with her, seeking cheap furniture for her flat. They delighted in looking for the whimsical old painted tin signs that designated a particular business. Enormous gray eyes peering through round spectacles signaled an eye doctor. They saw huge scissors above a tailor's door, a Napoleon-style red and gold bicorne hat outside the milliner's, a black tin lobster for a fishmonger, and an enormous fork for a hotel restaurant. When they found a sign portraying a chair, they knew they were in the right neighborhood. Mr. Hendricks ordered the driver to halt.

"I'm an old hand at making silk purses out of sows' ears," Fanny told her friend, who looked confused standing in the middle of one dusty shop after another. Hendricks was clearly an innocent when it came to junk stores. "It just takes some imagination," she explained. She bought the cheapest possible chairs and tables, after which the sweet fellow whisked her into his waiting carriage and called out to his driver the name of a restaurant in a better neighborhood, where he treated Fanny to a meal of oysters, *mignonnettes d'agneau,* and vintage Veuve Clicquot, interspersed with tender squeezes of the hand.

"YOU GET GOOD light in here," Margaret Wright said the first time she visited Fanny's apartment. They stood looking out the window of her parlor, with its view of windmills at the top of the hill, and below, the city's battered buildings.

"It's not the Paris my friends back home crowed about," Fanny said. Dora and Virgil Williams had seen Paris in the days before the Prussians blasted the city to rubble.

"It's a ruined battlefield," Margaret observed. "I know a woman who was one of the Commune people. She's quite poetic when she talks about those glory days. All the workers rallying to be heard in the new government after the siege, women demanding new rights . . . This neighborhood was a main outpost for them, you know. Awful how it

all ended. So many Communards executed, maybe right around here—
and only, what, five years ago?"

"Five years ago," Fanny said thoughtfully. "I was carrying Hervey
and setting up a new household in Oakland. I knew almost nothing
about it."

"How brave those people were, to stand up that way," Margaret
mused.

Fanny realized that when her new friends talked about the siege and
the uprising afterward, she lost interest. She saw signs every day of the
war that had been waged in these streets; on either side of her building,
the former houses were piles of stone and boards. She had only to walk
around the neighborhood to see abandoned cannons strewn here and
there. But it was somebody else's war, not her own.

"Your Communard friend would probably despise me," Fanny said
to Margaret. "I'm not very political. I can't bear the type of woman who
makes a profession of going around giving speeches. Oh, I believe in
women's rights in a general sort of way. But truth be told, I'm more of
a clinging-vine type."

Margaret burst out laughing. "You? A clinging vine?"

Fanny shrugged. "I don't want to be a stately oak that stands alone.
It makes me lonesome to think of the oak with no shelter, no support,
except what it provides for itself."

"Now, that surprises me," Margaret said. "You are the woman who
left her husband and brought her children over here so you could *paint*,
for goodness' sake."

"I know. How can I say it? I don't want to live the rest of my life
without a man. Someday I would like to find another . . . a good man.
Right now, though, what I want from Paris is some beauty in our lives,
some peace and happiness. And do you know? I think Paris, after what
it has been through, wants the same things."

Once Fanny had settled her family in Montmartre, once Hervey
began to return to himself, a wave of freedom washed over her. Away
from Sam and her family and neighbors and even her artistic friends in
San Francisco, she felt a sense of contentment unlike anything she had
known since she was a child. Six thousand miles it had taken, but at
last, the seething hurt inside her calmed. She commenced taking notes
for a story she would write about the new Paris growing up around her.

Maybe a story about construction of the basilica of Sacré Coeur, which was under way at the top of Montmartre. People seemed to like stories about European cathedrals. There wasn't much to see yet, but she might be able to sell a piece on the hilltop church to a magazine, the way Margaret had done, and make a bit of money to supplement Sam's monthly check.

She loved the anonymity of Paris. In Antwerp she had been a curiosity. Here, there were single women from around the world, going about their business with nary a second glance. Fanny was not new to the bohemian style of life; she had befriended writers and painters back home who fit the category. But the women at the San Francisco School of Design were subdued compared to these free spirits. *We are living among the lotus-eaters,* she wrote to Rearden.

She and the children were surviving cheaply, as most of the artists were, yet they hardly noticed it at first. For very little, she could buy cooked vegetables and slices of meat that required only heating. Her mother had always been fond of the saying "You can't get blood from a turnip." *Well, there's one point on which you and I don't agree, Ma.* Fanny had always possessed a knack for making something out of nothing. When the spirit moved her, she threw together onions, chicken backs and carrots into a pot and invited a group of students from the atelier to a jolly dinner.

Later, when she tried to recall the early weeks in Paris, she wouldn't be able to remember one moment of pleasure from that time. For by December, Hervey had fallen desperately, deliriously ill.

CHAPTER 6

It had begun with chills and swollen lumps in his neck. Then red patches appeared on his skin.

"Scrofulous consumption," Dr. Johnston said.

"Scrofulous?"

"He'll develop ulcerations. He will bleed. It's possible it is in his lungs as well. He may recover, or he may not." Johnston, whose kindly face sagged with sadness, looked directly at her. "Do you understand?"

"Yes," she said. But she didn't. Not then.

"Give him seven grains of quinine mixed with water to make a teaspoon. And spread this on him." The doctor put a jar of salve into her hands.

"It burns my eyes," Sammy cried, running out of the room when Fanny applied the claylike stuff all over Hervey. Belle had already made haste out the door on a pretext of getting a newspaper.

"I won't lie," Fanny said. "It is not the best smell on earth, but it's no bother if it makes you well. Isn't that right, Hervey?"

The boy nodded, covering his eyes with a washcloth.

"We have to do what the doctor tells us." Fanny bustled around the room. "You're going to be in bed for a while, sweetheart. It's no fun being sick at Christmas, but we have one another. That's the main thing."

There wouldn't be any Christmas at all, but it wasn't yet time to tell the children. Sam had written recently that he had no money to send them that month. With Hervey's illness, medicine came first and other needs after. The food she and Belle and Sammy ate was the simplest possible: black bread, smoked herring, soups.

At seven, Sammy suffered most from the lack of money. He was a sturdy boy, but he'd developed a wan look as he'd grown older: pale hair and eyelashes, light skin beneath freckles. In Paris, his pallor had grown even more pronounced.

Once, when Fanny went out to get medicine, Sammy accompanied her. Emerging from the chemist's, she found the boy, nose pressed against the window of the patisserie next door, eyeing the glazed fruit tarts. He was hungry for something besides stew and bread, and it grieved her that there was nothing she could do about it. Each morning he ate only a roll and milk before he walked out the door in his little uniform to attend his private school. At least he got lunch there and had a happy place to be during the day. Thankfully, the tuition was paid up through May. They were all growing thin, including Hervey, who had lost his appetite. Fanny gathered together a few pieces of jewelry and pawned them, then bought expensive foods to encourage the child to eat, but to no avail. When Hervey left untouched some grapes—plump violet greenhouse grapes that Sammy eyed for two days—Fanny quietly put them on the older boy's bedside table.

The winter days passed slowly. Her admirer, the surgeon, had departed a month earlier for Italy, and she wished she had not restricted herself so much to only his company. Without him, she had no male protector in Paris.

On his last visit to their apartment before his departure, he had looked at Hervey lying on the sofa, looked at her and the children growing thinner, grimaced at the shabby furnishings, and blurted out, "What will become of all of you when I leave?" It was not insincere, his concern. But it wasn't enough to keep him there. She couldn't blame him for fleeing troubles that he didn't want as his own.

Fanny fought off melancholy with sewing projects during the gray winter hours—patching stockings, making a costume for Belle. Mr. Julian announced that he would give a fancy dress party for the ladies at the New Year, and everyone was encouraged to come. There would be piano music, and the students already knew the refreshments: brioche, wine, and fruit. Fanny's stomach growled to think of it. She pieced together a colorful dress for Belle out of two old ones, and a headdress from the leftover material. Fanny wanted the girl to feel as festive as the others. She would stay home, but it would be a chance for Belle to escape the dreariness of evenings in the apartment.

Every few minutes, Fanny looked up from her sewing to observe Hervey. He was so thin now. Once his cheeks had been fat, and he'd had the sunniest disposition. She had carried him in a sling when he was tiny, when his head was smooth as an egg, and they fit together as if they were one piece. How vividly she remembered the day he was born! The midwife had held him up by the feet, and Fanny had fallen instantly in love with that little upside-down petal-pink face. He was her final vote of confidence in her marriage and the last good thing she took from it. How, in the face of such beauty and hope, could Sam have taken on yet another woman? Fanny knew then that Hervey was her last child, and she would keep him for herself. She would never say it aloud, but of the three, he was her best beloved.

During those lonely Paris hours, she sang every song she could think of to Hervey, and helped him hold a crayon in his hand to draw the lions, always in cages, that he preferred as his subject matter. When the boy slept, she kept herself awake by composing lengthy letters, cajoling her friends to write. *Do send me some gossip,* she wrote to Rearden. *You know I love to hear about our literary friends. But no bad news. I could not bear it right now. Above all, don't tell Sam that Hervey is sick, I beg of you.*

Day to day, she debated whether to alert Sam. The strange reality was that she could not discern how serious Hervey's illness was. In the past week the boy had been delirious with a fever, but then yesterday he had recovered. He'd sat up, smiling, played with Sammy, and seemed nearly well enough to go out for a walk in the park.

Rearden sent a letter scolding her for the reckless trip; he had put down on paper the words Sam was surely thinking. But her old friend—old sparring partner, more like it—included money to buy Christmas presents, and for that Fanny could forgive Rearden his cruel remarks. When the envelope arrived, she was sitting in a chair with the remainder of their cash in her lap, trying to imagine how they would make it to the end of the month. The surprise funds briefly brightened the miserable household. Fanny bought toys for the boys and new drawing pencils for Belle, and filled the kitchen cupboard.

Through the bitter cold of January, she kept two fires going in the parlor during the day to keep Hervey warm as he lay on the sofa. At night, she and Miss Kate took turns staying awake beside him. His sores had begun to bleed and had to be dressed constantly. His frail little body had to be shifted to take the pressure off new sores.

When Belle and Sammy returned home from their classes, they kept vigil by Hervey's side. One day Belle brought a newspaper and sketchily translated an article about a wealthy California woman who had taken over a whole floor at the fancy Hôtel Splendide. A picture showed a woman in a white dress and feathered hat, surrounded by her entourage.

Fanny studied the faces in the paper. "I know this woman," she said. "I knew her when she didn't have a nickel. In Austin, Nevada."

Belle perked up. "Truly?"

"Tell about the camp!" shouted Sammy, who never seemed to tire of the old stories.

"It was winter," Fanny began. "Belle and I hadn't been in camp with your father all that long. We heard there was going to be a party in the next settlement, a few miles away. I had brought a trunk full of dresses with me, only to find that they were far too fine to wear in Austin, Nevada. The camp was just a gulley of falling-down shacks, and the few women living there had to wash their things in the brown river water. No plumbing. No furniture. Nothing but a makeshift bed and a couple of pots in your father's cabin when I got there. But I did get to wear one of those nice dresses the night we went to that party. Somebody had made a sled out of a big wood box with some runners on it. There wasn't a mirror to be found in the whole gulley. When the other women came to get me, one of the girls held up a lantern and a metal pie pan so I could see to fix my hair." Fanny touched her finger to the newspaper. "This woman in the article—she was the one who held up the tin pan."

"Oh." Belle sighed, struck by the fairy-tale ending. "And now she's rich."

"At least somebody got rich," Fanny mused. "I bundled you up in a blanket that night, and we piled onto the sled with the other ladies and sang all the way to the next camp."

"Did I dance?" Belle asked.

"Like a dervish. I'll never forget you swirling around that room. You were too little to need a partner. Oh, and I remember that was the night I met that preacher, Reverend Warwick. He had two gold front teeth. I said to him, 'I didn't know there was a minister in these parts,' and he said, 'You musta heard of me by my nickname. It's Smilin' Jesus.'"

Sammy knew that part of the story already, but he laughed heartily, as they all did. How desperately they needed to laugh.

Fanny remembered the night in Nevada as if it had just happened.

At that party, she had danced until dawn, with a different partner for every tune. Some of the women, she learned, were from the whorehouse in the next camp. Later, Fanny wondered if Sam's philandering had already begun by the time she and Belle arrived in Austin.

"Will you call on her at the Splendide?" Belle asked.

Fanny knew that her daughter was wondering if she might work herself into the rich woman's good graces. "No, I won't," she replied. She studied the photo of the woman she had known. How strange to think they had been together in that hardscrabble mining town, each of them part of a couple bent on striking it rich. How could she have dreamed then that she would someday end up in Paris, camped nearby and yet a world apart, in a suite of cheap rooms with her three children and without her husband?

She realized then how much she really did miss Sam and how afraid she was for Hervey.

CHAPTER 7

B y mid-March, Fanny was frantic; Hervey's condition had deterio-rated badly. Three different times she hired a carriage to go out into the countryside to find a farm where she could get fresh oxblood to replenish the iron Hervey was losing through bleeding, then hurried back to the flat so he could drink it while it was warm. For several days she searched the apothecaries of Paris, looking for the ground-up bark of some tropical tree that supposedly could cure tuberculosis. None of the treatments—not the doctors', not her own—could turn the tide for her beautiful child.

Some nights during her vigils, she had to fight to keep her eyes open, she was so exhausted. Alone and scared, she made promises. *Please,* she prayed. *Please.* Strange events began to occur in the dim light. Staring at the fireplace mantel, she saw a vase and jug about to fall from the edge. Time and again, she jumped up to rescue them only to find nothing in her hands. During the day, she felt as if her feet were not touching the pavement. Instead, she floated just above it, weight-less. She did not mention the weird sensations to Belle or Kate.

One night while she was keeping watch over Hervey, the boy woke and asked for water. When he reached out to take the cup, she saw light streaming from his fingers. She wired Sam the next morning: *Come im-mediately, regardless of expense.*

Every two or three hours a new wound appeared. "Blood. Get the things, please, but wait until I'm ready." Fanny fetched the washbowl, bandages, and probe to clean each new opening in her boy's delicate skin. He squeezed his eyes shut and said through gritted teeth, "Now, Mama."

The pain of treatment was so shocking to his body that he would become violently sick to his stomach. Others in the household could not bear to stay in the room. Sometimes when he went into seizures, the joints of his legs and arms made a sound like the snapping of brittle branches. It seemed his skeleton and organs were disintegrating. Blood rushed from his ears.

Fanny lay with him in her arms, murmuring words of comfort through his hours of agony. She prayed that if there were indeed a merciful God, He would strike the boy unconscious so he would feel the pain no more. But the child never lost his mind. Despite his agony, he never cried out, not even when his bones, near the end, pushed through his pale skin.

When Sam arrived the second week of April, his knees buckled at the sight of his son. Fanny had tried to prepare him ahead of time, but at first Sam could not bear to look upon the child. It was Hervey who patted his father's head to comfort him.

Fanny watched in dumb wonder as her shy boy became precocious in dying. He said goodbye to Belle. He kissed the hand of Miss Kate, who had shown herself to be a storybook heroine in her devotion to him. He gave his toys to Sammy.

At the end, Hervey said, "Lie down beside me, Mama." And then he was gone.

CHAPTER 8

F anny's breath came slowly. But for an intermittent shiver, she sat
perfectly still. At the request of the other students, she had returned
to Mr. Julian's studio to pose for the morning head study. It was four
weeks since Hervey's death.

"So sad," the Russian girl remarked as she studied Fanny's face, running her forefinger along the contour of her cheek. The other students
gathered around. "Can you bear to sit?" they asked.

She could have said no. But these women had comforted her like
sisters during her boy's illness. Anyway, it hardly mattered where she
was. Here, at least, they understood her stupefaction. If they wanted to
draw despair, it did not trouble her to face them.

For two days she bore witness to her son. Sitting for the artists, she
did not see them. She saw only the gentle, heroic Hervey. How could
any of them begin to understand what she had witnessed: a five-year-
old boy with more courage in his tiny, wasted body than she had ever
seen in an adult.

It haunted her that his was not a proper burial place, but there wasn't
enough money to pay for a headstone, let alone a decent site. Fanny,
Sam, and the two children had walked through the streets to the Saint-
Germain cemetery behind the little white casket. There, amid headstones and statues of weeping angels, they clung to one another as her
baby was lowered into a small unmarked rectangle of French earth. As
they were leaving, the cemetery superintendent approached, followed
by a dolorous nun who translated for him. "Your lease will expire in five
years," the nun explained. "If you can't keep up the grave permanently,
the remains will be moved into a common grave with others." The
word "pauper" was not uttered, but Fanny assumed that was what the
official meant by "others." He pointed approvingly at a child's grave
surrounded by a small iron fence. Lying flat on the ground, the stone

was etched with the outline of a cradle and one word: *Regret*. The superintendent led them to a nearby grave where the figure of a sleeping woman, her arms crossed over her breast, topped a grave. *"Le gisant,"* the man said. He turned to another marker. *"Un obélisque."* The nun translated in a monotone. "The reclining statue. An obelisk, perhaps. These are some of the possibilities you will want to consider for your son's grave marker." Looking at the superintendent's pitiless expression, Fanny wanted to spit in the man's face.

"He died peacefully," Sam said repeatedly when they returned to the apartment.

"He did not! What do you know?" she shouted at him. She wanted to pummel him, though her husband had been only kind to her since his arrival. What use was there in recrimination? The man was suffering badly. But the loss did not bring them closer; they grieved at opposite ends of the apartment.

In the days that followed, she suffered searing headaches, collapsed from dizziness, lost her memory. She found she couldn't spell when she tried to write notes on the black-bordered stationery Belle brought home. After nights of wakefulness, when slumber finally came, she dreamed Hervey was uncomfortable, lying so long on his back in the coffin; he needed to be turned.

"You kept getting out of bed, trying to turn over your mattress all night," Belle told her in the morning.

Sam feared she was going mad; he said as much. "You don't seem to know I'm even here," he told her.

He was right. His voice was the buzz of a fly in the next room.

"You must go away someplace warm and rest," a doctor told her. "Your nerves have experienced a terrible shock. Sammy is pale. Too thin. He could fall sick, as Hervey did." The last sentence snapped her into awareness. She got up out of bed.

"I know of a quiet place not far away," Margaret Wright told Fanny. "An inn at Grez, on the Loing River. It's close to Barbizon but away from all the bustle, and cheap. It's near the Fontainebleau Forest. I'm going there sometime this summer."

The future, such as it was, assumed a shape. They would leave these heartbreaking rooms and take in the country air for a while. Miss Kate would not accompany them; she had turned up an old aunt in Paris who offered her a room.

In May, Sam delivered his family to the inn. Before he returned to America, Fanny argued for more time in Europe. "I want Sammy to be a gentleman. He has a chance at that if he attends school here."

"One year," Sam said. "That's all I can manage or tolerate."

CHAPTER 9

It was still cool when they arrived in Grez-sur-Loing. Nestled in the midst of vast farm fields, the village was a smattering of stone houses, a picturesque bridge, and a ruined twelfth-century tower with ferns growing in its cracked walls. In those first few weeks at the Hôtel Chevillon, they bundled in coats and wool scarves and arrayed themselves along the bank of the river—she and Belle with paintbrushes and Sammy with a fishing pole. Within speaking distance but silent and worlds away from one another, they gazed fixedly at the water.

The Loing River was just beyond a long garden behind the inn, a rambling stone building that was empty except for them. Madame Chevillon, a motherly sort, took it upon herself to fatten up the children, who cooperated with gratitude. Fanny expected her own plumpness—her loveliest feature, Rearden once told her—was gone for good. She was so reduced from her previous self that Sam had paid a seamstress to rework her old clothes and make an inexpensive dress.

The Chevillon was an eating place for a few men from around the area. They came in wearing muslin shirts soiled from the day's work, washed their hands in the kitchen, then settled down to mutton, wine, and local gossip. With its crackling fireplace, rows of pickled vegetables huddled on the windowsill, and pots huffing on the stove, the small room reminded her of an Indiana farm kitchen. The smells and the hum of conversations she couldn't understand offered some succor.

Margaret Wright had told her the Hôtel Chevillon was the most bohemian of the bohemian gathering places near the Fontainebleau Forest. "Barbizon has become too fashionable. It's overrun by poseurs more interested in the mise-en-scène than in producing any actual art. The real painters go to Grez," Margaret had assured her with authority, although she'd not yet been there herself. "And you needn't worry. They will leave you alone, I think."

As the weather warmed, Madame Chevillon prepared for more guests. White sheets flapped on the clothesline; broth simmered on the stove. On a morning in late May, Fanny and Belle looked down from a window on the staircase landing to see a black-haired young fellow step out of the *diligence* that had brought him. Bob Stevenson, a twenty-nine-year-old Scot from Edinburgh, was the first of the regular summer crowd to arrive, and he looked every inch the artiste type Margaret had described. He wore trousers that ended at his knees, stockings with red and white horizontal stripes, and a smirk.

Seated next to him that evening in the dining room, Fanny found him rude.

"There's an onslaught about to begin," Bob Stevenson remarked, filling his glass with wine. "Once the others start to arrive, you'll discover this isn't the place to be if you are hoping for a little peace. Madame Chevillon said you had come for the quiet."

"Oh," Fanny said.

"Is that right?" the man persisted. "There are places not far from here that would serve you much better if you are here to rest . . ."

"I was *sent* here to rest," she said, squinting at him across the table. Though he was just another young fool, he spoke English. "I had a son." Her voice sounded dull and distant. "My children had a brother. He died . . ." She looked up at a corner of the ceiling, counting. ". . . six weeks ago."

The young man turned crimson. "I'm sorry," he said.

"Strange that they prescribe rest when you lose a child. There is no comfort in resting. One only thinks more." She lit a cigarette. "Do you believe in heaven, Mr. Stevenson?"

The man was disarmed. "No," he said. "I'm sorry."

Fanny let out a bitter little laugh. "Well, I guess I've got a foot in the same camp nowadays. I'll tell you one thing," she said, inhaling deep. "If there is a heaven? My boy has jewels in his crown."

Belle stood up then. "Come along, Mama. You, too, Sammy. Let's walk down by the river."

When they appeared at breakfast the next morning, Bob Stevenson rose from his seat and bowed slightly. "You and your daughter are painters, Mrs. Osbourne?"

"We are."

"Might I interest you and Belle in a little outing? There is a certain place I like to sit to get the perspective of the main street. Your son can come along. We'll give him a brush."

Fanny shrugged, nodded.

Later, when she understood that Bob Stevenson had come to the Hôtel Chevillon ahead of his friends in order to frighten off the intruding Americans, she comprehended the shame he must have felt when he learned of her loss. For Bob was a decent man, it turned out, from decent people.

After that first day of painting, Belle stayed behind with Sammy, who preferred to fish. For about ten days, only Fanny and Bob went out to paint. They sat together for hours on the main street of Grez, discussing art and life and passersby while painting the quaint stone buildings. Bob's canvas was the better one, but he complimented her work. For short stretches of time, Fanny's gnawing sorrow eased.

In his gentle way, she realized later, Bob brought her along in small steps to the point where she could talk to people again. There was no obvious show of gallantry, no sign of pity on his part. They had merely conversed like normal people. But it felt as if he had flung a rope bridge across the chasm that had formed between her and the rest of the world since Hervey's death.

When his friends began arriving in June, Fanny didn't retreat to her room. She felt a measure of her old self returning. She was able to greet each one warmly. And they, in turn, made her family part of their peculiar circle.

CHAPTER 10

Bourron was a short train ride from Paris, but Louis Stevenson nearly missed the stop. His damp cheek had stuck to the window in his sleep, and it was only the abrupt separation of skin from glass when the train halted that shocked him awake. He grabbed his knapsack and leaped onto the station platform, still groggy. It was dinner hour, and the plangent sound of pots rattling in a house nearby made his belly growl. If he were to catch the end of supper at the Hôtel Chevillon, he'd have to step lively, but Grez-sur-Loing was only four and a half kilometers away, a snap for a walking man. His legs—unfurled after three weeks in a canoe—rejoiced in the freedom.

Louis climbed down an embankment next to the tracks and found the path through the woods toward Grez. He remembered the trail from a year ago. He and his cousin Bob had followed it to a pub in Bourron, then staggered back to the Chevillon, singing "Flow gently, sweet Afton" and baying at the moon. It had been a perfect summer idyll, an escape from Edinburgh and parents, a wild splash into *la vie bohème.*

Now, as the darkening violet sky drew down upon the horizon's last strip of gold, he picked his way over fallen trees and brush until he spotted an open field next to the main road into Grez. It was August, and he had already missed two months of raucous pleasure with the friends who'd arrived earlier. He shouted, "I'm coming!," laughed at the hoarse caw of his voice in the evening silence, then broke into a run. In a few minutes, the hotel came into sight, its yellow windows and doors beaming like campfires in the gloaming. Louis went around to the side of the building and entered the back garden through the carriage doors so he wouldn't be noticed. As he crept across the stone terrace, he could see familiar faces at the dining room table, as well as an equal number he didn't know. Madame Chevillon's niece Ernestine languidly cleared plates. There was Henley with his great, unruly red beard and his hogs-head of a chest, shaking with laughter. Charles Baxter, Louis's old uni-versity comrade, who'd clearly had a snoutful, was smiling at a robust young woman with olive skin and wavy hair—Spanish or Italian, per-haps. And Bob, looking handsomely disreputable in his newly droop-ing mustache, was listening to a small woman at the end of the table.

Louis moved a step closer. The woman appeared to be a sister of the other, for her straight nose and dark hair were similar and her skin the same pale caramel shade. She was sitting sideways, with her feet propped on a slat of Bob's chair, and between draws on her cigarette, she leaned near to his ear to speak. Bob's usual sardonic expression was nowhere in evidence.

Louis watched for several minutes before stepping toward one of the open French doors. He stopped and turned to the garden. In the dim moonlight, he made his way to a small fountain, where he splashed water on his face and neck and raked wet fingers through his hair. Then he knelt, opened his knapsack, and recovered from its bottom a rolled-up black velvet jacket. Shaking the coat, he pulled it on and smoothed it as best he could. From a pocket in its lining, he produced an embroi-dered felt smoking cap and placed it on his head. Once more Louis's hand went into the bag, this time coming up with a red sash that he tied around his waist. As a last touch, he tucked his white linen pants into his high boots.

He walked quickly to the house, pausing to consider each of the two doors. Rejecting both, he chose the open window. With the grace of a high jumper, he threw one long leg and then the other over the win-dowsill and hurtled himself into the dining room.

CHAPTER 11

Noise exploded in his ears—whoops, cackles, clapping, the sound of chairs scraping the floor as one friend after another entered the fray of bear hugs and backslaps.

When the chaos subsided, Bob stepped forward and spoke to those still seated. "Ladies and gentlemen—those of you who don't know our newly arrived guest—may I present to you my cousin Robert Louis Stevenson, Louis to his friends. And to the lads in this room who know him best, the Great Exhilarator!"

"Hurrah!" they shouted. "Exhilarate us, Lou!"

Someone passed a glass to Louis. "To guid-fallowship," he said, lifting his voice along with the wine, "to guid health, and the wale o' guid fortune to yer bonny sels!"

He threw back his head and let go a giddy laugh when the wine hit his tongue. Pure gladness coated his mouth, slid down through his chest, lit up his arms and legs. My God, how joyful a picture the dining room made. It looked as warm as a Flemish painting, all golden and peopled by dear friends and ragged, lovely strangers. They smoked pipes and cigarettes, a company of exiles with paint-speckled forearms that united them into a band and declared their intentions.

Will Low, the sweet-tempered American painter Louis had met the previous summer, gestured to the end of the table where he was chatting with a young boy, the only child in the room.

"What took you so long?" The boy looked up at him through pale lashes. "Everybody's been waiting."

Louis crouched down near his chair. "And what might your name be?"

"Sam," he said. "Sammy. But these people call me Pettifish." His shoulders went up in a question. "I don't know why."

Louis laughed. "Is it short for *petite* fish? I'll wager it is. You know, my father had a name like that for me—called me Smout. It's a Scottish word for a small fry."

"Why do grown-ups want to name us after fish?"

"Ah, that *is* a good question. I haven't the faintest idea. But I'll tell you how I ended it. Charged him a penny every time he said the wretched word. You might consider that."

"Sam's here with his sister, Belle," Will explained, nodding toward the pretty, dark-haired girl next to Baxter. "And at the end of the table," he continued, "that lovely lady . . ."

". . . is my mother," the boy said.

Louis stood up to have a better view. "You don't say. I thought they were sisters."

The child rolled his eyes. "Everyone says that."

So these are the Americans. Could they possibly know the displeasure they had caused his circle of friends, sight unseen? When Bob got word from Madame Chevillon that an American woman and her children had taken up residence at the inn for the summer, he had fumed with indignation. The only reason the fellows were assembling at Grez in the first place was because they had been driven out of their last summer haunt by a swarm of lady painters. The bourgeois art students from the school in Barbizon had filled the inns and cafés and turned up behind every other tree with an easel and paintbrush.

News of the American woman and her brats had landed like a lead weight on their collective fantasies. So much for a summer of *la vie bohème* on the banks of the Loing. Bob was so irritated by Madame Chevillon's announcement that he'd come to Grez before the others, intent upon behaving badly enough to chase away the intruders. He was the right man for the job; he had a slicing wit when he chose to unsheathe it.

While Louis was out paddling the *Arethusa* from Antwerp to Paris, Bob had sent him two letters in care of Will Low's studio in Paris. Louis collected both right before he came to Grez. In the first letter, Bob's rage was palpable. By the second letter, though, his indignant tone had disappeared. *They're all right,* he'd written.

"Come with me." Bob had Louis's arm now and led him directly to the lady interloper.

"Fanny Van de Grift Osbourne," she said when she stood. The

crown of dark brown curls at the top of her head came up first (how tiny she was, nearly a foot shorter than he), and then the smooth honey-colored face tilted. He examined the curving upper lip—like an archer's bow—and the deep brown eyes. "I feel as if I know you," she said, grasping both of his hands. Everything about her was exotic, from her lively gold-ringed fingers to her tiny blue kidskin slippers peeking from beneath a black skirt. She might have been a Sephardic shepherdess, to judge from her features, but the voice was different. American, to be sure. It had a touch of grassy prairie in it, riverboats, he didn't know what all. Maybe Tennessee walking horses.

Louis grinned. "May I ask where you are from?"

"Originally? Why, I grew up in Indiana." The dark eyes, full of sex, danced first toward Bob and then Louis. "Your cousin tells me you're from Edinburgh. He also says you're . . . What's the expression? *All right,*" she said.

Louis was taken aback. Those were the words Bob had used to describe *her* in his last letter. Had Bob told her how they had all dreaded her? Louis felt strangely out of step for a moment, as if understandings had been reached in his absence.

"I'll get some food for you," Bob said, and disappeared.

"Have you been to America?" Fanny asked Louis.

"No, I regret to say I haven't. But when I was in Cumberland some years ago, I met a Highland spaewife who predicted I would go—"

"A spaewife?"

"Oh, a mad old crone who claimed she had second sight."

"Be careful what you say," Fanny said. "I have a touch of it myself."

Louis laughed. "She was nothing like you, but I liked her predictions. She said I would visit America and I was to be very happy and I would spend much time on the sea."

"You don't say." Fanny Osbourne turned her attention to a pear-shaped mesh bag suspended from a link of the silver chatelaine around her waist. She unhooked it and pulled out a small sack of tobacco. "Cigarette?" She peeled six papers from a booklet and put them on the table.

"Absolutely. I'm not accustomed to a lady making her own."

Louis watched her boyish fingers shake a line of tobacco onto a paper. She rolled the cigarette evenly with both thumbs, then lifted it to her mouth, where her cat-quick tongue sealed the edge. Six times a stuffed rolling paper went to her lips; each repetition was more expert than the last. "That should do us," she said, reattaching the little purse to her belt.

He noticed several objects hanging from other fine chains on her waist, including a folding knife and a pouch full of drawing pencils.

"You are the very spectacle of self-sufficiency," Louis said.

When Fanny raised her eyes to his, he caught his breath. She focused her gaze on him as if sighting a pistol. "Are you mocking me?" she asked.

"No, no, not at all! I'm admiring you. Have you always rolled your own cigarettes?"

"Ever since I started smoking. A miner in Nevada taught me."

"In Nevada?"

"I lived for a while in a silver mining camp."

"My goodness! How . . . bracing."

She drew on her cigarette. "That's a delicate expression, Mr. Stevenson." Her eyes remained unwaveringly on his.

"I meant you seem so ladylike, and to be such an adventuress—"

"Oh, it's not that unusual to find women in mining camps. But I wasn't in the same line of business some of the others pursued, if that's what you're wondering."

Louis shook his head. "I am wondering why you take whatever I say and misconstrue it, madam. You have known me five minutes, not nearly long enough to despise me. It usually takes at least ten."

She laughed then, and small, perfect white teeth flashed across her face. "I'm only teasing you, Louis." *Lou*-us, she pronounced his name, soft and slow, as if stroking it. "I liked you the minute you jumped in."

Bob returned with a plate of food for him and a bottle of whisky. "To Louis the Canoeist," he said, tapping his glass to his cousin's. "Give us the plums, Lou."

There had been an abundance of plums to pick from along the banks of the Scheldt and the canals of Belgium and then, at the end, the upper Oise. Louis had traveled for twenty days in the *Arethusa* with his shy, athletic friend Walter Simpson, who manned another sailing canoe, the *Cigarette.* Their voyage had provoked furious note taking on Louis's part—from observations on the free life of the barge captain to his own near-kidnapping by the mad young oarsmen of the Belgian Royal Nautical Sportsmen's Club, whose enthusiasm for boating was almost frightening. For the sake of a warm clubhouse dinner and a bed for the night, he and Simpson pretended to know the great English rowers whose names the Belgians reverently recited. As they were escorted to their sleeping quarters by one of the club members, Louis and Simpson, under pressure, agreed to give a morning demonstration of the proper English stroke. At dawn, they fled rather than be found out as rank amateurs.

There was so much Louis had saved up to tell Bob, but how could he say it now, in front of this new woman? He longed to say, *If you want to find out who you really are, then go travel. To move is the thing.* He wanted to say, *Something important has begun.* Every chance encounter, every change of landscape in the journey, offered itself up to his pen. He could see a way now to go out and have adventures, to pour all that he witnessed through his soul and onto paper, a way he could make a living doing what he loved, in spite of his father's plans for him. At the end of the journey, after he had maneuvered the *Arethusa* to a dock in Pontoise, it was raining. He hated wet weather. Yet he had put his face up to the drizzle and thanked it for falling on him.

Louis looked at Bob and Fanny's expectant faces. "French rain is different from the stuff that falls in Auld Reekie."

Bob laughed, but Fanny said, "It takes leaving, doesn't it, to see things through fresh eyes."

"It *does,*" Louis said. He saw she had two or three wavy silver strands, like sprung coils, at each temple. "I felt free, truly free. Just to be out in the open air . . ."

"Do you know that Whitman poem 'Song of the Open Road'?" Fanny asked. "'I think heroic deeds were all conceived in the open air . . .'"

"'. . . I think whatever I shall meet on the road I shall like,'" Louis responded, picking up the verse, "'. . . and whoever beholds me shall like me.'"

He saw the faintest smile flicker across her somber mouth as she took his measure.

"So, you're a travel essayist now, are you?" Bob injected into the quiet moment that followed. He sucked hard on his pipe and released a cloud above their heads. The sardonic grin he had developed at Cambridge was in full display. "Your father will be thrilled to hear that." He turned to Fanny. "Our friend here recently completed his legal studies."

"I am not suited to be an advocate," Louis said, suddenly cross.

"You're not much of a vagabond, either," Bob observed. "Look at you with a knapsack. No self-respecting Gypsy carries a freshly pressed shirt."

"When we were younger, perhaps sixteen," Louis explained to Fanny, "we would go adventuring for a couple of days without anything but a toothbrush. Not even a comb. Considered it bad form to be encumbered."

"We couldn't stand ourselves after a while," Bob added, "so we'd have to go buy shirts and underwear and visit a barber rather often, just to get the hair combed. It got expensive."

"Our fathers were underwriting our adventures in those days," Louis said.

"Let's be honest, they still are." Bob swilled back a whisky.

"So you were close as little boys," Fanny said.

"Like brothers," Bob said.

"But I want to know about *you,* Fanny Osbourne. How did you decide to come to Grez?"

She flicked her wrist, and the vivacious face went slack. "There's plenty of time for that. How long are you staying?"

"I have to go back to Edinburgh in a few days."

"We can talk tomorrow," she said. "I must put my boy to bed. He's looking weary down there." Louis watched her collect the limp child from his seat and depart the room.

"She's quite something, isn't she?" Bob said when she was gone. "The locals call her *la belle Americaine.*"

"Indeed. What is she doing in Grez?"

"Ordered here by a doctor."

"Lungs?"

"No, it's not that. She came over to the Continent to study painting, along with her daughter and sons. While they were in Paris, the youngest boy died of consumption—the kind Henley had."

"Ah," Louis said. "What a pity."

"She broke down, and they sent her here to rest."

"Where is the husband?"

"Back in California."

"And . . . ?"

"Rather raw, from what I can gather. Fanny doesn't say much about him. I get the feeling it went cold a long time ago."

"Did you tell her we all dreaded her presence here?"

"I did just recently. She found it quite funny."

So they are confidants, Louis thought, *probably lovers. And once again, here am I, floating around in Bob's wake.*

He poured himself a glass of whisky, drank it down, and then threw back a second. "A guid dram, laddie," Louis growled playfully. But his heart stung. He waited for the burning to pass before pulling himself up to go talk to the others.

CHAPTER 12

Morning at the hotel was nothing like the night before. Louis remembered this fact from last summer, when he found the previous night's comedians and revelers creeping around the dining table at ten, drinking coffee, surveying the tartines and croissants, assiduously avoiding intercourse with any early bird hanging about in the room.

Since he'd been canoeing, Louis had become a dawn riser, and it took every bit of discipline he could command not to launch into cheery banter with his mates. It wasn't a terrible sacrifice. He took his volume of *Don Quixote* and wandered into the woods, where he could read in the presence of pines.

By eleven, when he returned, he saw that the guests of the inn had divided into tribes. The painters were strung along the banks of the Loing, eyeing the old stone bridge that spanned the river. Close to the small pier where the inn's wide canoes were tied up among the bulrushes, Bob, Fanny, Belle, and others sat beneath white umbrellas, a few feet apart, dabbing at their canvases. If he strolled too close, he could find himself a motive of some painter's work. "Motive" was the word the painter types used to describe that day's subject. A motive could be a boat or a bridge or the river, or him, if he weren't careful. Louis walked up the long, narrow lawn toward the ragtag little group of writers and poets gathered on the inn's terrace.

What a merry mess the whole lot of them were, dressed in wooden sabots, blue fisherman shirts, waistcoats, scarves, berets, fezes, tam-o'-shanters, and wide-awake hats. They smoked cheroots, cigarettes, meerschaums. Men, mostly, they were—a mélange of English speakers from Britain and America, mixed with some French and Scandinavians, plus a Spanish fellow, a German, and an Italian. Two colorful women, mistresses, lounged with the writers while their lovers painted. A woman journalist from America scribbled in her notebook. Many of the artists were fashionably cynical, yet he could see the truth: They were giddy as little children to be here, playing with one another.

Louis suspected each of them, in his or her own way, was an exile—from bourgeois values, family crests, unhappy love affairs, childhoods too long spent in church pews. He wondered if they had started as social outcasts who found the artist's life an acceptable way to be in the world; or if their passions for painting or sculpting or writing had shaped them into outsiders. He had never been quite sure how the chicken-versus-egg question played out in his own life.

It seemed he had spent half his childhood in bed with a hacking cough. It was the stories read to him, and those that he eventually read himself, that had saved him from the worst of the loneliness. *God, how pale and thin I was—a glasshouse seedling. Just different.* His illnesses had cut him off from the society of other children too often. But the stories had made him different, too. They had shaped his appetite, his moral prejudices, who he was. Those sick days when he had listened to the joyful sounds of football on the street below, he'd longed to be an ordinary kid. But at eleven or twelve, when he went out into the neighborhood dressed in pants too short and hair too long, his appearance set off taunts among other children—oh, he could hear them now, *Hauf a laddie, hauf a lassie, hauf a yellow yite!*—Louis knew he might as well be tattooed all over. The question of how he got that way was moot. It was around then that he began using his tongue as his sword, as small, fragile boys tend to do.

He waded among the wooden tables where a small gaggle of writers leaned on their elbows, immersed in conversation. "*There* he is," William Henley declared, pulling up a chair next to him. "Sit down, my good man, and tell us if Zola is taking us all to the dogs."

Louis drew on his cigarette and grinned at the Londoner, whose disheveled, bearded head was as large and friendly as an otterhound's. "He don't find much to like in humanity," he said in a wry tone.

"All that ugly realism not to your taste?" Henley asked, shifting his stump to get a better purchase on his seat.

"Give me a rousing romance. Entertain me."

"Who've we got with us this mornin'?" Henley turned his friend's book face-up to see the title. "Cervantes . . . ha! I should have known."

"I wanted to look at his style again. To try it on."

"Comment?" A French writer, who was recovering from the previous night's excesses, raised his head from the tabletop where it had been resting next to a potted red geranium. "No man is a writer if he *imitates!*" he exclaimed, pulling himself upright.

"I have taught myself the writing craft in just that way," Louis said, "by aping the greats."

"To write is to give the soul," the man objected. "Truth comes from this place." He jabbed his chest with a forefinger. "No French writer says, 'I ape this man. I ape that man . . .'"

"Perhaps he does not *admit* it." Louis grinned. "Come now, what does it matter? Let us hear what your souls are saying today."

Laughter, followed by silence. Then the sound of paper unfolding, as one after another of the writers took a turn reading aloud his verses and paragraphs to the others on the terrace.

Henley leaned over and spoke softly in his ear. "Have you been wandering in the forest pitying yourself?"

"No." Louis smiled. "Well, maybe. Actually, I am thinking about starting a story."

"You are going to abandon your essays?"

"It's the law I want to abandon." Louis sighed. "I'm simply in the mood to try something different, and fiction—"

"Magazines buy essays," Henley said.

"An adventure story—"

"I don't begrudge you your adventures, lad. Why don't you write a little story about setting out in a canoe?"

"Better still," Louis said, his voice growing dark with conspiracy, "set out with me in one of the canoes after lunch."

Henley glanced dolefully at his abbreviated limb.

"Forget the game leg," Louis said, "you've got a mighty pair of arms on you, man." He turned to the others in the group. "Gentlemen and ladies, I propose we writer types take on the painter types in a friendly boating contest this afternoon. What say you?"

"Yes! Yes!" the cry went up.

Later in the day, when the canoe wars had been waged and the paddlers had retired to their rooms to nap before dinner, Louis paced his bedroom. Something had come over him when Fanny Osbourne had emerged from the inn wearing her bathing costume. More than the

magnificent form she made in her black cotton suit, it was the red es-
padrilles with laces tied around her ankles that nearly undid him. When
he saw her, he'd wrapped his towel around his waist and tried to think
about the Napoleonic code. Now the red shoes batted around in his
brain like flies. He was a fool for footwear and he knew it. But could a
pair of scarlet shoes render him so hopelessly smitten? Or was it the
way Fanny's somber focus on her paddle broke under his teasing? How
she screamed helplessly when he tipped her over, then emerged from
the water slick as a seal and, grabbing on to the bow of his boat, up-
ended him with the power of a man. The scene as it replayed in his
mind was almost perfect, except for the part where Bob lifted her wet
and lovely body into his own canoe.

Louis could not bear it any longer. He poked his head out into the
hall and found it empty. He stepped over to Bob's door, knocked, then
entered when he heard his cousin's steady snore. "Bob . . . Bob." Louis
shook his shoulders.

"What is it?" The voice—a frog's—croaked his annoyance.

"We need to talk."

"Can't it wait?"

"Here," Louis said, and handed him a glass of water. "Wake up."

Bob sat up in bed, yawned. His hair was wet and flattened on one
side. "Did somebody die?"

"Are you in love with her?"

"Who?"

"Fanny Osbourne."

Bob yawned. "Hell, no." He scratched at his head. "She's fetching,
all right, and—"

"Because I am," Louis said.

"You're daft, Lou."

"I knew you would find humor in it."

"Well, her name is Fanny—"

"Of course you would have to say that."

"She *is* married, and she *is* a good twelve years older than you."

"Ten and a half. And she's separated from her husband."

"So was Fanny Sitwell, but that didn't get you into her pantalets."

"I know, I know." Louis's voice was low and urgent. "But this is different. I swear it, Bob, she's the one."

"Christ's sake, Lou. You've known her for how long, a day and a half? Must you always fall so hard? Can't you just play?"

"You two are together a lot, and I assumed you had something started."

"Naw." Bob laughed. "I must own she has a mischievous wit, but the daughter"—he let go a soft, admiring whistle—"the daughter is a minx."

"So you don't mind if I . . ."

Bob shrugged. "Have a try at it."

Louis leaned over and grabbed his cousin's arm. "Will you talk to Fanny, then? Not yet, of course. But when the time is right, will you make my case?"

"I'll try," Bob said, "but the woman appears to have a mind of her own."

Louis lit a cigarette and waited for his comeuppance.

"Don't you already have a perfectly fine mother?" Bob asked.

Louis dropped his cigarette into the water glass, sprang onto his cousin, and put him in a headlock. Ever the superior specimen, Bob flopped him around like a fish.

CHAPTER 13

B elle Osbourne, wrapped in a robe, collapsed on the old stuffed chair in their bedroom. "There is nothing for me to wear tonight," she said to her mother. "Nothing."

"Wear the blue check dress, why don't you?"

"It makes me look as if I'm ten."

Fanny was seated at the dressing table. "You're moving too fast, Belle." She turned around in her seat. "These young men here . . ."

"I want to wear something pretty for once."

Fanny's palm made a dipping arc. "A lady keeps her voice low and sweet."

Belle hissed with frustration.

"When I met your father," Fanny mused, "I was your age, and—"

"And you were standing on stilts." Belle sighed.

"The point is . . ."

". . . you were just a child. I know all that, a hundred times over, Mother."

"In those days, they started things too early. It was too, too early."

"No, they didn't."

"Isobel!" Fanny directed a look at the girl that instantly set aright their positions. Belle had always been a pleasant child, eager to help. Lately, she had grown willful, and in a heartbeat, the air between them could thicken with tension.

The animosity wasn't constant. Today, for example, they had all gone canoeing on the river. A contest evolved, and Fanny's boat was overturned. When Bob Stevenson pulled her out of the water, Belle laughed and called to her, "How pretty you look all wet, Mama!" Soon enough, Belle was dunked, too, but Fanny could not return a tender compliment to her daughter. The mother, as well as anyone else with eyes, saw the blooming girl's anatomy prominently outlined beneath her black blouse. It had left Fanny feeling oddly sad.

"You can't go back, is what I am saying to you." Fanny's voice softened. "You sashay out of your childhood, and the world makes sure you can't have it again. Think about what you're doing."

"It's too late for that, Mama," Belle murmured. She walked into the adjoining room and shut the door.

Fanny brushed her hair absently. Too much had happened. How could a shred of childhood be left in Belle after she'd witnessed her brother's long death? Even before that nightmare, Belle's naïveté had peeled away in the acid atmosphere of the Oakland household.

When the girl stomped back in, she was wearing her mother's melon-colored dress. It was clear she had borrowed a corset, too, for her elevated breasts threatened to unleash themselves from the neckline.

"All right, Belle," Fanny said wearily.

"Then I can wear it?"

"Come here, sit down." The mother stood up and allowed her daughter to sit on the stool in front of the mirror.

"Do you see how your eyes appear rather prominent when your hair is pulled back tight?"

"It crinkles up if I don't pull it back after I wash it."

"First of all, never say 'warsh.' That is the worst sort of twang."

Belle looked puzzled. "Isn't that how you say it?"

"Not anymore." Fanny yanked strands loose from the band that held her daughter's hair up in a knot. Belle flinched but kept quiet. With small nail scissors, the mother cut pieces of hair around the girl's hairline. "Short curls around your face will soften your features."

Fanny ran the brush through her daughter's hair, pulled back the black mass, and shook it. Small snippets of wavy hair fell around the girl's brow and cheeks. Belle beamed at her reflection.

"When I was little," Fanny said, "my grandmother was ashamed of me because my skin was dark, at least compared to hers. Every morning she sewed a sunbonnet into my braided hair and made me wear long nankeen gloves up to my shoulders. Imagine going out every day like that! Everyone knew *why* I had to wear the gloves, and no one else had a hat sewn on her head. I was a shy child at that point, and I felt terribly embarrassed. When I came in from playing and my face had turned the color of a pecan anyway, she scrubbed my skin raw. It wasn't enough that everyone wanted blond looks; my grandmother believed people with dark skin were naturally wicked."

Another memory flooded Fanny's mind; she was surprised that it still wounded her. "What are you?" a neighborhood girl had once asked her.

She'd known even at the age of seven that the girl was inquiring for one of her parents, since Fanny had overheard the child's father use the phrase "some kind of half-breed" when she was visiting once.

"Who wants to know?" Fanny asked in response.

"My pa."

"Dutch and Swedish," Fanny had replied.

The girl had seemed unsatisfied, as if she'd heard that answer before. "But what are you *really*?"

"My mother never stopped telling me I was beautiful," Fanny told Belle. "I didn't believe her for a long time. Now I prefer my dark skin to that unnatural 'flesh' color in my paint box." She replaced the scissors in a small leather case. "You got my coloring, honey, just as I got it from my own mother. Don't bother with mauve, no matter what the French tell you is fashionable. It doesn't set off your skin. Always wear a spark of color, and find some touch that is all your own. Maybe it's a particular way you wear your hat. Something." Fanny reached over her daughter's shoulder and yanked up the bodice of the melon dress. "A collarbone is far more alluring than exposed breasts. A man wants to imagine. Did you see that local girl who came around yesterday and was talking to the writers? She was all dressed up, poor thing. And do you know what the men did when she left? They laughed. One of them said, 'She's wearing her hunting clothes.'"

Belle stood back from the mirror to study her new hairstyle from different angles. "Mama, do you think that Irish painter Frank O'Meara likes me?"

"Did you even hear what I just said, Belle?"

"Yes, I did."

Fanny sighed. "I don't know what Frank O'Meara likes. Except maybe that thorny shilalagh he carries around."

"Oh, his singing voice . . ."

"It won't put bread on the table, darlin'."

"He's rich, too."

"Well, that helps."

"Helps? Aren't you the one who always says it's as easy to fall in love with a rich man as a poor man? I thought you would approve."

Bob Stevenson had told Fanny that O'Meara had wealthy Irish Catholic parents. She tried to weigh the parts of that equation. He might be rich as Croesus, but the parents would never permit the boy to marry a Protestant girl. There was no harm in allowing Belle her point for now, though. "He does have a nice voice," Fanny said.

Belle turned and gave her mother a conspiratorial look. "Louis Stevenson was sparkin' on you last night."

Fanny waved away the remark. "I don't care a particle about that."

A grin spread over Belle's face. "Frank says he's from a wealthy family and is in line to inherit a lot of money, but he won't live that long because of his dissipation. Frank thinks Bob and Louis are both mad."

"Do you know what I think? I think this inn is full of gossips. Go down to dinner. I'll be there in a few minutes."

At the closet, Fanny reached for one of her black dresses but pulled out the white instead. *It has been three months.* She had allowed herself a blue shawl or white blouse since she'd arrived, but not without the black skirt or gray jacket. Fanny sighed bitterly. Why did any of those rules matter? Her baby was gone. No mourning clothes could begin to express the weight of that loss. There would never be another day in her life when her mind and heart were not bound up in black weeds. She put on the white dress.

Fanny heard loud conversation coming from the dining room when she descended the stairs. As she entered the room, Louis Stevenson stood up and called out, "Guid een'!"

"Good evening," she returned.

"Ah, this one is going to take a bit of work," Louis said to his cousin. He pulled out a chair between his and Bob's. "Tonight, Fanny Osbourne, with your permission, I suggest we undertake a wee lesson. In fact, we shall all undertake a lesson in the Scots tongue," he said to the rest of the table.

"Hopeless," said the German artist. "You can't teach an American or a Frenchman to pronounce Scots."

"Nonsense," said Will Low. "Give us a try."

Louis's eyes went bright. "All right! Let's start with the simplest phrase. 'Guid een'.' It starts here." He pointed to his neck. "Guid," he growled, fingering the tendons beneath his jaw. "One gags from the nether folds of the throat."

"One could strain oneself," Fanny replied.

"Ah, now, give it a try."

"Ged eeenin'," she said, her lips stretching.

"She's on to it!" Bob said.

"Got eenen'," someone ventured.

"Try it," Fanny said to Margaret Wright, who had arrived the day before, but her friend demurred, uncharacteristically shy in the midst of these madcap jokers.

Sitting beside Margaret at the end of the table was Joseph Howard, a famously homely Louisianan whom the others had found strange from the start. Fanny suspected the Europeans had never heard a true Southern accent, for when he spoke, they tended to gawk in wonder at the large square-headed man. He was not the least bit strange to Fanny. He might have been one of her eccentric uncles, proud of his backwater roots. While the others painted the bridge, he sat before his easel, creating a blazing scene from the Battle of New Orleans. In the afternoons, when everyone climbed into canoes, Howard would squeeze into a washtub he had persuaded Madame Chevillon to part with and merrily paddle in their midst.

"Gooood evenin'," the contrarian called out now in his Southern drawl.

Fanny began to smile along with everyone else. She felt as if she had fallen into some hollow that might have been in the remote hills of either Scotland or perhaps Tennessee. She couldn't remember the last time she had felt so silly. As the pot-au-feu was passed, Bob served her from the tureen while Louis refilled her wineglass. Oh, it felt fine.

Was it the accents that gave the mad Stevensons their charm? They clearly loved speaking in broad Scots, switching from their Edinburgh English into a tongue that was nearly incomprehensible to her ear. And they reveled in playing off each other, finishing each other's sentences. The two of them did not look to be kin. Louis had dark blond hair and wide-set brown eyes that went hazel in the light, full lips, a narrow chest, and a wispy patch of hair beneath his mouth. His face was a theater of emotions, his features shifting in a twinkling from gay to tragic as his supple mind ranged across subjects that moved him. He seemed to have no protective veil; his feelings lay open as a child's.

Bob was three years older than his cousin and the more sophisticated of the two. He had dark, handsome features and a tall, athletic body; he was, quite simply, one of the finest-looking men Fanny had ever seen. He was adept at everything—art, music, philosophy. Everyone regarded him as the best talker in any room. How different his tone was now, compared to his clipped formality when she first met him.

She found it touching when she remembered how Bob, dead set against her at first, had gently helped to revive her. Oh, the others had been attentive and kind. But it was Bob's company she wanted most. Lately, she'd allowed herself to imagine what was unthinkable before. What would it be like to live in London or Paris with a man like Bob Stevenson—a refined, educated, charming European? Over here, divorce was not the moral failure it was in America. What would it be like to never go back, to raise young Sammy over here, to send him to fine schools?

She would want a modern man who wouldn't expect an old family dowry. What she had to offer was herself—no innocent, to be sure, but wise and still pretty at thirty-six. Her sisters and even Sam told her she was at the height of her beauty. It wasn't too late for her to find another husband, and it wasn't a selfish impulse to be on the lookout for one. The best thing she could do for her children's future would be to remarry, and well.

Fanny's reverie fell away as the hilarity in the room grew louder.

"Dae ye speak Scots?" Louis was shouting. He was leaning forward in his chair, his lank hair falling over one eye.

Her tablemates brayed the phrase back to him.

"Juist a wee," he replied.

"Joost a way!" they sang back.

"Awa', an' bile yer heids!" he said.

The diners stared at one another, confused.

"What did he say?" Belle asked.

"Go boil your heads," Henley said matter-of-factly.

More laughter followed, but within the noise, Fanny heard little choking sounds coming from her left. She turned to see Louis holding his chest and gasping for breath.

She had seen real choking once when her father had saved a man by lifting him up and squeezing him; a chunk of meat had popped like a cork from the man's mouth and shot across the room. She stood up, prepared to pound or squeeze Louis, just as he slid from his chair onto the floor. Tears were running from his eyes.

"What is it?" Fanny shouted to Bob above the din.

"*Madderam,* madam," he said. "Bend back his hand."

She didn't know the word, but bending his hand wouldn't help. She dropped to her knees, wrapped her arms around his chest, and squeezed. When she glanced at Louis's scarlet face, she realized he was laughing hysterically, like a man possessed.

"Bend back his hand!" Bob shouted again.

Fanny felt disoriented. She looked, confused, from one cousin to the other.

"Never mind," Bob said. "I'll do it." He took Louis's hand and bent the slender fingers back so hard, Fanny thought they would snap off. When Louis's laughter coughed and sputtered to a stop, he climbed back on his chair and began chatting as if nothing had happened.

Fanny looked around the table when she sat down. Had more wine been drunk than she'd realized? Louis's friends seemed unperturbed by such a strange scene.

"What is *madderam*?" Fanny asked Bob.

"Old Shetland word. Means 'madness.' Pure, joyous insanity."

After dinner, the crowd convened outside under the arbor, where Chinese lanterns hung from the lattice. There was a hammock where Fanny settled when it was offered to her. In the canoe-dumping games, her foot had been caught between two boats, and her ankle was throbbing. The others arranged themselves in chairs around her or sat cross-legged on the ground. One fellow shared a bottle of wine with his pet monkey. A pretty grisette, an expert at swallowing goldfish, circled the group with a new amusement. She dangled a grape on a string over their heads while each person tried to catch it in his teeth.

A voice said, "I don't want this day to end." And another: "Let's tie the canoes together, climb in, and see where we wake up in the morning."

They talked into the night about Monet, Degas, and Millet. Balzac's novels and Irish independence. Money. Love. Photography. Did pictures or words have more power? Fanny, like the others, spoke freely into the near darkness, the circle lit by only the moon and a few candles guttering in the warm breeze.

Someone asked Bob Stevenson if he still intended to commit suicide when his inheritance ran out. Just a few days earlier, Fanny had heard Bob's outrageous declaration. When his father died, he'd left his son a small sum of money. Bob had been spending it over the years in creative, pleasurable ways. Fanny calculated that his merry march toward cessation was approaching its end.

"No man has the right to toss away his own life." It was Louis's voice, tremulous with emotion. "Just as he has no right to dispose of his neighbor's. It's still a murder."

"Your life doesn't belong to just you," Fanny said.

"Obviously, I disagree with you," Bob said. "I got thrown into life without my consent, and I have every right to decide when and how I will leave this earth. What's more, suicide is a fine subject for a story, Lou." He drew on his cigarette thoughtfully and tipped his chair on its back legs. "Let us imagine for a moment that there is a private organization, not advertised in any way but known by word of mouth among a certain group of men—a club . . . a suicide club. Once a month there is a card game run by the president of the club. The attendees pay a fee to get in, have their fill of champagne, and then sit down to a game of cards. They take turns drawing cards from the stack at the center of the table. The fellow who draws the ace of spades is the honoree that month. The winner, you might say, of his own demise."

"Why does he need to join a club to commit suicide?" Belle asked.

"Because there is another important card player at the table," Louis said, picking up the thread of the story. "That is the man who draws the ace of clubs. It falls to him to dispatch the first winner that very night."

"Kill him, you mean?" Belle asked.

"Exactly," Louis said.

"That's an interesting twist," Fanny mused. "I think it is harder to be a murderer than simply a man who wants to end his own life."

Louis and Bob played back and forth with the idea, embellishing here, rejecting there, until someone produced a guitar and quieted the talk.

Fanny looked up through a circular opening in the arbor at the black sky, awash in stars. She considered the idea of staying right where she was, of sleeping in the hammock so as to breathe in the fragrance of the trellis roses. Soon enough, couples were standing, saying good night. She noticed Belle and Frank O'Meara slip into the shadows. Fanny sat up in the hammock and climbed out. Louis leaped to his feet, took her arm, and helped her back to the building.

"Upon my soul," he blurted, "you are the most magnificent woman I've ever met." He was looking down at her, and in the dim lantern light of the inn, she saw tears in his eyes yet again. "I think I am falling in love with you," he said.

Fanny felt her chest shrink with embarrassment. Happily, the stairs to her bedroom were only seconds away.

"Louis." She patted his shoulder. "You are sweet. Now get some sleep."

CHAPTER 14

⁓

Fanny,
Might I pull you away from the riverbank later this morning for a walk
in the woods?

Bob

Fanny had found the invitation slipped under her door as she went down to breakfast. If there were a more enticing way to spend a sunny September morning, she could not think of it. In the past couple of days, since Louis returned to Edinburgh, the friendly intimacy Fanny enjoyed with Bob had revived. She contemplated the prospect that he might speak his feelings at last.

Around eleven, Bob was waiting downstairs for her, wearing a battered plaited-straw hat. They set off into the forest, where streaks of sunlight shot through oak and pine branches, splashing the ferns with a quivering glow.

"I have a question for you," Fanny said finally. "I hope it is not too personal."

"Ask it."

"Are you serious about all that suicide talk?"

Bob took off his hat, scratched his head glumly. "My money's going to be gone soon enough."

"Perhaps it's time to start earning some of your own."

"Perhaps."

"No one will hold you to that talk. You have too many people who love you."

"Louis wouldn't allow it, anyway," Bob said. "Say, how do you like Louis?"

"He's charming. Nearly as clever as you," Fanny said. "But my word, one minute he's weeping, and the next, he's so hysterical he can't stop laughing. I don't know whether to give him a handkerchief or look out the window. Does he have some condition?"

Bob's laughter pealed through the clearing where they stood. "A variety of them," he said. "Being a Lighthouse Stevenson is one."

"What is that?"

"He's an artist in a family of proper engineers—my father was one of them. They're quite famous for the lighthouses they build, by the way. But his main condition is being giddy with life. He's suffered, you see, with his lungs—been near to death a few times. But that's made Louis who he is; a bit of a bedlamite, you might say. Hungry for living life and oblivious to caution sometimes. Never, never has he let his illnesses cripple his spirit. He's always got a zany story or joke saved up for me. And the laughing? Well, haven't you ever laughed so hard that you lost control? When you were simply gasping for air and thought you would never stop?"

"Possibly as a child. Not lately."

"I'm sorry, Fanny. You haven't had much reason to laugh."

"Frankly, I found your cousin a little frightening."

"Oh, he's perfectly all right. The thing is, once you've laughed that hard, you will want to do it again. It feels so grand. Lou and I spent a good part of our youth laughing our heads off. He would look at me, and I was doomed."

They were walking along a path overhung by branches of a great-trunked beech tree.

"Do you suppose Monet came to this spot to paint?" Fanny said.

"When he was about nine . . ."

"Monet?"

"Louis. And I was twelve, we would set up lead soldiers and wage huge battles in his bedroom. Not just maneuvers; we would give the wee men grudges, bad habits, valor—whole histories, not only military ranks. I could play at his bedside as happily as if I were outdoors." Bob laughed to himself. "A huge imagination he has; that's why he's never bored."

"I can see you love him, Bob."

"He's got his foibles, don't get me wrong. He may have abandoned the church, but he's a moralist of the first water. I remember one time we came upon a man on the road who was beating his dog. Louis was horrified and told him to stop. The man growled at him and said, 'I'll do what I want. It's my dog.' Louis, mind you, was a mere boy, but he said indignantly, 'He's not your dog. He's God's dog.' That pretty well sums up Louis's attitude about unfairness. Can't bear it. He's going to be famous someday, mark my words. If he can keep his health."

"He appears to be perfectly fine."

"I think the canoeing, being out in the country air, is good for him." Bob caught her eye as they continued on. "He's awfully fond of you, Fanny."

"I do not need another child."

"Fanny," Bob said gently, "I am a lazy, vulgar cad. I haven't any ideas about what I can really do. I don't think I will ever be a first-rate painter. I may be older than Lou, but he is far more mature."

They walked on for a few minutes. Up ahead, Fanny could see the path that led back to the garden. Disgusted, she stopped and turned to him. "Were you assigned this task, Bob, or have you undertaken it on your own?"

Bob's eyes passed over her face. "You are a beautiful woman, an accomplished woman. A man would be blind not to see that." He paused. "I would not make the case for anyone except Louis. He has a soul like that of no one else I know. And I am not what you imagine, Fanny."

In the garden, Bob put his hand at the small of her back and walked quietly with her to the dining room, where the midday dinner was in progress. Fanny saw at once the knowing glances darting among the people gathered there. She knew what they were thinking: that something deeply intimate had happened on the forest walk. Her whole head was burning. She tipped up her chin and looked neither left nor right. *Let them think they have caught us in a tryst.*

What she knew by the time they had reached the inn was something else entirely. In a fashion that only a man of Bob's genteel breeding could have managed, she had been passed like a slab of cheese on a plate from one diner to the next.

CHAPTER 15

When Louis arrived at the iron gate in front of 17 Heriot Row, fear gripped him. *What an absurd sensation for a man of twenty-six.* Yet here he stood like a child of eight, dreading going into the place as if it were a setting from a Poe story. It was, in fact, a perfectly pleasant row house in the New Town, built of beveled sandstone blocks, distinguished from its neighbors only by an arching fanlight above the door. Otherwise, his father's house locked arms with its fellows in a show of seamless solidity. These were homes occupied by judges and lawyers and other stewards of Edinburgh, and their basements were quarters for the servants, not dungeons. Lately, though, when Louis came back to the house where he had grown up, he felt a prisoner's panic upon crossing the threshold. He had endured miserable inquisitions in recent times—usually at the dining table and at his father's hands. Now it was his wretched lot to be coming home with his hat in hand, for he was nearly out of money.

He closed the big front door gently, stepped quietly through a second set of glass doors, and walked into the empty dining room, where coals glowed in the grate. He stirred the fire with a poker, hoping for a few moments of solitude before his mother appeared and commenced one of her pleasant interviews, a mixture of good-humored small talk and family gossip, followed by delicate, abstract forays into his personal life ("How does a handsome young man like you keep the girls at arm's length?") and his cheerful, edited confidences. The real interrogation would begin later, when his father returned home from work, and all niceties would fall away. Louis sank into the big chair by the fire and closed his eyes. Within a minute or two, he heard the distinctive shuffle of the butler's shoes.

"Good afternoon, Mr. Stevenson," the man said.

"John," Louis said, "how are you?"

"Very well, sir. Your parents are not at home just now. They went out to Swanston. But Miss Cunningham is here. I'll get her."

Soon a different but familiar step clicked on the staircase. Louis jumped up and went into the foyer. Against the oval skylight on the third floor, he saw the sprightly figure of his childhood nurse—a tiny gray-haired woman in a neat brown dress, flying down the winding stone steps, her arms open.

"Master Lou?" she called out. "Is it really you?"

"Cummy!" he shouted. "I had no idea you would be here." He lifted her in an embrace before she got to the bottom step.

"Your mother asked me to drop by in case you arrived while they were in Swanston. They went out yesterday and will be back by supper tonight. They weren't sure what time you were coming. I was just up in your room, fluffin' the pillows."

"Alison Cunningham, I am past the need of fluffing."

"Every man likes a little pampering once in a while. Look at you," she said, smoothing his lapels. "Did you add more height in the past twelve months?"

"I stopped growing some years ago, my friend."

"I must be getting shorter, then. I have an old lady's bones. Sit down with me, Lou, and tell me all about your trip. Are you hungry? I asked Mildred to have tea ready in case you got here in time. I haven't seen you since you had a wig and robe on, the day you passed advocate."

Louis winced. "Ah, Cummy, did you have to remind me of that? I have blissfully blotted it out of my mind for six weeks. Well, mostly."

They settled at the dining room table where they had spent so many hours of his boyhood, coloring and printing out his earliest stories. Soon platters were coming up the dumbwaiter from Mildred in the kitchen below, and Nora, a sweet-tempered servant who'd been with them forever was trundling trays of food to the sideboard. Cucumber and egg sandwiches, smoked salmon, and toasted cheese on bread— "Orkney cheddar, Master Lou, yer fauvrit," Nora confided. She sliced the fruitcake and spread clotted cream over a piece for him. "Juist as ye like it."

"Thank you, Nora. You spoil me." They all spoiled him, he knew. It gave them something to do in this quiet household.

"I've had my tea. But you know how much I like to watch you eat," Cummy said. "How was the canoeing on the Scheldt?"

"It was an ordinary-sized adventure, no high drama," Louis said. "But I have enough material to do some essays for magazines. If all goes well, I will wrap them up into a book. I think it could sell."

"I'm *sure* it could," she said. Her eyes blinked rapidly, as they always had when she was stirred up about something. "You're the finest writer I have ever known."

"How many others have you known?"

Louis watched her think about it. "None," she said. "Still . . ."

They both laughed. Cummy hadn't any idea what he wrote now. Though she had always crowed about his boyish scribblings, she was truly proud of the religious history on the Covenanters he had written when he was sixteen. She privately took some credit for it, having indoctrinated Louis in the brutal martyrdoms of the Presbyterian heroes who fought against the Episcopal monarchy. It was the first thing Louis had published, even though his own father had paid for the printing. To Cummy, *The Pentland Rising* ranked among the important books of the ages.

She was a believer in him the way only mothers and nurses could be. Once, about a year before, his mother had chided him for not responding to one of Cummy's letters. "Alison Cunningham had more than one marriage proposal she turned down so she could stay at her post." He knew he was "her post," but it hadn't occurred to him that Cummy had ever lost anything except sleep for him.

Their fondness for each other had been forged during the feverish nights of his unrelenting, croupy coughs. Cummy had comforted him tenderly through it all. Now that he was grown, they remained close friends. Never mind that she was a ferocious Calvinist and he a nonbeliever. He forgave her the bloody tales that haunted his childhood, and she forgave his recent lapse in faith as a temporary complication. "Even John the Baptist suffered doubts," she told him. "You were always a pious boy. God hasn't forgotten that. Just don't keep Him waiting too long."

Louis could not look at Cummy without thinking of drafts, cures, blood, and terror.

She had been a fierce opponent of drafts. She could detect the faintest incursion of cold air and could instantly rig a blanket as a hanging to seal off his room. Whole winters he had passed inside that hothouse, too sick to get outside. It was bronchitis; it was pneumonia; it was incipient tuberculosis—the diagnoses changed over time. What was agreed upon by everyone was that he had inherited a bad set of lungs from his mother, and drafts, above all, were to be defended against.

Cummy would stand at the window, whatever the season, cheerfully pointing out anything that moved to the sickly child bundled in a blanket. By day, they studied the Edinburgh sky, umber-colored from factory grit, and scanned the trees in Queen Street Gardens, trying to locate the one blackbird sending up a song. Or he would lie facedown on the floor and paint pictures. At night, awake and hacking, he listened as Cummy spoke of the hideously persecuted, half-naked and freezing Covenanters who were run through with swords by King Charles's soldiers on Rullion Green in the Pentland Hills. She told of their corpses being axed to pieces and the heads and hands sent to different parts of Scotland, and she told him of "the boot," an iron torture device placed over the leg that was used on some of the battle's survivors. When pressed by the boy, she explained that the torturer squeezed an iron wedge between the martyr's leg and the iron cage, then hammered it until the leg was pulp. For months, when he closed his eyes, Louis saw free-floating, mutilated limbs. He prayed for sleep, and when it didn't come, he prayed for morning. His little rag of a body would finally fall unconscious just as other children were heading to school.

He wondered now if his parents had any idea of what was going on during those wide-eyed nights. Margaret and Thomas Stevenson were observant Presbyterians but happy enough to be lumped together on Sunday with all the other Church of Scotland burghers on their street, unlike Cummy, who belonged to the more evangelical Free Church. Could his parents possibly know their fair-haired darling had knelt next to his nurse and prayed for their souls' redemption because they played whist? Could they have imagined the menu of horrors Louis had been provided on a nightly basis while they slept? The images were as vivid now as they were then, the blistered skin of the unrepentant roasting on a million spits. Did his parents guess that the night terrors that plagued him—his vision of the devil riding furiously past their house on horseback—had roots in the nurse's tales of damnation? Cummy's heaven was a pale thing compared to her vivid images of a roaring, devouring hell.

All of Cummy's stories had been administered to him as she sat on the counterpane of his bed and dosed him with castor oil, cough syrup, the dreaded antimony wine that tasted of metal and sometimes made him vomit, and the strong black coffee she brewed to calm him in the night. All the good of the woman was mixed together with the dark and bitter.

Yet Cummy was as dear to him as his mother was. She had never allowed a novel or play into his room, but she had read to him with drama and gusto the things she loved: long passages of Scripture and the Shorter Catechism; a poem called "The Cameronian's Dream" whose singsong first lines he could recite even now: "In a dream of the night I was wafted away / To the muirland of mist, where the martyrs lay . . ."

Sometimes she had broken her own rules by reading aloud to him from *Cassell's Illustrated Family Paper.* It was a periodical full of articles about art and science and, best of all, delicious made-up stories. Cummy bypassed her scruples by choosing to view the tales as true. She had seen firsthand the magic such stories exerted on him.

"I'M NOT GOING to practice law," Louis said, blotting his mouth with a napkin.

Cummy waited a while before she responded. "Have you told your father?"

"I will tonight."

She patted his hand, then drew in a big breath. "Well, now," she said, exhaling the words thoughtfully.

"And I have met a woman."

"Oh!" Cummy struggled to conceal her surprise. "You don't say."

"She's an American and she has children. Divorced." Louis watched her eyebrows quiver slightly at the announcement. "I'd appreciate if you didn't mention it."

"Of course, Master Lou, I won't say a word." She glanced at her watch as if she had an appointment, then hurried to the foyer to get her coat. When she came back to hug him, her eyes were wide and blinking. "I shall be saying a prayer for you about suppertime."

When she was gone, Louis went upstairs to change clothes. In his bedroom he noticed what a lot of junk there was, things from his early years that embarrassed him to look at now. His mother had made the room a museum of his childhood. He had never bothered to pitch any-thing himself, and he commenced doing so. Picking up the little card-board figures from a play theater he'd loved as a boy, he considered throwing them into the wastebin, then rejected the idea. His eyes fell on a stack of papers next. He knew the pile intimately but spent the next couple of hours reading through the pages anyway, walking down that avenue of history one more time.

It was no accident that he'd become a writer, he thought when he glanced up from the pages. In his bookcase, he spotted *The Arabian Entertainments,* a book he had borrowed repeatedly from his grandfa-ther's library before he finally owned it. Next to it stood a row of ro-mances that had been his friends: *Robinson Crusoe, Gulliver's Travels, The Three Musketeers, Don Quixote, Rob Roy,* and a half-dozen other historical novels by Scott that had swept him away at thirteen. Walt Whitman's *Leaves of Grass* was crammed in among the romances, though it should have occupied a shelf of its own, so completely did it turn his seventeen-year-old world upside down with its unblushing sexual imagery and manly thinking. By then he knew he wanted to be Robert Louis Stevenson, author. Had known for some time, actually, as he'd carried around a notebook in his back pocket for the purpose of describing things since he was a boy. When it came to writing, he'd been obsessively practicing for years. He had set himself the task to imitate the best writers, including Hazlitt, Wordsworth, Montaigne, and Hawthorne. He was convinced the exercise would help him pene-trate the mystery of what made good writing great. You went to the masters to study their technique, whether you were a painter or a woodcarver or a writer. You learned the basics. And when you were schooled in the craft, truly practiced, when you had exposed yourself to the best, you might be ready to utter your own thoughts. He laughed to remember how he had driven everyone mad during his Charles Lamb period, when he blathered on like an insufferable prig, imitating how he thought the great essayist would have spoken, and interjecting "If I may so speak" into any pause in a conversation. How did his family put up with it? Yet it wasn't for naught; he'd profited considerably from aping the masters.

Now he stacked his old pages in a neat pile and left them on the desk. Perhaps someday, someone would be heartened to find his early attempts. It was vanity to think that way, he knew. And he cringed at the memory of asking Bob to save his letters without saying why; they both understood what Louis was hoping for. It was a measure of Bob's friendship that he had not peed his drawers at the pride of the remark. Yet there it was—fat ambition.

He was eyeing the cardboard theater figures again when a knock came at his door.

"Darling!" His mother swept in and wrapped her arms around him, beaming in the way she used to before all the arguments took over. He was struck by how little her oval face had changed since he was a small child. She kept herself girlish and slender for his father. Not all women her age did that. "Come to supper, Lou. We want to hear all about your trip."

DOWNSTAIRS, THOMAS STEVENSON already occupied the head seat at the table.

"Louis." His father spoke his name matter-of-factly, as if identifying an object. When Louis and his mother were settled, his father lifted his knife and set to work on the lamb chop before him.

"Hello, Father," Louis said pointedly, when it became clear that there would be no cordiality. "And how was *your* trip?"

When Thomas Stevenson spoke, he had the look of a weary academic finishing a long lecture. He kept his head bent and tilted slightly to one side while he glared up from heavy eyelids. His eyebrows winged at an angle, forcing deep horizontal lines to etch his forehead. One always had the sense that he was using every shred of patience he possessed to make his point to a thickheaded audience.

"You've had your holiday. It's time you take on clients." Thomas pushed mashed potatoes around his plate. "Monday morning, get yourself over to the Parliament House and—"

Louis took a deep breath. "I've decided to try to make a go with the writing. I began a book of essays when I was in France, and I thought we might talk about—"

His father's head tipped farther forward, as if he were confused. "Let me understand this. You abandoned engineering because you were bored. But you agreed to study the law if I paid for your legal studies. I did so, believing that your writing would be secondary to the law. Now you are saying you won't practice?"

"It was a compromise. It was never a true calling to me."

"It was an agreement," he thundered. "Have you forgotten that?"

"I told you when I was fourteen that I wanted to write, and you wouldn't hear of it. You looked at me and saw another lighthouse builder. And when engineering school didn't work out, you looked at me and saw a lawyer. I entered the bar for your sake. The truth is, I have no desire to walk the boards of the Parliament House for the rest of my days." Louis tried to modulate his tone. "I have so many ideas to express. What I want is to become a good writer—a great writer, if it may be. A writer of influence. I don't feel that way about being an advocate." Louis waited for the usual rejoinder: How do you intend to feed yourself?

"Your personal commitments are as fickle as your faith?"

Straight to the old wounds. Louis measured his words. "We have been through this all before, Father. It isn't the ideals of Christianity I disagree with, it's the intolerance of a religion that won't permit questions. How can you live with that? If you believe, then believe. But don't tell me I can't use the reason I was born with. *You* are the one who taught me about science, to explore and question."

His father stood up slowly. "I have made all my life to suit you," he said, his voice an agonized rumble. "I have worked for you and gone out of my way for you, and the end of it is that I find you in opposition to the Lord Jesus Christ. I would ten times sooner see you lying in your grave than that you should be shaking the faith of other young men and bringing ruin on other houses as you have brought already upon this."

"So that is what I will do as a writer? Shake the faith of other young men?" Louis's eyes filled with tears. "Have you ever once done something for the joy of it? Or is it all just degradation and damnation with you?"

Thomas Stevenson looked stricken. It was an unfair remark, and Louis knew it. His father had nursed him through the nights when he was sickest. He had laughed and played with him as if he were a child himself. But this matter of religion had wedged them apart. *You are a good man,* Louis thought, *but you are cowed by some strange Calvinist devil.*

Louis observed his father's hunched shoulders, his face red with distress. He had long worn a neat beard like a stirrup around his ruddy face, without a mustache. In the lamplight, the bitterness in his heart showed on his naked, downturned mouth.

"I thought to have had someone to help me when I was old," he said.

His father left the dining room, the food on his plate gone cold. In the past, it was usually Louis who stormed off, running to his room or racing outside. Thomas Stevenson lumbered to his study and shut the door. Louis had heard it slam in the past after their exchanges. Now he sensed defeat in the dull click of the latch.

Maggie Stevenson eyed her son, her pretty features tortured. She had not spoken up for Louis; these days she rarely did. It did not surprise him. His parents had long enjoyed their own society, and even as the adored only child, he often felt left out. Her silence simply confirmed what he'd known for some time. *My mother is my father's wife. And the children of lovers are orphans.*

"Excuse me," Louis said. He stood up, fetched his jacket in the vestibule, and headed into the night.

CHAPTER 16

Out on the street, Louis felt a chemical mix of rage and freedom in his chest. It was the same dangerous brew that had propelled him at seventeen into raw adventures. He remembered the first time he stormed out after his father shamed him. He'd been so full of outrage, he frightened himself. He had not known then where he would go— it was ten o'clock—but he wasn't going back in, that much he knew. That night Louis discovered confidence, or perhaps recklessness, within himself. He had walked for hours through the old section of Edinburgh, repeating his father's words in his head until the night world around him erased the dispute. In the neighborhood he knew so well by day, new faces appeared after nightfall. He went back often after that, sneaking past his parents' bedroom door, creeping home at three or four A.M., until he felt the Old Town was his and he could stride through its dark landscape like a tiger surveying its territory.

Louis stormed along Princes Street now, kicking a light pole in his fury. *Sick of it! Sick of you!* The old man's insults crowded his brain. It was on Princes Street a few years back that his cousin Bob had come close to being pummeled by Thomas Stevenson. Louis's father had discovered an incendiary piece of paper while pawing through his son's room when he was away at school. It was the constitution of Louis and Bob's Liberty, Justice, and Reverence Society. Bob had drafted the LJR's irreverent, tongue-in-cheek manifesto that rejected everything their parents had taught them, but Thomas had made the leap that it was Bob who'd caused Louis to reject his faith.

"You have tampered with a man's soul, the worst sin!" Thomas had shouted at his nephew upon encountering him on Princes Street. "How could you do that after all I have done for you?" Stunned by the transformation of his amiable uncle Tom, Bob had held up his hands to fend off any blows that might be coming at him.

"I understand what you are contending with," Bob later told Louis when relating the events, and it had given Louis comfort to know that someone else could see the vein of repressed violence that throbbed in his father. Not once had he seen it physically expressed, but it was there, deep and ready to burst.

"VELVET." LOUIS HEARD the familiar name from a voice just behind him and turned to see who had spoken it.

"Mary! How are you?"

A young woman with a wide gap between her front teeth smiled and extended a gloved hand. "I'm weel," she said. "Juist oot gettin dinner makkins."

"You look wonderful, Mary."

"Thank ye." She averted her eyes for a moment. "Ah'm gaun tae America. In juist twa weeks. Gaun tae to live with relatives in Michigan. Hae ye been there?"

"No, never."

She shifted from foot to foot. "It was lovely getting tae ken ye, Velvet."

"I'm glad I know you, too, Mary. And glad for you that you're leaving this place. I wish you a wonderful life."

"You hae a fine yin, tae," she said. She squeezed his hand, then walked on ahead of him, her great hips swaying beneath her skirts.

It was on one of his earliest angry walks, when he was drunk on beer, that he'd met Mary. She was a country girl whose soft hands, blue eyes, and honest Scots tongue seduced him instantly. They had stepped around graves in the Calton cemetery, looking for an unoccupied patch of grass. Louis could see vividly, even now, the moon-washed shapes of entwined couples lying on the ground between graves, like toppled stone statues.

Mary was the first girl he had ever lain with. After a few trysts at the graveyard, she'd stopped meeting him, and he'd moved on to spend his allowance at the brothels in Leith. One in particular, run by a woman named Flora who managed the business for an absent owner, became his favorite. The place was full of a changing cast of businessmen, petty thieves, sailors. Flora took one look at Louis and named him "Velvet Coat." He realized in time that everyone acquired a new name in that house. It made sense; nobody wanted to use his real name. Flora sat Louis down at a table in the kitchen, where she got an earful of his playful, bright talk. "This seat at this table is yours. Any time. Any day," she told him. He took to bringing a notebook and penning bad verses while the prostitutes—young and old—fussed over him between their assignations. In time, when he came through the door, the women would gush, "Velvet Coat!" Or simply, "Velvet!" He took comfort with a number of them.

In the past, Louis's feet would have walked him directly to Flora's on a night such as this. But he was a different man inside his skin now. It struck him that in the rages of his youth, he might have gotten himself into real trouble. Ironically, it was probably the moral compass Thomas Stevenson installed in his son that had kept him out of jail.

His anger at his father had begun to look like the kind of sorrow the Greeks wrote about—something that couldn't be fixed. Why had he chosen to tell the truth about his waning belief, especially since he'd lied to his father about so many other things? Louis once used the word "atheist" to describe himself when, in fact, "agnostic" was more accurate. But "atheist" was more hurtful; it was the juice of a lemon in his father's wounds.

If he were free of his financial indebtedness, he might be able to strike a new relationship with the great lighthouse engineer, man to man. But here he was, twenty-six, not yet a writer of any worth, and still relying on his father for money. It was nothing to be proud of.

The thought of Fanny Osbourne came to him again. He kept hearing her voice, a running brook under ice. She was like no woman he had ever known—a real American girl, unimpressed by class and all the things he hated. She was a brooding listener, and when she spoke, she flickered new light on his understanding of a thing. And good Lord, she looked like a Mayan goddess. He wanted to stroke the dark, smooth loveliness of her shoulder, gone brown and shiny from the sun; he wanted to know the soul behind those eyes. Some men would run away from a woman who had lived life. He wanted to dive into that deep pool.

Louis's mind ran to another woman he had loved not so long ago, Fanny Sitwell—Claire. That was the private name he had given the patrician dark-haired woman who had taken him under her wing a couple of years before. She was staying at the time in a cottage in Suffolk, grieving over the loss of one of her two sons, and trying to separate from her idiotic vicar-of-something husband, though divorce was out of the question.

Louis had gone to Suffolk during a holiday to escape the pressures of home and law school. Fanny Sitwell was eleven years older than he and a nuanced woman, yet she'd been instantly kind and accepting of him, never calling attention to the gulf of years that separated them. "You're a born writer," she told him with an enthusiasm for his work he'd never known. "I want you to meet my friend Sidney Colvin. He can help you. He has publishing connections."

For hours she had listened as Louis poured out his misery, detailing the battlefield engagements at his father's house. Always, Claire had taken his side. He would lay his head in her lap while she listened with the tenderest sympathy. It was what he had needed three years ago. He was a little embarrassed now to think of the noisy letters he'd written to her in fits of passion and depression from 17 Heriot Row.

"Things sometimes get exaggerated at twenty-three that will seem less significant later on," she said to him a few months later when he saw her in London. Claire was thirty-four at the time and, in her gracious way, adept at letting down an admirer who was behaving like an immature fool. She was a true friend, but he had mistaken her solicitude for romantic love. He might still be pining for her if Sidney Colvin had not come to him and asked rather directly that he step aside. Sidney himself was smitten by Fanny Sitwell and let Louis know he was prepared to wait as long as it took for her wretched husband to die.

What was this attraction to older women? Louis couldn't explain it, nor did he think it really mattered. He was ready and willing to love. Claire had not wanted to be the object of his passion. Why would Fanny Osbourne want him? He had made a barking fool of himself by declaring his feelings for her.

He remembered something that had happened on the canoe trip with Simpson. Somewhere along the Scheldt, they had come upon a couple lying on the hillside, wrapped in each other's arms. Louis's eyes had grown accustomed to reeds on the shoreline and cows hanging their heads over the bank. He was unprepared for the sight of the lovers. Paddling along, he'd been playing with some rather satisfying words in his head that he meant to make a note of—*It was a fine, green, fat landscape . . .*—when he realized he was looking at a man's naked white flank resting atop a pink dress with a pink-cheeked woman in it. The two were gazing at each other, talking, when they realized they had been found in their secret spot by two *voyageurs*. *Voyeurs*, really, for Louis could not take his eyes off them. He was captivated by the dream-like scene. His heart and groin in unison set off a racket of thumping longing.

Louis had arrived at Grez just after that. Had Fanny Osbourne noticed the galloping desire that seemed to have made an idiot of him? There was no shame in longing. But what had he shown to Fanny Osbourne except the longing? He wanted to return to her, to let her see he was capable of higher feelings, that he had serious bones in his body.

He needed to prove he was worthy.

CHAPTER 17

At a table on the Chevillon's long lawn, Fanny was working on a new story. Beyond her, the river mirrored perfectly the ten sunlit arches of the graceful old bridge. From where she sat, the reflected curves created the illusion of a row of ellipses. She loved those arches for the way they framed the landscape beyond, and for the cool shade they provided when she canoed through them on a hot day a couple of weeks earlier. Just now the sun was hitting the inside of them, turning the old gray stone a rosy terra cotta. She had seen the bridge painted from every angle, and she'd painted it herself, yet its moods continued to mesmerize her. Today she would put it into a story rather than on canvas. She'd begun a tale about a woman staying at an old hotel that was frequented a hundred years earlier by a group of artists. Somehow Fanny wanted the woman to encounter the ghost of one of the long-ago painters. The woman wouldn't know he was a ghost, and she would fall in love with the reclusive artist who came into the parlor to talk with her only late at night, after everyone else had gone to bed.

Fanny closed her eyes and tipped her face up to feel the late-September sun on her skin. Maybe she should put the bridge in a travel story about Grez. She'd have a much better chance of selling that.

"How happy you look out here."

It was Louis Stevenson's voice, and it startled her; she'd not heard the sound of shoes brushing through the grass. When she opened her eyes, his midsection came into view, in particular his hands. The fingers were so long and thin, hanging there like string beans next to his trouser pockets. Fanny nearly welcomed Louis with a smile, then remembered her hurtful conversation with Bob and that she was angry with both Stevensons.

"Bob has gone back to London," she said curtly.

"Yes, I know."

"Will Low is gone, too. They all left a week ago."

"I came to see you," Louis said.

Fanny put down her pencil. She wished he would go away. When she looked up, there was that persistent, earnest face awaiting her reply.

"Is it your turn now, Louis?"

"What do you mean?"

"You and Bob seem to be under the impression that I am a movable feast, to be shifted around at your convenience. Isn't that right?"

"Fanny. No. Did Bob . . . ?"

"Bob did your bidding, Louis."

"What did he say?"

"Enough to get his message across."

"I didn't want to interfere if he had begun something with you."

Fanny sighed. "Well, isn't that loyal of you. Nothing had begun, but I'm sure Bob thought he was letting me down. Frankly, I've had many men in love with me, and except for an unfaithful husband, I have never had occasion to feel rejected. Quite the contrary. So I found it amusing to be let go of, so to speak, *and* handed over to someone else in the bargain."

Louis rubbed his forehead. "This is all my fault. I told Bob I was in love with you."

"How is that possible? You don't know me."

"I want to know everything you are willing to tell me, Fanny. Everything you love and hate, your whole life. Just talk to me, please. And I will talk to you. I want you to know me as something more than"—he sighed—"a blundering fool."

Fanny waved her hand dismissively. "You're a good man, I can tell that. But you're mistaken if you think you can simply walk in and claim me. I don't belong to Sam Osbourne and certainly not to Bob Stevenson."

"I am here to see you because I have never felt so joyful in the presence of a woman."

Fanny regarded the warm eyes, devoted as a spaniel's. Aside from the fact that he was slender, Louis appeared perfectly fit, not the sickly specimen Bob spoke of.

"I'm sorry if I've troubled you." His fists went into the pockets. "Forgive me."

Fanny rose from her chair. Louis grasped her hand and held it. They stood still for a moment, their eyes downcast.

"I don't know what you want from me, Louis. You're a young man, and I am a married woman. I can only be your friend."

"That would make me incredibly happy," he said.

BACK IN HER room, Fanny was surprised to find her daughter packing. "What are you doing? We have another two weeks here, Belle."

"That's what I want to talk about. The landlady said the flat would be empty by October first. I thought I would go and get the place set up before you and Sammy come in."

"Nonsense. You can't be alone in Paris."

"I'm so bored here, Mother. Everyone has left."

"Louis Stevenson just came back."

Belle shrugged.

"I thought you found him entertaining. You said when he was here before that you would rather listen to him than read a book."

"He's nice-looking for an ugly man," she said. "But I'm ready to go back, Mama. The school session has already begun. It seems my whole life, I have started my classes late. Everyone will know one another."

"Where is Frank O'Meara going to be October first?"

"Mother!"

"Well . . ."

"He won't be in Paris yet," said Belle. "He went back to Dublin. And Mrs. Wright has already moved her family into the flat next to us. She said I could stay with them if I came back early."

Fanny knew then that she would let Belle return on her own to the city. Margaret Wright was the kind of woman who didn't miss a thing; she could be trusted to act as a substitute mother in a pinch. "I suppose you can get the coach tomorrow to Bourron."

Belle threw her arms around her mother. Over her daughter's shoulder, Fanny's eyes fell on the open satchel, where one of her best shawls was poking up in a corner.

"No," Fanny said.

"Oh, all right." Belle pulled out the shawl and returned it to her mother's closet.

"I'm desperate for a nap. Will you go look for your brother? I haven't talked to him all day. He might be hungry."

When the door shut, Fanny fell into bed, exhausted. Belle wasn't near finished. She had to be watched for nuances, listened to in the spaces between sentences. This happened with girls; they developed secret lives and behaved mysteriously and worried you to death. Fanny didn't know if she had the strength at the moment to oppose it. Sammy was an altogether different matter. He was no trouble, never had been. That was the thing about good children. If you got busy, you could forget to watch. Hervey had been sweet and easy, too.

THE NEXT AFTERNOON, while Sammy fished from the bank of the Loing, Fanny met Louis in the dining room at four, as they had agreed the night before. Ernestine was bustling in and out, preparing dinner. In the kitchen, Fanny could see chickens beginning to roast on a spit in the fireplace above a pile of crackling twigs. Madame Chevillon's ancient grandmother sat silently beside the fire, occasionally taking a bellows from a hook to squeeze at the embers.

"Ask Ernestine to give us jobs," Fanny said, pulling two chairs up beside the woodstove. Louis spoke in French to the young woman, who seemed surprised by the offer from the American lady. "Tell her my hands like to be busy." The young woman returned in a few minutes carrying a basket of apples and a small tray with two glasses of vermouth.

"You skin those so expertly," Louis said when Fanny set to work on the apples.

She glanced at him. "Tell me something about yourself that people don't know."

Louis answered quickly. "I was a pious child," he said.

"Weren't we all expected to be pious?"

"No, you don't understand. I was *morbidly* pious. When I was five or six, I couldn't sleep for the sorrow I felt from the suffering of Jesus. Oh, and I was terrified, too. I feared I would die during the night and slip into hell for some offense. So I'd fight off sleep by counting up my sins and praying for forgiveness. When I think of it now, I pity that sad little chap."

Fanny whistled. "So do I."

"I never should have told you that." Louis put his face in his hands. "You must think I am thoroughly damaged."

"I think you are one of the cheerfulest men I've ever met, actually."

Louis sat up and smiled broadly. "A philosophical choice," he said. "Tell me about your own family."

"Let's see," Fanny said thoughtfully, sipping the vermouth. "I was raised by parents who believed a child was born with a nature that was either good or bad, and nothing they did was going to alter it very much. Oh, they inoculated me with a proper sprinkling in the Whyte River. Henry Ward Beecher did the honors, in fact. Our house was right next door to his church." She tossed a long curling peel into a bowl set on the floor between them. "My mother was sweet as pie, and she convinced my father that all seven of us children had sterling characters. So, we were free as birds—there wasn't a shred of discipline in the house."

"I never would have attended school if I were in your family."

"My schooling was"—she weighed her words; she did not want him to think her stupid—"spotty."

"Mine as well," he said. "One year my parents hired a French tutor, and all we did was play cards. It's not a bad way to learn French."

Fanny laughed. "I never learned French, but I started to read in English when I was four. My father would sit me on a stool and have me read aloud for the neighbors."

She remembered just then one of those occasions. The local newspaper editor, a friend of the family, had questioned her after she read a passage from a book called *Familiar Science*. "If the world is round, why don't we fall off?" he'd asked her. "Gravitational attraction," she'd piped up, much to the glee of her father.

"The adults were appalled," she recalled to Louis. "They thought it highly unnatural."

"You were precocious."

"Only in some areas. I went through high school, but all I cared about was reading. That and being outside in nature." Fanny looked at his face, seeking a trace of judgment. "It may sound like I come from bumpkins, but I don't. My ancestors arrived in Pennsylvania before William Penn. Truth be told, I spent a lot of time running free with my cousin Tom, who was as rough-and-tumble as they come. We would ford streams up to our necks, climb trees, swing by ropes. I was a wild thing—always had to jump off the highest rock into the river."

"A tomboy."

She nodded. "I was a shy girl child and dark-skinned, which was not the standard of beauty in Indianapolis, let me tell you. I knew early on I was different, and I had got the idea that I wasn't pretty. So I gave up on the whole business of trying to be pleasing in a girlish way. It seemed to me that boys had a lot more fun. It was a relief. I didn't look at myself from the outside. I just lived inside my skin, looking out."

"You had the kind of boyhood I craved," Louis said.

Fanny took a deep breath. Thinking of it now, she could almost smell the odor of sticky pinesap from the forest near her house. She pictured the same woods in winter, when hoarfrost feathered the pine needles. She wanted to tell Louis how she'd felt the world in those days, how the conversations of birds made sense to her, the clouds spelled out messages, the bright ripples of lake water moved through her the way sound did. Would he think her a silly fool?

"There were summer nights . . ." Fanny remembered aloud, pressing fingertips to her lips. "Do you have lightning bugs in Scotland?"

"No. But I've seen 'em in the south of England."

"Then I don't have to explain the magic of—"

"Do."

"Well, I was the neighborhood storyteller. I probably got my taste for ghost stories from my granny. She was an unpleasant, domineering woman, and unfortunately, I had to share a bed with her. At night she told hair-raising tales about bodies rising from graves and the horrors of hell. I learned to tell stories from a gifted terrifier, you might say. Children would start gathering in our backyard while we were still eating supper. I must have been about eleven. Once I finished helping with dishes, I'd go outside, and there would be a pack of sweaty youngsters, waiting. I'd hold off until it was dark, when you could see the lightning bugs. The little ones sat close together because they knew things were going to get scary. That's about all I knew, too, because you see, I never made up the stories ahead of time. I just trusted they would come to me, and they did. There were the usual appearances by giants and talking animals in the stories, but what was going to happen was as mysterious to me as to anybody else. Right in the middle of things, a little one would slide down the wooden cellar door and scare the wits out of the fella sitting below. Or an older boy might reach out and grab somebody's wrist, and there'd be pandemonium." Fanny laughed. "My, it was fun. The feeling of it, you know? Because I was waiting like everybody else for the story to reveal itself. And then to get going, and to feel like I was up on a draft of air like a bird, just sailing along with the flow of it. Not to mention the feeling of having the whole crowd in my palm . . . it was a giddy feeling for a girl of eleven." She breathed in deeply. "I reckon I've been trying to get that feeling back ever since."

"The feeling that you just touched something divine?"

"Oh, I'm talking about fairy tales and ghost stories, after all. But yes, I knew there was a wonderfully mysterious sensation to be felt when you create something. I knew even then it was an artist's life I wanted." Fanny stared into the fire. "There were probably four summers like that. And then my life turned upside down. Suddenly, I wasn't ugly anymore. Boys were coming around to pay calls." She shrugged. "I got distracted—got married and had a child." She put up her hands. "What more is there to say?"

"You were fearless."

"Foolish, too."

"Fearless enough to live in a mining camp in Nevada," Louis said.

"Well, foolish enough to marry a man who went off to find gold. I didn't know he was going to do that when I married him."

"So you followed him."

"Yes."

"And then?"

"And then there were snakes and angry Indians and raw winds whistling through the boards of the shack, and I learned to live with it all. I could have stood anything, I think, except his philandering."

"Even there?"

"There were prostitutes in the camp. Whether it was going on there or not, I'm not sure. But when he gave up on the claim in Austin, when we moved to Virginia City, there was no doubt about it."

Louis studied her. "You stayed with him. You had more children."

"Always after a reconciliation." Fanny sighed. "He swore he had changed . . ." She shook her head. "On my forgiving days, I think it's a sickness with Sam. There are times, though, when I wish he were dead."

She bit her upper lip, regretting those last words. No one should say such a hideous thing about anyone. Louis certainly wouldn't. She remembered him walking around taking up a collection a few weeks ago for a couple of stranded minstrels. He was above such remarks.

Something Bob had said about Louis popped into her mind: "He makes everyone around him a little better, a little brighter."

Watching Louis peel an apple, Fanny realized she was glad he had come back.

CHAPTER 18

In the morning, he was waiting for her when she appeared in the dining room.

"Would you like to take a walk?"

"I'm wary of walks in the woods with you Stevenson men," she said. "Anyway, Sammy is still asleep."

"It's going to be a warm day. I think it would be good for you."

Fanny finished her cup of coffee, stepped into the kitchen to confer with the cook, then went upstairs. She thought about the walk and felt an odd little palpitation. Stopping at the mirror in her bedroom, she pinched her cheeks for color, tied a red kerchief around her neck, then turned sideways to study her figure. She was surprised that her looks had not gone down, given the past year. She pulled her heavy boots out of the closet, the flat-soled ones she wore for walking. On the floor of the closet lay a small case. Impulsively, she opened it and removed the revolver Sam had given her back in Nevada. It was heavier than her pistol and did not fit in her pocket. She put the gun into a cloth bag, threw in a handful of bullets, pulled the drawstring, and slung the thing over her shoulder.

"Where are you going?" Sammy appeared in the bedroom doorway in his nightshirt.

"Louis and I are going for a walk."

"May I go?"

"Ernestine said she would make you an omelet while we are gone." Fanny hugged the boy. "If I know Louis, he will want to fish with you this afternoon."

Downstairs, Fanny collected the lunch the cook had prepared and put it in a knapsack for Louis to carry. "Sammy will be all right here for a couple of hours. He just woke up."

"The chicken we had last night?" Louis asked, patting the bag.

"And croissants."

"You're brilliant."

"I'm hungry."

They walked from the inn toward the path into the forest. There were a couple of dogs waiting at the opening. She had noticed before that they didn't go into the forest on their own, but they would follow people in. "Come on, then," she said to a mutt, and two followed. Louis went ahead of Fanny, moving along confidently, like an explorer. He stopped now and then to hold back branches that hung over the trail. They walked for a half hour without saying much, the dogs trotting along behind them.

It was a path neither of them had walked before. When Louis stopped, they were in a clearing near a stream. Fanny found a rock on which to lay out the picnic food. She used her small knife to cut up the chicken and put it on the bread. Louis had brought a goatskin of water. They ate quickly. It was nothing but bread, chicken, and water; still, they were content.

Louis sat on the ground against a rock and tilted back his head. Suddenly, he shouted out, "I love this forest! I love France!"

The echo of Fanny's laughter reverberated in the clearing. She sat upright and surveyed the ground around them. Soon she was on her feet, collecting pinecones, four of which she placed in a row atop a flat rock near the base of a tree. Next she came back to where Louis was and sat down, reached into her bag, and pulled out the smooth-handled gun.

His face registered the desired effect: The cigarette nearly fell from his lips. "I didn't know I had come among revolvers," he said.

Fanny emptied the bag of bullets into her lap and loaded the gun. She stood up and took her position, about twenty yards from the rock. With her back straight and both eyes open, Fanny blasted four shots, hitting each of the cones.

The air smelled of gunpowder. Her ears rang. When she turned around, she saw that the dogs had run off and Louis was on his feet, his expression registering something between alarm and marvel. She offered him the handle of the gun.

"Not my forte," he said, holding up his hands, as if in surrender. He lit a cigarette for her. "Do all the girls in Indianapolis carry guns?"

"Just the ones who like to shoot things." She put the revolver back into her sack. "I like to shoot things."

"Was that some sort of warning?"

"Take it as you wish," she said in an imperious way, but she couldn't sustain the pose. She put her head back and laughed. "I was trying to impress you."

"You did that. Where the devil *is* Indiana?"

"It doesn't matter. I don't know where home is anymore. We leave in a week for Paris, but we can't stay *there* forever."

"Don't think about it," he said.

OUTSIDE, THE DAYS were growing cooler. The last flowers of summer were fading, and the horse chestnut was dropping its spiky green balls. In the river, red berries fallen from bushes on the shore drifted in lines with the water's ripples and collected along the banks.

There were things she did need to think about. Getting Sammy a tutor in Paris was one, but the bigger worry was money. She dreaded the prospect of another threadbare winter in Paris, never knowing if Sam would send support or not. All the years they lived together, he made her ask for the week's household money; he would never give her the allowance outright. First he would demand an accounting for the last amount he'd given her, then look in her purse to see if she had some money left. He said it was only fair. But it made her furious to remember the humiliations. Sam had taken her dowry, along with money borrowed from her father, and thrown it down a mineshaft that he eventually walked away from. Where was the fairness in that?

I mustn't think out loud about Sam anymore. That couldn't be what Louis wanted to hear. As the days at the inn wore on, she found herself withholding stories if they involved Sam. Was Louis keeping to himself such stories of his own?

Now she woke every morning feeling calm, knowing she would see him first thing. They'd meet at the breakfast table, where he would concoct some adventure for the three of them. They paddled the river and fished, mostly tangling their lines in the thick sedge. Out in the woods, Louis reverted to eight—Sammy's age. They chased around playing hide-and-seek among the trees. "What was that about living inside your skin?" Louis asked her, pulling her into the game.

In the afternoons, Fanny and Louis sat beside the dining room stove. He told her about the lighthouses his father and grandfather had built. She told him about her own father's lumber business. Louis talked about how he had known at fourteen that he would be a writer. She told him about the art school in San Francisco where the creative impulses she'd always had veered toward painting.

She felt herself softening. Over the years she had made a near art of listening to men, no matter how boring; she perfected the interested gaze. But Louis was not boring, not ever; he was an extraordinary talker. And the pleasure was, he listened to her. Closely enough that after a time he seemed to be reading her mind, anticipating what she would say next. They came from entirely different worlds, yet they shared a surprising number of common experiences.

One night while she was mending stockings next to the stove, Louis and Sammy sat on the floor nearby and sculpted wads of wax into small human figures.

"This is a Confederate lieutenant who lost his boots in the last battle," Louis said to the boy. He had retrieved a matchstick and stuck it in the wax man's hand. "He may be barefoot, but he still has his trusty sword." He held up the soldier for Sammy to see. "What do ye think of this fella, mannie?"

The boy was on his belly, molding something. "He's perfect, Luly. I've got his horse right here."

Luly. Sammy has already given Louis a new name.

He read to the boy from *The Pilgrim's Progress* and *Tales of a Grandfather* and deftly spun stories out of his head. There wasn't a drip of condescension in his voice when he addressed Sammy. One night Louis led both of them down to the river. They gathered dry sticks from along the bank and built a fire, where they cooked apples over the flames.

"We're Crusoe-ing now!" Louis shouted. "If it weren't so blasted cold, mates, I'd say we should sleep outside tonight."

It had been hard to get the boy to bed after that. Once Sammy's eyes finally closed, Fanny returned to the dining room, where Louis was clutching a stack of papers.

" 'The Suicide Club,' " he said.

"You finished the story?"

"Close enough. Would you have a listen?"

"I'd be thrilled."

As Louis read, she realized he had taken Bob's idea and transmuted it into something entirely new. It was now the tale of a penniless young man without prospects who resembled Bob quite a bit. He had spent the end of his money to buy tarts and pass them out as a last act of generosity before he headed over to the suicide club. By the end of the story, the young man was saved from death, and the club closed down.

"I love happy endings," Fanny said, lifting her wineglass to him. "Bravo! You are a fine writer, and I am not just saying that because you wear a velvet jacket and a red sash. You are very good. Truly."

Louis looked as if he had just won a boxing match. They spent the next hour taking apart the story, with Louis asking her questions about whether a particular line worked or if a scene made sense. Now and then, he made note of her responses with rapt attention, saying softly, "You have a wonderful ear."

When they said good night outside her room, he kissed her on the cheek. Fanny was surprised he had not pressed himself upon her more, despite her initial warning. Most men would have made stronger overtures. She was grateful for that; she didn't know if she wanted him to. With Sam Osbourne, there had never been a question. This slender, cerebral young man with the soft white hands confused her. She wondered if Louis was hankering after some idealized notion of a woman but, in the presence of a real one, lost his nerve.

"I have started writing again," Fanny said one afternoon as they stood on the stone bridge near the inn. A cool wind from upstream blew against her face.

Louis was tossing orange peels to cackling mallards below. "Since you got to Grez?"

"Yes. Only in the past few weeks have I been able to put words together again."

"Why did you wait so long to tell me that?"

"I'm not like you, I'm a novice. I have sent stories in to some journals," she said sheepishly. "I still like stories of the supernatural."

"Nothing to be ashamed of. Scots have a weakness for ghosts and dungeons and blood. That we do."

"I've only managed to get one small thing published—not the least bit mystical—in a magazine you've never heard of."

Louis shook his head. "It's very hard to get published."

She shrugged. "Everything has been hard."

He touched her shoulder. Below them, the river headed toward the little rapids where they had taken canoes a few weeks before to shoot over its edge.

"As sick as he was, I refused to believe Hervey would die," she said. "He suffered for five hideous months but never complained. My boy never complained." Fanny leaned on the bridge rail with her face in her hands. "I keep thinking, if I hadn't brought Hervey to Europe, his health would not have broken. Or maybe if I had taken him back to the States from Antwerp, he might have made it. My brain won't stop asking, what if?"

"I'm so sorry, Fanny."

She wiped her eyes with the heels of her hands. "My boy will never have the chance to canoe down a river or discover if he likes to paint or to write. Why should I be happy? How dare I?"

Louis took her in his arms and rocked her there on the bridge. Peasants returning from the fields stared as they clomped past in their wooden shoes, with hoes and shovels in hand.

That night, when the inn was silent, they lingered near the stove. The coals spilled a circle of light on the floor.

"What is it you want, Louis?"

"I want to travel and have real adventures. And when death comes, I want to be wearing my boots." He leaned forward in his chair, gazing intently into the fire, and after a pause admitted, "The bigger truth? I desperately want to go in for literature! I don't want to waste any more time, and certainly not on the law."

"Well, you have a gift with words."

"My father doesn't think I can survive on writing."

"Hmm. I don't know about surviving on it, but when you have a gift, it isn't yours to keep to yourself. It's the reason you're here. It's your purpose."

Louis studied her face. His eyes were the most disarming thing about him. Often he seemed to be noticing something just beneath one's epidermis.

"Have you been eavesdropping at the door of my heart? Because that is what I believe with every chamber of it. You *understand,* Fanny Osbourne. You're good, and wise, and flaming courageous." He took hold of her hands. "Can you fault me for falling in love with you?"

She did not venture another word. She rose to her feet and went with him up the dark staircase and past her room where Sammy slept. In his room, Louis eased her down on the bed. He held her for a good while, moving his lips from time to time to her ear to kiss it. The warmth of his breath, the comfort of a man's arms, caused her nearly to weep. Her hand brushed against his belt, and he took it as a sign. She let him unbutton and unlace her, and when her garments were a pile on the floor next to his bed, she welcomed his body to hers. She felt his hipbone press against hers as he whispered how he had wanted her so desperately that day in the woods. When he spoke her name, it sounded like an intimate foreign word.

Fanny found herself a little stunned afterward. Louis was not the boy she had first taken him to be. He was a confident, generous, hungry lover. Clearly experienced. The past hour was not like any time in her life before.

Lying next to Louis, she remembered herself as a young bride. What had she known about love at seventeen? It was a wordless, crazy attraction that had flung her from stilts into adulthood. Sam had never talked to her about her spirit. He had devoured her in bed; hatched big plans about their future; impregnated her; been jealous when other men showed interest. He had given her the big revolver to protect herself, and bragged of her skill as a marksman. He had bragged, too, that she was the best-looking woman in Nevada and could cook beef fifteen different ways. But had Sam Osbourne ever really liked her? She didn't know.

That this brilliant, warm, funny Scotsman said he loved her spirit was enough for the moment. She didn't want to think about his unfitness as a marriage prospect, his lack of money, or his youth. Good

Lord, he was closer to Belle's age than her own. *You are thirty-six, Fanny. You've lived long enough to know better. He's no solution to your problems.*

Someday years from now, she imagined she would read in a newspaper about Louis's important new book or his latest lighthouse and would then feel a twinge of regret for their ill-starred timing. But for now, before she had to get up and go to her own room, she savored the comfort of his shoulder, where she rested her drowsy head.

~~~

1877

It was the green hour in Paris, when people drinking emerald-colored absinthe filled the cafés. As he hurried along the snowy streets of Montmartre, Louis glimpsed couples inside bars sipping the elixir, their arms draped lazily around each other. The absinthe lovers flooded his mind with memories of Menton three years earlier, when he had gone south to recuperate from lung troubles. Alone, free from his parents, he'd drunk absinthe and smoked opium into blissful stupefaction. It hadn't helped his health one whit, but he briefly felt as untroubled as these people looked.

When he turned now onto Rue de Douai and spotted Fanny's stone apartment building, a vein in his neck began to thud like a steam hammer. He looked up, hoping to spot her in one of the tall windows, leaning over the black iron balcony and waving at him, but he caught no glimpse of her. She knew he was coming. Was her heart galloping the way his was right now?

By their last day at Grez, they had nearly stopped talking. It seemed anything of importance had already been spoken or didn't need to be. He could see in her face what she was feeling. The night before she left, he'd written a farewell poem for her.

> . . . On the stream
> Deep, swift and clear, the lilies floated; fish
> Through the shadows ran. There, thou and I
> Read Kindness in our eyes and closed the match.

She had cast that pensive gaze of hers over the paper, nodded knowingly, and put it into one of her pouches. Then she'd boosted Sammy into the old donkey cart headed to Bourron, climbed up, and waved goodbye.

Louis realized his nerves were wrecked from the fear that their separation over the past few weeks might have rubbed the bloom off the rose. He shook away the thought and bounded up the four flights of stairs to Fanny's flat.

"Louis!" Fanny shouted when she flung open the door of her apartment. Her kisses—unabashed, even loud—settled the matter. He lifted her tiny body and whirled her around like a doll. When a woman next door poked her head out into the gritty-looking hallway, Fanny slipped from his grip and straightened her dress.

"Margaret," Fanny said. "You remember Louis Stevenson."

The woman nodded, greeted Louis, and retreated.

"She was in Grez for a bit, wasn't she?" he asked.

"Yes. She's a writer," Fanny said. "We met in art class, and now we're neighbors." She pulled Louis into the parlor, a bare little room with a ragged sofa and an ancient pair of chairs with punctured caning.

Louis put his hand through a hole in one seat. "You could get your bum caught in there and never get out," he said. He loved watching her laugh at his paltry jokes.

She leaned back and clasped her hands together, her round eyes half-mooning with glee. "Flea-market treasures," she said. "I'm going to make cushions for those chairs."

"Aren't you a clever girl. And where might Sammy be?"

"With Belle at the circus for another hour or two. They went to see the trapeze men."

Louis looked toward the open door to her bedroom.

"What is it you have in mind, sir?" she teased.

"You," he said gently. "Us." He withheld what was next on his tongue. *French acrobatics.*

With a measure of awkwardness, they went in. The last of the day's light was fading through the sheer curtains as Fanny removed her dress. He was struck by the white lace of her chemise, how it appeared to glow against her skin. He wound his arms around to her back to dispatch the corset, then pulled the chemise over her head. He tried to keep his eyes on hers as he undressed her, but it was a complicated set of moves that he managed with limited grace. Once she was naked, he couldn't help gawking at the splendor of her full breasts. "Bless my eyes," he muttered.

Fanny pulled back the sheets and lay down, stretching one arm slowly across the far pillow. Her small hand, the color of old ivory, sank into the white down. He put his cheek on her neck, felt the warm pulse of her. His mouth went down to the marvelous breasts, around and into the moist spot between them. Soon she was moving in rhythm with him, and he thought, *What else matters but this?*

After their lovemaking, she rose from the bed and kept her back to him as she dressed. When she was covered, she turned. "I don't want Belle and Sammy to—"

"Of course not," he said.

"The neighbors here . . ." she warned.

"I'll see you in the parlor."

Fanny. Fanny. Fanny. How quickly she could shift. She was the most passionate woman he had ever shared a bed with—leading, following, losing herself in trancelike forgetfulness. How then could she suddenly become modest?

Louis reached down to his trousers on the floor to remove a pencil and notebook from a pocket. *On Falling in Love,* he wrote, and underlined the words. *And so we go, step for step, like a pair of children venturing together into a dark room—with both pleasure and embarrassment.*

LATER, WHEN THEY went out to walk, he told her, "I am French."

"And the Scotch accent?"

"Well, I *feel* French, anyway." He pulled up his collar to cover his ears. "A while ago my father changed my middle name to the French spelling. It was L-E-W-I-S before. I took terrible ribbing from Henley who finds it pretentious. He still writes to me and uses the old spelling. I don't care. 'Louis' suits my soul.

"God, how I love Paris! I love every hair on its head. The street names alone are fit to open a novel. Rue de la Femme-sans-Tête— Street of the Headless Woman. Street of the Bad Boys. Street of the Bridge of Cabbages. When I was a child visiting Paris with my parents, my father used to make a game of finding street names like that. We used to go over to a crèmerie in St. Germain. It was amazing, not only for its tarts but because the owner kept the napkins of his regular customers locked up in a drawer behind the register. How I wanted to have my own napkin stashed there!"

He remembered one of those early visits, when he had spied a boy of about sixteen wearing a black velvet jacket and a beret. The moment had been spiritual. In that glimpse, he had found his style. How old was he then? Eleven?

Even then when he came to Paris, his senses, like a bird dog's in the field, went on high alert. In those days, it was swords and military paraphernalia displayed in a shopwindow that could stop him in his tracks. Now he was a collector of characters. When he happened upon a big personality in a café, and he often did, he moved in close to watch and listen. He scribbled down the remarks of quieter types, too, like the dipsomaniacal bartender who adored discussing Flaubert. "I love books," the man said, his eyes growing misty, as if he were talking of his mistress. He lifted his shoulders in resignation. "And I love gin."

Other days, Louis was satisfied with smaller hints of character: ambiguous smiles, arrogant nostrils, elegant diction emerging through bad teeth. He saw venality and courage played out on Paris's streets, and he filled up notebooks with the details: a cheese merchant furtively sweeping the day's detritus from his sidewalk over to the chocolatier's doorstep; a woman with a port-wine stain over half of her face, singing "Vive la Rose" on a street corner; a well-tailored old man with a telltale red nose whipping off sad little watercolors of hens and chicks for drinks in a café.

During the years when Louis was ailing and needed a sunny climate, his parents had bundled him off with them to the South of France, but they always scheduled in a visit to Paris. It occurred to him that they had come here because they needed to fill their own lungs with a little freedom from everything back in Edinburgh. His mother and father always seemed more relaxed in France.

French was sweet and liquid on his tongue. Sentences, paragraphs, coherent ideas flowed naturally, and he found himself in many a charming exchange. He read the great French classics with a dictionary at hand, but he gathered his spoken French from butchers, waiters, and landladies.

The French could be brilliant conversationalists, honest and free from hypocrisy. But they kept a distance; he didn't know if he would ever share a close friendship with a French person. He felt deep affection for Parisians nevertheless, because in their city, more than any other place, a man could devote his life to art—and be taken seriously.

Fanny admitted that she did not love the city as he did.

"I'm going to show you *my* Paris," he told her. He did not have to say, "So you will fall in love with the things I love." She understood that, and he could see she wanted to.

He took her to his favorite booksellers near Pont des Saints-Pères on the Left Bank, where he bought Victor Hugo's *Les Travailleurs,* and from the slim offerings of English-language volumes, Fanny chose a book she loved, *Middlemarch,* and a children's book for Sammy. In a public square, they warmed themselves near a blazing brazier, along with a circle of ragged women and men with whom he commiserated about the cold. On they went in the chill air, stopping often at shops and cafés where he knew the proprietors.

Following the advice of Will Low, they went to hear his friend Emma Albani sing the title role in *Lucia di Lammermoor* at the Théâtre des Italiens. Later, they paid a visit to Will's studio, where he was painting a portrait of the Canadian soprano. At the doorway of the building, two battered stone lions straddled the entrance wearing painted-on mustaches, courtesy of art students who lived there. Upstairs, they found the raven-haired Albani, dressed in her silk Lucia costume, standing erect with folded hands in front of Will and his canvas. The air smelled of mineral spirits; dust particles from ground pigments floated through streaks of afternoon sunlight. Louis and Fanny quietly made their presence known, crept up to view the painting, then slid back into the shadows where he could still see, even in the dim light, the look of pure joy on her face.

Every park or café became their own private place. They made up stories about the people around them. "That villainous fellow over there," Louis would begin, glancing at a portly gentleman drinking his morning coffee at a nearby table. "Do you see his walking stick resting on that chair? Look at the top of it."

Fanny glanced surreptitiously at the handle, a carved ivory Turk's head. "A courier, obviously," she said, picking up the bait. "The shaft of the cane is hollow. He's carrying rolled up sheets of paper inside . . ."

"Antique erotic prints from Japan?"

"Your mind does run in a certain direction, my love," she teased. "They are priceless drawings, stolen, of course, and intended for that woman over there. The two of them are in cahoots."

Louis eyed the potential co-conspirator, a plain freckled girl eating a croissant at the next table. "She does not know what she is to intercept. She has come from Marseilles at the request of her lover," he said, "a deserter from the Legion who was hired on as a spy for . . ."

The games lasted as long as their own coffee and rolls, and then they were out on the streets, where the rhythm of life swept them along past flower stalls and boulangeries, past display windows full of glinting paperweights, gloves, Japanese silks and fans, past doorways where baking bread or perfume or chocolate sent fragrant fingers out to the sidewalk to fetch them in by the nose.

Sometimes remembered buildings were gone. They wandered around the blackened stone remains of the Tuileries Palace that had been burned nearly to the ground during the suppression of the Paris Commune. "I was here when it was intact," he said with wonder. "How changed Paris is in just fifteen years." Elsewhere, he discovered that the mazes of crooked little streets he remembered from that early visit had been leveled by Baron Haussmann, the formidable mind behind the reshaping of the city. Now in their place were wide, arrow-straight boulevards lined with streetlights that imbued nighttime in Paris with a theatrical air. They walked along the lit streets as if they, and every other person on the pavement, were players in a grand, romantic drama.

CHAPTER 20

"I have good news," Louis said when he visited her apartment a few days later. "You remember Henley, of course. He's starting a publication called *London*. And he's going to publish the story I read to you."

" 'The Suicide Club'?"

"As soon as I polish it up. I think the length will be good for the magazine. I want to do a series of these shorter stories for him. Then, if luck holds, put them together as a collection for publication."

"That's grand, Louis."

"I don't know if publishing in *London* will mean much money, but it's one more foray in the right direction. He's going to need a lot of help. I was thinking you could do some work for him to get the thing off the ground—find writers, do some editing, perhaps. He could pay you a little something."

"Yes!" Fanny sat up wide-eyed on the sofa. "Say yes to him. I will absolutely help. It's perfect timing, Louis. Sam can't pay me next month. And I *want* to do it."

"Then I will pay."

"But you haven't got any money for—"

"We'll find a way," he said.

Walking back to Will Low's studio for the night, Louis tried to figure how much was left of the thousand pounds his father had given him upon graduation from law school. It had seemed like a solid amount when he got it. He hadn't been a spendthrift, exactly, but he'd picked up the bill for a group dinner now and then, loaned friends money, and pitched in for this or that. The biggest chunk of it, he'd given to Colvin when someone stole a set of valuable prints in his keeping. Louis loaned him 250 pounds, lest Colvin be sued. Poor old Colvin probably would be paying that loan back for a good long time.

Louis had given a fair amount to Bob and his sister as their money ran out. None of his generosity, he thought, was out of the ordinary. His friends had done the same for him when he was short of funds; it was how all of them lived.

He could sleep and work at Will's place and toss a few francs his way. At least he'd had the sense not to accept the invitation to stay in Bob's flat. The place was crawling with bohemian friends and hangers-on. One fellow was sleeping in a closet. They were drunk by afternoon and up until dawn. Louis had pledged himself to work every morning until dinner, and he knew he could do it in this city.

The next afternoon, when he walked over to the Montmartre apartment, he found Belle in the parlor entertaining Bob. One look at his cousin confirmed what Bob had already admitted: He was smitten. Louis burst out laughing at his stupefied cousin watching the American girl, whose free-limbed storytelling had Bob gazing at her as if she were an exotic bird.

"Luly!" Sammy shouted when he saw his friend. Louis and the boy bear-hugged.

Fanny's eyes met his in the round of chatter that followed. They went out into the hallway together.

"I wish we had our own parlor, just for you and me," he said.

She pecked his cheek, then drew back and crossed her arms. "Did you know your eyes are red?"

"I went back to Will's last night and wrote until three or four in the morning."

"The canoe essays?"

"*Inland Voyage.* That's the name I came up with last night. I have two hundred pages so far. Added about fifteen last night."

Her smile was coquettish. "Have I told you today that you are amazing?"

"That's all I want to hear. Ever." He put the back of her hand to his cold cheek. "Who was your model at the studio today?"

"A man dressed as Napoleon Bonaparte."

Louis tittered. "And your foot?"

"Still achy," she said. "The price of canoe wars. I probably shouldn't have been out there in the first place. I can't swim, you know."

"Fanny!"

She shrugged. "I wasn't going to miss the fun."

"I love you because you're game." He put his lips on her neck. "I love you because you have the heart of a man inside the body of a luscious—"

"No," she said. "Not here."

"Fanny . . ."

"A woman's reputation is a fragile thing. Even in Paris." Her eyes darted toward the parlor. "Speaking of which, Bob has added a whole new wrinkle to my daughter's life."

Louis reluctantly drew back. "Where does Frank O'Meara stand?"

Fanny shook her head. "She's in a complete dither about which one she loves better. She can hardly concentrate in art classes. Frankly, she's driving me mad with her chatter about them."

"It's so beautiful outside. Let's round up everybody and go to the crèmerie to get a bite to eat," he said.

They walked out into the street, and Belle took Louis's arm. Just ahead, Fanny linked arms with Bob, while Sammy scampered around making snowballs.

"Do you love snow, Belle?" Louis asked.

"Yes, I do."

"That's good. Because we couldn't be friends otherwise."

"You have strong opinions about the oddest things," Belle said.

"Some people look at snow and think about catching their death of a cold or how a person could get lost in it and meet his end. What could be better than to be wrapped up warm in a coat and to see the soft flakes coming down?" He nodded toward Fanny and Bob up ahead. "Come to think of it, I believe I love my friends better when snow is falling on them."

Belle, who had been ambivalent about Louis's presence in their lives, allowed a grin. Her enormous eyes peered at him from beneath her fur-lined hood. "You have made my mother laugh again. I haven't heard her sound so happy since Hervey was a baby."

CHAPTER 21

"Mother," Belle said when she came in the apartment door. It was afternoon, and Fanny was scrubbing Sammy's school uniform shirt in a sudsy bowl. "What is it?"

"I had lunch with Frank, and he said Louis is sick."

Fanny dropped the shirt and wiped her hands on her skirt.

"It's his eyes. Will Low told Frank that Louis is in bed and he can't see a thing."

Fanny hurried into the bedroom to pull her boots on. "Go to my sewing box and get out a thimble. Fill it with boric acid crystals and wrap it in a clean napkin."

She'd noticed Louis's eyes growing worse in the past day or two. Yesterday morning she had mixed a few grains of the white stuff in water and dripped it into his eyes, then sent him home to rest. When he hadn't shown up at two o'clock, as he usually did, she assumed he was writing away. Fanny threw on her coat. "Watch Hervey!" she called over her shoulder.

"I know who you mean," Belle called back.

Snow had brought the cabs and trams to a crawl. When Fanny got to Will Low's studio, she saw the large white-haired head of an otherwise tiny doctor bending over Louis's bed. The man was disheveled, and his spattered shirt cuffs gave proof that he was at the end of a long workday. In profile, his nose was a bony ridge upon which stiff bristles of hair stood up like porcupine quills.

Louis was talking gaily in French to the old man. "What does he say?" Fanny asked Louis.

"There's my lady," Louis said. "Hello, sweet one." He stared blankly in her general direction.

"Louis, what does he say?"

"I got meself a roarin' eye infection. Fever, too."

"What are we to do?"

"Drink a pint a' whisky."

"Please, Louis . . ."

"He says I need to have the bandages changed every fifteen minutes," Louis said.

Will Low's jaw worked furiously as he watched.

"Tell me what the doctor just said, can you, Will?"

"He says Lou could go blind if he does not care for his eyes. He shouldn't have any light." Will covered his wispy mustache with a paint-splattered hand. He looked around his studio, dismayed. "I could put sheets over the windows . . ."

"Will, kindly ask the man precisely what we are to do and when. And ask him where I can get whatever medicine I need."

"Of course," he said. His face, boyish beneath a sealskin toque, registered his profound relief that she had arrived.

"I know how to do this, Will. Between the two of us, we should be able to get Louis into a cab and over to my flat." Fanny patted Louis on the shoulder. "You're coming home with me."

" 'My young love said my mother won't mind,' " Louis sang.

Will Low blinked nervously. "I thought a little drink might take his mind off the burning."

Fanny glared at Low. "He's pixilated. Get his trousers on him, will you?"

Fanny set him up in her bed and pulled a chair next to it. During the night, light from the streetlamp fell on his body. She had never seen him asleep, and she couldn't take her eyes off him. His face was as beautiful as Raphael's. She had seen a painting once of the artist as a young man, and his face was oval, with pensive dark eyes, like Louis's. *Here is a man so full of life and goodness and gifts,* she thought. *And utterly reckless with his health.* He had ignored the burning in his eyes for a week, just kept on working.

Ten days ago he had come with pages to read, and she'd felt almost immediately that a new door was opening for them. He began with his canoe essay and read sections of it aloud over a period of a week. But yesterday he had arrived with a piece about falling in love.

Falling in love is the one illogical adventure, the one thing of which we are tempted to think as supernatural . . . She had pursed her lips to suppress the greedy pleasure she took in the words. The essay was written in generalities, but there was no doubt about it: It was an open love letter to her. Louis planned to send it off to *Cornhill* magazine.

She ran her hand over his forehead. He was twenty-six and she was thirty-seven. She had spent a good part of her life being regarded as the young one. "Such a young bride, such a young mother, so young to be traveling alone," people had always said to her. How odd to find herself the older one. She didn't feel finished yet. She felt as young as he was. What did age matter, anyway? Not a scintilla. Except that it had allowed her to walk into love this time, eyes wide open—there was no falling about it.

In the morning, when she stood up, she nearly dropped over from want of sleep. Belle was lounging in the parlor. On seeing her mother emerge from the bedroom, the girl clasped her hands and said, "I'm not judging you, Mama."

"There's nothing to judge," Fanny responded testily. She put her hands to her waist and stretched backward. "Ten grains of boric acid mixed with water." She pointed toward a cup on the windowsill. "You watched me do it last night, right?" She yawned. "Oh, do I need to move these legs! If he wakes up, tell him I will be back soon to make breakfast."

Fanny made it down to the newsstand and was on her way to the bakery in the next block when her ankle buckled. It was the right foot, the foot that had ailed her since Grez. She gritted her teeth and hobbled back to her building, hoping against hope it was not a real sprain.

Four flights. Up to an awful apartment. Sam had made certain they couldn't get too comfortable in Paris. When she had returned from Grez, her Paris doctor had told her she was still fragile from Hervey's loss. "You will need a housekeeper," he'd said. "You're much too weak to do that sort of work." Ha! Housekeeper, indeed. She had dared not tell him they lived on the fourth floor and felt lucky to have it.

When Fanny returned, Louis was sitting up. "They're much worse today." There was despair in his voice. "A man can write with bad lungs. But what does he do without eyes?"

Fanny took his hand. "Louis, I think you should go home." She waited for a response, but none came. "We'll get Bob to take you to your parents' house," she said finally.

"Bob isn't in Paris, Mama," Belle said. "He's gone to Scotland for a week."

"Two weeks," Louis corrected her. "He left yesterday."

Another silence.

"There is a good doctor in London I have gone to," Louis said. "I have close friends there who have taken care of me before. Colvin, my editor friend. And Fanny Sitwell. She would help us, I'm sure of it. Henley is there, too. He owes me a little fussing."

CHAPTER 22

It was the curtains Fanny couldn't help staring at. Sitting on a chaise in front of the drawing room window, she pretended to look out on Brunswick Row, but her gaze went only as far as the lush brown velvet that framed the view. The curtains were pure simplicity; Fanny could have sewn them herself. But the fabric made her want to bury her face in it. The velvet would feel soft as a baby's thigh, she was certain; it was that fine. Subtly layered refinement—that was the atmosphere Fanny Sitwell had achieved with the pieces in her drawing room, from the leather chairs worn to a mellow shine to the pale blue damask wallpaper. That summed up the lady of the house, too.

"How is the pain today, Fanny?" Mrs. Sitwell asked. She moved over to the divan, where she adjusted the pillows under Fanny's foot cast.

"Gone," Fanny said. "Thankfully gone. I would have had the operation a month ago if I'd known I would feel so relieved."

"Dr. Evans is a miracle worker."

"That he is," Sidney Colvin concurred. He sat by the fireplace in a chair that was clearly designated as his, since no one else ever approached it. He was a pinched, sober man, an intellectual type who buried himself in journals and books when it was just the three of them, tossing a remark now and then into the conversation. It was when Louis showed up that the fellow blossomed. He was a real Cambridge professor of some sort. Everything about him was neatly trimmed, from the hairline below his bald pate to his close-cut beard to the tailoring of his coat.

"He may come across as a cold fish," Louis had warned her, "but he is the soul of decency. They both are. Oh, they're proper types. You must never smoke in front of them, for example. But they have been extraordinarily kind to me."

Fanny and Louis had shown up in London like a pair of injured birds; he nearly blind and she limping and queasy with worry. Louis's old friends had gone into action, arranging visits from the finest doctor in town. They brought in food to their hotel room during the fortnight Louis was laid up, with Fanny at his bedside. It was during one of the doctor's visits to the hotel that the venerable physician had spied Fanny's limp, examined her foot, and pronounced her an ideal candidate for surgery.

Now she was the patient. Returning from the hospital, Fanny had come to recuperate in the home of Mrs. Sitwell. The pair insisted she stay there and showered her with concern. They set her up on the sofa by the window, where she served as a splash of color in the subdued decor. They had thrown a tiger skin over the upholstery before settling her there, tied a yellow silk scarf around her head, swathed her in bright shawls, then sat down and gaped at her across the tea table as if she were Pocahontas.

"Mrs. Sitwell," she said now, glancing at the piano, "might I persuade you to play?"

"If you can bear my little errors," the woman said. "I have been working on a Mozart Sonata."

"If there are errors, I won't know."

"Do let's hear it," Colvin piped up.

"Do you play, Fanny?" Mrs. Sitwell asked.

"I don't have a musical bone in my body."

The woman laughed. "Louis doesn't have much of one, either. No sense of pitch whatsoever. But he does *adore* music, doesn't he? He puts his heart into that little flageolet of his."

"Oh," Fanny said. She realized she did not know he played anything.

Fanny Sitwell had an appeal of the Pre-Raphaelite sort, with sculpted cheekbones, straight brown hair parted down the middle and knotted at the back of her neck, and limpid blue eyes framed by brows fixed in pretty concern. Apparently, she had retired her bustle, for there was none to arrange when she sat down on the piano bench. Instead, she wore cream-colored tea gowns in her home. She was all patrician loveliness: her carriage, taste, flawless manners. In fact, she used the word "lovely" all the time, whether speaking of the sky or a friend or a rib roast.

Thank God for the piano. There were three more days to be gotten through on the sofa in this overheated flat before Fanny and Louis could return to Paris. These people had been ever so kind, petting her and waiting on her every desire, but she was no good as an invalid. Never had been. And the whole situation was strange, staying in the home of a woman whom Louis seemed to have desired rather heatedly at one point. "I worshipped her," he'd told Fanny in explaining their close friendship. "But it was merely a boy's crush; I was so young." "So young," as Fanny calculated it, was only three years ago. It hadn't been such a long time since Louis was coming to this house, pouring out his soul to his nurturing angel, and resting his head in his Madonna's lap.

With his eyes healed, Louis was spending time with Henley, working on the magazine. In the late afternoons, the two men would show up, brimming with excitement and ideas for *London*. That was when Sidney Colvin would look up from his book with a spark in his eyes and plunge into some literary debate with them.

"Do you think the Purist Movement has lost its momentum in Britain?" Henley had said over tea yesterday, in a tone that the others apparently took as provocative. Colvin's color seemed to heighten, and he pursed the rim of his cup in his lips for a good long moment before he replied flatly, "No, not at all." Fanny didn't dare ask what the movement was, for fear of appearing ignorant, but it dawned on her as the conversation proceeded that she was sitting among the vanguard of the Purists.

Now the music allowed them all a brief respite from polite conversation. What an odd relationship her two hosts had. They seemed to share pleasure in being "literary discoverers." They acted like an old married couple, yet they were careful to a fault not to show overt affection. Fanny doubted that any real intimacy existed. Just the promise of intimacy, probably, if only the Reverend Sitwell would kick the bucket. To be perceived as having a lover, given Mrs. Sitwell's marital state, was out of the question. Much better to be viewed as the nourishing goddess in her salon, with her friend ever at her side. Colvin, for his part, appeared content as a spoiled cat with the arrangement.

Fanny wondered if her feeling was simply raw envy. Louis had said she and Mrs. Sitwell would find they had much in common: both of them separated from wretched husbands; both grieving the recent death of a child. But Fanny suspected they shared very little. Mrs. Sitwell was from a different world entirely—a world of soirees peopled by the literary lights of London. Judging from the adoration of the men around her, she was the ideal Englishwoman: a person of delicate sensibilities whom they trusted to be discreet, a woman whose presence was calming. She appeared to have no artistic ambitions of her own. Instead, she was the Great Appreciator, stoking the egoism of each one. If she must work now, as Louis said she did—secretary to the College for Working Women—there was no sense that the wolf had ever been at her door, as it had been for Fanny.

She didn't long for Fanny Sitwell's life; she just wanted a little more comfort and security in her own. She had been making do for so long, scraping together what she could. An unpretentious life but genteel in its way, literary and artful—how nice that would be. She was tired of troubles. She had a pretty little falling-down house in Oakland and a sweet garden, but nothing like this place. *Imagine what I could do with a touch of money.* She let herself sink back into the cushions and picture what life as the wife of a successful writer might be. Louis would work in his study during the day. She could run the household and do her own writing. She would be his confidante, his editor, his counsel. She was nothing like Fanny Sitwell, but she knew well enough her own attractions. Louis loved her because she *wasn't* overtamed.

When Mrs. Sitwell stopped playing, Fanny applauded. Colvin had been sitting with his eyes closed, once in a while letting his toe fly up in time to the music. "Soul-stirring," he murmured.

The doorbell rang, and a servant ushered in Louis and Henley. They paused at the door as Henley, wearing a high-crowned hat with a floppy brim, leaned his crutch against the wall, placed his hat on it, and used his cane to get to a chair. Louis, to Fanny's astonishment, was wearing new clothes. "You've been shopping," she said.

"Am I no a bonny writer chap?" he asked in an exaggerated brogue. He stood back, pointed a dandyish toe, and modeled for everyone the double-breasted dark blue suit and stiff bowler.

"Lou, you look handsome in that hat," Fanny Sitwell said. Her voice turned kittenish. "Do you remember the hat you were wearing when I first met you?"

"A straw hat, as I recall," Louis said, looking uncharacteristically embarrassed.

"A wide-awake hat, it was. You were coming up the lane to your cousin's house with a knapsack on your back and reading a book, oblivious to the world."

Louis smoothed the jacket. "Well, I can't be going around London to see editors in ma auld tatters," he said. "And I'm celebrating a bit." He pulled out a piece of paper from his pocket and waved it. "This is a contract with none other than Leslie Stephen at *Cornhill*. He's going to publish my essay 'On Falling in Love.'"

Fanny's eyes welled with tears. *I miss you,* she mouthed to him across the room. He shot her a tender smile and put his hand to his chest.

"Fabulous," Colvin was saying. "An editor of Stephen's standing can make a career for a young writer."

"Now, come," Mrs. Sitwell said, "sit down and tell us everything."

They pulled chairs around the sofa where Fanny lay, and Louis recounted the details of his meeting and the taciturn Stephen's remark that he was a fine stylist.

"That must have cost him quite a bit, to let loose with a compliment," Colvin remarked. "Quite a stellar day for you, my friend."

"And Henley here is going to publish 'The Suicide Club,'" Louis said. "It's possible we could see a few pounds from it all."

Henley's big face puckered with delight. "It's not out of the question. If all goes well, I intend to have the best of the new crop of writers. Louis, of course. And Henry James, and some of the others. I shall give Leslie Stephen a run for his money!"

"I don't know if James will last," Louis said. "His *Roderick Hudson* was a fair start—"

"Fair start? I thought the characters were brilliantly drawn," Fanny protested.

Mrs. Sitwell turned to her, her face barely masking her astonishment that Fanny had uttered a literary opinion. Colvin and Henley ignored the remark.

While everyone chatted, Fanny settled into the pillows at her back. She was so happy to see Louis excited and well. She saw relief on his friends' faces, too. Clearly, Louis's charm loosened them from their stiffness. He was their Great Exhilarator. And Lord above, they needed one.

"Lou," Mrs. Sitwell said warmly, squeezing Louis's hand, "*your* time is coming. I always knew it would."

Fanny put her hand into her skirt pocket, found a cigarette, pulled matches from her waist pouch, and in the spread of thirty seconds, was savoring a mouthful of smoke. Louis stopped midsentence and stared at her, his face gone slack. Fanny Sitwell appeared to bite her inner cheek, then said, "I didn't know you smoked, Fanny."

"I seem to have quite forgotten myself."

"Why, it's all right. You can smoke here." She fetched a china saucer and placed it on the tea table for ashes.

"This will be the only one." Fanny laughed. "I'm out of tobacco."

"You make your own?"

Fanny drew on her cigarette. "I do."

"Sidney," Fanny Sitwell said, "might I prevail upon you to go out and get some papers and tobacco?"

"Of course."

"I should like to learn how to roll a cigarette," Mrs. Sitwell said. "And if you can put your hands on some champagne, I do think this crowd would appreciate it." If she was only being polite, Mrs. Sitwell, nevertheless, was managing to rescue the moment, judging from the look of relief on Louis's face.

With Colvin gone, the hostess drew her chair closer to Louis's, and they fell into conversation about "art for art's sake." Fanny bristled when she saw how easily they talked. She felt an urge to burst out in her mother tongue, "It's too blamed hot in here," but she held herself in check. William Henley was left to hoist his great trunk up out of the little gilded chair on which he was perched and to push it nearer to Fanny. *You're quite agile for a one-legged man,* she thought, and in the next instant, *Thank God I didn't say that out loud.*

"I understand you might be willing to give us a spot of help with the magazine," he said to her. "Louis says you've done some writing?"

"Oh yes, I have written for any number of publications. I'm an editor, too. Of course, I could find other writers for you. Margaret Wright comes to mind. She's an American journalist who writes a column called 'Paris Letters' for some newspapers. She lives in my building. There are several of us writers at that address, actually. Our building is something of a haven for artists."

Henley seemed to lose track of the thread of conversation. He grabbed hold of either side of his chair to lift his body with his mighty arms, once again trying to get comfortable on it. He wore a barely suppressed grimace much of the time, she realized. And she was struck by how big he was. No wonder Louis called him Burly. The man filled the eye.

"Are you in pain?" she asked him.

He looked at her sadly, not responding to her question. Instead, he said, "I know you lost your son. I didn't say anything to you in Grez because I knew you were trying to get back on your feet. But you have my sympathy, Fanny."

Fanny stared soberly at him. "How I wish I might have found a doctor as astute as yours."

"I had lost one leg already, and my doctor wanted to take the other. When I heard Lister was having success with scrofulous tuberculosis, I went to his Edinburgh infirmary to get treatment. That's where I met Louis, you know."

"No, I didn't know. He told me that Leslie Stephen introduced you."

"Except for Leslie Stephen, who had seen a couple of my verses, I was friendless in Edinburgh. I'll tell you no lie. I was poor as they come and desolate with loneliness. My only companions were a couple of little boys laid up in that place alongside me. Then one day Louis appeared, unannounced. He told me he was Leslie's friend. He was the jolliest fellow, smart and full of mischief. It was as if Puck had just walked into my room.

"I wasn't supposed to leave the hospital, but before I knew it, he had me out of that bed. We had to get down a long stair with me like this." Henley waved a hand at his stump. "But he did it. He had a carriage waiting, and it was spring outside." His eyes watered. "I had been in hospital for eighteen months. He drove me around to look at the cherry trees blossoming and the blue sky. I shall never forget his kindness as long as I live. Look at me, then look at him, and you will understand the act of will it took to cart me out of that place. And not just once did he take me out. Oh, no. He came back and back."

Henley produced a handkerchief and blew his nose furiously. "Don't ever take the man for granted," he said to her. "Understand what you have, Fanny Osbourne. There's not another one comes near him."

Later, after she had taught everyone to roll cigarettes, after they had merrily smoked and finished off three bottles of champagne, Fanny regaled them with stories of her ancestor Daniel Boone and tales of life in a Nevada mining camp. She told how she served barley coffee to the Paiutes who came to the window of her cabin every morning; how she'd battled bothersome varmints; how she'd befriended the minister called Smilin' Jesus. The whole group burst into fits of laughter as she talked, especially when she used words like "varmint." She wondered briefly if they knew she was speaking tongue in cheek.

"I didn't know you were related to Daniel Boone *and* Captain Cook," Louis whispered when he bent over her to say good night.

"Loosely," she said. "Daniel is on Sam's side, and the captain on my mother's. But it makes a better story."

"Fanny, Fanny," he murmured indulgently.

She smiled up at him. "I was simply obliging the audience, darlin'."

"I'll see you in the morning," he said, kissing the top of her head. He began to leave, then turned back. "First impression?" he asked.

On the train to London, she had told him that her first impression of a person was practically infallible. Louis so wanted her to embrace his world. She had wanted to be embraced by it. How to tell him now that she felt out of place among his friends—that they were strange, overly mannered, and a little frightening?

She reached out her hand and rubbed the curtain fabric between her fingers. "Lovely," she said.

CHAPTER 23

⁓

The day after Fanny returned to Paris, she discovered an opened letter from Sam among other mail sitting on the entryway table. "When did this letter from your father come?" she asked.

"A week ago." Belle and Sammy sat at a table near the window, playing with a traveling chess set Fanny had bought them in London. "He's coming over in the spring."

"When in the spring?" Fanny's heart began to thrash about in her chest.

"Probably May. He said he would write soon with more details."

Sammy's eyes lit up. "He said he bought a pony for me for when I get home."

"A pony," Fanny muttered. *How predictable.*

"YOU'LL HAVE TO be gone when he comes," she told Louis when he came to visit that afternoon. They were sitting in the parlor of the apartment, speaking in low tones so as not to be heard by Belle or Sammy. "It must be done exactly the right way, or I shall be left with nothing."

"I understand." Louis shifted in one of the battered chairs. "I had my own letter today. From my father."

"Yes? Is he coming to see you?" While they were in London, she had encouraged Louis to make amends with Thomas Stevenson. When his eyesight improved, Louis had written to his father, explaining that there were new complications in his life and inviting him to visit Paris.

"He'll be here in March." Louis took her hand. "Have I mentioned how brave you were to take me in like that when my eyes went bad?"

She nodded solemnly.

They had not talked about Louis living with her. He had stayed the night before when they got in. But it was clear, after their enforced separation in London, and after a night of passion and tender declarations, that neither wanted to be apart again.

"My father can be a reasonable man, and I believe he'll help us if I ask. But I can't present you to him just yet. He would love you, Fanny, he will love you when he meets you. But this arrangement"—Louis swept his gaze around the tawdry parlor—"he wouldn't understand. It would work against us."

Fanny winced at the remark. She fastened her eyes on his. "I don't play the fallen woman very well. I have known the real type, and I don't admire it."

"It isn't what I want, but I am asking you to trust me. Look at what you are asking of me—to disappear while your husband visits. Can you possibly think I am not offended by that prospect?" Louis's frustration smoldered in his words. He struggled to calm himself. "Look, I won't have to depend on my father much longer, Fanny. I'm going to support you and your children. I'm going to marry you and we'll live together properly. For now, if my father gives me a decent allowance, I can cover your rent and have enough to tide us over until you can get a divorce."

At that moment, Sammy came into the room. The boy looked at both of them and turned to leave.

"Come along, my friend," Louis said, making his voice gay. "I am going to take you and your mother to dinner."

"I HAVE HEARD they serve good food that's not too dear," Louis said of the café he'd chosen. When they entered, Fanny noticed the maître d' was curt, as if he disapproved of something—Louis's coat, no doubt, which was showing wear. The waiter was equally haughty. Almost in reaction, she suspected, Louis ordered a bottle of Clos Vougeot. It was an extravagant choice; they would be living on soup for a week as a consequence.

"It's superb," he promised Fanny, who knew little about wine.

Now the bottle was on the table. Louis sniffed the poured wine, leaned back in his chair, and crossed his arms. "It is corked." His voice was matter-of-fact.

The waiter stiffened. He smelled the wine and insisted it was not.

"Indeed it is," Louis said, his tone growing indignant.

The waiter turned on his heel and marched off.

"How infuriating," Louis fumed, "to be treated like a gullible . . ."

". . . hayseed," Fanny said.

"It boils my blood."

When the waiter returned, he placed a bottle in front of Louis and walked away. Louis tasted the wine, and his face flushed. "It's the same goddamned bilious stuff he served before. He simply put it in a different bottle."

Louis stood up from his seat. He called out, "Monsieur!" and *"Monsieur!"* again when the waiter did not respond. In a hot fit, Louis leaped from his seat, grabbed the bottle by its neck and smashed it against the wall next to the table. Fanny and Sammy ducked as glass chunks flew. All around them, diners ran from their chairs. Louis was shaking, staring at the bottle neck in his fist and the red streaks dripping down the yellow wall.

Fanny pulled Sammy up and put on her gloves. "I need to leave now." She took her boy's hand, swallowed hard, and walked past the staring diners and maître d', out the door of the café.

"It was outrageous—" Louis began when he caught up with them outside.

Fanny shook her head emphatically. There would be no discussion on the way back to her flat. Louis hailed a cab, and they rode in silence. At the apartment, she sent Sammy scurrying up the steps. "I will be there in a minute," she told him.

"What in God's name happened in there?" She stood facing Louis, her hands curled into fists on her hips.

"I won't stand by and let someone be taken advantage of," Louis said, "including myself."

"But that *rage*—it wasn't moral indignation. It was an unholy tantrum. Completely out of proportion, and in front of my son."

Louis's shoulders sagged.

"You are feeling pressure. Well, so am I. That is life, my dear. You say you want to marry me, and then you act like that?" She shook her head. "You are a good man, when you behave like a man, but I do not need another child. Decide which you are."

CHAPTER 24

Sam Osbourne filled the doorway of the parlor, wearing a banker's suit and a felt Stetson. One arm held a suitcase and the other his beaming daughter, whose own arms were wrapped around her father's neck.

"Might just choke your pa." He laughed, then took Belle's hands and stood back to look at her. "My, goodness," he said, shaking his head. "My baby girl's all grown."

Sam peered into the dim parlor, where Fanny stood with her son, who huddled beside her, his thumb looped through the back of her belt. "Come in, Sam," she said.

The man took off his wide-brimmed hat. "Fanny," he said with the slightest bow.

"Say hello to your father." She moved the boy around to the front of her and put her hands on his shoulders.

Sam mussed the child's hair. "Something for you," he said. He knelt down in front of them and riffled through his satchel until he produced a small braid of horsehair. "That's from the mane of your filly, son. She's waitin' for you to give her a name."

Sammy took the braid and rubbed it between his fingers. "Is she this color all over?" he asked.

"Chestnut, with a little white blaze between her eyes," Sam said. "She's the prettiest little filly I ever met, and calm as they come. Gonna be big someday. Could be sixteen hands by the time she's grown."

The boy wet his lips. "When do I get her?"

"As soon as you get home."

SAM OSBOURNE WAS still handsome, the pale-lashed blue eyes framed by crow's-feet now, the rosy cheeks gone a little leathery. The mining years showed more on him than the years inside an office. But Sam hadn't grown fleshy. He retained the muscled frame, the square jaw, and the straight nose that had made him seem so much finer than the other Indiana boys she'd known all those years ago. As for his legendary charm, she had only to look at her children to know it still worked. They hung on his every word; they hung on him.

She knew too much to be seduced by him again. Before she'd left Oakland, she had asked a neighbor friend to watch the cottage. The woman reported by letter that within two weeks Sam had installed a woman in the family house who was, no doubt, still sleeping in Fanny's bed. It was important to keep bad memories alive, lest she feel guilty about her love affair with Louis. She recalled the time she'd found a beautiful pair of women's shoes in Sam's satchel. She'd been excited—it was just before Christmas—and then enraged when she unwrapped the tissue around them. They were probably four sizes bigger than Fanny's small foot. She had gone into the kitchen and poured hot boiled jelly into the shoes, then thrown the sticky things back into his bag. Not once did he mention it.

WHEN SHE MULLED it over later, she was annoyed by how easily Sam slipped back into their lives, as if the separation had resulted from some fluke of scheduling. Sam had been clear in his letters that he wanted a reconciliation. In her responses, she had made clear that she had no intention of reuniting with him. But she could not wish away the facts of her own life. She needed his monthly checks, and he was growing mightily impatient sending them. How could she negotiate if she didn't welcome him? And the children deserved to see their father. The first night, though, she set down the rules. "You will sleep in Sammy's bedroom. Belle will sleep with me," she said.

The beginning of Sam Osbourne's visit was feeling like a family vacation. He spent his mornings with his son, strolling through different neighborhoods, visiting parks, and trying new pastries. When Belle and Fanny returned from the atelier, he took them all out to explore Paris. Fanny was thrown off by the strange pattern of their days together: tense conversations punctuated by bouts of gay sightseeing. Several afternoons spent at the newly opened Paris exposition only enhanced the unreal quality of their hours together. They wandered through halls displaying paintings and Alexander Graham Bell's telephone and other modern inventions.

They moved on to an ethnological exhibit that made Fanny wince. The *village nègre* was an actual human zoo, a series of tableaux that showed hundreds of Africans dressed in animal skins, supposedly portraying their normal daily lives. "They make them out to be primitive freaks," Fanny said to her boy as she pulled him away from an iron fence through which the white Europeans and black Africans gawked at one another.

"In America, they put Indians in shows like that," Sam Sr. chimed in. "What you just saw, son? That wasn't real. It's somebody's mixed-up idea of who they think those folks are."

There is the Sam Osbourne I once knew. It was one of the few remarks he had uttered since his arrival with which she could concur. Long ago she had admired Sam's solid decency. He had become unreliable over the years, but his progressive attitudes and geniality still won him admirers. He'd been one of the founders of the Bohemian Club, where he socialized now with some of the biggest names in San Francisco. People tended to like him until they had a business deal with him. Or married him.

For a man who claimed to have limited funds, he showered his family with little gifts and treated them to good food during outings. Waiters in restaurants took them for tourists, which annoyed Fanny. After two years in Paris, she spoke limited French, but she could read it. It was always Louis who ordered for them with his flawless pronunciation. But Sam, in his big hat, was immediate evidence that they were Americans and wouldn't know the difference between a crepe and a croquette. Sam complained that French beer was inferior and French manners were prissy. One night as they walked back to the flat, Fanny encountered a fellow artist from Monsieur Julian's school and greeted her in the way all her friends greeted one another in Paris, with a kiss on both cheeks. Sam snickered in disgust. "You don't even talk like you used to, Fanny. What are you doing here among these people?"

It was the first shot across the bow.

"What does it look like? I am living in a miserable little apartment, barely scraping by on the money you send us, so that Belle can study art."

"Oh, come now. So *you* can live the 'creative life.' You are having a fine time here with all your arty friends."

Fanny fingered the chain at her waist. "Nobody knows you here, Sam. They don't know about your sordid little peccadilloes. They don't pity me. Believe it or not, people here like me for who I am. That must be hard for your narrow mind to comprehend."

"You hauled away the whole goddamn family," he growled. "If you don't bring the children back, I will sue for custody."

Fanny batted away the remark with the back of her hand. "I thought you liked the arrangement. We're out of your hair. You're free as a bird to have any whore you want. And I don't have to know about it."

She used the word pointedly. She knew Sam hated it, and that fact enraged her more. It wasn't just sexual adventures he pursued. He fell in love with the women he kept, the women who siphoned off the family's grocery money and sucked away Sam's attention and protection, who dressed him in the latest styles and sent him home to Oakland smelling of violet perfume. They weren't whores to him. He had even defended the virtues of one to his wife. "She wants to be your friend," he had said at the time.

"Let's not do this to each other." Sam's voice was weary now. "Can't we have a moment of peace?"

Up ahead, Belle linked arms with her brother. Fanny slowed so they didn't overhear bitter words. Nearly an adult, Belle knew of her father's infidelities; she understood the complexity of the situation. But Sammy had never understood why they were living abroad. He was so innocent, in fact, that Fanny feared to think what the boy might reveal if he got on the subject of their new friend Louis. If Sam learned she had shared a room with another man, if she lost her claim to higher moral ground, she stood to lose everything, including custody of the children. She hadn't been thinking about that possibility when she'd welcomed Louis into her bed.

"IT WAS GOOD times, all right," Sam was saying. They all sat in the parlor. "Do you remember going down the mine shaft, Belle?"

"I think I do. But maybe it's just that I heard the story all these years."

"Tell me." Sammy lay on the floor with his head propped on one hand.

"It was the first mine in Nevada we had. I went down every day and—"

"We sent Belle down there in a bucket once," Fanny said. "I can't believe I allowed it, when I think of it now—maybe because I was so young. I stuck a lump of clay on the bill of her cap and set the candle into it. Then I watched my little girl go down that shaft until she was just a tiny flickering light in a black tunnel."

"It was how we all did it." Sam laughed. "I caught her on the other end, and she was perfectly fine. She brought me down some lunch, as I recall."

"You didn't show one bit of fear, Belle," Fanny said. "You had a wonderful time."

"I remember the stagecoach ride to get to the camp," Belle said. "And I remember music. A fiddler and a squeeze-box."

"The squeeze-box was Charlie Craycroft's," Sam said. "He was a real loner. Rumor was he'd been involved in a shooting in California and the law was looking for him; he kept to himself. Had a shack near ours, and he was sweet on your mother, like a lot of the fellas were. That's because your mama was the prettiest girl in camp."

Sam was trying to worm his way into her affections with old memories. It was his preferred method of softening her up.

Fanny again saw the eagerness in Sammy's young face. "Charlie used to make cookies for Belle," she said finally. "He shaped the dough into little animals. But he was too shy to give them to us. He'd leave them outside the door."

"Oh, but he could play that squeeze-box," Sam went on. "Late at night, usually. It was just about the lonesomest music a man ever heard."

They sat in the parlor long after Belle and Sammy had retired.

"I want to find a way," Sam said. "I miss you, Fan. I want my family together."

She sighed wearily. "Do you know the name I call you in my mind? The Man with No Shame. I am the one who carried the humiliation all those years. Isn't it funny how that works, Sam? There you were, sleeping with your latest whore five days a week in San Francisco. And there I was, ashamed, as if it were my fault. I'm still trying to make sense of that."

Sam looked out the window, where streetlamps made bright blurs in the foggy air. "You cut me off, Fanny. You know it."

"Any woman would." Fanny shook her head. "You were never left out in the cold for long."

"You did your own flirting. With my friends, no less."

"Nonsense."

"Don't lie to yourself, Fanny. What about Rearden?"

Fanny waved away the remark.

"You wrote to him so he would pass on to me what you said, didn't you? To make me jealous that there are men falling all over you here." Sam's voice was rising. He got up and paced. "What were you thinking, Fanny, to take the kids like that? Off you went half-cocked, just like you always do. How could you drag three children halfway around the globe and not know that fancy art school didn't even *take* women? What kind of planning was that?"

"The only bad planning was being born into this world a woman," Fanny lashed back. "That and marrying a whoremonger."

"He never would've gotten tuberculosis in California," Sam shouted. "And if he had? He wouldn't have died of it." He stood still, fixing her with a cold stare. "Rearden told me you knew for months Hervey was deathly sick. Long before you told me. Rearden said you begged him not to tell me because you didn't want me over here." Tears ran down his cheeks. "Wasn't he my boy, too? Didn't he love me, too?"

Fanny felt the anger in her chest shift, in that second, to aching remorse.

"Did he ask for me at all in those months?"

She looked down at her lap.

"What did he say?"

"He called out for you," she admitted. *Over and over again.* "I didn't know those first couple of months he was so sick. He'd sit up and eat and seem to be getting better." She heard the pleading in her own voice. "He was far too sick to travel back home by the time I understood. I was keeping the truth from myself, not just you. I would sit by his bed and think, *There, he took that milk. See how the color is coming back to his face.*"

Sam fell to his knees beside Fanny. She put her hand on his heaving shoulder. "I missed you during that terrible time, Sam. I realize I had no right to have Hervey so far away." Her throat felt like it was closing. "Forgive me," she whispered. "I should have wired you sooner."

Fanny slid to her knees from the chair. She put her head on his chest as they leaned in to each other, weeping.

~

CHAPTER 25

The next morning, Fanny waited on a bench in the vestibule of her building for the mail. Sam was out with the children and, with luck, would return after it had been delivered.

Since her husband's arrival, she'd watched for the postman downstairs, lest Sam happen upon a letter addressed to Louis at the flat. The suspicious old concierge seemed perturbed by her presence. Wearing two coats, with a ring of keys at her waist, the woman watched every day for the postman in a chair outside her loge; apparently, she did not want company. She lifted her small head like a tortoise, turning her kohl-circled eyes toward Fanny. *"Il y a un problème?"*

"Un petit problème—en Amérique," Fanny replied. That seemed to satisfy the woman. An American woman's family problems back home held no interest for her.

Fanny felt drained from the previous evening. She had not told Sam she wanted a divorce. He would fight it hard, and so would her family. Her parents and sisters seemed to think a divorce was more scandalous than the way Sam had been treating her all these years. *It will leave you defenseless, and mark you and the children,* her mother had written. How could she say to her mother: I love another man, a kind and good man who will shelter us?

When she pondered what had been said the night before, she was not surprised to know Sam carried a gulf of sorrow over Hervey's death. That was the thing about Sam—he was capable of deep emotion. He was a mass of contradictions, a jumble of tender and heartless impulses. For so long, the two of them had been entwined at some elemental level. She had come to think they were as connected as Siamese twins joined at the gut. Back in California, she'd known it would require miles—thousands of them—to break free from him. A great distance was needed not only to discourage him from coming after her; it was necessary to keep her from going back to him. Even now she was vulnerable to Sam Osbourne, even after two years and Louis Stevenson in her life. She no longer had any illusions that her connection to Sam was love. It was something stronger, like tangled veins and shared blood and unholy patterns that couldn't be escaped.

Thank God he will be going back to California in two more days.

Fanny remembered the night she and the children and their nanny had sighted Antwerp from the steamer's deck. She'd looked at that foreign city and thought, *I am free to be somebody new.* Free from being Sam Osbourne's wife, the disgraced woman who kept taking her husband back. The shame she had borne for so long seemed to float away into the Belgian air. Standing on the ship in port, she'd felt young in her skin again.

Loving Louis was utterly different from loving Sam. She felt clean with Louis. His goodness brought out the goodness in her. With Sam, the opposite was true.

Last night, as she stood up from the floor and headed for her room, Sam had taken hold of her wrist. "Don't you see? Losing Hervey changed everything," he said. "I want back what we had. Yes, I've made mistakes; I admit it, and I'm sorry. But you've had me on trial for the past ten years. You made it impossible for me to stay in the house with you." He let go of her. "I know you better than anybody in this world. I know your heart. I wouldn't ask you to come back if I didn't love you."

"*BONJOUR!*" THE POSTMAN'S voice echoing in the cold little vestibule roused her from her thoughts. She watched as the concierge divided the mail into piles for the various occupants of the building. Fanny took her pile and hurried up the stairs. There were no letters addressed to Louis, only a literary journal, *Scribner's,* and a telegram from San Francisco for Sam. Fanny sat on her bed and perused the magazine's table of contents. "Bird Architecture," "Camping Out at Rudder Grange," "Topics of the Times," "Bohemian Days"—Fanny's eyes stopped there—by Margaret Wright. Margaret! She felt a little thrill of pride. Her friend, her dear neighbor, and here she was in the pages of a premier magazine. Best of all, she had written an article on Grez! Fanny flipped to page 121 and found the most delightful illustration entitled

"Catching the Sunset," in which comical-looking artists dabbed at their canvases. On the next page was a cartoonish depiction of a "Scotchman" reading a thick book. It had to be Bob, for the funny fellow in the illustration was wearing his trademark striped stockings. Fanny took a deep breath and settled in.

She smiled to read the beginning, where Margaret portrayed herself as Philistina, a city-loving Parisian who goes out to see what all the excitement is about in the Fontainebleau Forest, specifically in Grez, a bohemian gathering place, *where human nature showed neither at its worst nor at its best, but simply developed by a broad freedom of action and expression into some of its most extraordinarily picturesque, angular, positive, original, beautiful, and unbeautiful individualities ever seen upon the face of the earth.*

That's exactly it, Fanny reflected. There was freedom enough in Grez to show who you truly were. Fanny remembered Margaret always hanging back a little, madly jotting notes. It occurred to her now that her friend had been working the whole time she was there. And here was the result, as wry as the woman herself. Fanny read down past Philistina's arrival by donkey cart in the village, then her description of the Hôtel Chevillon, where artists gathered around the dining table and let fly with unreserved conversation.

Fanny tried to match each outlandish character in the story to her friends.

Fairy in size, like a hummingbird in movement and in purpose of life, her Majesty seems, to the not too clear-sighted observer, in spite of her thirty-eight years, scarcely more than a girl. Her Majesty is not a sumptuous queen, as her raiment proves . . .

Fanny flinched as it dawned on her that *she* was being portrayed as "the Queen of Bohemia" and the most ridiculous person at the inn.

. . . though her Moorish blood, streaming for centuries through conquered Spain and invaded Netherlands, to reach by strange channels far-off California, and leave its swarthy stain upon her complexion and its fiery gleam in her eyes, gives the impression she has a barbaric taste for splendor, for leopard and tiger hues, and glories of flamingo and bird-of-paradise in all her appertain-ings.

Her Majesty is smoking a cigarette between the soup and the roast. Her Majesty is generally smoking a cigarette when she is not sleeping, and when dining usually has her little feet upon the rungs of her neighbour's chair, while she tells strange stories of wild life among the Nevada mines, where feverish brandy and champagne were cheaper than cool water and sweet milk . . . There is subtle suggestion of castanets and guitars in the queen's voice, even somewhat monotonous as it is—a faint shadow of the ca-chuca and the cracovina in the free motions of her arms above her head.

Fanny felt dizzy but kept reading. The words—vicious, damning—wouldn't stop.

In the highly civilized old world she may seem a lost princess, a stray daughter of the Incas, come only to shabby queenhood in Bohemia by right of her uncivilized blood and her royal birth. Before New World eyes, looking from nearer into barbarism, there is none of the glamour which sees romance and poetry in simply dusky skins, wild, free motions and turbulent lives, so that real, unromantic barrenness and poverty of nature is as visible to them in a deposed daughter of the Incas or Mexican dancer as in the pale factory girl who toils and spins and knows nothing else.

Stunned, Fanny sat up on the bed and took a deep breath. She read the piece to its end. Apparently, in Margaret's "New World eyes," Fanny was the most unbeautiful of individualities in the whole lot, for no one else fared as badly as she.

Poverty of nature. Uncivilized blood. Barbaric. Fanny leaped up from the bed and went to the bathroom, where she took Sam's razor from the cabinet. She slit out the contents page first, then the pages of Margaret Wright's article, and crumpled them. When she saw how mutilated the magazine looked, she decided to put all of it in the trash, hoping Louis wouldn't miss it.

She tried to remember the last time she had seen the brisk little

American. She could think only of the many times Margaret had popped her head out into the hall, snooping. Had she seen Fanny and Will Low carry Louis into the apartment that night, drunk and singing and nearly blind? Probably. Her door was cracked often enough. Surely she had seen Louis coming and going since then. Surely she knew he lived there. Fanny had considered her a friend; she had made no great efforts to conceal the situation.

Even as she crushed the hateful pages, she shivered at the possibility that Louis had already seen the article. It was his habit to read his journals the moment they arrived, cover to cover. Without his own copy, he would read it at a friend's. Louis considered it a plum to be published by *Scribner's,* something he hadn't yet managed. But Margaret had managed. At the moment, all Fanny wanted to do was ask her why. Why? But she was gone—moved back to England a few weeks ago without so much as a goodbye, a rebuff that Fanny had attributed at the time to a hurried departure.

She felt as if she might be sick. She opened up the balls of paper and forced herself to read the pages again. Some would consider the essay a witty parody, but the woman's remarks were as raw as the racial cartoons Fanny had seen in the newspaper when she was growing up. How could one's skin color prompt such vitriol? There was ferocious contempt running through the piece; Fanny suspected it was because she had been living openly with Louis, right next door to Margaret, who surely found the arrangement more evidence of Fanny's "barbaric nature." Fanny had always prided herself on judging a person's character correctly from a first meeting. She'd believed Margaret was a friend who understood her circumstances. How had she been so wrong about the woman?

She put the wadded papers and magazine in a bag, then raced downstairs, bumping against walls in her frenzy, and out into the street, where she dumped the bag into a pile of trash. When she climbed the four flights of steps, she returned to her bed, this time crawling under the blankets and pulling them over her head. She was shaking, and her teeth were clattering. Fanny knew that it would be no secret to any of the Grez crowd whom the piece was about. They were probably buzzing in cafés right now. Had they all viewed her as Margaret did, a pretentious fool? Weren't any of them her true friends?

In her head, she heard Sam Osbourne's voice: *What are you doing here among these people?*

Fanny climbed out of the bed, washed her face, and went out of the apartment building before Sam and the children returned and saw her distress. She walked through Montmartre, dabbing at her eyes with a handkerchief, trying to dispel the panic she felt. Wandering through a park, she noticed a mother sitting on a bench, gently rocking a pram. A wave of shame washed over her.

Looking at her situation from the outside, Fanny didn't like the picture she saw. Regardless of Sam's repeated betrayals, there was no excuse for her laxity; she should have been more discreet in front of Belle and Sammy. The portrait Margaret Wright had painted of her as a merry seductress, living loosely so soon after her child's death, was hideously unfair. Still, she saw how unseemly her life might appear to people who didn't know her.

I have been living in a dream world, she thought. *This can't go on.*

CHAPTER 26

When Louis planned it, a long walk seemed the best salve for his troubled heart. A twelve-day 120-mile trek through the Cévennes would be daunting, but the sting he felt would not be soothed by meadows and summer. He needed to exercise himself against terrain that pushed back. The stretch of mountains in southern France matched the state of his soul—desolate and rocky, a cold expanse of steep hills and mournful valleys.

"I'm going for a walk," he told his friends who questioned the wisdom of a trip into the wilderness alone. "A book is in it." They knew it was peace he was after. He had been a sad case since Fanny left to return to the United States.

Louis could not make sense of her departure. He'd heard what Fanny *said,* but it did not satisfy. "I love you," she had assured him. "But there are the feelings and needs of other people to consider." While she was packing her trunks to leave Paris, she was already framing their love affair as a memory. "I shall never forget the time we've had together," she said.

Louis looked dolefully at Modestine, the mouse-colored little pack donkey he had bought in Le Monastier for sixty-five francs and a glass of brandy. In that small town of lace makers and wineshop proprietors, the donkey was attested to as a fine specimen. Louis had fallen hard for her gentle eyes and austere elegance, but it wasn't more than an hour into his journey that he discovered the nature of the beast: The donkey took small steps and few commands. In one day, the animal had grown deaf to Louis's ongoing, one-sided, out-loud conversation with Fanny, for she ignored her new master's pleas to "Go!" as just more blather from the skinny human with the stick. She curled her lips back, baring her brown teeth as she enjoyed a hearty hee-haw at his predicament.

The local peasants along the way were no more cooperative. They were unfriendly, sometimes ignoring his requests for directions. Even the children seemed contemptuous. Having gotten lost repeatedly while following stony mountain paths that seemed to circle back from whence he came, Louis felt fury in his gut. He and the donkey were stuck together in this most inhospitable corner of the world in a farce worthy of Molière. Modestine refused to move despite his exhortations. Louis realized he was a laughingstock when a passing peasant cut a switch, whacked the donkey's rump, and yelled, "Proot!"

"You have to show her who is the boss," the man said when he stopped laughing.

"Argggh," Louis groused. He didn't like hitting anything, certainly not a shuddering, winded creature, least of all a female creature. When he'd set out from Le Monastier a day earlier, he had taken her mincing steps as the gait of all donkeys and resigned himself to follow her pace through the wooded slopes and river-crossed valleys. But now, with the man applying his switch and Modestine leaping forward and running without pause, Louis suspected he had been fooled by the Sarah Bernhardt of hoofed mammals. Once the peasant left the path and bid adieu, however, Modestine slowed. Louis found himself in an isolated dale with a steep hill to climb, and no amount of prooting could get the stubborn donkey to move faster. He was desperate to set up camp at a lake ahead before night fell. He switched the animal harder and was immediately sickened by his own brutality. Compounding his misery, the bag he had made for sleeping, strapped as it was over Modestine's back, kept slipping off and scattering the provisions stuffed inside it.

One egg whisk, two loaves of black bread and a loaf of white, a bottle of brandy, a leg of mutton. Spirit lamp, jackknife, lantern, leather flask, pilot coat. Tins of chocolate and sausage. These were the necessaries he had packed in his clever sleeping sack and flung over the back of the wretched Modestine. The supplies yet again were strewn all over the dry and rocky ground where the ass grazed on tufts of grass.

Louis sat down, smoked a cigarette, and took a few swigs of brandy. "Ah, Fanny," he said out loud. He pictured her sleeping right now, her eyelashes quivering as they did when she dreamed. Louis closed his own eyes and saw Sam Osbourne lying next to her. He leaped up, shook out his limbs to throw off the image, and furiously retied the bag on the donkey. This time he loaded some of the supplies on his own shoulders and set out once more.

The walking was easier but Louis grew discouraged when darkness came on and he'd found no lake. He cursed the indifferent stars as they began to appear. In time, he happened upon an old stone inn at Bouchet-Saint-Nicolas where he gladly took the one bed available in a room shared with a young married couple. He was so embarrassed by their proximity that he averted his gaze, but not before glimpsing one pretty white arm hanging over the side of the bed. Louis didn't know if she slept nude or in a gown, but he didn't need the young woman's nearness to stir thoughts of Fanny.

Why did you leave?

It mystified him. They were so close to making their dream happen. Yes, there were obstacles. Sam Osbourne was cutting off money to Fanny until she returned. Sammy was eager to go back. And Louis wasn't even close to being financially independent. Still, none of it seemed insurmountable to him. Only a few weeks earlier, he had been filled with hope. He'd just published *Inland Voyage* and gotten positive reviews—reviews that startled him with their enthusiasm. True, no real money had materialized. But his meeting with his father had gone well, and he now had a modest monthly income to count on. Fanny was already his bride; a marriage certificate would be a mere formality. She knew he was pledged to supporting her children as his own once he had his sea legs in publishing. Why, then, was she saying a union was out of the question? Why now, after resisting Sam for so long, had she given in and returned to California?

He tried to put himself in Fanny's shoes. Any woman in her position would be fearful. There was much to lose on a nameless chap like himself. Maybe she felt their differences were too great, that her very soul was at risk. He remembered something she'd said once: "I'm not remotely close to being Scottish or French, Louis. I'm made from different clay."

God knows there have been enough missteps on my part to frighten her away. The bottle-smashing scene in the café hadn't helped his cause. He cringed at the memory of another moment. Early during their time together in Paris, they were in a carriage when one of his fits of laughter overtook him.

"Pull back my fingers," he had said to her between gasps.

"I won't," she replied. "Now stop this nonsense."

Louis's voice kept rising as he laughed. "Dammit, Fanny, bend my hand! I mean it! If you don't, I shall bend yours back until I break every bone." He grabbed her hand and bent back her fingers until they clearly hurt.

"Stop it!" she shouted. She pulled his hand to her mouth and bit it hard, breaking the flesh and causing him to cry out. The shock of seeing blood rise up out of his punctured skin had brought him to his senses.

What a stupid, immature fool I was! And yet she had not left him then. He'd asked her forgiveness, and she had given it.

In the weeks leading up to her departure, their life together in Paris had been heaven and hell. She'd confided to Louis that she was going to return soon to the United States so she could begin divorce proceedings. He was stunned but comforted himself with the thought, *At last. The wheels are moving.* As the days wore on, though, her intentions became less clear. She seemed to be struggling mightily within herself. "You're a *dowie* lass," he said, "ain't ye?" She admitted she was depressed. And then one day, as they sat in a café on Boulevard de Clichy, he saw a calmness come over her for no apparent reason. After that day, she turned her gaze to California with a stony resolve.

Belle, who had no idea that her mother was intent on moving them back, was stricken with anger and hurt, but Fanny seemed to ignore the girl's pleadings. By the time Louis put her and the children on the train, headed for a steamer, Fanny was offering him no words of encouragement. Walking down the platform away from the train that day, he could not bring himself to look back at Sammy leaning out the window, waving to him with a small paper American flag.

LOUIS TURNED HIS back to the couple's bed and slept fitfully. In the morning, the innkeeper's husband, a simple, gentle man who once worked as a muleteer, fashioned a goad for Louis. "The problem is that she can't feel your switches on her hide," he said. The goad had a tiny metal point, only an eighth-inch high, whose prick was all the motivation Modestine needed to move. "The goad is not the only thing," the man said. He argued that Louis should discard the bulk of his sleeping sack and distribute the remaining weight evenly on her back. "Do you see how hard it wears on her?" the man asked with surprising compassion, given the metal point he had just honed. Indeed, Louis could see raw spots on the mule's hindquarters. Out went the mutton, the empty bottle, the white bread for himself. He kept the loaves of black bread to feed the donkey. After that adjustment, Modestine went on at a steady trot, with the help of the occasional prick. She was freer without the heavy load, and he felt a new sense of freedom, too, out in the cold air with miles ahead—free to walk, free to ponder, free to hope.

In the nights that followed, the sack he had concocted allowed him to sleep, in spite of roaring winds. He congratulated himself again on its cleverness: a six-foot-square bag made of green cart cloth on the outside and blue sheep's fur inside that kept him warm and dry. The landscape began to work its spell on him. In the mornings, he woke with wonder at each new setting.

Near the end of his trip, he camped among a stand of pines. It was late by the time he fed the donkey and spread out his setup. The pines formed walls that encircled him, and the sky was a ceiling of jittering stars. He laughed to himself over his absurd meal: a bite of Bologna sausage alternated with a bite of chocolate, washed down with sips from his single precious bottle of Beaujolais. He listened to the sound of water tripping over stones in a burn nearby, listened to the last calls of birds as darkness blacked out his sylvan room.

A year ago he had written an essay arguing that the best way to walk was alone. Who wanted to have one's solitude disturbed by someone else's talk? Lying in his bag, he thought it was a different man who had written those words.

Louis dug through his pack in the darkness, feeling for his journal and a taper he carried. He rolled over and struck a match. The brightness was sudden, almost alarming. He lit the candle and began to write.

I wish a companion to lie near me in the starlight, silent and not moving, but ever within touch. For there is a fellowship more quiet even than solitude, and which, rightly understood, is solitude made perfect. And to live out of doors with the woman a man loves is of all lives the most complete and free.

That night, as on every night of his journey, he fell asleep with Fanny as his pillow-thought. How happy they had been in Paris! Talking, laughing, walking together for hours through the streets until the night cast them into their bed, where they were happiest.

At sunrise, he reread what he had written so far during the journey and realized it was filled with private coded messages to her: *I love you. I want you. Don't forget. Don't forget.*

He tied up his pack and looked around at the green floor of the glade and the walls of spired pines. It was one of the loveliest chambers in which he had ever passed a night, and it had been entirely free. He felt a sense of gratitude and debt to someone for the privilege of the accommodations. Louis reached into his knapsack and pulled out a handful of coins, then arranged them in a pile at the center of the room. Hopefully, they would fall into the unexpecting hands of someone in want of them.

CHAPTER 27

"I need money, Burly," Louis said.

"We all need money," Henley replied.

The tavern was almost empty. They had been coming to the pub in Shepherd's Bush every afternoon since Louis returned to London from the Cévennes and settled in at the Savile Club. It was afternoon, and the bright gray October light outside made no inroad into the tavern's interior. In the dim, smoky room, the pub owner was polishing his bar to a high shine; across the room, the only other customer, an elderly chap, was talking to himself.

"It will take three hundred fifty pounds if I am to breathe freely," Louis said.

"Have you asked your father?"

"Naw. I'm as like to get a fart of a dead man as money from my father for a trip to California."

"Then Deacon Brodie it is!" Henley boomed. "How many times must I say it to you, lad?" he asked, pounding the establishment's much abused table. "Your best idea is sitting at the bottom of a drawer. You could be rich right now."

Louis looked across at Henley's great pale face, bent and cackling into his pint as the man imagined the brilliant reviews they would garner. Though the two of them were burning the midnight oil to put out the magazine, it was the play Henley talked most of every day.

"You're going back to your parents' for the holiday," Henley said. "Pull the damned thing out and look at it. Or don't look at it. Just start over with me. I tell you, the idea is meant to be a play, and we are meant to collaborate on it. It will be a roaring success, and you shall have your three hundred fifty pounds. And much, much more."

"Ah, but the buggers have to talk to each other," Louis lamented. "A play is all dialogue and I'm not good at it yet. Not in my stories, anyway."

"Go to some of your old haunts in the Old Town and take your pencil. You'll get your thug talk there. Or have you lost your stomach for slumming?"

Louis recoiled. Henley knew how to plant little blasting caps. He was overly fond of reminding Louis of his affluent upbringing.

"You think it's that simple, do you?"

"You write the first draft, and I will make it sing," Henley said. "If you want, I'll make it rhyme."

Louis stroked his mustache absently. It was rich territory, Deacon Brodie's double life. Ever since he was a boy, Louis had heard the legend of the cabinetmaker who was the deacon of his Edinburgh trade union by day and a burglar after dark. Brodie loomed large in Louis's childish imagination. He'd thought of him nearly every night, in fact; Thomas Stevenson, an avid antiques collector, had bought an old wardrobe handmade by the scoundrel and placed it in Louis's bedroom.

At fifteen, Louis had looked into Brodie's life and learned he had a gambling problem; the stealing began as a way to pay off debts. His nightlife, in time, included more than robbery. The deacon had two mistresses who knew nothing of each other, as well as many offspring, in addition to his legal family.

"It's a hell of an ending," Henley mused. "Foxy old Brodie hanging in gallows that he himself carpentered—now, that's a poetic touch."

"When he didn't get caught, the burglar in him grew bolder," Louis said. "He felt more alive when he was stealing, don't you think? I want him to be an everyman who slowly slides over to the other side."

"Don't wait until the holiday," Henley said excitedly. "You're here. Start it now." To toast the idea, he ordered another round, which Louis paid for.

He didn't know if Henley was right about plays being lucrative, and he doubted the poet would make a great playwright. But he knew his friend needed money as badly as he did. Visiting Henley and his new wife in their tiny flat, Louis could see how meager their circumstances were. Henley had put what little he had into *London,* and it was faltering. Yet he was happier than Louis had ever seen him, with his adoring bride in his life.

"All right. I can devote my mornings to it over at the club."

Henley beamed. "Wait until I tell Anna."

"Do you know what I think, Burly?" Louis said. "I think a special tax should be levied on all you grooms who grin so gloatingly in front of less fortunate lads. Baxter is just as bad."

Henley let out one of his shaking laughs. "You've changed your tune. What was it you used to call marriage? A friendship recognized by the police?"

"Ah, hell. I envy you."

"Have you heard anything?"

"Yes and no. Fanny writes and says nothing. I can't fathom what is happening over there." Louis slumped in his chair. He remembered how he had raced with his heart in his throat to Alais to collect his mail after selling Modestine. It had been a surprisingly bittersweet parting; he had grown fond of the little donkey. Only one letter was waiting, in which Fanny talked about the weather in Oakland and seeing her old friends. It might have been written by a new acquaintance.

"This woman is different from you," Henley said.

"Fanny?"

Henley pursed his lips. "She is from a different world. America is an entirely different beast. Far more . . . primitive than Scotland."

"I love her! And I can't bear all this waiting. I want to talk to her in person. If I could get to California, we would resolve it. If I were there, she'd have the strength to move the divorce along. I'm a lawyer, for God's sake, I could advise her." He rubbed his temples with both hands. "I want, I want, I want . . . But there's no encouragement from her. Some days I think I'll go mad from it."

By December 20, Louis had handed over his third draft of the play to Henley and headed for Edinburgh, where he found Thomas in an expansive mood. He was obviously pleased by his trip to Paris in the fall, pleased to have been taken into Louis's confidence about the new love complication in his life. And it had all worked out as he'd hoped: The father had been able to support the son in a moment of personal crisis, and the troublesome woman had eventually gone away. Two wins for the father. A victory for the mother, too, who was ecstatic to have Louis home after a six-month absence. She set about making the

Christmas holiday festive, arranging gatherings at which a number of dull young women—unmarried daughters of friends—appeared serially in the parlor.

On Christmas Eve, the patriarch's spirits lifted higher, and Louis was touched to see how glad his father was to be on decent terms with him again. After he'd downed a pint, the old man's face turned serious as he spoke about love and loss.

"I've never faulted a woman for divorce. Never held a bad opinion of a divorced woman. Men who abandon the home, on the other hand, should be shot." Thomas Stevenson stood with one elbow propped on the fireplace mantel of his study, entirely in his element. "But a woman doesn't divorce lightly. No, no. I would not hold that against your lady friend." He walked over to where Louis sat and patted his back. "It's for the best, son, the way things have worked out, I think you will see that. Someone will come along who will light up your heart, and you will know, the way I did with your mother."

Next to his bedroom, in a little study his parents had created for him, Louis holed up to work on a new story. He found himself, instead, looking back on what he had already written.

New Year's Day, 1879, he wrote in his journal. *At least I've worked. I have no shame about that.*

Louis laid out periodicals on his desk, everything he had published so far, as if counting money. His mother had kept a copy of every journal, and he pulled out the issues of *Cornhill* and *McMillan's*. He saw progress in his work. He saw some sentences he liked in the essays he'd written about Victor Hugo's romances and about Edinburgh, among others. He liked very much his first fictional story about François Villon.

And then there was the book, *Inland Voyage,* in all its imperfect glory. But it was a book, by God, a true book. He took a copy of it from his bookshelf and placed it in the middle of the desk. He couldn't help running his hand over its cover with childish pleasure. Soon he could add *Travels with a Donkey* to the pile. There were a few good parts in it that he felt he would be willing to claim twenty years from now.

He leaned back and studied the stacks of magazines. What did they really amount to? An honorable start. It wasn't coin, though. The money he'd earned for the whole pile amounted to almost nothing. His heart sank when he recalled how he'd promised Fanny that he would support her. Had she seen how impossible that task would be and simply given up?

He had been wanting to write a full-length novel, but the idea seemed laughable. How would he support himself through such a long process? *I'm twenty-eight. Men build bridges by that age. Find cures for diseases. Build lighthouses.* Suddenly, the pile of periodicals and the lone book looked small indeed.

CHAPTER 28

1879

In May, Louis arranged to meet Bob in London, knowing it was his cousin's understanding he wanted most. When Bob met him at King's Cross Station, he was ebullient, full of talk about the Paris and London art crowds. In a pub adjacent to the train station, he announced his real news: One of his paintings had been accepted for exhibit at the Royal Academy of Arts.

Louis raised his glass. "To the overdue recognition of your genius."

Bob toasted happily and continued gabbing about the art world. After a while, he took in a satisfied breath. "And you?"

"I want to go to California."

Bob looked up at the ceiling.

"I'm convinced if I could get over there, I could—"

"It's an insane idea."

"So you're in their camp."

"Whose camp?" Bob asked.

"You know who I'm talking about. Henley and Colvin. They think Fanny is giving me the dodge. Henley actually called her 'that woman' the other day."

Bob spoke carefully while recalling her past kindnesses. "She nursed me when the black dog was on my back." He fingered a button on his vest, remembering that deep well of depression before changing the subject. "Do you have any word of Belle?"

"I've had three letters from Fanny. They might as well have been from a government office."

"I was in love with Belle," Bob said.

"I know."

"She was mad for O'Meara, though. He's probably been on a bender since she left."

They ordered another round. Bob lit a cigarette, leaned back, and blew smoke toward the ceiling in the worldly way that women found so fetching.

"Henley said you have a girl in Paris. A model?"

Bob nodded soberly. "Most sensual creature I've ever known."

Louis pictured Bob romping in bed with his luscious nymph. He looked away from his cousin at the dark room that filled and emptied quickly as people dashed for trains. At the next table was a man in no hurry, a fellow intent on charming his lady companion, who was rather ordinary compared to him. The man sported dashing facial hair: a wiry brown beard that he had divided down the middle of his chin and trained into two upward-swooping points, and a mustache, equally optimistic. Louis watched the fellow maneuver the woman's pale hand through the whiskery shoals toward his lips. He felt his repulsion turn to pity for the poor fellow. *Lord God,* Louis thought, *what fools we men are made by our cocks.*

"Why can't a man have both?" Bob was saying heatedly. "With marriageable ones, you sign away your life before you know what you've got. Could be cold as a mackerel." He sighed. "Belle could have been both."

"Man, I am sick, sick, sick of this past year," Louis said through gritted teeth. "I'm sick from waiting. I look at Gosse and Baxter and Henley, and I am saturated with envy. I'm jealous that they have wives and houses and happy little domestic lives."

"Ah, Lou, what happened to my ribald cousin?"

"He became a saphead. A weepist."

Louis stared thoughtfully at Bob. There was a time in their lives when Bob would have backed him no matter how preposterous the plan. Now he seemed unsympathetic, almost uninterested in Louis's dilemma.

"I read *Deacon Brodie,*" Bob said.

"Yes?"

"I can't lie to you. It needs work."

"How polite you've become. Colvin says it's pure rubbish."

THAT NIGHT LOUIS went out to walk and smoke. In the Haymarket area, he saw a rag-and-bone man sorting through a pile of garbage. Louis thought of a French phrase he loved—*pêcheur de lune.* Moonlight fisherman. This old man would sell on the street tomorrow what discards he found in garbage heaps tonight. When he walked away from the pile, Louis pulled out what the *pêcheur* had left behind: filthy trousers; a jacket with sleeves that hung by threads; two large cracked-leather shoes, half torn from their soles. He gathered up the smelly things, and the next night, he went out into London wearing the rags and the oversize shoes. He lurked in doorways, shuffled up and down the street, snarled at passersby, and generally attempted to look suspicious. When he passed near a police officer, he felt his pulse quicken. Surely he would be arrested as a vagrant! But the officer merely called out, "Good evening, sir." Louis flip-flopped in the absurd shoes back to the Savile Club, where he was staying. "What on earth now, Stevenson?" a dandy at the club remarked, looking him up and down with a withering glance. The comment was the only satisfaction Louis felt all night.

He turned over the events of the evening as he fell asleep. Did Deacon Brodie get away with his crimes for so long because he occupied a higher social rung than the average thief? Most likely, Louis's little experiment simply proved what he suspected: that a man was marked from birth—by appearance or mannerism or accent or vocabulary—in such a way that he was trapped in that state like an insect in amber. There were plenty of exceptions. But human beings had an uncanny knack for labeling their fellow specimens. And yet emigrants were pouring out of London and Edinburgh and Dublin, out of the depressed farmlands onto steamers bound for America, bent upon defying their classifications and finding new lives.

Judging from her letter, Fanny had gone back and gotten lost in her *old* life. She vacillated from letter to letter. He had seen the effect of indecision on her; it nearly drove her mad. He guessed that she was seeing her whole life in front of her, dangling on the thread of this decision. She had made a bad choice in Sam Osbourne. Might she make a mistake again? Meanwhile, he was the decision at the end of the string, and he was feeling badly swung about.

THEN A TELEGRAM came from California. *Louis. I'm lost and sick. Need you.*

Louis stared at the stark words. They were a cry from her heart. They were a mandate.

"I can't wait anymore," he told Baxter the next day.

"Have you told your parents you plan to go?"

"Lord, no," Louis said. "My parents are planning a holiday at a spa in Cumberland. Low in your ear, man, but when they leave, I'm going over."

He looked for affirmation in Baxter's sober, beefy face. It was impossible to tell from his expression what his old ally was thinking. Charles Baxter had always hidden his essential self behind a serious countenance, yet he had a wonderfully irreverent sense of humor when he let it out. In their law student days, he was an infidel and adventurer, the sort of fellow who would have dressed in rags and happily passed as a pauper right along with Louis for the sheer fun of it. It was at Edinburgh University that Louis recognized in him a fit successor to his cousin Bob—a partner in insolence and play. Looking at him now, Louis was transported back to the days when they would walk out of lecture halls in a show of contempt for the dusty old professors who stood at the front. Sprung from class, they'd entertained themselves with practical jokes. Baxter was "Thomson" in those days, and Louis was "Johnstone"—two old Scottish coots they invented as new identities for themselves. Conversing in preposterous dialect, they went out on the streets, bought salves and health devices from quacks, wrapped them up, then mailed them to prominent citizens in Edinburgh. A package might contain a bottle of anti-fat syrup or a remedy for impotence, flatulence, or baldness, depending upon the public figure in question; perhaps a set of old artificial teeth, a cheap Indian necklace guaranteed to ward off thunderbolts, or any number of oddities found in the junk shops of the Old Town. Afternoons were spent at Rutherford's pub, where Baxter's phlegmatic mask would crack into lines of hilarity over the day's hijinks. When he became a solicitor and joined his father's law firm, Baxter seemed almost apologetic about it, as if he were a failed bon vivant, as if he were letting down his best friend. To anyone who hadn't known him then, Baxter appeared these days to be the most ordinary of ordinary fellows.

"Thomson," Louis said now, putting a slip of paper into his friend's big paw, "here is the one contact in America. This is the address of someone who knows Fanny. Don't tell even the queen if she asks."

Baxter looked uneasy. "Everyone is worried about you, Lou. Henley thinks . . ."

"What does Henley think?"

Baxter sputtered.

"Tell me what Henley thinks, Charles."

"Henley fears . . ."

"Say it out. What does he fear?"

"That you are going to face a life of alarms and intrigues and perhaps untruths, and it's no good for your health." Having unburdened himself, Baxter let out a sigh. "To Henley, the very notion of California is blasphemous."

"And so, by association, Fanny is blasphemous."

"He is a pigheaded man who is wed to his prejudices. And he loves you as I do, Lou."

Louis shrugged. "I'm going. And I will know in a few weeks: Either Fanny wants to spend her life with me, or it is over. It's as simple as that."

He would make the trip in steerage. It would be the least expensive way to go, but beyond that, he could write about what he saw and earn some money. He was enticed by the prospect of a book about the *idea* of America, where emigrants could meld with others in the great classless pot called the United States. Did it work, really? More to the point, could he pass as a workingman in steerage? He would see soon enough.

Without Fanny, a piece of himself was missing; he could wait no longer. Once, in a bar, full of drink and bravado, he had told someone— maybe it was Colvin—that no man was of any use until he had dared everything. Now he was about to do just that. Louis closed his eyes and thought a prayer. *God, if You exist, keep me brave and single-minded.*

~

CHAPTER 29

1879

"Make way! Move!" At the dock in Greenock, porters wheeling carts loaded head-high with baggage struggled through the throngs of people pushing to board the *Devonia*. It was the first week of August, and Louis thought he might die of heat prostration as he was swept along with the sweating people around him. In the distance beyond, he saw that the crowd was being funneled through a narrow gateway as they approached the steamer. On his back he wore a knapsack; in one hand he clutched a valise and, in the other, a railway rug. Half carrying, half dragging the rug, he rued his decision to carry books in it. Six heavy volumes of George Bancroft's *History of the United States* weighed down the satchel by a good stone and a half. What had he been thinking? He was glad for the valise he'd brought, though. When the snaking mass of humanity stopped, he sat down on the valise and for a brief moment congratulated himself on his impromptu seat. Just as quickly, he saw the folly of his ingenuity. The crowd began moving again, and he was nearly run over by the human wave. Louis fought his way back to his feet, heaved up his bag, and pushed onward with the others, past luggage carts that had been abandoned by a few frustrated porters. Ahead, the steamer loomed black and long as a city block. Three masts it had, with a red stack in the middle. At the starboard side of the ship, the mob tapered itself into a docile stripe that moved upward and into the steamer.

Onboard, Louis followed the directions to his second-cabin bunk. Carved out of the steerage section in the bowels of the ship, the second cabin was cordoned off by a perforated screen of wood. Other than the table he got for his extra two guineas, and the thin partition, Louis's lot as a second-cabin inmate was not so different from that of the men and women in steerage. Bodies were stacked into what looked like cages set into the walls of the ship, each with sixteen bunks. It didn't take long to discern that people had separated themselves into sections according to their languages: Germans and Scandinavians in the starboard pens; English speakers mostly forward. In Steerage No. 1, down two flights of steps and set into the nose of the ship, he found mostly single men.

Once he'd settled into his place, he walked around to have a better look at his fellow passengers' accommodations. People were loading their belongings into their bunks and taking out of bags the tin cups and utensils they had brought for dining. That was the other part of the second-cabin bargain: Louis didn't have to provide his own eating implements, nor his own bedding.

The mood of that first day was almost gay; there was a hopeful feeling in the air as the *Devonia* moved out of the harbor. In his second-cabin section, Louis's fellow travelers introduced themselves. There was a Scotsman called "Irish Stew," a newly married young English couple, and a frail woman bound for Kansas who continually consulted her watch, which was set to Glasgow time. There was also a pair of young men traveling together, a Scot and an Irishman who claimed to be an American until his charade was detected. Affronted by the notion that any man would deny his homeland, Louis could not bring himself to talk to the fool for the rest of the voyage.

It was in the evening of the second day that the other passengers began to reveal their various talents. There was a fiddler sleeping in the nose of the boat, where the ship's most violent bucking occurred, who had played a few tunes the first night before being taken terribly seasick. The fiddler couldn't be roused from his bed, so the others did what they could. They gathered up by the main deckhouse; Louis discoursed upon his flageolet, while a few men produced pennywhistles, a small drum, and an accordion to offer up their repertoires. But it was the singers—mostly Scots—who claimed the day. One by one, they overcame their shyness to stand up and sing a Scottish verse that touched upon everyone's hearts; "O why left I my hame?"

Louis ate the same porridge for breakfast as the men and women in steerage; at dinnertime, atop a dirty tablecloth, he downed the same soup, croquettes, beef, potatoes, and excellent bread. He was taken aback by the complaints about the food. The workingmen in steerage insisted that the slop was inedible and resorted to their caches of tinned fish. Louis was puzzled, for he considered his palate fairly well traveled.

This was steamer fare, to be sure, and the difference between the coffee and tea was negligible, but he found the food quite good. On pudding days—Tuesday and Thursday—the emigrants voiced their pleasure. More often they complained about the lack of niceties as if it were a social injustice.

The only second-cabin passenger whom Louis befriended was one Mr. Jones, a Welsh blacksmith in the act of reinventing himself as a salesman. At first Louis took him for a countryman, as his dialect was hard to pin down. He was a widower who once had money enough, though it was all gone now. Yet he was going forward and felt confident that the patent medicine he intended to peddle in America would save his hide.

"Golden Oil, Mr. Stevenson," he said. "If you have the croup or a broken fingernail, come to me, sir, and I shall cure it."

Louis had not officially declared his own line of business until Mr. Jones inquired.

"A writer chap," he answered when pressed.

"What are you writing?"

"A story."

"You don't say! A made-up story?"

"Yes."

Mr. Jones let out a hearty laugh. "Oh, I could help you with some lyin' stories."

"This is about a man who is like me," Louis said, "a man who enjoys observing and collecting 'types,' so to speak—big personalities. He's fascinated by all sorts of people, and he comes upon a man who is a complete fraud, a man who takes advantage of foreigners in Paris by—"

Mr. Jones looked stricken. "Say no more. I shall read it when it is published."

Jones seemed content to simply observe a writer working. When other steerage passengers gathered around Louis and joked about his enterprise as he hunkered down over his notebook, Mr. Jones hushed them. One afternoon, though, the man caught Louis furtively taking notes in the shadows as a group of men spoke about abandoned mills and plows, about factory girls nearly starving.

"I know what you're up to." Jones's whisper was testy. "You're goin' to tell about us. About where we come from and what we eat and what torments our pitiful souls must endure. You're spyin' in the slums, ain't ye?"

Louis felt his neck and face flush hot.

Jones shrugged. "I shan't tell anyone," he said, waving the bottle of Golden Oil. "We're all imposters, one way or another."

"Thank you," Louis said softly.

After that, they talked deeply at the end of the day, each sharing what he had experienced. Jones, it turned out, was a flaneur of sorts, walking about observing what he could, given the restrictions on the boat.

"Seasickness is the great equalizer," Mr. Jones remarked one evening. "I caught a glimpse of first cabin today when I went up to speak to the steward about the food. He told me there's plenty of 'em prostrate up there."

"Aye, but it's a universal condition down here," Louis said. In the stuffy, common air of steerage, one man's seasickness was everyone's. Music seemed their only comfort. At one point Louis linked hands with a group of men who encircled a group of women to help reduce the swaying motion that was making them sick. The men sang "Lassie Wi' the Lint-White Locks" sweetly enough to make Robert Burns weep, wherever he was.

Music could not save them, though. By the seventh day, the bunks smelled and looked like the pens of animals. A mess of tin cups, rotting food, filthy clothes, and soiled rags and sheets shared space on the shelves with the resident bodies in steerage. Louis took note of every unsavory detail. Among the ghostly faces with eyes at half-mast, he found men and women whose fine characters shone through the bleak circumstances.

Above his little writing table, a single dim lantern swayed in the cabin's perpetual twilight. Louis sat reading his notes and gloating over the embarrassment of riches that steerage provided. At last, real material! A book was building in his mind. It was beginning to flow, yes, he could feel it coming. He would call it *The Amateur Emigrant*.

He went up to sleep on the deck when he could and invited others to join him, but no one did. Up top, he could lie looking at the stars and think of Fanny without tainting her memory with the terrible smells below. The fresh air, cold as it was, calmed his stomach, cleansed his lungs. Eavesdropping among the emigrants, he had pitied them for their vague, unfounded dreams. With his head clear, he wondered if he was as big a dreamer as the rest. Here he was, rushing to see Fanny, with no real assurances from her. Was he on a fool's errand?

When he returned to his writing table, he scribbled out a new paragraph for a story he'd begun, "The Story of a Lie."

> . . . the woman I love is somewhat of my handiwork; and the great lover, like the great painter, is he that can so embellish his subject as to make her more than human . . . To love a character is only the heroic way of understanding it. When we love, by some noble method of our own or some nobility of . . . nature in the other, we apprehend the loved one by what is noblest in ourselves.

One Tuesday morning the sea grew placid. Relieved passengers emerged on deck and strolled in their allotted space. Color returned to faces, and the fiddler played his Celtic tunes. How emotionally intense the music of Louis's homeland was, veering from exuberant joy to haunting sorrow. He felt his heart leap and sink as the tunes changed, and he wondered if the airs struck the hearts of those passengers not from Scotland in the same way. Around him, people chatted merrily about what they would do first after their feet hit the land. In the midst of the gaiety, three unfamiliar faces appeared. They were a gentleman and two young women from first cabin who had come to have a look at the steerage crowd. As they stepped around the outstretched legs of people sitting on the deck, one of the women held a delicate forefinger to her nose.

Louis felt his chest swell with outrage. "If we are not allowed to enter their section of the deck," he said indignantly, "they should not be allowed to enter ours."

"Aye!" other voices chimed in.

At teatime the next day, when the steward came around with broken pieces of meat that had obviously been scraped from the plates of first-cabin passengers, the crowd sent up a cry of disgust. Louis joined them. He wanted a nice joint of meat as much as the next fellow.

As the steamer neared America, Louis's brain fairly itched with excitement for his essay and then he realized he simply itched. All over.

The wretched linens he was so pleased to get for free as part of his two extra guineas were, no doubt about it, filled with mites.

When the ship pulled into New York, it was midday. Louis put on a pair of clean trousers he had reserved for the occasion, which promptly fell to his knees. He had lost fifteen pounds, he guessed, and red welts crisscrossed his skinny legs and arms and belly where he had scratched himself to a pulp.

CHAPTER 30

⌒

Rain soaked Louis and Jones as they left the *Devonia* and hurried through Manhattan's gritty streets in search of a hotel. After all the dire warnings on board about murderers lurking on every corner, they were relieved to find a friendly Irish family running a cheap boarding-house not far from the docks. In the morning, when Louis went to collect waiting mail, he found a telegram from Monterey. It was from Fanny's sister, who was staying with her there at an inn. The message was simple and direct: *Fanny sick with brain fever.* Frantic, Louis grabbed his bags from the hotel, raced to the ferry terminal, and bought a ticket to Jersey City, where he would begin his train journey west.

Later the next day, relieved to be ensconced in his train seat with heads nodding around him, he pensively watched the lights of Phila-delphia come and go before he fell into his own slumber. When he woke, the train was at a complete standstill in a hilly green stretch of country that looked not unlike England. An accident on the tracks up ahead had brought everything to a halt, and for an entire day, Louis sat in the train cars with the other frustrated passengers, unmoving and without food. It wasn't until the next night when the train pulled into Pittsburgh that he went to a café at the station. He'd not eaten for some thirty hours.

The emigrant train might have been merely uncomfortable if he had been in reasonable health. But the privations of the ocean voyage had come home to settle upon his profoundly reduced self. He was ill with fever, chills, and aches, but the worst of it was the itching. Louis ex-pected he could forgive an itching man nearly anything.

He grinned darkly when he remembered he had packed a small bot-tle of laudanum. It wasn't enough to last the whole ten-day trip, but for now it was a miracle. Louis cursed the pharmacist he'd sought out in New York who had looked at his bitten arms and issued him useless pills for his liver, of all things. In San Francisco, he would find whatever oil was prescribed for the itch—if, in fact, this hell was caused by mites. Periodically, the other possibility sent shivers of terror through him: The itch might be syphilis. People with the disease often got a rash that looked a lot like the one he had. *If this be the pox, I know where I earned it—in the Old Town.* Louis drank down a dose of the laudanum and, fighting despair, took out his pen and notebook.

Dear Colvin, he wrote as he waited for his misery to subside, *I never knew it was so easy to commit suicide.* Certainly, Henley and Bob believed he was doing just that when he set out on his journey. Sobered by their concern, he had written a quick will before boarding the *Devonia.* Now, in the grip of depression and pain, he thought, *Where would I be buried if I died on this train tonight?* Without hesitation, he wrote, *Under the wide and starry sky.* Below the line, he began composing an epitaph for his gravestone. *Robert Louis Stevenson, born 1850 of a family of engineers. Died . . .*

He stayed awake as a poem came to him.

> Under the wide and starry sky,
> Dig the grave and let me lie.
> Glad did I live and gladly die,
> And I laid me down with a will.
>
> This be the verse you grave for me:
> Here he lies where he longed to be;
> Home is the sailor, home from sea,
> And the hunter home from the hill.

When he woke, his fingers were covered in ink, and the conductor was shouting "Chicago!" As the train jolted to a stop, he tried to stand but fell backward into his seat. After a while, a newsboy came by and gave him a hand getting up. On legs intoxicated by the drug, Louis made his way into the train station, where he found a plate of ham and eggs. Waiting to board the next train, he lay down on marble stairs with his arms outstretched and watched himself as if from the outside with a removed sort of curiosity, to see what would become of him.

Another train appeared, this one running as far as Council Bluffs and the Pacific Transfer Station, where he would board his final train to California. Somehow he got himself on it.

At a hotel in Council Bluffs that night, he spent part of his dwindling money on a decent room, where he ate, drank, and fell asleep picturing Fanny sitting under the arbor at the Chevillon. In the morning, feeling revived, he joined a hundred other emigrants outside the station waiting to board. Here was the great melting pot of America everyone talked about, right on this platform. What an assortment of humanity! Irish, German, Italian, and Swedish types—but these people were not fresh off steamer ships, he discovered after a couple of short conversations. They had been in America for a while. They were from the eastern and middle states, failed farmers and factory men headed west with nothing to lose.

The train had two dozen cars, three of which were for passengers, the rest for baggage and cattle. As people moved forward in line, they were dispatched by the ticket taker to specific cars. It became evident to Louis that a sorting process was under way, and soon enough he found himself in the middle car of the three for passengers. His fellows on that car, it turned out, were all men traveling alone, with the exception of a small boy, perhaps eight, who had whooping cough. Women and children, along with a few men traveling with their families, boarded in the car behind his. The third passenger car, just ahead, was filling with Chinese.

Louis surveyed his new accommodations. Rows of wood benches on either side of the aisle allowed two sitters, but just barely. At the front, a stove occupied one corner, and at the back was a toilet closet. As the train moved out of the station, a white-haired conductor appeared at the front of car. "Gentlemen!" he shouted. Then, lowering his voice, "Gentlemen. I will explain this once." The crowd silenced itself. "These here wood benches you're sittin' on? You can make 'em face each other. Even better, you can make 'em flatten out and join into a bed." The conductor held up a flat piece of wood. "Now, this here is the board that will connect 'em." He chased two men from their seats and demonstrated how the benches collapsed. "Let me explain how we do things on this train. You need to find a chum to share your bed with. Between the two of ya's, you buy one board. Okay. Then each man buys his own cushions." The conductor put down the board and held up three square straw-stuffed, gingham-covered cushions. "Each man puts these on top, you got yourself a bed. One board and three cushions costs two-fifty." As the information sank into the heads of the emigrants, the men began to look around warily for a suitable bedmate with whom to split the cost of a board.

"No need for shyness now, boys." The conductor laughed. "I'll do the matchmakin', if you ain't got a partner." He proceeded to pair up travelers as he walked along the aisle. When he got to Louis's bench, he solicited a nearby gentleman in a suit who appeared alarmed that he might be paired with the ragged-looking Scot.

"I talked to this fella up here already," the man protested, standing and scurrying over to the side of a boyish traveler. "Feel like I know him. I believe me and him will be bunkmates, what do you say, young fella?"

The conductor moved on in his mating game. "Any offers?" he asked, looking around for another prospect. Louis felt himself blush and, in that moment, understood the plight of every woman who faced an arranged marriage.

"I don't mind," said a strapping young Pennsylvania Dutch youth, stoically stepping up like a volunteer for a chancy military maneuver.

That night, as the train chugged through the dark hills of Iowa, the men in the car swigged from bottles and listened to the lonely tunes of a cornet player. The booze and the music loosened them, and they shared where they were headed. In short time, everyone in the car had a new train name. Louis's bunkmate was "Pennsylvania"; the young fellow going west to cure his asthma was called "Dubuque" for his hometown; Louis was dubbed "Shakespeare."

The heat inside the train was blistering, so he wore only trousers and a shirt left unbuttoned and open. Every morning he went out onto the platform at the back of the train car with a tin dish of water and the cloth and bar of soap he had bought at the same time as his bedding. It was a risky operation to bathe on the back platform of a moving train, with one arm looped through the wood railing for stability. Louis quickly apprehended who was bathing and who was not: There appeared to be a direct relationship between how much flesh one exposed and how much one smelled. He found the stench of the men in his car profound, but when he came into proximity with the women and children, he felt near to fainting. The least offensive were the Chinese, who were more thorough in their daily toilets and actually washed their feet, an idea that had not occurred to any of the men on his car, including him.

And yet it was the Chinese who were reviled in one vicious "joke" after another by the white emigrants. It was common for men to make gagging sounds in proximity to a Chinese passenger. Not long before it had been the Irish who were hated, yet here was a race even more despised in the land of opportunity. Never mind that the Chinese had invented gunpowder and printing and a thousand ideas that the Western world was glad to imitate. It puzzled Louis, and he jotted down: *Their forefathers watched the stars before mine had begun to keep pigs.*

Perched up top of a train car, where he could escape the closeness of the passenger section, Louis felt the terrible itching ease some. He looked out at the flat, near-naked Nebraska plains and pondered his notions about the United States. Like a lot of young Europeans, he had for some while viewed America as a promised land. Any place declaring from the outset that it was dedicated to the proposition of all men being created equal had a foot up. Places like Edinburgh seemed staid and passé compared to, say, Chicago, where a man could capitalize upon his native talents in grand fashion, regardless of who his father was. In the scheme of things, it was hard not to feel some jealousy that America was on the ascent, and Europe was wallowing in decline, thanks to its own bad behavior.

Judging from the people he'd encountered so far, the American personality was gruff and suspicious until it became suddenly, inexplicably kind. Just this morning, he had experienced the dichotomy. Louis had positioned himself at the back of his car to catch fresh air through the door. Because the latch was broken, he held open the door with his foot. When a newsboy passed, he kicked Louis's leg hard, causing him to cringe in pain. But when the boy figured out just how sick Louis was, his cruelty vanished.

"Have a pear," he said when he passed later, and handed Louis the fruit. "You can borrow one of these, if you want," he added, giving him a newspaper. "Just keep it nice so's I can sell it."

Dubuque, who had observed the encounter, moved a wad of tobacco out of the way of his tongue. "Most folks here got leather hides, Shakespeare. But inside? You're gonna find a sack o' feathers."

It was true. Americans as a people were decent types at heart. But their generosity did not extend to the Chinese. Nor to the Indians, who came in for particular ridicule. At a station near Omaha, a small family approached the idling train to sell trinkets to the passengers. The tiny woman was wearing a dirty print dress and a man's bowler hat. The man looked strange and displaced, standing there in red suspenders and a dandy's striped waistcoat with a watch fob dangling from the buttonhole. The children were merely dirty, wearing rags of indecipherable origin. How could American citizens witness such humiliation and not rise up in outrage? Louis was seething with that question when Pennsylvania joined a group of other male passengers outside the train car and began dancing behind the Indian family while whooping wildly, much to the delight of the men inside.

Louis might have downed the whole bottle of laudanum at that moment were he not out of the stuff. How could the human heart hold within its chambers at the same moment such grand measures of nobility and baseness? He wrote in his notebook: *Indians at Omaha station: I am ashamed for this thing we call civilization.*

"What just came over you?" he fumed when Pennsylvania made his jolly return. "Did you leave your decency in your pocket when you got off the train?" Shamed, the boy turned his head away from his seat partner.

Louis stared out the window after that, watching the plains turn into the stark black hills of Nebraska. When the train slowly pulled into a station in Wyoming, he saw an eastbound train reloading its passengers. Weary-looking people hurried to return to their cars on the other side of the platform, but not before shouting into the windows of Louis's westbound train, "Go back! Turn around and go back!"

CHAPTER 31

⌒

"Fanny, are you awake?"

"Hmmm?" Fanny sat in a chair in Señorita Bonifacio's stucco-walled garden. She had nodded off to the drowsy hum of bees among the yellow roses covering the arch over the gate. "Funny," she said, yawning, "I was half-dreaming just then."

"You have a telegram." Nellie Vandegrift's blue eyes beamed at her from underneath a curtain of blond hair across her forehead. The girl put the envelope in her sister's hand.

Fanny sat up straight and ripped the telegram out of the envelope.

August 18, 1879. Departing New York today. Due Monterey by Aug. 30th. RLS

"Louis is coming," she said. She looked around the inn's garden as if seeing it for the first time. "What day is today?"

"Why, it's August twenty-seventh," her sister replied. "Is that what you mean? It's a Monday."

Fanny's fingers went to her mouth, her cheeks; she ran her palm over her head. "My hair!" she groaned. "It's positively grizzled."

"You're just as beautiful as you always were. Don't get yourself worked up. Dr. Heintz is coming over here any time now."

"No, no, I've got to put myself together." She glanced down at the dressing gown and slippers she wore. "I look like an old nana in this nightgown, like Aunt Tidge."

"You know what the man said: Rest. Come, climb into your bed and stay there. Once he leaves, you can get up again."

"There's so much to do. Louis could be here in what . . . three days?" Fanny stood up to embrace her sister. "At last," she said. "Something good."

. . .

"No fever," the doctor pronounced when he began to examine her. "What about the pain in your head?"

"Long gone," Fanny said. She sat at the edge of her bed perfectly still, trying to ignore the stethoscope pressing her breast. The smell of chili peppers roasting over a flame in the kitchen came to her, and the raspy sound of a scrub jay scolding some other creature outside the window.

The man turned to Nellie. "Any sign of delirium?"

"Not since those first two days."

Fanny closed her eyes, remembering the time she and Louis drifted in a canoe downstream from Grez. It was the day after they first made love. They had looked into each other's eyes and *known*: This is love, this is real.

"Convulsions?"

"No."

The doctor widened Fanny's eyelids, his own eyes boring into her pupils. "Does the sunlight bother you, Mrs. Osbourne?"

"Not a bit. Makes me happy."

"How is your sense of balance?"

"I'm all right now."

"I must say, you appear to be on the mend. What it was, I'm not so sure."

Fanny looked at the young doctor's already careworn face. "When you were here before, you said inflammation of the brain."

"It probably was brain swelling caused by anxiety and general wretchedness," he said. "It can happen to people who are going through a struggle, as you said you were. But it could just as well have been a bad case of influenza. Whatever you had, you need to eat now. No meat, eggs, or sweets. No coffee or tea." The man stood up and put away his stethoscope.

"Tell him about the crying," Nellie said, twisting one of her long braids nervously. When Fanny didn't speak, Nellie went on. "She breaks down a lot."

The doctor looked wearily at Fanny, as if he had seen too many crying women in his time. She could see he wanted to go home to his wife and dinner. "I'm perfectly fine now," she said, managing a smile. "I haven't cried for days."

"Cold sponge baths," the doctor advised, putting on his hat. "Nothing like a cold cloth to activate the skin and chase away the melancholy. Brightens the eyes and cheers the soul."

Nellie saw him out the front door. When she came back to the room, Fanny took her sister's hand and squeezed it. "There's one thing that can cheer my soul right now, Nellie, and it's not a sponge bath."

"Louis?"

"Oh, Nellie, you will love him. He is the kindest, most decent, wittiest . . ."

"It won't be long now."

"Nellie," Fanny asked cautiously, "what happened when I was out of my head?"

"You saw things that weren't there."

"I have no memory of it at all."

"You were talking to Pa."

Tears pooled in Fanny's eyes. "I feel terrible I wasn't there at the end."

"Pa never doubted you loved him. You know, not long before he died, he said you had every right to leave Sam. He was on your side."

Fanny blotted her eyes with a handkerchief.

"You've got a lot of Pa in you." Nellie's face grew pensive. "I think I'm more like Ma."

"You mean I got the temper," Fanny said sardonically, eyeing her sister, "and you got the sweetness?"

Nellie laughed. "I was thinkin' of how Pa stood up for what he believed in. Do you remember when I would have to go to the grocer's for Mama, and there were those two big boys—awful bullies—who threatened me? They said I had to pay a nickel to walk down their block. That's all I had in my sweaty little palm! I was terrified to walk that block, but I was almost as scared to go home without the groceries. Pa wouldn't abide a coward in the family."

"He told me it was my job as the oldest to go out and fight them," Fanny said, "to teach them not to fool with us."

"Oh, you were a sight when you came home."

"I guess it was a draw. They were bloodied, too."

"Pa wouldn't stand for nobody being treated unfairly. He was two-fisted when it came to that. You were the one Pa counted on to settle a score if we were picked on. Why do you think us girls looked up to you, Fan? You were brave. You were the one who really took care of us."

Fanny shook her head. "I'm tired of being strong."

Nellie chewed on her lower lip before asking. "Have you told Sam yet that Louis is coming over here?"

"He knows."

Bathed and dressed, Fanny went back to her chair outside. The courtyard garden was a tribute to the señorita's tender care, bursting as it was with a fat hedge of fuchsia shrubs and the Gold of Ophir rose over the gate that the lady said had been a gift from a suitor, Lieutenant William Tecumseh Sherman, during his assignment in Monterey. The house on Alvarado Street was like so many others in this sleepy coastal outpost. It was in the Mexican style, with a clay tile roof under which mostly Spanish was spoken.

Sam Osbourne had been so pleased with himself when he brought Fanny to Monterey. He knew she would love the adobe houses and the arches made from bleached whalebones that led to lush private gardens. He told Fanny the story of Señorita Bonifacio's love affair with the young Sherman, little suspecting that the story of a failed romance would touch her so. Apparently, Sherman had given the beautiful girl the rose shrub as a token of his love and a promise of his return when he was transferred out of the town. Maybe the young officer and the belle of Monterey courted in this garden. Did the famous general crush her when he married someone else? There was no hint of it, though she had never married. The señorita, thirty years beyond the romance, remained slender, arrow-straight, and handsome. Flitting around the garden like a hummingbird, watering this, clipping that, she appeared to be among the happiest of God's creatures.

Fanny had returned from Europe with heavy-hearted resignation. One more time, she told herself. One more try, for the sake of Sammy. She and Sam agreed to go away from the Oakland house to try to mend. They stayed at the inn in Monterey, which seemed a wholesome place to heal a broken marriage. They had sat in the señorita's romantic garden and spoken about trying to make a future together. They had walked the beaches for hours and talked about who they once were, who they were now. "Nobody understands you like I do," Sam had told her. "I knew the soft, shy girl. Still know her." They stayed in their big Castilian bed, tangled up in each other.

In one of his grand gestures, Sam rented an entire wing of Señorita Bonifacio's house for Fanny, Belle, Sammy, and Nellie, who had come out for a visit and decided to stay. He even installed new horses for all of them at a livery stable nearby. Sam seemed calm and confident now that he was on solid ground with a job as a court stenographer. He promised to come down on weekends from San Francisco to be with the family.

For a brief while in Monterey, the four of them played their parts in the Osbourne family with grace. They rode into the hills together, and Sam acted like a real father, adjusting Sammy's stirrups and making a point to ride beside the boy while keeping up a kindly conversation. Belle put aside her bitterness toward her mother for "snatching" her away from the arms of Frank O'Meara. They all behaved as if they were a normal, happy clan.

"I'll come clean with you, Fanny," Sam said one night during that time. "There were others you didn't know about. I don't know why . . ." He shook his head, as if as puzzled by it all as she was. "I am a changed man now. That I am."

Fanny drew in a deep breath. "I have made my own hurtful choices," she blurted out. "I had a relationship with Louis Stevenson."

Within a couple of weeks, Sam's visits to the rooms in Monterey began to taper off. Fanny suspected her admission cooled Sam's ardor. And then, a month ago, he admitted he had another woman in San Francisco.

FANNY WRAPPED HER fingers around the warm cup of coffee the cook had set out for her. She wondered what Louis would think of her now. She had put on a few pounds; she was thirty-nine years old. They'd been apart a year, but Paris seemed a lifetime ago. She was haunted by the idea that she had betrayed him—betrayed his faith in *them*. No one would condemn her for trying to reconcile with her husband. But she felt as tawdry now, having let down Louis, as she had felt after reading the vicious parody of herself in *Scribner's* magazine. Margaret Wright's article had cut her to the quick.

It was then that she'd decided to return to the States. She'd reasoned that she owed one more try to the marriage. If it could not be repaired, she planned to pursue a respectable divorce. None of it had gone according to plan. She was simply outplayed by her husband. Lost was the piece of higher ground she had clung to for so long. Her confession to Sam about the affair had divested her of that real estate.

"Sam has me right where he wants me," she said to Nellie, "in a rented place where he won't have to see me very often. He can charm his children and lure them away while waffling about a divorce. So much for high hopes."

Her dreams for Belle had been dashed as well. The girl had fallen in love with a rakish San Francsco youth named Joe Strong. He was a good enough painter and sweet, but he drank too much and was perpetually broke. Fanny saw something in Joe that was in Sam Osbourne's character as well: He was weak as water and a professional repenter, the kind of man who would be offering apologies for the rest of his life for the mistakes he kept repeating.

Belle sniffed her mother's disapproval. "*Papa* likes Joe," she said to Fanny, setting her jaw. Living in Monterey, Belle lately found many reasons to adore her father and to dislike her mother. One day, when Fanny persuaded her daughter to go to the beach with her, she had made a picture of the girl sitting on the sand. When Belle saw the sketch, she seethed with contempt. "What kind of mother makes her child look ugly in every drawing?" she demanded.

Belle was soon going off to the beach, not with her mother but with Joe. When Fanny objected, Belle exploded. "I'm eighteen years old! You can't control me anymore! It is hypocrisy to tell me I can't see a young man who is just beginning to make his way. You chose Louis Stevenson, who is penniless. And you've *lived* with him already."

Fanny gritted her teeth but remained silent, so Belle chose a new angle. "Frank O'Meara desperately wanted to marry me. I loved him, and you dragged me away. You have tried to break up everything good in my life. Worst of all is how you've tried to turn me against Papa."

"I wanted for you what I didn't have," Fanny argued. "A chance to enjoy something of your own before you start taking care of other people. Maybe a chance to actually shape your own destiny. You are an artist, Belle. You don't have to find yourself by *marrying* an artist."

Belle looked at her incredulously. "You know nothing about Joe Strong. You are an old woman, Mother, full of bitterness and talk of doom. And this is one time you will not have your way."

When Joe got wind of Fanny's disapproval, he hustled Belle off to San Francisco and married her. Fanny took to her bed, while Sam welcomed the happy couple with open arms and set them up in a fine hotel for a honeymoon stay.

How had the one thing Fanny wanted most in all the world, a happy little family of her own, slipped through her fingers? Sam lost long ago, Hervey dead, Belle estranged despite all the love and work, despite everything Fanny ever did to make a home. She had been too free with Belle. She had let the girl drift away from her.

Thank God she still had Sammy.

Fanny was in the garden when the boy returned from a visit to the stable. "Can you keep a secret?" she asked him.

Sammy's eyes widened. "Yes."

"Louis Stevenson is going to pay us a visit sometime soon," she told him. She watched as the news registered: His pale, long face lit up. He leaped in the air and shouted, "Luly is coming!"

"Shhh. Now, don't tell. You are the only one who knows."

CHAPTER 32

⟿

In the early-September sunlight, Fanny stood on the wooden sidewalk in front of the house on Alvarado Street and watched for Louis. She knew his route. He would take a train from Oakland to Salinas City, then transfer to the narrow-gauge train that dumped its passengers rather unceremoniously a few miles outside of Monterey. There he would get a wagon to bring him into town. Exactly when this would happen was anybody's guess.

Alvarado was the main thoroughfare in a town with only three real streets, and these were paved with a top coating of beach sand. At street corners in either direction, Fanny could see the old Mexican cannon barrels that had been plugged upright, like cigars in spittoons, to serve as hitching posts. The air smelled of horse droppings and fried beans wafting from Adulfo Sanchez's saloon. The seaweedy odor of the ocean was there, too, and when the horse traffic quieted, the sound of the crashing breakers could be heard. Alvarado Street was alive with traffic at this hour, with vendors, shoppers, children walking home from school, and the occasional *vaquero* seated on a fancy-tooled saddle, riding by too fast.

Fanny didn't know everyone in town, small as it was, but she was beginning to recognize faces—the local restaurateur, the newspaper editor, the neighborhood women who nodded when they passed, the handful of stupefied men who stumbled out of Sanchez's bar in the late afternoon. She knew personally some of the bright lights in town, including Adulfo Sanchez himself, who was officially engaged to her sister Nellie. Adulfo was a sweet man from an old Mexican family with deep roots in Monterey. Nellie had met him at one of the town's weekly public balls.

Another local character was Jules Tavernier, a well-known landscape painter. Early on in Fanny's stay in Monterey, Sam introduced her to

Tavernier, whom he knew from the Bohemian Club, and took her to his studio on Alvarado Street, where she found some local "artists" lazing on Persian rugs, drinking whiskey, and talking about French Impressionism. One of these reclining idlers was Joe Strong, the young man who was already sniffing around Belle. Joe had jumped up and spoken respectfully to Fanny, but in that moment she felt the essential wrongness of him. Even then she could see he was the kind of young man who would burn himself up early and become an albatross for some girl when his bohemian ways lost their charm. Fanny reflected now that she should have shipped Belle straight back to Indiana at the first signs of their affair.

"Fish! Fish!" A Chinese youth with a bamboo pole over his shoulder passed in front of Fanny, and she hailed him. She had purchased from the boy before and was fairly certain that "fish" was the only English word in his vocabulary. Examining the catch inside his net, she pointed to a shad, and he held up six fingers. Fanny reached into the small purse at her waist and paid him six cents.

She went inside the house, where the thick walls kept the room cool. For two days now she had bathed, dressed, and perfumed herself as if expecting company. Each day they waited for Louis to arrive. Sammy behaved like someone with Saint Vitus's dance, so jumpy was he with the secret. As the dinner hour approached, Fanny cut onions into a frying pan, then went outside to watch one more time. The fog from the sea was already rolling in. Carpenters carrying tools walked along Alvarado, and some of the drinkers from Sanchez's bar exited noisily through the doorway. One of the men coming toward her had a familiar gait. He was a wraith of a fellow, with dark hair and . . . Fanny squinted. It was Louis.

She let out a cry, and then he was standing there before her: Louis Stevenson, looking as if he had lost one half of himself. His features, always so lively, were strangely still, as if his eyes and mouth were too weary to dance. He was wearing the blue serge suit he had bought in London to call upon publishers. The jacket was a wrinkled mess that hung off his bony shoulders as if from a wooden hanger; a belt cinched at his waist kept the gathered pants aloft. Her face went slack as fear raced through her chest.

Louis did not touch her. "It's good to see you, Fanny," he mur-

mured. The sweetness of his Scottish accent was the only thing about
him that seemed intact.

"Where is your baggage?" she asked.

"I'm happy you're up, Fanny. I expected you'd be in bed."

"I'm better, Louis." She looked up into his sallow face again, prepared not to gasp.

"I was afraid you'd be . . ."

He put out his hand to hold hers, and when she grasped it, she saw
his wrists were covered with red welts. She pulled her hand away. "What
is it?"

"Ah, the emigrant's curse," he said. "The itch. I need to get some
medicine."

"Is it all over you?"

He sighed. "Unfortunately."

"We can go to the pharmacist right now, Louis."

"I need to sit down for a wee bit, is that all right?"

"Yes, yes, come in."

When they went inside, they found young Sammy standing near
the table. His head tilted slightly to one side when he looked at the
man with his mother.

"Sammy," Louis said.

The moment the boy heard Louis's voice, he stepped partly behind
Fanny. Stunned, mother and son ogled the apparition that had collapsed on a chair.

"I have all the makings for a fish dinner—just what you like," Fanny
said, forcing cheer into her tremulous voice. She bustled about finishing supper, while Louis's dazed eyes followed her. No clever quip came
from his mouth, only a rattling cough.

"What are you going to do?" Nellie whispered when Fanny went
into the hallway.

"Send him over to the boardinghouse. Will you go to Adulfo's and
ask him to bring Louis's bag? He left it there, he said. I suspect he's too
weak to carry it."

"Weak?" Nellie said, grasping her sister's hand. "Honey, that man's
half dead. Who knows what that rash is. What are you going to *do*?"

Fanny knew what Nellie was asking. *This is the man you want to
make a life with, the man who is going to support you? Are you insane?*

Through all the turmoil of the last months, during the battles with Sam, during all the letters from home condemning her for even considering divorce, Fanny had clung to Louis's memory. She had prayed for this moment, but now that it was here, everything felt wrong. Looking into the front room from the hallway, she saw an emaciated creature she didn't recognize, a tall man weighing perhaps 115 pounds, a thoroughly sick man.

"I don't know," she said soberly. "I thought I knew, but now . . ."

BY NOON THE next day, Louis had recovered some strength. He came by the house to collect Fanny. "Do your parents know you are in America?" she asked when they went out onto the street.

"They do now. I had a brutal letter from my father in New York. He told me to stop this 'sinful enterprise.' He's cut me off, and do you know? I'm relieved."

"Have you any money left?"

"Not to speak of. Colvin owes me. He wrote that he would send some as soon as he is able."

Just then Jules Tavernier emerged from his studio onto the sidewalk. "Mrs. Osbourne," he called out.

"Mr. Tavernier," she said, composing herself, "this is Robert Louis Stevenson, a friend of mine, and a great Scottish writer, I might add. He is in this country on a lecture tour."

"Well," the man said, appraising Louis none too subtly, "will you be speaking here?"

"Oh, no," Fanny interjected. "He's just down from San Francisco for a little respite."

When they had walked another half block, Louis asked, "Where can we go to talk freely?"

"To the beach," she said. "It's a small place, this town. People do not speak kindly of one another behind backs."

"I don't give a tinker's damn."

"I still have to care," Fanny said.

They walked down Alvarado Street to the soft sandhills that ran between the town and the ocean. She tried to cheer him as they walked, but he would have no part of small talk. The sound of the booming waves echoed like cannon reports in her ears.

"It was not an easy trip," Louis said when they reached the beach.

"I can see that."

"I was afraid you were in grave danger when I got the telegram. People die of brain fever."

"Nellie sent it. She shouldn't have frightened you. We don't know what it was, but it passed."

Louis stopped walking and turned to her. "Where are you in the divorce proceedings?"

Fanny caught her breath. "I haven't begun."

Louis looked at her incredulously. "Don't tell me that, Fanny. You asked me to come."

She looked at her feet, half buried in the sand. "It's not that I haven't talked to Sam about it."

"And?"

"He's resisting it despite everything. The truth is, I have been under siege from my family, too. Everyone is opposed to it. They're like your father, Louis. They think it's a sin."

"What do you want, Fanny? Not what do *they* want, for Christ's sake—what do *you* want?"

Fanny set her chin, looked into his eyes. "I want peace in my mind."

He kicked the sand. Whether from anger or the rash, Louis's neck was flaming red. "Are you going to marry me or not?"

Fanny put a hand over her mouth and stared out at the ocean. Her mind raced as minutes elapsed. When she did not answer, Louis walked away, up the beach, and she turned back toward town.

⌒

CHAPTER 33

Two figures were hovering over Louis when he woke.

"Here he comes," said one, an old man who leaned in close.

"Can you see me, mister?" said the other, whose face was as pocked as a beach stone.

"You been out for days," said the first. "We 'bout took you for dead."

Louis looked around. It appeared he was in the upper chamber of a rustic cabin. "How did I get here?" he asked.

"English," the old one declared.

"Scottish," Louis corrected. He tried feebly to sit up from the makeshift bed where he lay, but merely fell back.

"Oh, you're goin' nowhere for a while, mister," said the old one. "You gotta eat somethin'. Jesus Lord. Look at you."

Louis looked down at his naked, ribby chest. "What foul paste have you gilded me with, gentlemen?"

"Man talks like a book," said the pocked one.

The elder fellow aimed a flinty blue eye at Louis, daring him to complain further. "You itch, buddy?"

Louis thought about it. "No."

"Damn stuff works, even when a fella's been flayed as bad as you." The man laughed, exposing a naked upper gum on one side. "It's bear grease and some other surprises. Tom's own recipe," he said, nodding toward a fellow in the background who appeared to be an Indian.

"How long have I been here?"

"Four days, and mostly not here," the old one said. "What the devil is a man like you doin' knocked out under a tree on this ranch?"

"First, sir, what is your name?"

"Cap'n Anson Smith. This here's my partner, Jonathan Wright."

"I am Louis Stevenson. And I thank you both for saving my life."

"Oh, that ain't decided yet."

Tom came forward with a steaming cup. "Tea," he said. "Drink it."

"You was cold when we found you," Smith said. "Now you got yourself a fine fever." Louis saw a look pass between Smith and Wright. "Did you mean to just go off and die?" The captain's voice was soft and respectful, as if he would understand such an impulse.

"I like to go camping out, take in the air." Louis smiled at the old man's look of disbelief. "And . . . I had little funds for an inn."

"Or grub, looks like."

"Captain of what, sir?" Louis asked.

"Army. Mexican war. Only thing I shoot now is bears." He laughed at his own wit.

"Me and him raise goats here," Wright said. "Angoras. What's your line?"

"Writer chap."

Wright ran a knobby hand across his mustache. "Is there a woman somewheres in this?"

Louis began to explain about the train trip, but a coughing fit took him for a good five minutes. The two men eyed him warily. "No more talking till tomorrow," Smith said.

Louis lay on the cot in the upper chamber, coughing between sips of the tea. Inside his head, the Pacific Ocean thundered unceasingly. He remembered, foggily, the state he was in when he hired a horse and wagon in Monterey. His heart felt cracked in half, and his mind was gone to shards from the itching skin. He set out into the countryside bent on relief. At one point in his hill wandering, he reached into his pants to see what he had left. "Pocket-cured nuts," he said out loud, and shared with the horse what was in his palm. His money was all but gone. When he collapsed under the tree, he wasn't entirely sure. He recalled lying in a stupor, getting up only to water the horse during the time—how long, two days?—that he lay there. Aside from the peanuts, he had consumed only coffee. He lost consciousness at some point and was awakened briefly by a tinkling sound, which turned out to be little bells attached to collars on some goats that had gathered around him to have a look. He could picture himself now as he had been when he was found—the fool on the heath with a horse, a herd of puzzled goats, and Cap'n Smith all staring at him.

Exhausted by the coughing, Louis felt too weak to lift his own head.

Tom was watching and approached to prop him up and spoon soup into his mouth. Louis was touched by the kindness of these weathered frontiersmen. As he began to doze, he sent off a mental thank-you into the ether that the terrible itch was truly, truly gone.

The days that followed were marked by other people coming and going around him. Captain Smith and Tom brought infused teas and soups and progressively more solid food, while a pair of little girls visited from time to time to have a look at him. When he was less muddled, he learned that he'd been brought to Wright's house, one of two rustic cabins in a clearing surrounded by a circle of big shade trees and, beyond that, hills dotted with pines and goats. Louis could not see the open main room on the first floor from where he lay, but he woke to the snap of kindling in the dawn fire, smelled coffee and frying eggs, and felt the pulse of frontier farm life through the remaining day, until darkness quieted the family and the tinkling of bells outside.

Obviously missing was the woman of the house. Mrs. Wright was away due to illness, and in her absence, her curious little daughters appeared to have nothing more to do than gape at Louis, like every other creature in this place. When he discovered neither could read, he set out to teach them how to decipher words. Mornings thereafter, with flies buzzing all around, he gave them a lesson, followed by a story.

One day he recited a little poem he'd written not long ago.

"More," the smaller girl said.

"All right," Louis replied. "This one is longer, if I can remember it.

> When I was sick and lay a-bed,
> I had two pillows at my head,
> And all my toys beside me lay,
> To keep me happy all the day."

The children tittered at the rhyme. "Another," the older one chimed.

"Oh, this one keeps going," Louis said.

> "And sometimes for an hour or so
> I watched my leaden soldiers go,
> With different uniforms and drills,
> Among the bed-clothes, through the hills . . ."

He paused. "I've forgotten the rest." Louis sighed and looked around. Every face was at attention.

"Ah," he said. "Let's see.

> And sometimes sent my ships in fleets
> All up and down among the sheets;
> Or brought my trees and houses out,
> And planted cities all about.
>
> I was the giant great and still
> That sits upon the pillow-hill,
> And sees before him, dale and plain,
> The pleasant land of counterpane."

When he finished, to the giggles and claps of the girls, he felt as if he had just sent a tiger through a fiery hoop.

"You done good there," said Smith, who had been watching. "I can tell you, they ain't the easiest audience."

Louis glowed.

"You always been sick?" Smith asked after he chased the children outside to feed some goats.

"Not always." Louis waved a hand weakly. "Aye, a lot. Bad in the lungs."

The captain scratched his cheek. "We're goin' to get you into town soon as you're able. You've run through my kit out here. Maybe next week. There's a doc in Monterey could help you. We'll see."

CHAPTER 34

"Louis is back in town." Nellie's face was flushed from running.

Fanny grabbed her sister's arm. "Where is he?"

"Adulfo told me he's over at Doc Heintz's place."

"Where has he been all this time?"

"Out in the country somewhere. Adulfo wasn't clear on it."

Fanny's eyes frantically scanned the kitchen. "What do I have that I can take to him?"

"Fanny!" Her sister shook her shoulders. "The man doesn't want food from you." She paused. "Adulfo says he's been very sick."

Fanny tore off her apron and ran down the sandy middle of Alvarado Street. At the doctor's house, a maid answered the door.

"Is the doctor here? I need to speak to him right away," Fanny said. When the woman went to fetch him, Fanny smoothed her skirts and hair, wiped the sweat from her upper lip.

"Mrs. Osbourne." The doctor was momentarily confused. "You are looking healthier since I last saw you."

Fanny summoned her dignity. "I am here to see Louis Stevenson. He's an old friend of mine."

"Oh? Well, I'm glad to know he has someone in town. I took him in for a few days until he recovers." He looked at her curiously. "Are you aware that he is quite ill?"

"He had a hard journey from England. He's here on a lecture tour."

"I can't be sure—there's no real test—but I suspect the man has consumption." He shook his head. "Compounded by pleurisy and malnutrition. Came mighty close to dying out on that ranch. The boat and train travel from England broke what was left of his health." He shrugged. "Follow me. He's upstairs."

Louis lay with his hands at his sides, palms down, white sheet pulled up over his chest. His eyes were closed, and his face, in profile, looked remarkably peaceful. Sick as he was, his features showed his boyish sweetness; he had in him a soul as pure as Hervey's. He was brilliant, just, and wholesome—the closest thing to a holy man Fanny had ever known. In rooms full of people, she had watched others expand with happiness just to be in his presence. He was the most *alive* person she'd ever met. And he was funny on top of it all. How useful a thing it would be to keep such a man in the world. How extraordinary a life would be hers if she stayed within that circle of light.

Fanny knelt by the bed and put his icy hand into hers. "Don't die on me, Louis," she murmured. "Yes, I will marry you. Just hang on."

She saw the eyelids flutter. She didn't know if he could hear her, but she kept talking. "I was afraid, Louis. Do you understand what it is for a woman . . . ? I was protecting myself, and I thought, *How will we live?* But when you left that day on the beach, I knew I had made a *terrible* mistake. Sam has agreed to a divorce. Do you hear me? He's asking for a 'decent' interval. Don't you enjoy that, darling—decent? Oh, Louis, you are going to be a great writer, I know it in my heart, and a healthy one, and we are going to be happy together, in our own home. I can't promise I can give you a child of your own, but I will try, I promise you I will try, if that's what you want. If you can just hang on . . . Only a few more months until the divorce can be finalized, and then a little while after that . . ."

Louis stirred, turned his head toward her. The radiant hazel eyes took her in. "You look beautiful today, Fanny," he said. "Forgive me if I am not at my best." He gestured weakly at his body. "I'm all to whis-tles. This is hardly the figure I had hoped to cut as a bridegroom."

Fanny swallowed back tears. "I shall fatten you up before then." She dipped a cloth in a bowl of water on the table near his bed and wet his dry lips.

"I don't want to misrepresent myself to you, Fanny." Louis's breathy voice was as tattered as the rest of him. "I am a mere complication of cough and bones. When we met in Grez, I was the healthiest I had been in some time. The truth is, I've been an invalid off and on all my life. It will not be easy for you."

Looking down at Louis, she remembered the months of caring for Hervey. It had been excruciating, and it had not been enough. How vividly she remembered the day they buried him at Saint-Germain.

Watching the little casket go into the ground, she'd felt like the perpe-
trator of a terrible crime. The child should have been at home in Oakland, nestled safely in his own bed. Perhaps at some deep level she
didn't want to look at, she hoped to redeem herself for letting Hervey
slip through her fingers. Maybe marrying an invalid would be a prayer,
an act of contrition. She didn't know. All she knew for certain was that
she loved Louis.

"I shall carry you," she told him. "And you can carry me."

He nodded. "You'll pardon me, Mrs. Stevenson," he whispered, and
in a few moments, he was sound asleep.

CHAPTER 35

⁓

1880

"A decent interval" was not only Sam Osbourne's request; it was on the lips of every member of Fanny's family. Her parents and sisters had vehemently opposed the divorce. Even Nellie had argued against it. The very mention of an impending divorce was being kept from Fanny's sickly sister Elizabeth for fear the disgraceful news would knock her over the edge.

"I don't mind waiting so much," Louis told Fanny. "Your family has come further along than my own."

It was true. His father had used a desperate ploy to get Louis to return to Scotland and his senses. Through Baxter, Thomas Stevenson had sent word that his son was murdering his parents with anguish and disgrace. The father pretended to be near death to draw Louis home.

Suspecting he was being misled, Louis refused. Slowly recovering his strength under Dr. Heintz's care, he continued to work furiously on what he thought would pay fastest, fables and short tales, knowing that Fanny and Sammy would be under his protective wing soon enough. When that would happen remained uncertain, for the actual divorce date was dangled and withdrawn by Sam. In October, Fanny traveled north to Oakland, taking Nellie with her as a "chaperone." In December, when the decree was official, the decent interval between divorce and remarriage officially began.

A couple of days before Christmas, Louis moved to San Francisco to a boardinghouse, where he worked and waited. Twice a week during that long winter, Fanny took a ferry over to meet him for dinner. They sat at a modest little restaurant and gentled each other out of their anxieties. "June," she told him when he asked what would make a respectable wedding date. "That will be six months."

"If I can finish the work I began in Monterey, we will be all right by then," Louis said.

"What do you eat during the day?" she asked him over dinner one evening in March. Louis looked terrible, his cheeks hollow and shadowed.

He hesitated.

"Tell me," she said. "You look as if you are starving."

He hemmed and hawed. "Enough," he told her.

"Not enough," Dora Williams insisted when she saw Fanny a week later. "Virgil and I ran into him last week at the Pine Street coffee house. He was having his usual breakfast there, he said. A cup of coffee, one little roll, and a pat of butter—a bargain at ten cents. He told us he's mastered the art of having the bread and butter expire at the same moment. We laughed, but then he laid out the rest of the day. He goes back in the evening for another roll and coffee—that's his supper. He's eating only one meal, really, midday, that he gets for fifty cents."

"Louis only tells me about the stories he's working on," Fanny said, shaking her head. "He's trying to save what little money he has for when he has to support me. But that has already begun. He gave me fifteen dollars recently to keep the house going."

"Isn't Sam supporting you until you remarry?"

"Didn't you hear? Sam lost his job a few days ago."

THE CONSTANT ANXIETY, the enforced diet, and the frantic work pace took its toll: Louis fell ill with malaria. Fanny moved him to an Oakland hotel room to be nearer her cottage. It was there that Louis's lungs began to hemorrhage. When she discovered him in his room coughing up blood, Fanny raised a handkerchief to her mouth, vowed to herself she would not faint, and immediately fetched a doctor.

Stroking his goatee, white and stiff as a brush, Dr. Bamford stood over Louis's bony, pain-wracked body and said, "The patient is not to move. He must lie on his back so that his lungs can heal." Before he left, Bamford handed Fanny a bottle of ergotin and showed her how to measure an exact dosage. "This will make the blood vessels contract during a hemorrhage. He will need to have this medicine by him at all times."

"So," Louis said sadly of the latest horrific twist. "He arrives— 'Bluidy Jack.'"

Fanny sat by his bed and held his hand. She knew what he believed, that he would die of tuberculosis, and soon.

"For the sake of appearances," another phrase her family liked to use, was now ignored. One idea loomed large: She must get Louis to a safer climate. If they stayed in the San Francisco bay fog, it would probably kill him. She promptly moved him from the hotel into her cottage, consigned him to the sofa where she could nurse him, and set the wedding date for May. Sammy was away at boarding school by then in Sonoma, and Nellie was living with her. What her family, friends, and neighbors thought of the whole arrangement didn't trouble her mind now. If she could nurse Louis to the point where he could travel, she could get him to better weather.

By day she dosed him with Dover's powder and made soups to spoon-feed to him. By night she sat next to the sofa, watching helplessly as the ruthless cough hammered deeper in his chest. She and Nellie paused in fear to listen when, past coughing, he made a sucking noise in his windpipe. She held her own breath at those moments, uncertain if the last punch had been deadly. There would be a little gasp of air as Louis—limp as a dishrag, drenched with cold sweat, unable to speak—opened his eyes to peer at hers intently. *I am not dead yet,* the eyes said.

What astounded her was how close to the gates of death he could be at one moment and how alive he could be the next. After a nightlong assault of coughing, he might awaken unable to speak; or, he might sit up, ask for oatmeal, and announce he'd come up with a new story idea.

It's going to be a wild, rickrack journey with this man.

Within a few days of the hemorrhaging, he was standing on a kitchen chair, reciting Robert Burns. Nellie had spotted a mouse and jumped up on a stool, prompting Louis to rise from the sofa in the parlor and mount another chair.

" 'To a Mouse,' " he announced dramatically, putting hand to breast, " 'On Turning Her Up in Her Nest with the Plough.' By *Rrrr*obbie Bur*rrr*ns," he said, stretching the R's like a Scottish drum roll.

> Wee, sleekit, cow'rin, tim'rous beastie,
> O, what a panic's in thy b-r-r-reastie!

"What are you doing?" Fanny called from the other room. She rushed into the kitchen, put her hands on her hips. "Get down this minute!"

> Thou need na start awa sae hasty,
> Wi' bickering b-r-r-rattle!
> I wad be laith to rin an' chase thee,
> Wi' murd'ring pattle!

"I'll murder *you* with a paddle," Fanny cried. "You're supposed to be flat on the sofa."

Nellie's laughter only encouraged him, and he held forth through two more Burns poems.

"Get *down*," Fanny said, but by then even she had begun to giggle. He went on to impersonate a clergyman asking questions from the Shorter Catechism of a frightened child, also played by Louis, and all of it in his best broad Scots. When he climbed down, their eyes were wet from laughing.

The morning after his performance, he was on his back on the sofa, with his feet buried under the family dog, Chuchu. Fanny, and sometimes Nellie, worked as his amanuensis, taking down a new book idea or writing out his letters. In his hours of wellness, Louis's joy in life was so acute it amazed Fanny. He loved the chaotic household of two women, an occasional child home from school, a dog, four cats, and two horses, and delighted in making Nellie and Fanny the subjects of his jokes.

It was not the same giddiness he used to show, though. She remembered his displays of uncontrollable laughter and the hand-bending it took to stop it. The last time it happened, when she'd bitten him hard and opened a cut, Louis had looked at her with such injured shock that she'd been flooded with shame. She had seen such a look once before, on the face of her son Sammy. Long ago when he was a baby, Sammy developed a habit of kicking furiously whenever she tried to diaper him. He was just under a year old and playing with her, really, but she'd been tired at the time and slapped his leg—pretty gently, yet hard enough to surprise him. The child had stopped moving and gazed in disbelief at his mother. It was as if the world changed in that moment for him, and for her. Had she knocked the wildness out of the little fellow with one slap? Made him cautious? For that was what Sammy was now. Or was he going to be a careful type from the moment he came out of her womb? He never kicked again; she never slapped him again. As it turned out, Louis never lost himself to hilarity after Fanny's angry bite.

Louis seemed a far more sober man now than he was three years ago, and his joy less frenetic. Having seen his suffering up close in the last few weeks, she understood better why he would have wanted to abandon himself to untamed gaiety. She could see why he hated the ugly realism of Zola. No wonder he wanted to write adventure stories.

When he was feeling stronger, Fanny walked him slowly through her cottage's garden. It was not only for the sunshine that she led him along the twisting stone paths on the Oakland hillside, where each turn revealed a distant view or an arrangement of plants that pleased the eye. She wanted him to see what she had made with her own hands, for it was a record of herself. She had laid every stone of the path, planted every fragrant delight, built the arbors and log benches, dug the beds for six great patches in which pumpkins and onions and tomatoes had grown large on the hillside. She could remember herself when she first laid out the garden—young and industrious, so pleased to be grafting roses and pickling her own cantaloupe. She took Louis to the photography studio she'd built in an old shack, where cobwebs covered the glass plate negatives now—pictures of trees and flowers that she'd left behind when she went to Europe with the children. She took him to the shooting range she had set up so he could see that she had been someone before she knew him. A woman of parts.

She and Louis stood quietly near a patch of orange lilies. "Do you know what my mother called me as a child? Tiger Lily."

He smiled. "How appropriate."

"Ma always grew them in her garden."

"Are you saying goodbye to yours?"

"Yes," she said. "But there will be another garden to make, and a better one."

On a sunny spring day, Fanny and Louis, dressed in his ulster against any possible chill, took the ferry from Oakland to San Francisco to be married. It wasn't anything like a wedding, mostly paperwork and a few words spoken by an old Presbyterian minister in his parlor. When she filled out the marriage certificate, she had to pause to think of the date: May 29, 1880. Below it, she admitted to being forty but wrote *widowed* rather than *divorced.* Whose business was it other than her own?

The minister read from Corinthians about love being patient and keeping no record of wrongs. They exchanged slender silver rings while her friend Dora Williams stood by as a witness. Afterward, the three of them went out for dinner. Louis raised his glass of wine and said, "I don't think many wives will be loved as much as mine." That was the extent of the festivities. Even their simple meal might have been out of the question a few weeks earlier, before Louis's father finally came around.

Apparently, Thomas Stevenson got wind through Baxter that his only child was broke and lying sick in America. Shamed and remorseful, the old man promised his son 250 pounds a year as an allowance. Before the conciliatory letter from Louis's father, Fanny's throat would constrict when she thought of money. Sam's monthly support payments for Sammy had ended when he lost his court stenographer job. Thomas Stevenson's promised allowance eased her anxiety.

The moment the first check arrived, she took Louis to an Oakland dentist to have his rotten teeth pulled and replaced. When the swelling disappeared, they went together to a photographer to have wedding portraits done. Louis looked thin but groomed, while Fanny wore her best hat cocked at a flattering angle, and a string of beads around her neck with a wooden cross attached, an effect she hoped would garner the Stevensons' approval.

When Fanny saw the portraits, she was pleased. Soon she would send the pictures along with a warm letter to Louis's parents, preparing them for the fact that, when his health permitted, they would be meeting their new daughter-in-law.

CHAPTER 36

"Napa County." Dora Williams's finger glided over a California map. "In the valley, just below Mount Saint Helena, there's a little town called Calistoga. They've got hot springs up there that will cure anything you throw in them. Go to the Springs Hotel."

"Honeymoon" was too fine a word to put on the trip to Napa. They planned to stay for a couple of months in the mountain air on the advice of the Oakland doctor. After getting a look at himself in the mirror the morning they departed, Louis understood the gravity of the advice, for he resembled more a candidate for the grave than a groom heading off on his wedding trip. Yet his heart felt light, and his mind raced with the possibilities ahead.

They took a train north as a party of three, including Sammy, plus the dog, Chuchu. Outside, rolling hills—May-green and naked of trees—undulated past.

"Let's look at land up in Sonoma and Napa, maybe buy a ranch," Louis said when they passed a farm. "We could live out in the hills, hunt and fish for our food. You could sketch."

"I'd like that," she said.

He turned away from the panoramic view, leaned back in his seat, and rested his eyes on her. "Just now, in the sunlight—my God, you look splendid in blue." He squeezed her hand. "You are a beauty who has married a skinny wolf. Don't you find my toothy new smile rather fine, though?"

"I do."

"Listen, Fanny," he said, suddenly serious. "I am done with travel books. Lately, all I care to write is action, with drama and *incidents*. Big characters with moral dilemmas."

"I think you already do that in your stories."

"I'm talking about something with more carpentry."

"A novel?"

"Wouldn't that be nice?"

Louis looked back outside and caught sight of a stone quarry where men stood like ants on giant boulders. *There* was true labor, the kind that broke backs. How dare he complain about travel writing?

It was idle talk, anyway. Fanny knew as well as he that they would starve if he devoted himself to novel writing. He had only to look at Sammy, twisting a lock of his blond hair in the seat ahead of them, to remember that there were three to feed, and one of them had to be educated.

Louis reached into his pocket, opened to a clean page in his journal, and listed the pieces of writing he had in the basket, finished or nearly so. *The Amateur Emigrant* and the travel book on crossing the plains on the train; essays on Benjamin Franklin, Thoreau, and a Japanese hero named Yoshido-Torajiro who'd captured his interest; and *The Pavilion on the Links,* a tale set in Scotland about a gypsying young man who hunts up a wealthy old schoolmate and soon finds himself hunted.

His work wasn't as backbreaking as prying gargantuan rocks out of the earth, but in fairness to himself, he'd pushed his body hard, writing that heap of words. And he'd been hungry through much of the duration. Fanny and Sam couldn't be expected to live that way. Nor could he any longer.

At the Springs Hotel in Calistoga, Louis took the waters early every morning before the thermometer rose too far above ninety degrees. When he returned to their white gingerbread cottage, Fanny was often just waking. She had taken to wearing a chain around her neck with a gold coin suspended from it, and it was, quite simply, the most suggestive bit of eroticism he had ever seen. Some mornings as he soaked in the springs, the mere thought of that coin against her tawny skin brought him hurrying back to the cottage, where he latched the door between their room and Sammy's. He made love to her then, despite his fragile lungs and her whispers of "Gently, now."

"Why gently? You are my medicine."

Free of scandal and sorrow, Fanny let her own caution drop away. With the sun pushing through drawn muslin curtains, she held herself just above him while the gold coin swung mesmerically.

"Dear girl," he murmured with wonder after these sessions. She

would rise and put his notebook in his hands as she did every morning, then bathe, dress, and head to the lodge kitchen, where, early in their stay, she had talked her way into the good graces of the cook. When Louis joined her and Sammy for breakfast, he could see Fanny's hand in the morning's offering. There would be butter aplenty for the thick chunks of bread, and an omelet the size of a bowler hat, stuffed full of bacon, cheese, potatoes, and whatever else she had spied in the larder. On the table would be Fanny's own strawberry jam that she had brought as part of her plan to fatten him. The other diners looked jealously at the spread.

Their habit, after breakfast, was to return to the cabin, where Louis could write in bed. For a while, Fanny had her own composing to do. She struggled over a period of days, writing a letter to his parents to accompany the wedding portraits. *Do not expect a great beauty when you meet me,* she wrote. *It's just that I can't seem to take a bad picture.*

With their funds running low and the summer days getting hotter, Louis asked around about other, less costly accommodations at a higher altitude.

Morris Friedberg, a local merchant, was short and distinctive for wearing a wool coat in the wilting heat, unlike other men, who were down to their waistcoats. He and his wife walked with Louis out to the middle of the main road, lined on either side by one-story shops with two-story facades. Louis made note of the false building fronts. He had seen them all across America during his train trip; they spoke of the hurry-up American attitude of trying to make something look bigger than it was, without taking the time to build it bigger. The facades, like so much about this country, seemed to be an expression of intent. All the talk was about the future.

"These hills are full of empty shacks that were abandoned when the mines didn't pan out." Morris Friedberg gestured at the mountains in the distance. "You see the big one?"

"Mount Saint Helena?"

"Yup. About halfway up, there's a place that was an actual town just five or six years ago—Silverado. Somebody found silver and gold about eight years ago, and before you knew it, we had, oh, a thousand miners and boardinghouses and hotels. I had a branch of my store up there. But"—he sighed—"the vein run out." He shrugged philosophically. "If you're looking for a place above the fog line, that's where I would go. Rufe Hanson has the tollhouse on the road just below the place. The stage goes there every day."

"You can get fresh milk from Mrs. Hanson," Mrs. Friedberg added.

The man sized up Louis. "Rufe was a consumptive, you know," he said. "The fresh air cured him. He does everything now. Shot a hundred and fifty deer up there last year."

Louis felt slightly humiliated to be searching for free lodging. There was Fanny's dignity to be considered. What could he do now, though, except put a good face on the whole enterprise?

"'Squatting' is such a deliciously unsavory word," he said when he returned to the cottage. As they sat on the porch swing, he rested his arm on Fanny's shoulders.

"I suppose somebody still owns those shacks. Probably the mining company," she said.

"Haven't you ever wanted to do something mildly unlawful?" Louis teased. "It's enticing to consider going rent-free into a ready-made house. And it will make up bright as a travel story. It's so American— *roughing it* and all that. We'll call it 'The Silverado Squatters.' What do you think?"

"I've lived in a ghost town or two. Their charm is overrated," Fanny said. "But if you are asking, yes, my love, I will camp with you wherever you want to go."

Louis carried two light blanket rolls on his back plus a broom that the toll keeper's wife had pressed on them, while Fanny bore the heavier sack of food and utensils. Following an overgrown footpath, they haltingly climbed up from the road, switching back and forth for a mile or so through brush and pine trees, until they reached the cabins. Three wooden shacks, built just above one another, leaned into the hillside. The floor of the bottom shack was covered with ankle-deep rubbish and mounds of dirt blown there by the wind. Poison oak pushed through the creaking boards. This section had been the assayer's office. The shack above it held eighteen bunks and was equally filthy.

"It ain't worth the borrowin'." Louis sighed.

"I've had worse to work with," she said.

Many of the buildings that once made up a settlement had been carted away to different locations, according to Mrs. Hanson. But there were a couple left, and everywhere, evidence of the mining operation—piles of ore and boards and iron. Not far off, a stream ran through a clearing where they could bathe and wash their clothing.

The first night, they all slept outside. "The Milky Way seems the wrong name for it," Louis said of the banner above them. "It's thick as clotted cream."

In the morning, a white fog roiled below them, covering any evidence of Napa Valley, its patches of farmland, or the forested foothills below Mount Saint Helena.

WHEN THEY RETURNED the following week, they brought a wagon full of tools and supplies. Louis swept out the bottom building while Fanny and the boy spread hay over the two bunks they would occupy. She covered the hay with sheets she'd brought from Oakland, then began more serious homemaking. The bottom shack, which was to be a dining room and kitchen, had no windows or door remaining. She began by cutting into strips a battered boot she found; the strips became hinges for a wood door she hammered together. She fashioned window frames out of scrap boards and covered them with white cotton. Sammy worked as her assistant while she sawed and hammered useless chunks of wood into tables and seats. Inside the mouth of the mine tunnel, she placed an icebox where she stored the milk. Near it, she hung sides of venison and wild duck that Rufe Hanson sold her. Rufe brought up a stove for her to use, and she designated one section of the assayer's office as a kitchen. Once when he came up, he found her making a cabinet out of logs. "She goes at it like a house afire, don't she?" Rufe remarked to Louis.

"That she does," Louis answered admiringly.

Great bubbling stews followed, and corn bread and pancakes; Fanny knew how to cook over a campfire without turning food black and hard, a fact that astounded Louis. At eleven o'clock in the morning and again at three, Fanny served him rum punch topped with whipped cream and cinnamon. "Elevenses!" she would call out in a bad English accent, and he would leave off his writing to down the rum. The food was only part of the health regimen Fanny enforced: She rubbed him down twice a day with oil and ordered him into the sun to rest when he'd been at his writing too long.

Near the remains of a blacksmith's forge, Louis stacked old boards against a boulder to make a flat wall to lean against as he turned his notes about Silverado into a narrative. The travel story was full of the characters he had met along the way, such as Petrified Charlie, the old Swede who had stumbled upon a forest of ancient trees turned to stone not far from Calistoga. Charlie knew an opportunity when he saw one and soon enough began collecting admission fees to his "museum" in the woods. Then there was Jacob Shram, the vintner who was bent on making his piece of Napa into vineyards worthy of discerning French palates.

"The Scottish enjoy clucking over strange American types," he told Fanny over breakfast one morning. "They will like Petrified Charlie."

"Is that so?" she said. "Look at yourself and see who's strange now."

Louis glanced down. He had thrown on the nearest warm clothing when he awoke so as to leap into his writing straight from sleep. He wore his long nightshirt, a shawl of Fanny's, and one of her hats, shaped like a mushroom.

"The hat, darling?" Fanny said. "You've got it on backward. The feather is not meant to touch your nose."

One day the stagecoach brought a pile of letters for Louis forwarded from Oakland to the tollhouse. The most recent letter, dated June 29, was from his mother. It was long and newsy, as if no sorrow had ever passed between them. *I hope you both understand that I don't care for ancient history at all. I'd love to hear about your lives right now,* Margaret Stevenson wrote. A separate letter from Thomas strongly urged the newlyweds and Fanny's boy to come back to Scotland for a visit. The old man would pay for it all.

The remaining envelopes were from Colvin and Henley. Colvin disliked his *Amateur Emigrant* book; in fact, he questioned whether anything Louis had written since leaving was salable, and urged him to come back to England to live among "his equals." Henley claimed his language was becoming too American, implied that nothing he'd written in Monterey was worth a damn, and that he was losing his power to make a living as a writer, the longer he stayed in America.

"How dare they hound you that way! Don't they understand a sea voyage right now would kill you?" Fanny asked in disbelief. "Henley especially. He has been ill himself." She was spooning lard into a frying pan. "And they are wrong entirely about *Pavilion*."

Both men had roundly rejected *The Pavilion on the Links*. The story he'd written while he was bedbound in Monterey was not a novel but the longest fiction he'd produced so far. Louis was proud of its chilling atmosphere and suspenseful twists.

"They don't understand," he said sadly, reaching for the last unopened letter in the pile. "I am just beginning to truly find my method as a writer."

Joy flooded his body, along with a mighty burst of smugness, when he read the final letter. It was from Leslie Stephen, who wanted to buy *The Pavilion on the Links* and publish it in *Cornwall*.

FANNY KEPT SAMMY active fetching groceries from the tollhouse, where he had struck a friendship with the Hansons. Louis gave him lessons in math and Latin in the afternoons, and they worked together on making a pamphlet with the toy printing press Louis and Fanny had bought for the boy some months earlier. Left to his own devices, though, Sammy seemed adrift as he shuffled around the hill with a stick in his hand, looking for something to do. He sometimes climbed up a pile of boulders near the camp and sat for hours on the highest rock. He had turned pudgy of late, as twelve-year-old boys were wont to do before they shot up tall and grew fuzz on their upper lips. Up there on his rock, Sammy looked as bored as a human being could be.

Surely it must be strange, Louis reflected, to go from having Sam Osbourne in his life after a long absence to having Louis Stevenson as his stepfather. How strange to sleep in a makeshift bunk above his mother and this man every night. Truth was, it had been strange for Louis. The boy's presence in the same sleeping room had put an end to his passionate interludes with Fanny.

"What do you suppose he thinks about this new setup?" Louis asked, gesturing around the humble shack where light peeped through the boards.

"I used to know what he thought on every subject," Fanny said. She took a candle she'd brought and plugged it into a hole in the table's top. "But not anymore."

"Perhaps the boy hardly thinks about us at all. Lord knows, I was that way. When I was a stripling like him, I regarded my parents as ancillaries at best."

"Were you happy?"

"Supremely. I remember we used to go over east to a fishing village at the end of summer for a long holiday. My cousins would be there. The boys tended to run in a pack, and it seemed that town was created just for our amusement. The stretch of beach was full of hiding places, and there were ruins of an ancient fortress at one spot. We were free, you see, to be hanging about the fishing boats, angling off the dock, or clambering over garden walls to knock on windows.

"There's one thing we did that I remember vividly. When the evenings began to get dark earlier, in September, and we knew our idyll would end soon, we would go out from our little cottages and meet on the beach. We all wore a tin bull's-eye lantern on our belt. Our innovation was to go out with a topcoat over the lantern so it was hidden, not a ray of light showing. Why we didn't immolate ourselves, I'll never know—you could smell the tin blistering. We'd sally out into the pitch black and, once in a while, flash our lamps. When we bumped into each other, we'd whisper conspiratorially, 'Have you got your lantern?' And then we'd go as a group and climb into some boat, bring out our lights, and, as I recall, curse up a storm and tell frightening stories. But the talk was not the thrill of it. To walk in the dark and know you had that secret lantern at your belt . . ." Louis put his hand on his chest. "Ah, there was the magic of it for a boy."

"You know, Sammy's not been in one place long enough to make any good friends," Fanny mused. "I don't think he's gotten his fair share of happy-go-lucky times."

LOUIS BEGAN BY taking the boy to explore the two mine shafts. With the sun hitting the upper crevice—a great crack between the red boulders—they could look down fairly far into the bowels of Mount Saint Helena. When they put their ears to the crevice, they heard water drops plip-plopping in the dark interior. Not far from the cabins was a blacksmith's forge to contemplate, plus a great iron chute down the hillside. Next to some railway tracks lay an overturned cart that once carried ore out of the tunnel to a stamping mill below, where tons of rocks were hammered into dust in the search for silver. Louis and the boy spent hours imagining adventurers who had come here to get rich. They pictured men playing poker and drinking whisky around dozens of campfires flickering on the side of the mountain. They imagined miners returning home on the stagecoach, either penniless or with pockets stuffed with sacks of gold.

Late at night by the fire, after Fanny had gone to sleep, Louis told Sammy the tales he had heard in Calistoga, of the Mendocino City dentist who removed teeth with pliers in the morning and robbed stagecoaches in the afternoon; and of Black Bart, a stage bandit who looked like a minister and behaved like a perfect gentleman as he robbed ladies of their jewelry. Louis told every ghost story and every bogeyman legend in his repertoire, sang every sea shanty he knew, and when those were exhausted, he issued Sammy a lantern and went out with him to see what moved about in the darkness.

He recalled aloud a book he'd read in San Francisco about Christmas in the West Indies; in particular, the words "dead man's chest" stuck in his mind. He couldn't remember the meaning of the phrase, but he quickly thought of the verse, which he sang out into the black night. "Fifteen men on the dead man's chest—yo-ho-ho and a bottle of rum!"

The boy laughed. "Tell me a pirate story."

Louis drank down his cup of wine. "Well, let me think on it, Sammy. You would have to begin with the main pirate. Let's say you name him"—he cast his eyes around for some inspiration—"Silver. John Silver."

"Does he have a saber?"

"Oh, yes, or maybe a cutlass," Louis said. He thought of Henley, whom he'd always felt would make a fine pirate in a theatrical, given his wild red beard and barrel chest and general huffing bravado. "Silver is a crafty, shifting sort of fellow. People remember him because he has a peg leg. The other pirates often hear the tapping of the leg on the planks of the ship before they see him."

"What's the ship named?"

Louis made a grand gesture with his arm. "The *Hispaniola*!"

"Are there girls in this story?"

"I have no idea."

"No Aunt Pollys. No girls."

"Very well."

Across from him, Sammy nodded with enthusiasm. He sat twirling his hair around his forefinger, mouth agape, wide eyes glinting in the light of the campfire. "Tell me more," he whispered.

Part Two

Margaret Stevenson's crystal glasses glinted up and down the dining table. Candlelight threw a yellow glow on the faces of twenty Stevenson and Balfour relatives as they offered one toast after another to the newlyweds. Midway down the long table, Fanny sat with Louis on one side and one of Margaret's brothers, Uncle George Balfour, on the other.

"I want Louis to come out hunting with me this year," Uncle George said. He petted a graying beard that hung like a bib on his chest.

"It will depend on the weather, I'm afraid," Fanny said. "If it's damp, I won't let him go. His health is too precarious. But if *I'm* here, I'll be happy to accompany you."

"My goodness, Thomas," the uncle said, "she's a besom, all right."

"Is that anything like a bison?" Fanny asked archly.

The two men fell into gales. "No, no, my dear," said the man, whose veined cheeks turned round and red as crabapples when he laughed. "I married a besom myself, and wasnae day I regretted."

"You mustn't take offense, Fanny," Thomas Stevenson said. "It's a compliment. Means an impertinent sort of girl. A woman who could run the world if she chose to."

A minute later, Fanny whispered to Louis, "I had a hard time understanding the toasts. It sounds like everyone is speaking through wool socks."

"They're being extra Scottish for your sake," Louis said. He looked at her eyes. "It means they adore you."

Fanny stared down at her place setting. "I'm starving," she whispered. "Louis?"

"Yes?"

"What am I to do with that?" She pointed to a ladle-like object above her plate.

"Pudding spoon. Mother's puddin' spoons are as big as shovels. When dessert is served, you hold it in your right hand, then push the cake into it with the fork in your left."

"Oh."

"Eat out of the spoon. You're supposed to keep your elbows down during the operation. Can't be done."

At the beginning of the party, she and Louis had stood in the large drawing room of the Stevenson house on Heriot Row, greeting relatives. They had all come to celebrate as they would for any newlyweds. Judging by the close examination she received, they also had come to have a good gander at the American bride. Clearly, word was out that Louis had married an older woman. A cousin's eyes would scan her face, settle on the crow's-feet, glance at the neck. Fanny regretted wearing a necklace that Louis's mother had pressed upon her. No doubt somebody in the room was making note that the daughter-in-law was already raiding the family jewels. Fanny regretted the dress she'd chosen for the evening as well, a shamrock-green satin gown that made her look like a Nevada dance hall girl among these subdued people.

When she stepped away from the drawing room to use the WC, she inadvertently went into a small pantry and surprised two servants, who redirected her. As she turned and walked away, she heard one say to the other, "He's merrit wi a black woman!"

Louis received the same curious scrutiny for a different reason. Many of the family's circle were under the impression that he was still near death.

"You look quite *well*," more than one guest remarked upon greeting Louis.

"It must be the new teeth," Louis responded when his cousin Bob said it.

Fanny took quiet pride in the happy remarks upon Louis's appearance. "You should have seen him a month ago," she said to Bob.

"He's still frighteningly thin." Bob sighed. "I think I could wrap my thumb and forefinger around his thigh."

"You don't know how close he came . . ." Fanny could not say the rest of the sentence. "But I'm convinced he's on the mend."

It was comforting to see Bob Stevenson, who cared so deeply for Louis. Any attraction Fanny had felt for Bob in the beginning had long ago settled into a sisterly feeling. His confident demeanor had changed. He was a touch faded from the glowing young lion who had dazzled her at Grez.

"Are you surviving this onslaught?" he asked.

"I'm busy putting the faces with the stories you and Louis have told me."

"Have you had a chance to talk with Katharine?" Bob asked. He and his sister, Katharine de Mattos, had arrived at the party together. She was a slender, high-strung woman with the same sharp-chiseled features as Bob's. Fanny knew she was divorced from a notorious philanderer and struggling to support her two children. On that information alone, she felt an affinity for her.

"I have heard so much about you!" Katharine had gushed earlier in the evening when she came through the door. She kissed Fanny on both cheeks and chatted gaily for a few moments. "I'm going to steal you away once you're done with your greeting duties. Don't be overwhelmed by all these relatives. If you can't remember their names, I shall help you. Your Sammy is adorable, by the way. Oh my," she said, looking around at the crowd in the room. "So much family excitement at once! And Bob tells me you are going to have your first grandchild soon."

How did this woman know that Belle and Joe Strong were expecting a child? Fanny and Louis had heard only a couple of weeks ago. Louis must have told Katharine; of his cousins, he was closest to her and Bob.

Fanny smiled grimly. "Yes," she said, "it's true."

THANKFULLY, MARGARET STEVENSON appeared unconcerned about the matter of age. It seemed the woman had been waiting for a daughter-in-law to come along for some time. If Fanny was not the dewy-eyed virgin they had all expected Louis to choose someday, Maggie, as she was called by her friends, showed no sign of disappointment. The pale lady of the house was awash in the glow of her son's marriage long after the dinner party ended. "You all need new clothes!" she declared, and soon enough, a seamstress and tailor were measuring Louis, Fanny, and Sammy.

"She dresses me up like a doll," Fanny complained to Louis when they were alone in their bedroom after a session with his mother. "Do you think she's embarrassed by my clothes?" The delicate Maggie had darted around in her embroidered dressing gown, fetching bonnets and sparkling hair ornaments to put on Fanny's head and draping her in Kashmir shawls and jet necklaces, all the while pressing her to keep them. "When I complimented a vase in her room, she said, 'It's yours! I shall send it to you the moment you get your own place.' I'm afraid to admire anything now."

Louis embraced her. "I think the lady doth protest too much. And all along I thought you adored making furniture out of logs."

Fanny grinned. "Your mother knows where my heart lies. She doesn't take me for a climber."

Over needlework in the sitting room, Maggie's genteel reserve fell away one morning. She took hold of Fanny's hand and declared in a heartfelt rush, "I am so happy to have a partner now." She didn't say "a partner in keeping my boy alive," but Fanny knew perfectly well what she meant.

"It's not so easy taking care of a genius, is it?" Fanny asked her. "It's very much like angling for shy trout, I think. You have to know when to pay out the line and when to carefully pull it in."

Maggie nodded knowingly. "He's a bright young man who is careless with his health. And he has pride, my boy. He does not take my advice gladly. But he listens to you, Fanny, I have seen it. I can't tell you how relieved I am."

On a Sunday morning, while Louis was out walking and his parents and Sammy were at church, Fanny moved through the house in her robe. She was dying to fry up a couple of eggs, but that was an impossibility. All the meals in this house were delivered by dumbwaiter, sent up by a cook who worked and lived with another servant in the basement. She would have to wait to eat breakfast when everyone returned.

In the dining room, she ran her fingers along the smooth walnut surface of an old claw-footed desk, one of the many antiques with which Thomas Stevenson had filled the house. She turned over china plates to look at the maker's mark, held up crystal decanters to the light, felt the scalloped hollow of a silver tea caddy spoon and the bumpy surface of an antler-handled knife. The house was stuffed with exquisite things. Her own childhood home had not been humble by Middle West standards. Jacob Vandegrift had fared well enough as a lumber merchant and raised his brood in a perfectly respectable brick house surrounded by perfectly respectable walnut furniture. But respectable in Indianapolis was a world apart from refined in Edinburgh. It was the difference between twine and silk floss.

When she returned to the bedroom, she poked through a closet that spanned one wall of Louis's bedroom. Inside, she found an entire wardrobe of fine things he had never worn in her presence: morning coats, smoking jackets, dressing gowns, wool neck scarves soft as rabbit fur, cloaks, an array of embroidered caps. The closet smelled faintly of leather; looking down, she spied six pairs of boots and shoes arrayed on the floor along the back wall. Fanny fetched a chair so she could reach a high shelf. Her hand brought down a set of underclothes made of fine silk cord that was netted. The drawers and shirt, so soft and airy, had never been worn. She threw off her nightgown and pulled on the garments. Pure heaven, they felt. And the fit was perfect. *These I will take for myself.*

Now that Fanny was in the family, the war between father and son seemed to have sputtered out. Thomas Stevenson, it appeared, had been waiting for someone to listen to him.

"I was not born to wealth," he told Fanny that evening in his study while attending to his whisky, sip by sip. "My father was a lighthouse man, and he had taken my brothers into the business. Well, and so I went. My father was experimenting with silvered reflector lamps, to magnify the beam, you see. It was the great quest in those days . . ."

When Thomas Stevenson spoke of reflector lamps, he might as well have been a preacher bent on saving souls. He was modest about his own role in getting the lamps to blink intermittently by revolving, but Louis let Fanny know it was an enormous achievement. "He's a true *inventor,*" Louis said, and she was moved by the pride in his voice. "He'd be famous if he'd gone after a patent for any of it. But he didn't. He wouldn't. It was a moral issue with him."

"He told me he once wanted to be a writer," she said to Louis before they retired in their room.

"From what I gather, he tried any number of things that failed to stick. Here's the story my mother gave me. My father was studying engineering at the university when one day his father found one of his made-up stories stuffed in his coat pocket. My grandfather was irate.

He told him he had wasted seven pages of perfectly good paper with his nonsense and that he had better get a profession while his father was still alive to support him because he would be penniless otherwise." Louis laughed at Fanny's sober expression. "Another one of those 'sins of the father' stories, eh?"

"It makes me sad," she said.

SINCE SHE WAS a little girl, Fanny had been able to pinpoint the one person in a room who needed to be won over. It was a challenge she made for herself when she encountered a shy or taciturn or difficult person, and rarely did she fail. Now she trained her eyes and ears on Louis's father as he gradually shared the story of his life. She observed the small details of Thomas Stevenson's person. He sat across from her in his study with his elbows on the chair arms, fingertips forming a steeple. A gas lamp illuminated his features from below, and when the steeple went to his lips, when he paused to consider his words before speaking, she thought he looked like a monk from the Middle Ages, contemplating Scripture by candlelight. He might have made a fine cleric if he had not been a "Lighthouse Stevenson." Fanny witnessed the moral rectitude that had driven his son away; Louis's forgiving nature must have come from his mother. She also saw the similarities between father and son. Louis was just as fierce as Thomas in his own moral convictions. And like his son, Thomas was a rascal. Behind his impassive exterior lived a terrible tease. He called Fanny a variety of names: Cassandra was one. He chided her for the occasional presentiment that something was about to go wrong. "And what chaos is Miss Cassandra predictin' for us today?" he would say.

After dinner, if she did not immediately go to his study for a cordial, he would shout, "Where is the Vandegrifter?" He'd be waiting for her with two fists on his desk and some artifact or book that signaled the subject of their conversation that evening. "Aha! She's wearin' her cordial face," he'd say when she arrived. He knew she liked a drink as much as he.

Fanny met his roguishness with measured impudence. "Master Tommy," she said at one such session, "your home is absolutely lovely, but I am taken aback by one fact: Your bath facilities are terribly out of date. Shouldn't the premier engineer of Edinburgh have a proper bathtub? Shouldn't he have a loo on every floor? Why, in America, even people of ordinary means are adding them to their homes."

Thomas appeared startled by her remark. The reference to his status as an engineer, the mention of Americans—one of the two kept him up late that night. The next morning he showed Fanny the bathroom he had drawn to be built out in a large room adjoining his bedroom. It was extravagant and featured an enormous tub with a wood rim where he could set his whisky glass if he chose, and a wood cover for the whole that could be lowered to keep the water warm as it filled. A toilet compartment would be built into the corner; cupboards would run up to the ceiling. Margaret would have a fine dressing table.

"It will be here when you next come," Thomas promised Fanny. "And there will be a choice of three loos to meet your fancy."

"You've disarmed the man," Louis told her one afternoon as he sat down to write. "In a single visit, you've accomplished what I couldn't in a lifetime."

She took her place across from him at the table they shared as a desk, where Louis was working on his *Amateur Emigrant* and she was writing a short story. "Well, I'm not his son."

"True. And you're alike."

"How is that?"

Louis did not detect that she was smarting. "You tend to look at the dark side sometimes. You have healthy tempers. And you both rather savor your indignations."

"Oh," she said, "don't hold back now. Is there anything else?"

Louis's face fell. "I'm sorry, Fan. I was only teasing. Let's be gentle with each other."

There was no pretense that they were equals. When he had first read one of her stories he said, "You have a colorful way of saying things." Her spirits had sailed high on that remark until the next time she showed him a story and he said, "This is perfectly awful." She knew she was not a bad writer, but she suspected Louis found her stories, with their supernatural twists, a bit beneath his literary standards. "Maudlin!" he had written next to one of her paragraphs.

After a time, she no longer asked for his help. He neither encouraged her to write nor discouraged her, though he admitted that two writers in one family was quite a lot. Still, Fanny cherished their time at that shared desk. The writing hours were boring for Sammy until Louis unpacked the printing press that had followed the boy since their time at Silverado. Now the whole family devoted mornings to words on paper, with Louis contributing stories to Sammy's little magazine.

When Mrs. Stevenson poked her head in the door and found them all engaged, she let out a frustrated sigh. "Who will be my playmate today?" she moaned. "Come away with me, Fanny. Just for a couple of mornings." Fanny regretted the interruption but dutifully followed her new mother-in-law.

As it turned out, Louis's mother had a gift for Fanny. It was a piano scarf to be embroidered. The two women sat down and began to sew. Mrs. Stevenson was only a decade older than Fanny, yet her ways made her seem older. She sat stiff as a clothespin in her lace-trimmed tea gown. It was in her sweet family stories that her warmth shone through.

"I often used to take Lou to my parents' home in Colinton for a few days at a time. My father was a serious-minded parson who stayed mostly in the house after my mother's death. The grandchildren were all terrified of him, but Lou would skip up the old staircase with me to see him in his study. He would brave going in with a little snippet of psalm to recite so he could look around at the Indian pictures in there, of warriors on horseback and such. My father was utterly charmed by him." Margaret Stevenson laughed to herself. "The other spot at Colinton that held Lou's interest was the old cemetery nearby. We always had to go look at the headstones. He liked to scare himself."

Mrs. Stevenson's stories were at odds with Louis's own memories of his mother. She'd been absent in many ways, he once told Fanny. Thomas Stevenson had cosseted her because of her bad lungs, which kept her in bed until noon in those days. Cummy took her place, Louis had told Fanny sadly, and he blamed his father for keeping his mother at a distance from him.

In the afternoons that followed, Fanny's fingers flew through the project. "You make such tiny stitches so quickly," Mrs. Stevenson commented, only partly in praise. Seven days after it was presented to her, Fanny held up a completely embroidered piano scarf.

Louis's mother goggled in amazement at it. "It's perfect," she said with distinct disappointment. "That cloth was supposed to take two months, Fanny."

A couple of weeks into the visit, Maggie suggested they all go to a resort in Strathpeffer, in the Highlands. There they met up with a few Balfour cousins and uncles, who dined with them and took the long walks everyone in the family seemed to thrive upon.

It was on one such outing that Uncle George Balfour, the doctor of the family and Fanny's amusing seatmate at the first dinner party, took her arm.

"He's too thin," he said soberly, staring at his nephew a few yards ahead of them. "If you can get him to go, you should take him to Davos, in Switzerland. Have you heard of it?"

"Yes," Fanny said. Davos was on the tip of the tongue of every doctor Louis had seen in London and Paris a year ago.

"The thinking now is that cold alpine air is the best medicine for pulmonary phthisis. Dr. Reudi doesn't coddle anyone at his sanitarium. Louis will be out exercising, and he'll have to stop smoking. The place could return him to some semblance of health. No better climate exists for tuberculosis."

"I don't think his parents understand how sick he was in Oakland." She stopped and turned to the old man. "I will speak honestly with you. He has been near death several times in the past year."

George Balfour looked toward his sister, who walked arm in arm with Louis. "Go immediately," he said. "His mother has been without her son. Naturally, she wants him near, but I shall make them understand. I know Thomas will want to help with the cost of it all."

It was decided they would go to Davos. As Fanny and Louis made their rounds saying goodbye, Walter Simpson—Louis's old friend and canoeing companion—and his sister presented the newlyweds with a cat and a dog. "To keep you company," the sister said. "It's a rare breed." Fanny took one look at the caged cat and knew she would leave it behind with someone, to be picked up at some point in the future. Or not. But the dog, a Skye terrier with wavy black hair over his eyes and ears that rose up from his head like small wings, snared her heart.

"He's a big dog in a small body. It's the short legs," Simpson said.

"Great heart, the Skye has, absolutely fearless. They're bred for hunting but a great family dog. He'll be easy to have around the house, though you can't ignore him. He'll let you know that."

"Walter, we will call him," Fanny said, and took him straightaway into her arms. Soon after their departure, Walter became Woggs and then, inexplicably, Bogue.

"He's the perfect dog," Fanny cooed.

Louis smiled. "He even *looks* like you, Fan."

~

CHAPTER 38

1881

On the way to Davos, they stopped in London at the Grosvenor Hotel for a week, where they took a suite with an extra bedroom for Sammy and a sitting room in which Louis could receive guests. When Bob, Henley, Baxter, Colvin, and an old literary friend, Edmund Gosse, showed up, Fanny detected the cautious attitude of the men as they gingerly embraced her husband. "We thought the devil had you, Lou," Gosse said. "But by God, you old stick, you're looking famous."

"Both the Louises are looking famous," Colvin said, pecking Fanny on the cheek.

It had been two years since she'd seen her husband's old crowd. Henley had put on more paunch. So had Bob. They were all changed by age, marriage, children, jobs, and some of the friendships had grown more complex. Baxter, a lawyer, handled legal and financial matters for Louis. Henley was his publisher at *London,* as well as his literary agent—albeit unpaid, but he had high hopes that their play collaborations would prove lucrative. Colvin, who was paying off a significant loan from Louis in small amounts, acted as an editor and a sort of well-connected sponsor. Together just now, though, they might have been carefree schoolboys.

They had come to see Louis, their beloved Puck, but Fanny enjoyed the talk and stayed through the first evening's conversation. There was a genial glow in the room, such tenderness toward Louis, and Fanny, too, for what she had been through with his illness in the States.

Louis, for his part, was elated. He had been among mostly women and children for the past few months, and Fanny saw how it lifted his spirits to be with his old cronies, especially before the "confinement" in Davos.

"You'll be surprised by the place," Gosse said. "Symonds is in Davos and plans to stay indefinitely. He has an actual life there. You'll like his company."

"Ah, he's a pompous ass," Henley opined.

"The man's earned the right. He's considered a great Renaissance scholar," Gosse explained to Fanny.

"Symonds is his name?" Fanny asked. "Does he have a family in Davos?"

"A wife and four daughters." Henley sniggered, waving a dismissive hand. "Professor Symonds is an expert on Greek love."

"He just did a translation of Michelangelo's sonnets," Louis explained as the others talked on. "As they were written—man to man."

"I understood Mr. Henley's remark," she replied.

"He's an impeccable scholar. He's all the talk now in certain circles," Louis said.

"Are we a little jealous of Symonds's fame, perhaps?" Gosse asked Henley.

"No more than you."

"I suppose I should be jealous." Gosse sighed. "I seem to keep hanging by my eyelids to the outer cliff of fame."

Fanny stifled a snicker. *What high opinions these fellows have of themselves.* She excused herself, put Sammy to bed, then retired to her own room with a book. When she returned to the parlor near eleven, she found the men in their cups.

"Do bring your wives next time," Fanny said, gently encouraging them out the door.

Next day was a luncheon at the Savile Club, from which Louis returned drunk. When he had slept off the effects, a new round began. Henley, who had not bothered to nap since lunch, arrived smelling of whisky, an odor he was now complicating with wine.

"I want you to hear the poem our friend here recited for us today at the club," Louis said. "He wrote it whilst in hospital with his leg—the year I met him. Do you mind repeating it, old man?"

Aiming his delivery to a corner of the parlor ceiling, Henley let loose a rant against death. He spoke the last lines with a defiant anguish: " 'I am the master of my fate. I am the captain of my soul.' "

"Thank you," Fanny interjected into the silence that followed.

Louis paced the carpet, a crooked finger over his lips, while Henley looked at his lap.

"You have traveled a hard road, William," Fanny said.

Henley muttered sadly into his beard, "I was a panther once."

"The man hasn't a shred of manners," she steamed when Henley was gone. "It goes straight to my vitals that he ignores your health. It's one o'clock."

"Yes, yes," Louis said absently. He was up then, and out of bed, knocking into furniture as he went for paper and pen. "I must light the lamp for a bit. Sorry, Fan."

"Can't it wait?"

"I need to write it: the maimed manhood of Henley." His voice was feverish. "*That* is the key to a great character."

FOR A WEEK the old friends came back to visit. Fanny kept Louis in bed much of the day, then stepped in and out of the evening scene in the parlor. Often she felt the air in the room was charged with something. Competitiveness? The men appeared to be jockeying for closer position to Louis. After the first night, she stayed in Sammy's room or her own until around ten or eleven, when she took a seat among them, hoping her yawns might signal that there were others in the suite eager for sleep. She listened silently to their repartee, which grew less clever with the ticking of the clock. What awful swells Louis had as friends! Colvin affected a look of bemusement most of the time. He kept his neat little head cocked and his nostrils half flared, as if he had picked up the scent of an overripe cheese. When he spoke, his words amounted to stiff nothings. Gosse's manner was smooth as silk, but he was hopelessly conceited. Henley, by contrast, revealed signs of a heart, mightily injured as it was. He bore the mark of suffering not only in his body but in his conversation. He had come from a big, poor family, and his childhood had been a sorrowful struggle. Despite it, he was a self-made man who turned his miserable luck into heroic poetry. And yet in the midst of all his high talk, he diminished himself when he gossiped, or when he chewed his food like a sheep, with his mouth half open and his chin rotating in a circle while he spewed cracker crumbs into his red whiskers, where they rode out the remainder of the evening. Baxter, the lawyer, whom Fanny found to be one of those brown-haired young men who was indistinguishable from the next, remained insistently drunk. Only Bob Stevenson still pleased her, though she wanted to strangle him for staying on. The room was so filled with smoke that she could barely stand it, and she was a smoker herself.

Their planned week at the hotel turned into two as the men's visits melded into one long bout of false humility and intellectual one-upsmanship. There were no pretenses now. When she made a rare comment, they talked over her. No one but Louis noticed when she retired to bed.

Unable to sleep, she sat up and was shocked when tears spurted from her eyes. *Why are you crying, you fool?* And then she knew. It felt like an arrow every time Louis's friends came and made her feel like an unwanted outsider. It *hurt.* When Henley got on to the subject of American culture, his frequent use of "barbaric" seemed aimed directly at her.

She wiped her eyes and comforted herself by formulating caustic remarks she wanted to deliver to each of them. "How fortunate for you, Mr. Henley, that you have never had to bother your head with the annoyance of notoriety . . . How perfectly suited you are to be a sponsor of talent, Mr. Colvin. Borrowed limelight is better than none."

She picked up a pen and began a letter to Louis's mother. *I cannot bear London,* she wrote. *It is unhealthy for both my body and my mind.*

One night Henley's shouts, booming like cannon reports through the thin walls, were especially infuriating. If they were keeping her awake, then Sammy was wide awake in his bed on the other side of the sitting room. Sammy adored Henley because he thought of him as a jolly musketeer; just now the boy was getting a full dose of the black-guard side of his hero.

She gave up trying to block out the voices and listened. They were gossiping about a journalist who had recently died whose name she didn't recognize. All of them were roasting the man on a spit. "I suppose I have some time left," Louis said. "God seems to want only the bad writers up there."

She would have smiled at another time, when her head wasn't throbbing. She got back under the covers. At two o'clock, when Henley's laugh roared once more, a rush of holy rage shot her out of bed and into the parlor.

"For God's sake, go home—all of you! Am I going to deliver a dead man to Davos?" she shouted. "You have kept him up until the morning hours every single night we have been here. And to what end? So you can assassinate someone's character! Have you no self-respect? Are you not *men?*"

Baxter sat up in his chair, bristling like a cornered cat. Henley set his jaw. Colvin leaped to his feet. In the space of a minute, the sodden party stumbled out of the hotel room, leaving behind half-finished cigarettes and whiskys. When they were gone, Fanny leaned, quaking, against the door. Outside, she could hear the men in the hall, waiting for the lift. "What did I tell you?" Henley's gravelly voice demanded.

It dawned on Fanny what she looked like. Her hair was undone, wild as Medusa's; her heavy breasts, hanging loose under a violet-printed nightgown, quivered with every thud of her heart.

In the bedroom, Louis held his tongue, though he was clearly crest-fallen.

"Don't look at me like that," she said, still shaking. "I'm not a diplomat! I can afford to say what I think."

There was no leaving the Grosvenor Hotel, however, until the stag-gering bill was settled. Fanny was stunned to see that they had burned through fifty pounds. That was nearly one fourth of the annual sum Louis's father had promised them. How was it possible? She could only picture Henley finishing off bottles of Talisker when she considered the bill. But he hadn't done it alone. In the hotel restaurant, she and Louis had ordered freely, with no eye to the budget. Now they would have to eat humble pie by asking his father for more money. Louis leaned on Colvin, too, to come up with some cash. Fanny felt better about that; it was owed to him, after all.

When Colvin showed up with a check, he enjoyed witnessing their embarrassment. "What innocents you are," he teased them, "taking the dearest suite in the hotel."

CHAPTER 39

Louis grasped the brass handles on either side of the clinic's large scale and mounted it. He was not naked, but for Davos, nearly. He wore no shoes or jacket, just trousers and a thin shirt.

"Let go of the handles now," Dr. Reudi said as he peered at Louis's official weight. "Two pounds," the doctor announced. The small group of patients gathered in the hall politely applauded.

Louis alighted with a sheepish grin. "Pathetic," he whispered as he took his seat next to Fanny.

"Your weight?" she asked.

"This gathering."

By the end of the meeting, every patient had taken his turn at the weekly weighing. Then they returned to their places in the community, as pharmacist, furniture maker, postal clerk, chocolatier. This working community of tuberculars in Davos was but one innovation of Dr. Reudi, who prescribed fresh air, exercise, and a positive outlook along with any medications he handed out. Dr. Reudi would have none of the old thinking about tuberculosis that romanticized the pale beauty of the afflicted, lying about on fainting couches.

When they arrived at Davos, the taciturn doctor had come over to the chalet where they were keeping house to have a look at Louis. He itemized the patient's conditions: chronic pneumonia; infiltration and bronchitic tendency; enlarged spleen. He did not say the feared word "tuberculosis."

"You will need to stay here a minimum of eighteen months," he said. "I make no promises, but you have a chance to stabilize your lungs if you stick to the regimen." Reudi prescribed a diet that called for warm cow's milk, red meat, and plentiful wine. He limited Louis's work sessions to three hours and outlawed cigarettes, though he permitted him three pipes per day. After giving Louis a good talking-to, he turned a cool eye on Fanny, pronounced her fat, and put her on a diet of meat, lemons, health tonics, and a low dose of arsenic.

"One of those custard pastries with apricots," Fanny said as they walked through the snow back to their chalet after the weighing session. "If I could have anything I wanted to eat, that's what I would choose."

"I wouldn't have food. I'd have six cigarettes straight in a row."

"I'm fat," she said, sighing, "but I want you to know I don't approve of it."

"Plumpness is fashionable in Paris, Fan," he comforted her.

"How many pipes have you smoked today?"

"All three."

"Mmmm. It's going to be a long night."

"There's wine."

"Ah, there's that," she said, linking her arm with his as their chalet came into sight.

Since their arrival in October, Louis had done his best to partake of what Davos offered. When she saw him heading outside with his ice skates or bundling up for tobogganing, Fanny demurred. She'd always hated cold weather. There were plenty of inside activities, such as whist, and charity bazaars to knit for, but Fanny mostly stayed on the couch in the big open room on the second floor, slowly reading her way through a pile of novels and *Lancet* medical journals she'd found at the sanitarium library.

As the weeks wore on, she began to worry aloud that Davos was not a healthy place for her son. Sammy was pleased enough to spend his days with Louis, printing stories on his little press and waging long military campaigns against him with lead soldiers. Though tutors were interspersed between the entertainment, she decided Sammy would be far better educated at a small private school in Bournemouth, England. Louis embraced the boy heartily as he departed, shouting to him as the train began to move, "Be diligent, Sammy, especially in play!"

Now it was down to three of them, counting Bogue.

WITH THE BOY away, the health resort full of sunburned optimists began to feel oppressively artificial even to Louis, though he tried not to show Fanny. She, on the other hand, could not conceal her growing misery.

"Did you ever see one of those snow globes?"

"The paperweights you shake? With the sparkly snow that swirls around inside? Yes, in Paris."

"I feel as if I'm living in one. I am the figure inside, wearing a frozen smile."

Louis patted her knee. "We won't be here forever, little man."

"What does that mean?" Fanny asked crossly.

"My health is much better."

"I mean 'little man.'"

Louis laughed. "You're tiny, and you have the heart of a courageous man. It's a compliment."

Fanny was losing her sense of humor—fearful, no doubt, that they would have to live out the remainder of his days in the Alps.

Symonds, the Renaissance scholar, was one of Dr. Reudi's patients who had accepted his fate and built a permanent home in Davos. "You will notice a certain nervous strain from the high altitude among the people who reside here," he warned one day as Louis sat in the man's study, "particularly sensitive souls like yourself. You may find yourself a bit grumpy."

"So that's what's wrong with us."

"You'll get accustomed to the climate because you must," Symonds pronounced.

Louis could not conceive of calling Davos home. The landscape presented itself in black, white, and blue, without a hint of natural smell. The snow had its own beauty but was nothing to the brown and green of a Highlands meadow fragrant with life. He would never concede defeat the way Symonds had, though he welcomed the man's company and gladly listened to his lectures about Shakespeare and Italy and the Council of Trent. They helped fill the time.

As the days stretched into weeks, people went missing. It happened without fanfare. A knitting companion of Fanny's would be unavailable. The man who regularly sat at the next dining table stopped appearing for dinner. A new postman replaced the old. All around, fellow inmates were quietly dying—many of them young, athletic, cheerful, and the least likely candidates for the undertaker.

Louis was positively spruce by comparison and tried to help the others with a good turn. He spent one afternoon desperately searching for a birthday gift for a twelve-year-old girl who was not expected to see another birthday. Hearing that another resident had received roses at Christmas, he went to her quarters and talked the woman out of her flowers, then delivered them to the sickly girl.

He was hungry for the company of his old friends, but only Colvin visited briefly. When an unexpected guest did show up at their house in January, it was Fanny Sitwell. She had brought her eighteen-year-old son, Bertie, for treatment. He had just finished a school term when he was stricken with a galloping consumption. It moved Louis to see his wife rise up from her depression to shower kind attentions on his first love. No one could better understand her sorrow. He tried to find hopeful words, but even Fanny Sitwell could see the boy's condition was plummeting. By April, when signs of a thaw began, Bertie Sitwell was dead and buried at Davos in a cemetery for boys and girls. Fanny Sitwell went home stricken, silent, and childless.

FOR THE FIRST time in his life, Louis found his writing pace slowing to a crawl. "Do you remember how I couldn't seem to write in this place when we first came here? Now all my little fishes talk like whales."

"How is that?"

"I find myself using big words to give some force to a thought. It's these peaks all around us. Never have I used such lofty polysyllables."

She did not respond or look up. The carved clock on the mantel ticked off a minute before she said dully, "Just write."

She resisted being joked into a happier humor.

"A good novel might cure your boredom," he suggested when he realized Fanny had stopped reading books or writing stories. Only the *Lancet* held her attention.

"This article says that some vinegars erode your intestine," she said, looking up from the journal.

"Does that mean I can't have vinegar now?" he protested. Sure enough, she moved the vinegar cruet away from him when they went to dinner that evening. Another day, she was in a shiver over the idea that salt hardened one's arteries and caused early death. Yet another time, she became highly exercised by an article on germ theory.

"Many diseases are spread by germs, it says. Well, we both know that; I've known it for years. It makes perfect sense. Your body's weak right now, so you're more likely to catch something."

"What next? Will you be making every visitor take a bath before he comes through the door?"

"You treat me like your jailer!" Fanny shouted, throwing down the magazine.

"Why must you always *expect* the worst possible outcome for everything?"

Fanny stood up and put her face close to his. "Why must you go around chirping like a canary, pretending everything is perfect? It is so wearisome."

"*You* are wearisome! Stop trying to manage every minute of my bloody life!" Louis stormed into the bedroom, slammed the door, and crawled under the covers. There he seethed, glad she was miserable on her diet, glad she was getting a taste of her own medicine. As the hour passed, though, he felt immeasurably sad that they had come to this point.

How I hate fighting with her!

Excitable. Both of them were. What was to be done about it? There probably would always be some snapping friction in the house, high altitude or no. At least they spoke openly, argued frankly. It was a damn sight better than the silent treachery that a lot of married couples practiced.

In Davos, in such close quarters, his illness brought out the best and worst in both of them. Fanny was her nurturing, wry self one day, and the next, a screeching hellicat. Or worse, so willing to find the dark cloud that she actually made him feel sicker. Fanny let out sighs that seemed to rise up out of a Slough of Despond. Her kidneys ached, her head went dizzy, she could never get warm. As she sat and stared at the beams overhead, her mind seemed to get stuck on a thing. "Will you look into getting a cross for Hervey's grave?" she'd asked Louis, and he promised he would. She was terrified that the cemetery officials at Saint-Germain would move the boy's bones into a common grave, even though the contract had not yet run its five-year course. "I've put Baxter on it," he assured her, and he had, but it wasn't enough to say that. "Have you heard from Baxter?" she asked again and again.

Louis realized he was far better equipped to survive solitude than Fanny. He could retreat for hours while buccaneers or truant sons played about the hills and furrows in his brain, even if they never made it onto the page. Louis had been escaping the stupefying lassitude of sickness in just this way for as long as he could remember. And when words were doing what he wanted them to do on the page, he could soar above everything, even the sickbed.

Not Fanny. Her whole life was about being busy, about things she touched in the course of a day. She had been this way all her life, continually experimenting, exploring, creating with her hands, whether it was a recipe for stew or a photograph or a mix of pigments for a better blue on canvas. Confined by cold weather, in a community of sick people, she had grown frustrated and then depressed.

Louis left his bed to go speak with her. He poked the fire, then went to her at the stove across the room. "What have I let you in for, Fan?" he said, putting his hand on her back. "I always expected I would be a rather dignified invalid. I've always believed it is a person's sacred duty to be happy. But this . . ." He shuddered. "I know you hate this place. Well, so do I; I don't want to die here. But what good does it do to complain about it?"

"You are *not* going to die in this place," she growled. She slammed down a wooden spoon and went outside.

So much for a quick reconciliation.

Through the window, he could see her leaning against the balcony rail. *What is she thinking about out there? Going over all her troubles?* Maybe it wasn't entirely him. Maybe she was regretting the distance between her and her daughter. When news came that Belle had her baby, it was Louis who wrote the standard congratulatory letter and who later kept up correspondence with Belle and Joe. She nursed her grudges, Fanny did. And then all of a sudden they would disappear. Just the other day, Fanny had apologized to him for exploding at his friends while they were in London. It had taken her months to get over that anger.

No doubt she was there in the cold, wishing for the peacefulness of the Monterey beach or the warm hills of Napa, where she could watch snails and bees going about their business. He remembered a remark she'd made at Silverado when they'd both stopped what they were doing to observe a spider weaving an intricate web. *"That,"* she'd said thoughtfully, "is a spider explaining herself."

Louis watched her standing on the balcony without a coat, her back to him. A gust of wind whooshed a fine spray of snow off the roof and over her. She seemed not to notice. The blinding sun lit up the snowflakes in her hair like sparks.

CHAPTER 40

"Louis, are you all right?"

Louis was splayed on the bed, his legs half on and half off the mattress, his arms spread like wings. "I'm preparing myself," he said.

"For what?"

"For the Brownies."

"Don't the Brownies come if you're just lying in your usual way?"

"This position always brought them when I was a child."

"I'll sleep in the other bedroom."

"Do you mind, Pig? I had a real crawler last night. Perhaps I can get it back again tonight if I go to sleep thinking about it. I was an injured soldier in a hospital in Spain, and the doctor sent me off to recuperate in a terrifying old house . . ."

She didn't mind. The bed was Louis's nest, his writing desk, his sitting room for receiving visitors during the day, and at night a playground for the Brownies, or "the Little People," as he called them. When he was under the weather, he took his meals there. Sometimes the sheets were stained with gravy from his dinner. On nights like this, she welcomed a retreat into another room. Here in Scotland, where they were sharing a cottage with his parents in Braemar, she would stay in the extra bed in Sammy's room.

By now she knew that dreams were as important to Louis as a bottle of ink. Sometimes a particular dream stretched out over three or four nights, unfolding as neatly as a finished story. When that happened, he credited the Brownies entirely. More often they left behind puzzle pieces from which he put together a story. Any moral element had to be created during waking hours. "The Brownies don't have a rudiment of conscience," he told her drily.

Fanny's dreams were nothing like his. Sometimes they were so humdrum that she was bored even as she had them. "How did you dream last night, love?" he would ask in the morning, and she'd have to report, "I laced my shoes and brushed my hair."

The morning after the Spanish dream, he said, "I got the rest of it. I woke up and wrote down what I could remember. It's a whole story."

"You're making me positively jealous."

"You have to train yourself to be ready for the Little People. Set yourself to sleep with a particular place in mind."

Fanny attempted the method for a string of nights, hoping to bring up a ghost tale. She remembered the gnarly black branches of an oak that used to tap on her bedroom window in Indiana and set loose waves of goose bumps. In the morning, no story suggested itself. Her own Brownies were stingy, having left behind a paltry image of herself as a girl of seventeen, looking all over the house for something she had lost.

"It doesn't work for me," she told him. They were sitting on the porch of their cottage.

"Don't let it get you down, Pig. You seem to have your own strange route to the spirit world."

"Make fun all you want."

"I'm not making fun," Louis said gently, rubbing the top of her hand. "I've seen your instincts run true a hundred times."

"Well, you *do* make fun of me."

"When?"

"Every time you call me Pig."

"But that's an affectionate term, love."

"And I'm much thinner now that we are out of the blessed Alps."

"You *are.* Stop all this, now. Let's go for a walk."

He took her hand and led her from the stone cottage, through the garden gate, and away from the other picturesque stone houses, past an open country field to where a birk wood began.

They sat on a carpet of soft grass in an unshaded spot. Above, an Indiana-blue sky spread itself out between the tall downy birches. "You are my own luscious *spaewife*," he said. "You know I adore you." She laughed and let her head fall back on the warm earth. He lay down next to her and rested her head on his shoulder. Lying still, she felt sunned all through.

.   .   .

"YOU CAN LEAVE Davos. Your lungs are in splendid shape," Dr. Reudi had told Louis. "But there are no guarantees. If you won't remain at a high altitude, then go somewhere in the South of France, fifteen miles as the crow flies from the sea, and if possible, near a fir wood."

They had danced for joy around the chalet when Louis came home with the news. In Davos, Louis's face had filled out; his cheeks had turned ruddy with health. The idea that he might not have tuberculosis made them buoyant. They left the Alps in a hurry, before the outlook changed, and headed for Scotland to summer with his parents and Sammy in the Highlands before they went on to find a place in France.

Louis had been writing like a madman since they'd arrived in Brae-mar. He finished two shockers—"Thrawn Janet" and "Body Snatchers"— and "The Merry Men," about wrecked treasure ships. It was the pile of completed work on his desk, rather than her own dreams, that inspired Fanny to finally finish a tale of her own, "The Shadow on the Bed," which she hoped would be included in his next collection.

Everyone in the family felt the creative whirl inside the cottage. Having lost his best companions to the writing table, Sammy some-times set up his paints to pass a rainy afternoon. "Come color with me," he pleaded one day when Louis emerged from the room where he'd been working. Louis spread out a piece of paper on a table and began painting an island with some watercolors. Below the drawing, he wrote "Treasure Island."

"Imagine that there is an island where a chest full of gold is buried," he said to Sammy. "There is a boy named Jim who, quite by chance, comes into possession of a map of the island. The map has been drawn by a crusty old sailor of questionable morals, a man named, ah . . . Billy . . . Billy Bones. And through some series of events, the boy goes off on a schooner to look for the treasure. He is traveling with a collec-tion of sailors, some of them decent fellows, and some scoundrels bent on killing the other men when they find the gold . . ."

"Luly, is John Silver one of them?"

"Aye, he is."

Louis turned out several chapters in a matter of days. When Fanny tiptoed into his room, he cried out, "There'll be widders in the morn-ing!"

"Widders?"

"*Widows,* madam."

At dinner, he complained, "The trouble with a boy's story is to write it without any cursing in it. And pirates do nothing but curse. I need tepid oaths, I suppose."

"Fiddlesticks?" Maggie offered.

"Carpet bowls!" Thomas thundered.

Soon they could hear Louis shouting in his study. "Son of a Dutchman!" he would yell. "Dash my buttons!" Passing by his door, Fanny heard him cackle: "Shiver my timbers!"

"THE SEA COOK," he announced one evening when everyone gathered in the sitting room after dinner to hear the first chapter. "Or 'Treasure Island,' as you wish. By Captain George North."

"A pseudonym?" Mrs. Stevenson asked.

"I can't risk my literary reputation on a piece like this."

When Louis read it to the family, he pitched his voice high for the mother's words—"Dear, dearie me! What a disgrace upon the house!"—and made the voice of the buccaneer Billy Bones as gravelly as a river bottom. Fanny noticed Louis seemed to be playing not only to Sammy but also to Thomas Stevenson, who tittered like a schoolboy at every plot turn. What made them all gasp was the arrival of Long John Silver, the pirate character who had been brewing in Louis's imagination for some time.

"'His left leg was cut off close by the hip, and under the left shoulder he carried a crutch, which he managed with wonderful dexterity, hopping about upon it like a bird,'" Louis read. "'He was very tall and strong, with a face as big as a ham—plain and pale, but intelligent and smiling.'"

"It's your friend Henley!" Thomas shouted.

"Aye, it is," Louis admitted. "But in body only."

Having brought the Stevenson household to its feet, he made an outline of the rest of the story, sent it off to a boy's magazine called *Young Folks,* and promptly sold it for serialization. It didn't pay much, but he was exuberant in the following weeks as he worked toward the middle of the story.

. . .

ONE EVENING AFTER dinner, Louis walked through the cottage sitting room where the family was gathered, waving a few pages of the manuscript. "If this don't fetch the kids, why, they've gone rotten since my day!" he shouted.

Everyone laughed but Louis's father.

"It's a fine story, Lou," Thomas Stevenson chimed in. He waited a beat. "But this *Amateur Emigrant* book . . ." He had been reading the *Emigrant* manuscript all afternoon by a front window of the cottage. His elbows rested on the arms of his chair; his fingers formed the steeple he made when he was deep in thought. "I don't want it published. It's not up to your standards, and it makes you look so . . . threadbare. It shames all of us."

Louis crossed his arms, his own characteristic response to his father's criticisms. After a moment, he excused himself.

"You just now got a taste of the bad Thomas Stevenson," Louis said when Fanny came to the bedroom.

"It wasn't nearly so bitter as the arguments you told me about."

"This morning he actually pulled me aside to say I should insert a religious passage in the pirate story. He followed up that bit of advice with the news that he hopes to buy the *Emigrant* back from the publisher. He's embarrassed that his son traveled in steerage. He thinks it reflects badly on him."

"Louis, Louis. Just ignore the first part. As for the *Emigrant,* I don't think he sees it as censorship. And you can always publish it later. It's a temporary compromise. They are supporting us, after all."

"That's just the problem, isn't it? As long as I depend upon his money, I am beholden to him. *And* his literary taste."

By morning, though, Louis had shifted. The *Emigrant* would be pulled.

In the days that followed, the price of his frantic writing pace revealed itself. His nerves were at a high pitch, and he had a whoreson influenza bout followed by a visit from Bluidy Jack.

Chastened, they returned to the Alps for the winter.

CHAPTER 41

⁓

1882–1884

The following summer in Scotland weakened once again the health Davos had restored. As fall progressed and the question of winter quarters loomed, they decided to take their chances away from the Alps.

Fifteen miles as the crow flies; near a fir wood, if possible. Louis had happy memories of earlier visits to the South of France. "The Côte d'Azur," he proposed. "Either Nice or Marseilles." Louis set out ahead to find a place to live, while Sammy went back to school in Bournemouth. When Fanny arrived in Marseilles in October, they found each other in much better health and joyful to be reunited. The separation had shaken them awake.

They made love tenderly and wide-eyed. She let go of the buzzing that usually filled her brain, the questions. *Is he thinner? Was that a different sort of cough? Has he eaten his breakfast today?* She pretended they were normal people on a holiday. Their reunion invigorated both of them.

"What a morning," Louis would say as they walked the rocky, dry hills above their rented château just outside Marseilles. "I want to take this day, fold it up, and put it in my pocket so I can have it again and again. What is really necessary in life? A blue bay to gaze on. Sun."

"We're rich," she said.

Fanny sent for their furniture from Davos, but it wasn't long before word came that typhoid fever was sweeping through Marseilles. In the wee hours she heard the thundering of wooden wheels on cobblestone. "What is going on at night that keeps people out in the city's streets?" she asked a neighbor who spoke English.

The elderly woman, whose chin bristled with white hairs, looked around as if she had a secret. "They're carrying bodies to the cemetery in the night so no one can see how many are dead."

One morning when Fanny went out to get milk, she found the

bloated body of a man at the bottom of their stairs. "Somebody has dumped a dead person in the street outside our house," she told Louis excitedly. She suspected he didn't believe her. He thought sometimes she exaggerated so as to get her way.

"How do you know he was actually dead?" he asked. "He might have simply fainted in the heat."

"We're leaving," she said firmly. The furniture had not yet arrived. It was easy for them to get out of town.

Hyères was only forty miles southeast of Marseilles, but she felt safer there. "Chalet La Solitude," the funny little house she found, was too small to stay in permanently, but for now it was a lovely, waking dream. They rented it at the beginning of 1883, and the move felt like a fresh start.

The house was toy-sized but possessed all the essentials of a real one. A wealthy man from the area had visited the Paris Exposition and seen miniature models of Chinese pagodas, Turkish mosques, and Swiss chalets. It was the chalet that stole his heart. Though it was intended merely as a model for a larger version, he bought the house on the spot and had it shipped to Hyères, where it was reassembled on the steep, rocky side of a hill. When she cooked, Fanny found the kitchen so small that she risked burning herself on the range or impaling herself on pothooks. Louis's parents visited shortly after their arrival. They all squeezed into the tiny dining room, where their chairs were pushed up against the walls around the table. A servant, hired for the occasion, handed plates to them over their heads.

By comparison, the garden was spectacular, rich with olive, orange, palm, and eucalyptus trees, nightingales, and a view of the ocean in the distance. Below their terrace, terra-cotta tile roofs rippled down the hillside.

The first day of their stay, Fanny woke at dawn to a blue sky marbled with pink clouds. She wandered through the grove of olive trees behind the house, touching her palm to the bark of each one. "Thirty-five!" she told Louis gleefully when he awoke. Everywhere she looked, she saw rosebushes and aloe. It was March. In a few weeks the carpet of fig marigolds would be beaming happily, like a nursery of little pink-faced babies. She wrote immediately to her sister in the States to send vegetable and flower seeds.

An old staircase led down to town. They stayed aloft, mostly, well above the old village. It was a filthy place below, unswept, with refuse blown about the streets by the hot mistral winds. Convinced that *Treasure Island* would be a greater success as a novel than the syndicated version in *Young Folks,* Louis spent his days rewriting the material to be published as a book. Only occasionally did he put on his short black cape to venture down for a visit with his friend LeRoux the wine merchant. He followed his usual routine, writing all morning until noon, while Fanny kept herself busy with the house. She painted several interior doors in a Japanese style with female figures. One of the painted women was yawning, and it set anyone who visited to yawning furiously.

Fanny loved marketing in the morning and always found the stalls full of prettily arranged vegetables despite the general disorder of the streets. In the afternoons when Louis stopped writing, they wandered with Bogue through the garden, inspecting Fanny's beans and lettuces. One night they sat out on the terrace and watched the clouds scudding overhead against the black sky.

"I'd swear the stars are moving."

"Put your finger on that star," Louis told her, guiding her finger up toward the sky. "Now keep it there. It's not movin', girlie."

"I am content," she said. "This is contentment."

WHY IS IT, she wondered a few weeks into their stay at La Solitude, *that whenever I say out loud I'm happy, something goes wrong?*

"Louis," she told him one morning, "I think I'm pregnant."

Louis was honing the end of a pencil with a pocketknife. He set them down, leaned against the kitchen table, and crossed his arms. "How late are you?"

"Two weeks. You could set a clock by me most of the time." Standing in the tiny kitchen, Fanny tried to count back to find the day when it might have happened.

"We could adapt," Louis said, summoning an encouraging tone. "Of course we could. I suppose we'd have to."

Dear Lord, don't let it be. She remembered how much she had wanted to give Louis a baby of his own. When they married, she'd thought it was still possible, if only his health would stabilize. But the past two years of illness had put that dream to rest.

When another week had passed with no menstruation, he asked, "How do you feel about having a baby?"

"Afraid. We said in Davos that children were out of the question. But I know you wanted a child when we met, and now we never talk about it. How does a baby fit into this traveling circus? I'm forty-four—I could be ill, and then what? And how could we afford it? As it is, we are continually short of funds—"

He put a forefinger on her lips. "Hush. I agree."

When she announced the next afternoon that she had begun to menstruate, his face broke into relief. But in the following few days, Louis seemed bereft, as if he had lost an actual child whose fingers and toes he had already counted.

SHORTLY AFTER THE turn of the year in 1884, Henley and Baxter came to Hyères to visit. Fanny's relations with his old crowd—other than Bob—had been politely strained since the scene at the Grosvenor Hotel in London. She thought it was best that way, and apparently, so did Louis's friends, for they'd made little effort to rekindle their old familiarity. She didn't trust Henley, in particular. She suspected him of a backstairs cunning he never showed to Louis, though she hadn't any proof.

Still, she found herself trying to win him over. She made a dinner of roast beef especially for him. When they squeezed around the little table at dinner, knocking elbows as they ate, she sought to find the common ground on which they might converse. *Treasure Island*'s recent publication in book form was a safe topic.

"We've received so many letters from readers since it came out," she said. "Not just children are reading it. Many adults, too."

"I heard Prime Minister Gladstone has read it through a couple of times," Baxter reported.

"Shouldn't he be running the country?" Louis said.

Henley cackled, knowing how deeply Louis despised the man. He maneuvered the bowl of potatoes toward his plate. "It's a pity about the book rights," he said. "Only a hundred pounds." The big man shook his head. "You could be sailing around in a yacht if you wrote plays. I heard recently that George Sims made ten thousand pounds on one melodrama alone."

"What are you working on now?" Baxter asked.

"A poetry collection," Louis replied. "I'm calling it *A Child's Garden of Verses*."

Henley nearly choked. "'A child's garden' . . . ?"

"Go write your damn masterpieces!" Louis shouted. Henley and Baxter laughed, but everyone in the room knew Louis was livid when he jabbed his fork emphatically at Henley as he spoke. "When I suffer in mind, stories are my refuge; I take them like opium. Anyone who entertains me with a great story is a doctor of the spirit. Frankly, it isn't Shakespeare we take to when we are in a hot corner, is it? It's Dumas or the best of Walter Scott. Don't children, especially children, deserve that kind of refuge? Even if it's poetry?"

Fanny savored the look of defeat on Henley's face. He was a poet, after all. "Good heavens, you're touchy. I was merely teasing!" he protested.

She was already thinking what she would say to Louis in bed that night. "He is so jealous of you."

Henley had been floundering since his *London* magazine folded, while Louis's literary reputation kept growing. The previous week, Fanny had received a copy of *The Century* containing a glowing review of Louis's newest stories. She could hardly sleep the night the review arrived in the mail. Everyone she knew back in California read *The Century*. She nearly burst with glee when she thought of the friends who had questioned her choice of a sickly, penniless writer as her new husband. All of them—Timothy Rearden, Dora Williams, Sam Osbourne, her whole blessed family—would finally see how prescient she had been about Louis's talent.

Fanny thought Henley might be right about playwriting. A melodrama could be the gold mine Henley claimed. And it was probable the two men would do better a second time together. Whatever came, Henley was going to be a fixture in their lives for the duration. So was Baxter. Louis trusted his old friend from law school, and in a moment of candor, even Fanny had admitted to Baxter, "I'm no better than Louis with money." Still, it bothered her that the lawyer held the purse strings.

"Burly, you look positively Brobdingnagian!" Louis remarked when he witnessed Henley's mighty frame crammed into the chalet's tiny parlor. The men quickly understood that there was little fun to be had in so small a house. With Fanny's tepid blessing and a bottle of ergotin in hand, Louis was off with Baxter and Henley to Monaco, Monte Carlo, and Menton.

IT WASN'T LONG before Fanny got word from Louis that he had fallen ill in Nice, on his way home. His friends thought it was merely a cold, left him at a hotel, and returned to London. Now he was hemorrhaging. She immediately caught a train to Nice, all the while cursing the hides of Henley and Baxter. Were they even bigger fools than she thought them to be? What would it take to make them realize how fragile Louis was?

When she reached his bedside, she found him sleeping; his cheeks were sunken purple shadows, his fingertips white as paper. The French physician attending him told her to go into the hallway.

"Mr. Stevenson has pneumonia, which has aggravated his poor lungs into hemorrhaging," he said, after closing the door to Louis's room. "You should notify a male friend or member of the family that he may be needed, in case your husband dies."

Fanny was stunned. She searched his face and found only dull resignation. "I need to contact his mother to get here right away," she muttered.

"Where is she?"

"Edinburgh."

The doctor shook his head. "She won't arrive in time."

Fanny sat beside Louis's bed throughout the night, watching in frozen panic as he struggled to breathe. By morning, though, her husband was performing his Lazarus impersonation once again.

"Would you kindly get me a newspaper, Fan?" he asked when he opened his eyes. "I feel as if I don't know a thing about what's going on in the world."

With the help of the hotel manager, Fanny arranged for a visit from a consulting doctor named Drummond, who gave Louis a good once-over and announced, "You could live until you are seventy, sir, but you must curtail the traveling. You are a writer, yes?"

"Yes," Louis replied. "A very seedy one, at the moment."

"We are going to have to bind your right arm so that you are not tempted to use it. In this way, you will be able to lie very still. No talking, either. That is how it must be until your hemorrhaging stops."

Fanny was unsure how she would succeed in transporting Louis sixty-five miles back to Hyères. In a panic, she contacted his old canoeing friend Walter Simpson; when he declined, she suspected what he thought: that she was a Cassandra and this was a false alarm. She called upon Bob next, even though she had enlisted him far too many times in the past. He was married now, like Walter and the others, but Bob said yes, he would come. They managed to get Louis home slowly, with intervals of rest along the train route. Fanny was relieved and moved when Henley arranged for his trusted English doctor to come to Hyères to treat Louis. Along with Baxter and Bob, he guaranteed to pay the doctor's fees.

As she nursed Louis in the weeks that followed, she acted as his amenuensis as well. He was forbidden to pace, let alone get out of bed, though that did not stop him from dramatizing the dialogue as he dictated pieces of a romance he was calling *Prince Otto*. He growled the prince's lines and spoke in a high pitch for the females. During the hours she wrote for him, Fanny fell under the spell of his storytelling. She found herself whiling away hours with him as he processed one plot approach after another. She loved collaborating with him, but it was not her only work; there were meals to cook, sheets to change, bedpans to empty.

Exhausted, she hired a local woman named Valentine Roch to help nurse Louis. After one week of caring for him, the plain French countrywoman, wasp-waisted in her white apron, said directly, "I am not leaving you." She melded into their lives as easily as a nice cousin might. Fanny taught her how to cook the food Louis could eat, and showed her how to lower him into bed on all fours when his back pained him. It was a godsend to have another strong person who could manage the job, and Louis liked her. He teased Valentine shamelessly and called her "Joe." She was a simple young woman who intuitively understood the conditions that arose when a person boomeranged between life and death.

Louis was heroic, and for his companions to be anything less was unthinkable. "Might you pin some paper to a board and put it in front of me?" he requested of Fanny one day. "I've come up with a couple of verses I'd like to set down." She provided him with the board and paper. He sat in the darkened room and defied doctor's orders by using his left hand to scribble out the poems.

"There is something else I want you to do for me."

"What is it?"

"Go out on a walk and think up some story ideas for me, Fan, even if you just walk back and forth in front of the house. We need the money, and Prince Otto has stopped talking."

"So I am to be your Scheherazade? I think you just want to be rid of me."

He smiled. "There might be a touch of that in it."

She found relief in the walks. She had been reading in the newspaper about some young Irish-American men who had returned to Ireland to participate in a bombing plot against the English. She tried to imagine what sort of people could allow themselves to be part of such a heinous scheme. Soon enough, a mysterious man in a sealskin coat was flitting about her head, followed by a wealthy girl using an alias, and a house exploding. At night she spun stories out of thin air the way she'd done as a child, and she glowed when Louis remarked, "My lady has quite the perfervid imagination, thinks I to meself." She could barely contain her delight when he began concocting threads to connect the disparate tales.

"I'm fairly sure I can publish these," he remarked at the end of her fourth night of tale spinning.

She jumped up and opened the best wine in the house. "To our first collaboration," she toasted.

Out and about every day, Fanny learned from two encounters with English speakers that cholera was raging in Toulon, just three miles away. When she told Louis, they both let down their brave masks. Early in the morning, they could hear the sound of patients in the town below being wheeled to the pest house with the other contagious people. They knew then that cholera was closer than Toulon; it had obviously reached Hyères. In bed, Fanny huddled close to Louis's left side.

One night in late winter, he began to hemorrhage again. By now Fanny knew what to do. For some time she had carried a small vial of ergotin in pockets that she sewed into her dresses; she was never without it. The sight of Louis filling a bowl with nearly a pint of blood sucked the air right out of her lungs. She raced for water to mix with the ergotin granules in a minim glass, but her hands shook so wildly that Louis took the medicine away from her, calmly poured himself the proper dosage, and drank it down.

He signaled to her to bring a pencil and paper. With his left hand, he scrawled out, *Don't be afraid. If this is death it is an easy one.*

Fanny kept watch through the night. Outside, the trees rustled uneasily. She imagined the wind was blowing up the hillside from the old town, bringing with it thick clouds of germs—cholera, smallpox, typhus, who knew what—from the damp streets and pestilential piles of garbage below. She got up and went to the window. Even the olive trees had taken on a sinister aspect, as if their leaves were coated with a sickening dust.

CHAPTER 42

⌒

Gypsies. Vagabonds. Nomads. Those were the words Fanny had used since their marriage to cast their wanderings in a romantic light. But the words didn't seem colorful or amusing or even accurate. The truth was, Louis's cruel illnesses whipped around their lives, pushed them toward places they didn't want to go, and pulled them out of places they loved. They had pursued the ideal climate from Silverado to Davos to Hyères, and she was depleted from it. Louis's sickness lived with them like an uninvited guest wherever they settled. Fanny couldn't be angry with him, but the tyranny of the illness made her feel murderous. She hated that it tethered Louis to a bed, decided he shouldn't have his own children, kept him from the simple joys other people took for granted. And then there was the fickleness, when it lifted for a while and let them *hope*, like fools, that they might live normally.

When they abandoned Hyères, they went to London, where Henley and Baxter claimed they'd located *the* specialist. George Balfour came down to be present at the consultation. As it turned out, the physician directed his remarks to Uncle George, rather than Louis or Fanny. Louis's lungs, he said, were clear of disease. "You can stop the ergotin now," the doctor said before taking a quick exit. And Uncle George had agreed!

"I don't believe it for a minute," Fanny fumed when they were alone. "You just lived through the worst hemorrhaging imaginable." She promptly found another doctor who agreed with her. "Most definitely you should return to Davos for the winter," he warned them.

"Mother says Uncle George believes you have exaggerated my condition," Louis told her after reading his letters one afternoon. "And Henley is miffed because it was his doctor you went against."

"I don't care what they say!" Fanny cried out. "No one could witness what you just went through in Hyères and believe you have no lung disease." She stormed around the bedroom, tossing clothing into piles.

"Why do they all talk about climate and good air, and none of these people ever talks about *germs*? Maybe it's germs that cause tuberculosis; that's what some articles in the *Lancet* say . . ."

"You and the damned *Lancet*," Louis moaned.

Fanny glared at Louis in the hotel bed. His hair, which he kept long to protect his neck from drafts, pressed damp against his skull. "Look at you. You shiver. You can't sleep. You cough constantly. The morphine they give you makes you nauseated . . . but 'throw away the ergotin,' they say. Your lungs are just ducky. What am I to do when you start *bleeding* again?"

Louis looked at her sadly. "My poor little man. You're so brave."

"Stop it! Stop the empty talk. I can't be a saint all the time, the way you are. Sometimes I'm just so . . . angry." She threw up her hands. "What do we do now? Where do we go?"

"Let's go see Sammy," Louis said, "as soon as I'm able. We're close. I think it would do us both some good."

WHEN SAMMY CAME to their hotel, she hardly recognized him. He was taller and thinner. Before her stood a handsome sixteen-year-old schoolboy wearing new gold-rimmed spectacles and speaking the King's English.

"Look what happens when a mother turns her head," she said proudly. He had gone away a year earlier, an uncertain, preoccupied boy; now he was a gentleman wearing an overcoat.

During dinner, Sammy talked of his tutor, who was putting him through rigorous instruction to test for Edinburgh University. If all went well, he would live with Louis's parents while studying for his degree. Fanny devoured every detail of her changing boy. The pale beginning of a mustache on his upper lip. The part down the middle of his light brown hair. The way he drank tea now—full of milk and with both hands on the cup. His sudden interest in Gladstone, Irish politics, Victor Hugo.

"Where will you go next?" Sammy asked when he understood they wouldn't be returning to Hyères.

His question hit Fanny like a blow to the sternum. It wasn't "Where will *we* go?" Her son had grown accustomed to being away from family. Or maybe he hadn't. Perhaps he desperately longed for a home, as she did. He'd been seven years old when she uprooted him from Oakland.

In the intervening ten years, he had lived in a half-dozen places. When she recalled her own childhood, she saw the brick house surrounded by tiger lilies where she spent seventeen years. She traced in her mind the pattern of the wallpaper in her bedroom; she scattered feed for her mother's chickens beside a shed painted red. What place could Sammy picture as home?

It dawned on her how little time she had left with him before he went off to university and then out into the world. It was possible he'd return to the States. His father had been trying to lure him to California to become the manager of a ranch he had bought there.

"What would you think of staying in Bournemouth?" she said to Louis that night.

"Has pine trees and health seekers," Louis said. "Has a boy named Sam. Has bathing machines tended by plump ladies in beach costumes. Has a path called Invalid's Walk. What more do we require? I hate the idea of Davos as much as you do. The place is full of germs."

They rented rooms in a boardinghouse. Louis wrote, while she used the kitchen to make meat pies and chocolate cakes for the boy's weekends with them. They had been in Bournemouth for five months when Thomas Stevenson and "Aunt Maggie," as Sammy called Louis's mother, came for a visit.

At sixty-six, Thomas Stevenson was frail-looking and had grown a little muddled. "Small strokes, they think," Margaret Stevenson told Fanny when they were alone.

One evening Mr. Stevenson stood up from his chair in the parlor and made his proposal.

"It would do Mrs. Stevenson and me a great favor if you found a way to be nearer to us in our"—he paused to find the word—"our dotage, I suppose you'd say." He patted Louis's head, as if he were a small boy. "Isn't that the proper expression for the decrepit state in which you find me?

"If you stay in Bournemouth," Thomas went on, "I shall buy a house for you." He peered at them through narrowed eyes. When no immediate response came, he added, "And I will provide five hundred pounds to furnish it." He turned his head to look squarely at Fanny. "Well, now, what do you say?"

CHAPTER 43

⁓

1884

Dearest Dora,

*We send greetings and a change of address. We are now moved
out of our rented rooms here in Bournemouth. Louis's father was so
pleased to have us nearby, he came from Edinburgh and bought a
house for me as a wedding gift! It is a two-story yellow brick
cottage with a blue slate roof situated at the edge of a wooded
ravine called Alum Chine that has trails down to the ocean. There
is a rudimentary garden I can improve upon, and a giant dovecote
that's as busy as a train station. Mr. Stevenson is a great collector of
antique furniture and has made it a wonderful game to go with
me in search of just the right pieces for this house. We have named
it Skerryvore, after a Stevenson lighthouse. Louis grumbles about
being a "householder," but I think he is secretly crowing inside to
be settled in a beautiful spot close enough to London that his
friends and family can visit. I am sending along a recent
photograph of myself . . .*

Fanny enclosed the portrait she'd just had made. It screamed re-
spectability, and she knew Dora would notice that, but Fanny also
knew her well enough to be certain she would show the picture to all
their friends. Six years ago, when Louis was living in San Francisco
waiting out Fanny's divorce, he had gone over to meet Virgil and Dora
Williams at their art school. When Virgil came to the door, he had
taken Louis to be a tramp and nearly turned him away. They became
good friends the moment the mistake was corrected, and it meant
nothing to Louis then or now, but the sting of that encounter still
burned for Fanny.

In the full-length photograph, Fanny wore a pearl choker above a white lace dress with a snug white belt around her recently recovered waist. In a previous portrait with Louis's family taken soon after their arrival in Scotland, she had looked unpleasantly thick around the middle. It had distressed her enough that she'd brushed black paint on the picture to reduce the appearance of her midriff. Happily, this photograph would require no doctoring. She knew it was vanity, but this image was how she wanted to be thought of by her old friends in San Francisco: composed, slender and beautiful at forty-five, and very much *arrived*.

FANNY LEAPED OUT of bed every morning now that they were in the new house. Maybe it had been a bribe from Thomas Stevenson to get them to stay near Scotland, but surely Thomas had also seen how desperate she was becoming without a house of her own. And Skerryvore was her own. It was a place she could make better, and she set about doing that the moment they moved in. First came a new bed for them and one for Sammy; then she went to work on the red dining room. She bought a Sheraton-style dining set, some decorative blue china pieces, two Piranesi prints, and spent fifty-five pounds on napery and silver utensils. When Louis came down one day from his study and saw the latest pile of stuff that had arrived from London, he drew on his cigarette and remarked, "Perhaps we can pawn it for food."

It was in the blue drawing room that Fanny released a pent-up urge to decorate rather grandly. She bought wicker lounge chairs, enough seating for a proper salon, and yards and yards of yellow silk the color of pale mustard. She imagined a beautiful window seat where Louis could work, where Sammy could read a book or guests could sit, drinking their aperitifs. The idea of hiring someone to do the kind of carpentry she could do herself seemed out of the question. Instead, she acquired several identical oak boxes, lined them along the study wall below the window bay, and topped the surface with cushions covered in the yellow fabric.

The results suited her. The house did not look as if it belonged to Margaret Stevenson. There was nothing precious about it.

When Louis saw the effect, he gasped. "It's so delicious I could eat it," he said, and then, "Isn't this too fine for the likes of us?" He looked hard at his wife, who was wearing one of her good dresses. "Too fine for the likes of me, I should say. You're a chameleon, Fanny. I swear, you take on your setting." He turned in a circle to regard the room. "I, on the other hand, feel a qualm coming on."

It was only a moment later that he threw off his reservations. He retrieved from a box a plaster sculpture that his friend Auguste Rodin had sent to him. It depicted a naked man and woman kissing and made Fanny squeamish to have it set out. Louis laughed off her sudden prudishness, placed the piece between a pair of smiling Buddhas, poured himself a whisky, and stood back to admire his cleverness.

Skerryvore. They had taken the name from the most challenging, the tallest and noblest, of all the Stevenson lighthouses. Against daunting odds, Alan Stevenson, father to Bob and Katharine, had managed to build the Skerryvore light station on a treacherous strip of submerged reef off the west coast of Scotland. The lighthouse had surely saved many lives. It was a symbol of indomitable spirit to Louis and Fanny. Outside, on the porch, they placed a model of Skerryvore.

Louis took such pleasure in going out in the evening, when he was able, to light the lantern that fit inside the miniature lighthouse. He would come back inside then, and they would rest snug by the fire, savoring the new chapter they felt opening.

Word spread quickly in Bournemouth circles that an Author was living among them. Women bearing cakes came up the stone walk to pay calls, their faces expectant. Fanny managed to thank them as graciously as possible while letting them know they would not be invited in, for the Author, whom they'd really come to see, was in delicate health and not to be disturbed. Ever.

Only two people managed to get into the house early on, perhaps the third or fourth day after their arrival. They were unpacking boxes when the doorbell sounded. Fanny peeked out the window through the side of the temporary curtain she'd hung and spied a girl of about ten on the porch, standing beside a timid-looking woman whose face was streaked with tears.

"There's a woman crying on our porch," Fanny remarked, wiping her hands on the old painting jacket she wore over her dress.

"We have to answer, then," Louis said. He was sitting on a wooden box, swathed in a blanket over his jacket, and pawing through another box.

Fanny stepped over piles of packing straw to get to the door. When she flung it open, the woman let go a startled sob.

"We thought you weren't home," the girl said. "We rang and rang."

"I'm sorry," Fanny apologized. "We didn't hear it. We were banging boxes around."

"We're your neighbors," the girl announced. "My name is Adelaide Boodle." She made a businesslike curtsey. "And this is my mother."

"Are you quite all right?" Fanny asked the shaken woman. She touched her arm gently. "Come in and sit down."

The girl sprang into the parlor and settled herself on a packing case before her mother could restrain her.

"I told my daughter you would not want to be disturbed, but she's an aspiring writer and admires your husband's work. I'm afraid I succumbed to her enthusiasm. I am so embarrassed to be bothering you."

"Come in!" Louis boomed. He led the mortified Mrs. Boodle to the only chair in the room. "Valentine!" he called out. "Valentine, dear! We need tea for our new neighbors."

Much later, when Adelaide was a regular fixture at Skerryvore, Louis let slip the name he and Fanny had given to the threshold where Mrs. Boodle had dissolved: "The Pool of Tears." In turn, Adelaide confessed that her family (far less inhibited in their own quarters) used nicknames for their new neighbors: "R.L.S." and "His Sine Qua Non." The girl revealed to Fanny how thrilling it was that first time to finally clap eyes on the Author.

"My mother is shy, but I am not," Adelaide explained to Fanny on her second, solo visit to the house. "I want to be a writer, and a writer must be able to go out and meet the world as it is. I am hoping Mr. Stevenson would like to take on a pupil."

Fanny suppressed a laugh. Adelaide was a dark-eyed child with soft brown ringlets and an aquiline nose that suggested character. She was bright and chatty, confident and curious, a lover of books with a tender spot for any animal, much like Fanny had been at ten. Even if Louis wanted a pupil—which he didn't—he was too weak to take on such a project. Worse, he could be ruthless with his criticisms, as Fanny knew only too well.

"Have you written stories?" Fanny asked her.

"Yes, a lot of them."

"I'm afraid Mr. Stevenson is not able to give time to tutoring. He must conserve his energy for his work. I'm a writer, too. I believe I could serve in his place. If you would like to come over next week and read to me while I do my mending, I'll give you an honest assessment of your writing."

So began one of their fondest attachments to Bournemouth friends, of whom there were only a handful. Louis's health didn't allow more; he was as sick as he had ever been, and for far longer periods. Many of his days were spent in bed, occasionally with one arm strapped to his chest so as not to set off a hemorrhage.

Sometimes Louis was so fragile after an episode that he dared not talk, so they had to communicate with hand signals. With his left hand, he wrote out on a scrap of paper the guidelines for the signals. A crooked finger asked for explanation. A pantomime should be followed by a statement of what Fanny or Valentine understood him to want. The third guideline hurt Fanny just to read it: *The case of the dumb patient is one of great inconvenience and suppressed wrath. When he has made you a sign you have failed to follow and he shrugs his shoulders, drop it forever.*

Louis had always hated being fussed over when he was ill. Her attentions—a shawl over the shoulders, a fluffed pillow—had to be done stealthily so he wouldn't notice them.

In the close atmosphere of Skerryvore, sealed off from drafts and visitors, Adelaide Boodle blew in most days like beach air. In between the informal writing lessons, she made herself useful by watering plants and helping Fanny feed her pigeons and the stray cats that lived in the chine below. She knew everyone in the neighborhood, and if a rented room was needed for one of Louis's friends who came down from London, Adelaide knew where to find one. Her reward was free access to the Skerryvore library. With Sammy gone during the week, Fanny took pleasure in having a child in the house; she savored afternoons spent with the girl in the drawing room, the sun slanting across the Persian rug as she read *Little Women* to her, just as she had read it to Belle at the age of ten. Later, she introduced Adelaide to stories she loved by other American writers—Charles Warren Stoddard and Bret Harte, whose Gold Rush prospectors amused the girl. The fact that Fanny had known both writers in her San Francisco days raised her profile considerably.

A couple of months into their lives at Skerryvore, Sidney Colvin and Bob Stevenson visited. Colvin had a new job title, "Keeper of the Department of Prints and Drawings," and occupied an apartment in the British Museum as a perquisite of the job. "Why don't you offer a course for aspiring young writers at the museum?" Colvin proposed to Louis. It nearly broke Fanny's heart to witness her husband's excitement at the prospect of getting out of the house. "I want it!" he said. "I could do it. Absolutely."

Fanny and Bob locked eyes in that moment.

"I didn't realize he was so terribly frail," Bob whispered to her later. "Do you think he is up to . . . ?"

"No," Fanny said sadly. "The doctor would never allow it. But it can't hurt him to entertain the idea. Maybe he'll improve if he feels some hope."

When Bob and Colvin were gone, Louis said to Fanny, "I will need to practice on someone. Sammy might tolerate it on his days at home, but . . ." His eyes brightened. "Get me Boodle!"

"It terrifies me a little to send you into the lion's den," Fanny warned the girl when she told her of the proposal. "Mr. Stevenson is not the easiest critic. I know from personal experience. You see, he considers writing a sacred calling—"

"I can accept criticism," the girl insisted.

"—and he hates bad writing. When you are learning, there is bound to be bad writing." There was something else she needed to say to the girl, though not yet. *A woman's imagination is different from a man's.*

"I am stronger than I look," Adelaide said. "I want to take lessons with him."

"All right, dear. I'll be in the next room. If he gets surly, you just come to me."

Fanny listened in on the first few lessons. She could hear Louis in the adjoining room, instructing Adelaide to write short paragraphs in the various styles of a few classical writers. After three weeks of such exercises, Louis announced that the girl had managed the assignments satisfactorily.

"It comes naturally," Adelaide explained. "We like to mimic people in our house."

"You're ready to write something in your own style," he told her. "Describe a place. No more than a page. We shall discuss it tomorrow."

"My mother's garden," the girl whispered to Fanny on her way out the door. "I know it front to back."

The next day, while the lesson proceeded in the dining room, Fanny lay down on the window seat in the drawing room. The cat jumped up and spread himself over her belly while Fanny fought off the urge to sleep. She remembered a few lessons in writing she'd had with Louis when they were at Silverado and, later, in Scotland. They were so contentious that Fanny and Louis agreed to abandon the idea.

"This is absolutely *appalling.*" Fanny sat upright when she heard Louis's raised voice. "Let us begin with the adjective *green,*" he said. He uttered the word as if it were bile in his mouth. She knew, if he were able, he would be pacing back and forth in high dudgeon.

"You say 'green lawn' in this paragraph," he went on. "Everyone knows a lawn is green. Never use green to describe a lawn. In fact, never use the word! Get rid of all these adjectives. Better to use active verbs. Don't say, 'Climbing red roses are everywhere,' as you do here. Make them *do* something. Say 'the roses clamber up the trunk of the elm, and redden an arbor that creaks under their weight.' Do you get my meaning?"

Louis sighed heavily. Fanny hated those sighs when she heard them. The poor girl must be melting with humiliation in there.

"The English language is old, Boodle. But a good writer owns every word he puts on paper because he makes it new and fresh, you see. It must be precise, though. Precision is everything. Why? Because words have power—to inspire or embarrass, or even to kill."

There was a terrible pause, and Fanny prayed for some gentler encouragement.

"Adelaide. You must promise me you will never, *ever* write anything this dreadful again."

"Stop that, you brute!" Fanny shouted from the drawing room. She bolted from the seat and went to fetch the girl. "Are you all right, child?"

"Yes," Adelaide squeaked. She departed in tears.

"Look what you've done," Fanny growled. "You were perfectly savage to her. And people think you are the Prince of Kindness. Ha!"

Louis waved off the rebuke. "Adelaide has backbone. She will return with something better tomorrow."

Fanny's head wobbled in disgust. "They will be having quite a mimic session over in the Boodle parlor tonight."

CHAPTER 44

"Are you up to a lesson with Adelaide?"

Louis was sitting, stuporous, at the desk in his study. "Is she here?"

Fanny nodded in the direction of the drawing room.

"Send her in, then."

He eyed the pile of correspondence he had intended to attack. It would have to wait. He had nearly as little enthusiasm for writing letters as he had for teaching writing to Adelaide Boodle. The wind had been out of his sails for a week, ever since the Forces—his doctor, Fanny, his lungs—pronounced the London teaching position mere fantasy to pursue.

"I came across something I want to read to you," Louis said to Adelaide, who sat in a wing chair opposite him. He pulled from a bookcase behind him a volume of essays by Shelley. "'A man, to be greatly good,'" he read, "'must imagine intensely and comprehensively; he must put himself in the place of another and of many others; the pains and pleasures of his species must become his own.'" Louis closed the book. "Now, I believe that is fine advice for a writer. Except, I would add, he ought to try to live inside the skin of other species, too. I suspect a pig has a point of view about a few things."

"I think that way—about the cats," Adelaide said.

"Oh, I don't doubt it. You are a naturally good girl, Boodle. It will be easy to put yourself in the boots of the hero. As a boy, I always imagined myself as the good fellow on a white horse who was coming to the rescue of the others. But if you want to be a writer, you are going to have to put yourself in the shoes of people who are not so good. Everybody has faults. Some people have a lot of them. Yet no one sees himself as a monster. You need to try *being* him—or *her*—to know how she feels and thinks."

Louis went to one corner of his study, where wooden crates his mother had recently sent from Edinburgh were stacked up to his height. They contained books, except for one marked "Skelt" on the outside. He removed a couple of boxes off the top to get to that one, then used his folding knife to pry it open. He laughed softly when he looked at the contents. On top of some smaller boxes inside was the collapsed framework for the toy theater he had played with as a child. "Have you seen one of these?"

"No." The girl moved over to the corner where Louis sat cross-legged on the floor, assembling the simple wooden stick framework that supported painted background scenery, props, and the little hand-colored figures of a particular drama.

"I got my first drama set when I was six years old," he said. "Now, what you see here are pieces of a number of different sets I owned as a child." He lifted out a painted scene. "This is a backdrop for a melo-drama called 'Three-Fingered Jack, the Terror of Jamaica.' Some of the characters in that little play have survived, but not all."

He began sorting through a box that held small hand-colored fig-ures from different dramas. "Here's Robin Hood. Here's Aladdin. Here's a maiden who works at an inn. You can see it's a mishmash. I think that is all right for us. I loved the little plays they provided, but I often departed from those outlines, and that's just what I want you to do. Start with a backdrop. There are a couple of others in the box."

The girl pulled out a castle scene, a prison vault, and an island/ocean scene with a warship among the waves.

"Good," he said. "Now look through these characters and see if you can fit together a likely setting for, say, four of them. See these little props? There's an ax, a bag of gold coins. A paper that's a will, from the looks of it." He rummaged about. "Here's a treasure chest. The way the plays always worked was that there was some contest to get at a trea-sure. Might be a pretty girl two fellows are after. Choose your—"

"I know what to do," Adelaide said.

"Have them talk to each other. Out loud. Even yell."

The girl got down on her belly in front of the wood structure. She slid the castle scene into the slot for the backdrop, then started poking through the colorful paper characters.

Louis departed the room so the child wouldn't be embarrassed to try out a few lines. Winded from the box lifting, he lay down on his day-bed in the drawing room to rest. Memories of his boyhood Saturdays flooded his head.

The day had always begun with the stated intent of "having a look at the ships." He went out to a corner near his house with his father or mother and others—Bob came, too, when he was living with them—and stood in the chill, whipping Edinburgh wind to admire from a distance the visiting ships in the Firth of Forth. The joy of those long-ago Saturday mornings was what came next: strolling to the window of a stationer's shop on Leith Walk that sold Skelt's Juvenile Drama toy theater sets. In front of that window, penniless, Louis suffered bouts of anguished longing. The scenes in the window changed regularly. There might be a forest with a halted carriage. Beside it would be a battle raging between a rowdy band of robbers and bearded fellows in dress coats, brandishing pistols. He studied the names displayed near the characters: "The Miller," "The Huntsman," "Long Tom Coffin." A person could buy a paper figure, unpainted, for a penny. There were colored ones available for twopence, having been painted by the wife and grown daughter of the shop's owner. But that would have stolen the pleasure—when he was able to buy some figures—of dipping his own brush, choosing his own colors, then cutting out the little people and pasting them to cardboard. And then the acting out of the play began. *What a bargain those childish dramas were for my parents!* The theater sets bought hours of solitude for the adults who lived at 17 Heriot Row, and incalculable happiness for the boy who was housebound there.

"She's having a grand time." Fanny's voice. She laid a blanket over his chest.

Louis focused his eyes upon his wife. "Who am I as a writer but what Mr. Skelt made of me? He taught me how to tell stories."

"Stand back!" came a holler from the other room.

"Shall I send her home?"

"No, God no. Leave her alone. Let the child play."

CHAPTER 45

1885

Years later, when they looked back on their time in Bournemouth, Louis would scratch his head and wonder at the fruit of his efforts. "I was sick to death half the time, yet I never produced so many *words* in my life." Fanny would remember him sitting in bed, churning out *Kidnapped,* trying to write fast enough to capture the dialogue of his wild Scottish characters. "Hoot! Hoot!" he would shout from the bedroom, transmuting the story's wretched old uncle's disgust into a whoop of joy.

Later, she would understand that he was, in bursts, doing the writing that would solidify his reputation. Afterward she would recognize something else that they hadn't fully comprehended then: the subtle shiftings beneath their feet that shook their certainties about who they were. While she thought they were happily expanding into house and garden, Louis felt his life slowly shrinking.

Throughout those three years, there were the usual fluctuations in Louis's health, the strangle of bills, the pressure of deadlines, squabbles that rose out of nowhere. Not that they didn't savor the day-to-day pleasures. They knew how to squeeze every drop of joy from linnets trilling outside, or visits by friends, or the heroics of Bogue. When the dog caught rabbits that ate Fanny's lettuces, Louis would pour him a cup of beer. And when Bogue got into a set-to with another dog, a frequent occurrence, Fanny could see that the master, cursed by physical frailty, beamed with pride at the outsize confidence of his terrier.

During a bout of wellness in their second year at Skerryvore, Louis announced one day after opening the mail, "Cousins coming!"

"Bob and Katharine?"

"Yes. Henley's tagging along as well. And don't arch that eyebrow at me," he said when he glanced at Fanny. "He knows his fate if he so much as sneezes."

When the party arrived full of gay spirits late one afternoon, it seemed the din and stir of London rushed in the front door with them. Katharine always looked chic, despite her economic situation. Today she wore pointed shoes with flowers embroidered on the toes. Bob brought champagne and cheeses one could buy only in the city. They sat down, popped corks, and bathed Louis and Fanny in talk. Valentine lit candles around Skerryvore's drawing room, and it took on the feeling of a city salon.

Henley recited from memory a positive review that their London production of *Deacon Brodie* had garnered, then went into a lengthy analysis of why it had failed with audiences. After a while, Katharine turned the talk toward another subject. "Did you hear?" she said. "Thomas Hardy has built a country house in Dorchester and moved there with his dreadful little wife."

"Dorchester is, what, thirty-five kilometers from here?" Henley asked. "You ought to go over and meet him. George Meredith could set it up. He knows him. I loved *The Mayor of Casterbridge.*"

"I didn't," Bob said. "Makes me feel gloomy."

"Is that all it takes?" Louis jumped in. "I'll tell you what makes me gloomy these days. The state of the British Empire. We're headed for another war in Burma . . ."

Over dinner they celebrated the publication of Louis's *A Child's Garden of Verses* in March and his new collection of short stories in April—*The Dynamiter,* based on the tales Fanny had invented for him at Hyères.

"Were you pleased with the reviews?" Katharine asked.

"Well enough," Louis said.

Fanny felt a flush of anger. "I would have been more pleased had just one newspaper mentioned my name in a review."

"Your name is on the cover of the book next to mine, Fan," Louis said. "That's where it matters."

"Katharine, you're writing more stories, I'm told," Fanny said, changing the subject. She had helped Bob's sister in the past with a story. Katharine was a clever, cultivated woman but a weak writer, Fanny thought.

"Yes, William is nurturing my poor efforts along."

"I'm scheming for Katharine to become famous." Henley chortled.

"It does seem to be one of the ways a woman can earn money these days," Fanny mused.

"I've just begun a new story," Katharine said, sitting up on the edge of her chair, wide-eyed and nervous as a squirrel. "It's about a puzzling little chance encounter. A young man on a train meets a young woman, an attractive woman who has something mysterious about her, something captivating but very different from the girls he knows. She speaks as if she is from a foreign culture, and he quickly falls in love with her. It will turn out that the reason she seems so unusual is because—"

"She's a water nymph, a nixie!" Fanny interjected.

Katharine frowned. "No. No, I don't think so. I think he falls in love with her for her charming way of saying things, and then . . . he learns that she has escaped from a lunatic asylum."

Now Fanny frowned.

"William here believes he can get the story into print for me when I finish it." Katharine flashed a fond look at Henley, who attended to her like a devoted pup. It occurred to Fanny that Henley might be a little in love with Katharine.

After everyone else had gone to bed that night, Fanny poured glasses of wine for Louis and herself as they lingered in the kitchen, talking quietly.

"Do you remember the story Katharine sent me, asking to see if I could get it published in America?" Fanny whispered. "I had to rewrite the whole thing. Even *she* knew how bad it was, I think."

Louis shrugged. "She seems intent on making her way by writing, it appears."

"Why did she divorce her husband?"

"Terrible ass. Unfaithful, a liar. She must have known it before she married him; everyone else did. Thankfully, she got out of the marriage, but she hasn't much money."

"Your uncle Alan was mad, you told me once. Maybe that's where she got the lunatic concept for her new story."

"He had a breakdown when the children were small—never managed to fully come back from it. I was too young to notice." Louis gnawed on a fingernail. "Since Uncle Alan's death, my father has tried to look out for them, in his fashion. He, Alan, and Uncle David were partners in the family firm. Now David has retired, and his sons are the only offspring who have continued on in the business. The money end of it has been awkward. They reached an arrangement where my father will get a fairly significant share of the profits while he is alive. When he dies, my cousins—David's sons—will have the business exclusively. So my father has been giving money to Bob and Katharine, though not enough to live on, to be sure. It hasn't been the easiest situation for any of them."

"How does Katharine live?"

"She gets by somehow." Louis shook his head. "People seem to think *anybody* can publish what they write. It's a *craft,* for God's sake."

After Louis went upstairs, Fanny stood alone in the kitchen, anger rising inside her. His parting remark was clearly intended for her as well as Katharine. She wanted to shout at him, *But I'm a better writer than she is, I know I am.* It burned her up to see Henley fawning over Katharine, making her part of their tight little coterie. No one would admit it, but Fanny was outside the circle. What was she to them? A nurse. A housewife.

Fanny pushed the cork into the wine bottle and put it in the cabinet. Maybe, in reality, that's all she was. Some days it felt that way; there was so much hard labor in taking care of Louis and the household. She had been trying to write a story of her own for months, but every time she got a head of steam going, some duty waylaid her. She had gladly signed on to this life when she'd married him, but if Louis were well, she suspected there still would be little encouragement from him for her writing ambitions.

In her free moments at Skerryvore, she had scratched her creative itch by decorating the house and making a garden, thinking that having a house of her own would spell contentment at last. And it did, to a degree. But that kind of work ultimately didn't satisfy her deeper creative impulses, and it didn't fetch any glory in Louis's circle. Lately she had begun to wonder if the work she did fetched much respect from Louis.

When her mind went in this direction, she felt as if she might explode with frustration. One minute she was longing desperately for time to realize her own gifts, and the next minute she was chiding herself for egoism. *Damn vanity. I am my own worst enemy.*

Surely it was their situation that was causing this wretched frustration. Any woman who had ever taken care of a sickly husband over a long period of time no doubt felt the same emotions. Louis's own frustration at being a patient was understandable enough. Yet his frequent surliness at being nursed hurt her and fed the nugget of rage in her chest. Why, he didn't even seem to notice she was suffering. There were times when she wanted to scream, "Do you have any idea what I give up every day for you?"

As it turned out, a new friend was to enter their lives who made Fanny feel a part of a far finer connection than she ever could have had with Louis's old cronies. Henry James, who had accompanied his ailing sister for a ten-week stay in Bournemouth, appeared at their front door one summer day. Valentine mistook him for a tradesman—inexplicably, given the fact that he was well dressed—and sent him around back. The incident mortified Fanny, but James enjoyed a good laugh and came by the house nearly every evening after that.

He and Louis had become acquainted when James published an essay on the art of fiction in a literary magazine. James insisted a novel should convey a sense of reality so convincingly vivid that one couldn't help but say "Yes!" when reading it. He mentioned two books he had just read, a novel about a cosseted French girl's upbringing and eventual broken heart when she failed to marry; and *Treasure Island,* full of buried doubloons and hairbreadth escapes. The psychological portrayal in the French novel caused James to say "No!" repeatedly, while he called Louis's adventure story a delightful success, though he added that he could not gauge whether it competed with real life: "I have been a child, but I have never been on a quest for buried treasure."

A couple of months later, in an essay for the same literary magazine, Louis delivered a playful thwack to James. *If he has never been on a quest for buried treasure, it can be demonstrated that he has never been a child,* he wrote. *There never was a child (unless Master James) but has hunted gold and been a pirate, and a military commander, and a bandit in the mountains; but has fought and suffered shipwreck and prison.*

Soon enough they were in correspondence, each perfectly gleeful to find another writer who pondered as deeply as he the art of fiction writing. Fanny thought nobody else came close to those two minds in exploring the subject. Now that the actual person of Henry James was in

Bournemouth, he had his own chair by the fire at Skerryvore, and the two men spent hours talking about their work. Fanny reveled in his calls, often sitting in on their conversations.

At first she'd been intimidated by James's regal bearing, the balding intellectual head, the serious eyes, and an expression on his full lips that she took to be condescending. But he quickly showed himself to be a kind man and still an American, despite his many years in Europe. Perhaps it was for Fanny's amusement that he slid into slang quite easily, saying "Well, hang me" when he couldn't think of a word, or calling faces "mugs," or claiming he'd been "bamboozled." Soon he and Fanny were sharing their perceptions about being outsiders, though Henry was not treated as such among the European social and literary sets. They discovered commonalities—they'd both been living in Paris in 1876, and Henry knew Montmartre as well as she.

Fanny took pleasure in pampering Henry James. He loved American foods; corn on the cob dripping with butter was his favorite. The fact that it came straight out of her garden struck him as a miracle. Veal loaf with mashed potatoes brought the man close to tears. "A working fellow needs proper belly timber," Fanny assured him when he accepted second servings.

He often arrived with a gift for her—a jar of chestnut puree or a box of pretty stationery—and once he came with a beautiful Venetian mirror to decorate the dining room wall. She loved how he interrupted a high conceptual thread of talk to gossip about a society woman at whose country house he had recently dined. Henry was different from Louis's other friends in many ways. For one thing, he understood a woman's mind so much better, as was evident in everything he wrote. But there was another difference: He'd not had a friendship with Louis before his marriage to Fanny.

"He doesn't long for the 'old' you," she told Louis one evening after James had left. "It's such a relief."

"I think you're sweet on him," Louis teased. "Ever since you wrote him a note and he called it clever."

Well, maybe she had swooned. How extraordinary it was for a girl who had attended the Third Ward public school in a bumptious upstart town like Indianapolis to be discussing ideas—in front of her own hearth—with the worldly author known for making hay out of American expatriates in Europe. Henry James's sensibilities were broad enough to allow that a woman like her might offer up wisdom of a different shade from what he heard in the company of barons and princesses. Fanny felt enlarged by his attentiveness. Was he listening so carefully because he would eventually turn her into one of his "American abroad" characters? She had read all of his books, and she had lived long enough with a novelist to know how friends' speech and mannerisms found their way into Louis's writing.

Once, after she'd regaled Henry with a story about her days in Nevada mine country, he'd said, "I haven't heard the word *shucks* for a good while."

"Are you taking notes for an upcoming novel?" Fanny rejoined. "*The Hoosiers,* perhaps?"

Henry merely grinned.

If that happened, it was a fair enough trade, for Henry James was the most splendid company, and every one of his visits had a tonic effect on Louis. The adorable, balding bachelor with the wickedly funny tongue brightened the house every time he entered it. The hours they spent with him were a reprieve in that time of struggle. For struggle there was.

MONEY TROUBLES LOOMED large and were uncomfortably interwoven with her family. Louis had taken on the expenses of Sammy's education, though. Fanny knew Sam Osbourne told people he supported his son over in Europe. The truth pained her: He had sent five dollars once to Sammy, and then, about two months ago, four dollars so the boy could have his photograph taken and sent back to his father. That was all.

Recently, he had sent to Louis an old unpaid bill for Fanny's flat in Paris. The bill reminded her vividly of her ex-husband's mean streak.

Louis had been magnanimous in paying for Sammy's private schooling, as well as the taxes on the Oakland house, which Sam conceded to her in the divorce. It was not these expenses that set Louis's teeth on edge; he took them on gladly and never spoke of them. It was the rare letters from Belle and Joe Strong to Louis, bragging of their important new lives now that Joe was set up in Honolulu as a painter, and then in the next paragraph asking for—demanding—money.

"What infuriates me," Louis seethed in a rare moment of complaining, "is that they insult me as they beg!" Standing in the foyer after retrieving the mail, he held the latest letter in his hand. "I am the cause of the Osbourne family breakup. And therefore, I must pay my dues. Belle is collecting on the damages."

"I don't know what's happened to Belle; I don't recognize her anymore," Fanny said. "Can't she see? Every coin we send her has first been minted in your brain. There she is, living in Hawaii, socializing with the royal set, while Joe drinks himself to death." The more Fanny talked about it, the angrier she got. "She writes more often to Dora Williams than she does to me. She cares not one bit for how I am or how you are. But mark my words: One of these days we will find ourselves strapped with supporting them."

The whole matter was thrown into a new light when a letter arrived from Belle describing news she had received from Paulie, Sam's new wife. Fanny read it aloud to Louis during lunch:

" 'I write with a heart broken. Paulie sent a letter saying Papa has gone missing. It has been a month now without a word from him, and his friends believe, as I do, that he is undoubtedly dead. He left one morning for work, asking that Paulie have a late supper for him, and he never returned.' "

Louis looked up from his soup. "Didn't he go missing once before?"

"Yes." Memories rushed at her. She could feel the desert dust in her nostrils. "We were living in Virginia City. He joined a party of men headed to Montana to work a new mine. It was his last fling at getting rich quick, he said. But months passed and no word came. He didn't come back and didn't come back. One day I looked outside the little cabin where we lived and saw wagons stuffed full of dressers and pans and children. All these people were clanging out of town, headed for San Francisco. I was barely getting by with my little sewing business. A friend of ours offered to help me get to the city, so I threw our few things into a couple of trunks, spread word around town where I would be if Sam came back, and got on a stagecoach with Belle."

Sitting across from Louis, she could picture vividly the dirty, run-down neighborhood she'd moved to in San Francisco. "We lived in a cheap boardinghouse. I went around to shops, looking for work. I took with me the pretty little smocked dresses I'd made for Belle as proof of my skill. Somehow I passed myself off as a French seamstress and got a job."

Louis looked stunned. "But you hardly speak a word of the language!"

Fanny shook her head at the memory. "I didn't talk. Mostly gestured, as I recall. We were near destitute, but I got Belle enrolled in a real school." A pang of sorrow passed through her when she remembered the lonely little apartment. "After a few weeks in San Francisco, word came to me that the men had all been massacred by Indians." She swallowed hard, remembering the agony of those days. "I was twenty-six years old and suddenly a widow. I worked long hours in a dress shop, sewing, and at night I took in fancy work for extra pay. My fingers stung from pinpricks. Some days I felt as if I were clinging to the side of a cliff, and the only thing keeping me from falling off were my wretched, worn-out fingertips."

Louis reached across the table and squeezed her hand. "You never told me all the details."

"I didn't want to sully our relationship with more talk about Sam. I figured you'd heard about enough."

"And, of course, he came back."

"Yup." Fanny snickered. "Walked into the boardinghouse one day with open arms. Told me that he and a friend had lagged behind the party of prospectors the day they were ambushed. 'Miraculously,' they escaped with their lives. He'd been in Montana for a year and a half."

"I remember that part," Louis said. He fell silent for a minute. "Do you believe he's dead this time?"

"He might be," she said thoughtfully. "It's possible he committed suicide. He was given to melancholy." She ran her hand over her mouth and breathed deep. "It will crush the children. Especially Belle."

"Are you going to tell Sammy?"

"Not yet. I'm going to write to a couple of friends to see what they know."

When she heard from Dora Williams a month later, Fanny realized she might never learn what happened to Sam Osbourne. A pile of clothes had been found on the beach; they were thought to be his. But a rumor of a sighting in South Africa was afloat as well. It was just as likely Sam had decided to cut and run once again. Fanny wondered if he was with some new young woman, far away from California.

When she finally revealed to Sammy that his father was missing and thought to be dead, the boy turned his head slightly to the side and looked at her through squinting eyes, as if he disbelieved her. He went out of the house for several hours. When he came back, his face was swollen from crying. He allowed Fanny to put her arms around him. He stepped back, then, and composed himself. "I want to change my name to my middle one," he said. "From now on, call me Lloyd."

CHAPTER 46

"No! Noooo!"

Fanny leaped up, her heart in her windpipe. Louis was flailing about in the twisted bedcovers. She pulled back the sheet and looked all around his face and pillow but saw no blood. Fanny shook his shoulder. "Louis, wake up!"

His eyes, open now, darted around the room.

"You're having a nightmare," she said, running her palm across his forehead to soothe him.

"Damm it! Why did you wake me? I was dreaming a fine bogey tale."

"You were yelling—"

"Get my board!"

Fanny padded over to the corner of the room where a rectangle of wood leaned against the wall.

"Hurry! Pen and paper. Now!"

She tiptoed out of the room and went to the extra bedroom. In the hallway, the clock showed 2:10 A.M. When she woke again around seven, she put her ear to the keyhole and listened for him but heard nothing. Carefully, she cracked open the door. Louis was sitting upright, his pen scratching furiously across paper.

In the kitchen, only Valentine's rump was visible. She was cleaning the oven.

"Quick," Fanny said, panting from her race downstairs. "Make coffee and toast on a tray." When she hustled upstairs with the food, he gave no sign that he saw or heard her. He wore his wine-colored poncho over his shoulders; his head was bent in concentration, a dark forelock drooping over his brow. She set the tray on a chair next to the bed and left.

The previous week, Louis had had a hemorrhage. "He's not to have any excitement," the doctor had said after examining him. "No guests. No speaking. Give him the morphine to keep him sedated for a few days." Now she remembered the usual addendum: "No movement of the arm." She knew better than to interrupt Louis. Once he had said to her, "A story should read like a dream you don't want to wake from." Right now he was writing about a dream, and he was in a dreamlike trance as he did it.

FOR THREE DAYS, the air in the house was charged, as if a fierce thunderstorm were roaring upstairs. Fanny, or sometimes Valentine, crept into the bedroom to leave food for him. Once, when Fanny brought in a new supply of ruled foolscap and ink, she noticed he was writing with his pen between his third and fourth fingers, the forefinger obviously gone numb. The finished pages of his story lay on the floor, punctured through by the steel nib of his pen as he furiously raced to record his thoughts.

She stayed away except when he needed something, sleeping in another room rather than risking a break in his fierce concentration.

On the third day, when Fanny brought him lunch, he spoke. "Sam—" Louis started, then corrected himself. "Lloyd is home?"

"Yes," she said brightly, "for the weekend. Do you want to see him?"

"Not now. But tell him I will read tonight."

When he came downstairs that evening, Louis looked feverish. He shook his red right hand all about, trying to relieve scrivener's cramp. She fetched some paper for Sam and herself to write down their responses, as was their custom.

Louis arranged himself in his favorite chair. He loved reading his work aloud. It was a self-indulgence, poorly disguised. He used Fanny's criticism and edits when he thought them right, though she could just as well have read his manuscripts. But he loved to feel his tongue shape the sounds of the words he'd written on paper. He loved to hear a voice out loud—Long John Silver's, for example—after having heard it only in his head. Reading was his reward after any day's work, and he savored the attention of his little troupe of true believers. It was with plot that Fanny's attentiveness helped. She would pepper him with questions: *How exactly did the chest get there?* Or *How would the others know?*

Louis began.

"'Henry Jekyll was a respected chemist in London town,'" he read, "'a tall, handsome man of fifty whose large, firm, white hands spoke of his profession in shape and size. At the moment, he was engaged in measuring out some white salts into a graduate containing a bright red liquid.'"

As the story continued, Fanny and Lloyd learned that Dr. Henry Jekyll was a spiritually bankrupt man who was frustrated that he could not indulge certain urges because of his standing in the community. He began experimenting with powders and eventually came upon a chemical formula that, when drunk, allowed him to assume the disguise of another person entirely, an ugly, primitive-looking, uncivilized man with hairy hands, an evil man named Edward Hyde.

It was as suspenseful as any story Louis had ever written, Fanny thought, but there was a strong aroma of sexual misconduct about Hyde's nocturnal adventures. Louis described Jekyll's struggle as a "war in the members" and a "spirit versus the flesh" problem. The sexual innuendo bothered her, but she knew Louis would dismiss her squeamishness as worthy of the worst prude.

There was something more deeply amiss in the story, though. Louis had made Dr. Jekyll a thoroughly bad man whose only purpose in transforming himself into Hyde was to benefit from the disguise it provided him. She wrote in her notes: *Shouldn't Jekyll be both good and bad, as all people are?* The understanding hit her like a bolt, and she did not know whether to tell him the truth. Louis needed to be propped up just now, but to lie to him, to mask her true feelings would bring down his wrath later. He called her his "critic on the hearth." He counted on her. She wrote her feelings as best she could.

Sitting on the window seat in the drawing room, Louis read while Fanny continued taking furious notes. Lloyd had started to but put down his pencil and stared ahead with a horrifed look as the plot thickened. Louis read straight through for nearly two hours. At the end, Lloyd was clapping wildly. "How on earth did you do that in three days?"

Louis gloated for only a moment before turning to his wife. It was obvious he could tell from her reticence that Fanny was disturbed.

"All right," he said, extending his hand for her written notes.

"I'm going to just say it, Louis."

"Yes, yes."

"I don't think you should specify the vice."

Louis waved a hand dismissively. "Thank you, Mrs. Grundy."

"You've missed the point," she persisted. "Dr. Jekyll should not be such a bad fellow; he should be someone who is a mix of qualities. You've said it yourself time and again, that good and evil both reside in every man and woman. That's why this story should be an allegory, not another bogey tale. You've written it as only one man's horror story. Furthermore, the potion doesn't ring true."

Louis looked baffled by her challenge. "The potion was in the *dream*. A dream doesn't lie," he said indignantly. "And of course it's an allegory, but it must be subtle."

"It is too subtle, Louis. You need to make Jekyll's weaknesses less defined, so that anyone can see himself in the story and feel uneasy. If you strengthen the allegory and make the vice more abstract, it can be a masterpiece."

He snatched up his papers from the hassock in front of him. "What do you know?" he shouted at her. "You don't own my mind!"

Fanny's face flushed hot as she watched him stand up and let his fist fly into the wall, then storm out of the room and up the stairs.

Valentine peeked around the doorway, wide-eyed.

"We mustn't speak to him at all now," Fanny told her. "Not a word."

FANNY TIPTOED INTO the bedroom around eleven to see if she might make amends and share the bed for the night. Louis was awake and appeared to be thinking. She could not read his expression in profile, though, and he did not speak. When he became aware she was in the room, he pointed a long bony finger at the fireplace. She misunderstood at first and prepared to add coals to the fire. But when she saw the scraps of burnt-edged paper with a few letters remaining in Louis's hand, the horror of the situation fell upon her.

"Why? Why did you burn it?" Her eyes filled with tears. "To punish me?"

He looked away.

She went back downstairs and sat by the fire in the dining room. The flames threw flickering light on the muskets and pistols on the walls. Well, it was done; he'd burned it. *Be honest, Fanny,* she mused. *You wanted to burn it yourself.*

Everyone looked at Louis and thought of the boyish fellow who wrote *Treasure Island.* The story he had read to her tonight touched on something she had refused to explore before. How perfectly named his evil character was—Hyde. What dark longings did Louis hide? Jekyll's compulsions in the story sounded sexual. The reader couldn't help but think of whoremongering, though Louis hadn't included any significant women characters.

The story left her deeply uneasy. It made her wonder if she really knew her husband. Over the years, she'd noticed that Louis had many friends who were homosexuals. She thought of Symonds in Davos, who was Louis's closest friend during their stay. If ever there were a man living a double life, it was he. He was married and a father of four daughters, but he kept male lovers on the side, and everyone knew it. "He publishes his own dirty little books," a woman in Davos had told her, "then he gives them out to his 'special' friends."

Fanny felt perplexed. *Lord knows, Louis doesn't condemn the disposition.* Neither did she. But it occurred to her that men fell in love with Louis the way women did. Gosse, Colvin, Henley. Even Henry James seemed smitten.

It was not something she wanted to think about. But she had made the mistake of averting her eyes from Sam Osbourne's dalliances, so she forced herself to contemplate the possibilities. When she first met Louis, she found some of his mannerisms woman-like—the way he moved his hands when he talked; his sensitive mouth; the private humor he seemed to share with his men friends that could spin out into high hilarity and leave her puzzled; more than anything, the way he showed his emotions so openly. He would fall upon the ground in tears and then be up the next moment, giggling out of control. She'd dismissed all that as part of his high-strung personality, especially since, from the beginning, he'd shown himself to be a hungry man in bed. When he was well, his appetite for her was voracious. And when he was ill? Of his earthly pleasures, lust seemed to be the thing he let go of last.

Early on in their relationship, Louis had confessed to visiting prostitutes when he was a young man. Wouldn't he have pursued men back then if that was his inclination?

No, she was certain her marriage was not a false front. Still, she wondered: *What unnameable impulses* does *Louis harbor?*

She knew what he would say about *her* Hyde. That inside the kind, loving girl from Indiana resided the Greek Furies themselves, who came out, ever so occasionally, seeking blood and vengeance. He referred to her as the Angry One. She couldn't deny it.

Louis, she realized, was one of the few people who had not disappointed her. Once she had thought him the closest to Jesus Christ of anyone she'd ever met; she knew now that he wasn't so perfect. He was vain, vulnerable to flattery. Henley teased him that he couldn't pass a mirror without looking at his reflection.

Louis was incapable of conscious cruelty, but he did have a temper. Few people knew how enraged he could become. She would never forget the scene in Paris when he overheard a Frenchman insulting the British. Fanny could still see the blur of Louis's velvet jacket as he leaped up and demanded the man retract his remarks. When the fellow stood to call his bluff, Louis slapped him across the face.

That is the man I married. Louis hated for anyone to be treated unfairly, including himself. Sometimes he overreacted. As for shadowy longings, if he had a desire for some other kind of life, it was hidden even from himself.

The longer she tried to understand it, the more she saw the subject as an enigma. She put out the fire in the dining room, collected a quilt, and, listening to the coo of doves in the chimney, fell asleep in a chair.

CHAPTER 47

L ouis awoke early. No new dream. But the old one wouldn't go away. It chilled him to remember it.

He could see them quite clearly. Two gentlemen pass through a wooden door and enter a damp courtyard. They know a man who lives in the house that faces the open court. When they glance up, they see a vexed-looking man who sits by a half-open window on the second floor. "Dr. Jekyll!" one of the men calls out to the fellow. "Do come down and have a walk with us. You could use the fresh air. You don't look so well." The man won't come down. And then a terrifying expression overtakes the doctor's face. He closes the window and moves away from it, but in that moment, both of the men on the ground understand they have glimpsed something—a transformation, inutterably horrifying.

The second part of the dream was vivid. A small man runs through the streets. His pants drag. His clothes are too big for him. He has a hideous, somehow malformed face and corded, hairy hands. A policeman chases after him, shouting, "Stop!" The man disappears into an old doorway off the street. Runs through a courtyard and up some stairs, past a surgical theater, and into a doctor's laboratory. He is frantic. He pours white salts from a glass saucer into a beaker half full of red liquid. He drinks it and his face appears to melt, change hue, then reshape itself with different features. His body grows large, into a different man's body. He is transformed. He is a whole and respectable figure. At the door, the policeman is pounding . . .

Louis scoured his brain for a few more scrapings of the dream. Nothing. The Brownies had left just those bits: the agonized Dr. Jekyll at the window, and later, the hideous Edward Hyde taking the potion.

The evening before, Louis had come up to the bedroom, itching to pound more walls, but his fist was aflame from the first punch. Instead, he fell into the bed to stew over his wife's remarks.

How galling that Fanny considered herself his ultimate critic. Thomas Stevenson was partly to blame for that. Long ago, he had said to Louis, "You really shouldn't publish anything that Fanny has not approved first." She had taken that endorsement far too seriously. Louis blamed himself, too, for he'd brought her along, invited her to collaborate on story collections and playwriting with him and Henley. Recently, Henley had said, "I can only collaborate with one Stevenson at a time."

Long ago, before he met Fanny, he had made up his mind that marrying another writer would be a mistake. A family could tolerate only one. Well, Fanny had been an aspiring writer before he knew her. Any qualms Louis might have felt about a life with her had inevitably passed. Their time together had become one long conversation—contentious sometimes, yes—yet she had opened his mind in many ways. And Fanny's mind was keen; she had a wonderful way of seeing things that was all hers. Sometimes her thoughts were so original that they took Louis aback. But she was more intuitive about human nature than skilled in literary nuance. He wanted to say to her, *I love you, I owe my life to you. But my writing comes first, even before you. Because I* am *my writing. And when you meddle in my work, you muck with my soul.*

Louis looked at the pile of paper on his lap. Earlier, he had felt so exhausted that he could not even contemplate rereading the story for errors. He had hoped to sleep tonight and read the next day with a fresh brain. There were at least thirty thousand words there.

Before he laid his head down, it hit him. *Goddammit, she's right.* As it stood, the Jekyll and Hyde story was merely a penny dreadful horror. The tale *should* be written as a stronger allegory. It held within it a germ of truth about the "other" in every man, a truth so powerful it could make any reader of the story flinch with recognition of his own weaker self.

After he had tossed the manuscript into the fireplace, he tried to sleep, but the new story would not let him rest. Louis sat up, mapping out the direction of the next version on his board. As soon as his note taking ended, his pen was writing a new version of the story. Ideas, whole paragraphs sparked around his brain; he abbreviated words to capture them on paper before another bolt hit him.

NEXT TO THE bed, a tray with food and medicine appeared. Someone, Fanny or Valentine or maybe even Lloyd, had delivered it during the day, and now Louis fell upon it with gusto. He kept his pen moving as he ate, noting down, *a horror that is knit to him closer than a wife, closer than an eye;* and *man is not truly one, but truly two.*

After a while, the food in his belly—or perhaps the morphine—made him dog-tired, and he fell asleep sitting up with his tray on his lap. When he awoke, it was black outside and raining. The house was silent. He picked up his pen, put it between his third and fourth fingers to alleviate the pain in his hand, and continued writing. The words did not stop. Morning came. Eggs on a plate arrived, warm and fragrant. He nodded to Fanny as she set the tray on his bedside table, but shook his head to signal no conversation. She had buttered a roll for him. He dipped it in the dish of jam with his left hand and ate it like a starving man while his right hand rushed across the paper.

He tried to imagine how it would feel to have one's body begin to change of its own volition. He remembered what it was like as a boy to emerge from a nightmare brought on by fever, seeing the clothes he had hung on a door hook take on ghastly shapes like the fearsome bodies of monsters. Jekyll must see himself in the mirror that way—ghoulishly transformed. Louis reflected on how his own body could turn upon him; in the space of a few minutes, he could become a sick, pathetic thing utterly unlike his well self.

The sun came into the window, patterned the room, went away. The night passed as the previous one had and the next one would, with Louis upright in bed, his hand cramped with pain as he wrote and wrote. In the late afternoon of the next day, he let his arm fall next to the bed; the pen slipped out of his hand.

He had been writing straight, with almost no breaks, for six days: three days on the first draft, three days on the second, for a total of over sixty thousand words.

When Fanny entered the room with another tray of food, she

found her husband standing at his mirror, touching his cheeks with both hands.

"What is it?" she asked him.

"I was so *emairsed*," he said, "I half-expected to see Hyde's face."

She eyed him cautiously, then saw the fat stack of pages he'd written. He rubbed his eyes. "I will read tonight," he said.

CHAPTER 48

The fame Louis had dreamed of as a young man did not strike him like lightning. Instead, fame arrived as a small swell that pushed itself up slowly into a proper wave until it had overtaken him. Even when *The Strange Case of Dr. Jekyll and Mr. Hyde* was published at Christmas, the story was received at first as one more holiday shocker. Not until January did the surge of enthusiasm begin, thanks to a review in *The Times* of London.

"Listen to this!" Fanny shouted one drizzly morning as she raced to Louis's bed with the newspaper. "'Nothing Mr. Stevenson has written as yet,'" she read excitedly, "'has so strongly impressed us with the versatility of his *very original genius* as this sparsely printed little shilling volume.'" She let out a whoop.

"Let me see," he said, gleefully taking the paper.

"Read out loud the sentence that begins . . . there." She pointed to the second paragraph.

"'Naturally, we compare it with the somber masterpieces of Poe,'" Louis read, "'and we may say at once that Mr. Stevenson has gone far deeper.'" He grinned, then let out a delighted chortle.

Throughout the day, Fanny found herself breaking into laughter. *At last,* she thought. *At last.*

By February, preachers were referring to *Dr. Jekyll and Mr. Hyde* from their pulpits. Newspaper critics saw encoded messages in the story about any number of topics, from hypocritical moral attitudes in British society, to Darwin's theories about the essential animal nature of man, to the tyranny of colonial powers, to buggery, to the horrors of drug and alcohol addiction. A stage adaptation was already in the works in America. Letters of praise poured into Skerryvore. Symonds wrote from Davos to say Louis had written something classic, something better than Balzac's *La Peau de Chagrin* or anything Poe had written. But he admitted that the story had so disturbed him, he doubted he could read it again; he wondered, in fact, if any writer should be poking around in such painful territory.

All the attention delighted Louis. But it was the awestruck comments about his writing style that lifted him most. Critics pronounced his dialogue worthy of Shakespeare. They praised the lapidary precision of his sentences, declaring that every phrase sounded like poetry. Henry James wrote that the story was a masterpiece of concision and eerily haunting because there were no women characters to speak of, though they surely must have been influential in the making of the story.

"Thank you, Henry," Fanny said aloud upon reading his essay.

BUOYED, LOUIS WENT back to work with a fury. He was not well at all and, more than ever, tethered to the pathetic four-by-six-foot real estate of his bed. The pretense that he was anything but an invalid was hard to support.

When Fanny wrote out the letters to his friends that he dictated, the words he used to describe himself dented her heart. He spoke of his body as his dungeon; he talked of himself as a spectral phantom, an abhorrent miscarriage, a paralytic ape, the wretched houseplant of Skerryvore. The cough was the most constant reminder of his ill health, but it rarely visited him by itself; it brought chills, insomnia, and rheumatism. Too often there was a doctor in the house and some new or old drug left at his bedside. He rallied when friends came to visit, then paid the price afterward, taking weeks to recover.

Only Henry James's visits seemed to have a positive effect. "He's enthusiastic for whatever I pursue," Louis said. "He never criticizes when I try to stretch and try something new."

"Henry likes new challenges himself," Fanny said. "And he trusts your talent." Louis would not merely add another horror story to the canon; he would write a horror story with such subtlety and depth that it would take the genre to a new height. That was how much Henry believed in Louis's gifts.

Once when Henry came to visit, Louis's parents were there as well. After witnessing the mother and father demand his every moment, Henry pulled Fanny aside. "I am simply boiling," he said. "They sit on him. Can't they see how they drain him?"

"*And* bring influenza to him." Fanny sighed. "No, they don't see. Most people don't see it. His mother sailed out of here saying, 'I expect you will spend the summer with us in Scotland.' Why doesn't she just shoot him?"

In September, Henry came down from London for a weekend visit. He settled into his usual chair beside Louis to talk about writing. Fanny slipped in and out of the drawing room, bringing a knee blanket for Louis, and later a shawl, but resisting the temptation to take a seat with them. It was a struggle, for she loved to be a part of the talk about books and ideas. Instead, she went into the dining room, where she could catch their words.

"I am haunted still by *Dr. Jekyll,*" Henry was saying.

"Came straight from the underworld, my friend."

"One finds strange objects floating around in that murky tank."

"I never know how much of my dreams have been seeded by real life," Louis said.

"How is that?"

"I've been thinking about duality and the double brain for a long time, so I may have suggested to myself the Jekyll and Hyde double-personality idea."

"Show me the ordinary man who does not carry around some other person inside, or at least some question about who he truly is," Henry said.

"What interests me is the borderland—"

"—where selves collide."

"You are mining the same territory, Henry. I can't tell you anything you don't know."

"Identity is the great topic, is it not?"

"For the novelist, yes. It's the province of the well, though. A chronic invalid has but one thought about his identity: He doesn't want to be a sick man. The rest of the discussion seems quite frivolous to him— an immense privilege of the healthy. Still, I'm a novelist, and so I pursue it."

The men were circling back to their old topic of romance versus realism.

"A novel must compete with life," Henry said with slyness, as if baiting Louis into a familiar argument.

"Ah, there is where we differ, my friend," Louis said. "I don't object to literary realism per se. But I can't bear Zola's sordid view of the world. He rubs the nose of the reader in ugliness. It's gratuitous." Fanny could picture Louis in the next room, shivering reflexively at the thought. "Anyway, I have rather recently escaped the clutches of Calvinism. I have no interest in joining the new religion of Pessimism. Ah, well. No doubt his admirers find me quite out of touch with real life. It's why Zola is regarded as a serious writer and why my books are found on the children's shelves at the bookshop."

"*Dr. Jekyll* has changed all that," Henry said.

"Obviously, I am not afraid to write about cruelty or violence," Louis said. "But for a writer to feed the reader great dank heaps of ugliness in the name of realism is dispiriting. And to foist such stuff on young minds? It's evil. Writers should find out where joy resides and give it a voice. Every bright word or picture is a piece of pleasure set afloat. The reader catches it, and he goes on his way rejoicing. It's the business of art to send him that way as often as possible. I have to believe that every heart that has beat strongly and cheerfully has left a hopeful impulse behind it in the world. If I cannot believe that, then why should I go on? Why should anyone go on?"

CHAPTER 49

John Singer Sargent was riffling through Fanny's wardrobe. The painter pulled out a gold-threaded white sari she had bought on a whim in London. "Do you mind?" he asked, holding it up to the light from the window.

When she appeared in the sari, Sargent seated her in a chair against a wall. "The shoes, Mrs. Stevenson. I wonder if you might . . ."

"Am I to understand that you want me barefoot?"

"Now, Fan, you know perfectly well you go around here in bare feet," Louis chimed in from the other side of the bedroom, where he was brushing off his velvet jacket.

"And the shawl," the artist said thoughtfully. He lifted the shimmering fabric off her shoulders, examined her without it, then draped it over her head so it partly concealed her face.

She had worked as a painter long enough to know what effect he was after for the portrait of Fanny with her famous husband: Sargent wanted to present her as truly exotic. If she hadn't been party to draping models herself, she might have refused to pose. It wasn't that she was afraid to cooperate with another artist's vision of "an artistic couple," as he phrased it. But she suspected that, sweet as he was, she could not entirely trust him.

Earlier, Sargent had done a portrait of Louis, and the end result was strange indeed. Louis looked like a weird, bony, girlishly pretty aesthete. Fanny had tossed the finished painting into the garbage bin after Sargent left. The artist hadn't liked the first painting, either, and was back to try again. The young man was a good friend of Will Low, and these sittings were a favor to Sargent in the wake of a scandal that had erupted the previous year at the Paris salon. He had painted a portrait of a socialite in a revealing black dress, with one tiny strap falling suggestively off her white shoulder. The picture's overt sensuality caused a furor at the exhibition and sent the painter scurrying to London, where he was now living and trying to rescue his reputation as a portraitist by painting his friends and acquaintances. It would not help Fanny's reputation among Louis's circle if she appeared uncooperative or haughty. Still, she couldn't dispel the creeping feeling she was about to be roasted and served up by John Singer Sargent.

Louis was more sanguine about the intrusion into their lives. He was feeling better, and the presence of the visitor summoned a burst of energy in him. To fend off boredom, he employed Adelaide Boodle to read aloud from *Adventures of Huckleberry Finn,* which Louis had just finished reading a couple of nights earlier, already reread, and was ravenous to read again.

"A novel?" Sargent asked glumly.

"Ah, he's brilliant!" Louis said. "You'll love the story." Fanny could tell the artist detested the distraction. Soon Adelaide's high-pitched English accent was wrapping itself around Huck's American backwoods conversations, full of *hain't*s and *reckon*s and *looky here*s.

Now Sargent was arranging her husband in the foreground. Louis managed to stand still for a while, though she knew he couldn't sustain it. In no time, he was pacing back and forth in his usual manner, one hand stroking his mustache as Adelaide read, the other hand fluttering in and out of his pocket, while the artist's brush darted like a hummingbird between his canvas and paints.

After the first sitting, Louis and Fanny looked at the canvas of their dual portrait. Only Louis had been sketched in so far, but the lines already captured his fitful bursts of motion.

"I believe he has done a good job on my hand," Louis said. "It appears to be moving even now."

"It expresses the whole man," Fanny said.

Three days later, when Fanny viewed the nearly finished painting, her enthusiasm vanished. Sargent had captured Louis's youthful face, his intense brown eyes, his preoccupied brilliance. On canvas as in real life, Louis exuded intellectual energy. The image of herself, however, deeply disturbed her. He had cast her as a sort of harem woman with painted rings on her toes and black lines around her eyes. It looked nothing like her. More disturbing was how insignificant she was in the painting compared to Louis. She was cut in half, pushed off the side of the canvas.

"I like it, though it is damned queer," Louis said staring at the canvas after Sargent had departed. "I look like a madman—a caged maniac pacing about—"

"—while I sit at the edge looking colorful. An urn might have served just as well. Where on earth will it hang?"

"In one wealthy woman's parlor behind a potted fern," he said. "No one will see it."

As it turned out, Sargent decided to give it to them. "I can't stand it," she told Louis when he hung it on the sitting room wall, "but at least it won't be exhibited in some gallery."

"Oh, come now," he said, "it's quite interesting. Let's live with it for a while."

The painting annoyed Fanny whenever it caught her eye. No one else would notice, but never had it been so obvious that she was being set out on the periphery.

It was not the first time. People befriended them because of Louis. She understood; he was so lovable. But she had grown weary of letters written only to him, after all the effort she had invested in his friends. She received the occasional letter from Colvin or Symonds and sometimes a chafing one from Henley criticizing her for some perceived misdeed—masked, of course, as friendly joking. To Louis's old crowd, she would always be an interloper.

The exceptions were Sidney Colvin and Fanny Sitwell. When they came to visit in the summer, Fanny poured out her soul to the woman she had least expected to become a confidante. And yet Fanny Sitwell was just that.

While Colvin sat with Louis in the garden, the two women headed to town for a walk. Around Fanny's neck hung a pair of field glasses for bird viewing. They walked down the chine through a stand of pines where the smell of resin filled the air.

"Louis's spirits seem good," Fanny Sitwell remarked as they gingerly descended a rustic stairway.

"You always put the best face on things, my friend. His health is just plain bad."

"I'm so sorry for both of you. You must be exhausted."

Fanny shrugged. "I have always taken care of other people. I suppose I am used to being tired. That's not what frustrates me most."

Fanny Sitwell's eyebrows rose quizzically.

"I am a cipher under a shadow," Fanny said.

"Oh."

"Don't misunderstand me," Fanny said. "I haven't any interest in despising men. I happen to like them, especially educated men. That's why it has come as a surprise to find such offensive attitudes among my husband's friends. Louis can't see it. He thinks I imagine it."

If Fanny Sitwell was surprised by the outburst, she didn't show it. She said, "We were raised to be selfless."

"If I seek to make a mark of my own, am I not a woman, then? Am I a monster for wanting something more? I've always found ways to move around the rules men make, but I am worn down by it in England. I'll never fit the British standard of womanhood. And I don't want to."

She searched her friend's face for signs she'd just insulted the one female companion she had.

"You know how I feel about all this," Fanny Sitwell said. "You simply have to move forward despite all the notions about how we are *supposed* to be."

"Heaven knows you have made a life for yourself . . ."

"I didn't have a job when I first met Louis. It would have been unacceptable for a vicar's wife to be out in the workplace. But when my first son died . . . After the fog, a clarity arrives. I knew I would separate from my husband, and I had to find work to survive. The secretarial job at the women's college came some months later, through friends. It freed me."

They sat down on a bench. She took Fanny Sitwell's hand in her own. "You are a boon to me. What would I do without you? Some days I feel like such an oddity in this place."

CHAPTER 50

⁓

Fanny watched the bowl of mashed potatoes go around the table. It was a wilting July evening in Bournemouth, and a new flock of guests was at her dinner table. Before Henley and his wife, Anna, arrived along with Bob Stevenson and Katharine de Mattos, Fanny had stood in the steaming kitchen beside Valentine, overseeing the miserable meal preparation. The girl was prone to mistakes when she was out of sorts. She spewed incomprehensible French curses into a boiling pot while Fanny sliced tomatoes and wondered aloud what had possessed her to choose lamb and potatoes for a hellishly hot evening.

"I sent it everywhere," Henley was saying as he scooped a fat spoonful of potatoes onto his plate. "The magazine market at the moment appears to be glutted."

"William is being polite," Katharine said with self-deprecating good humor. She was cool-looking in a fashionable linen dress, except for the beads of sweat across her upper lip. "Let's be honest among friends. Mr. Henley has had little success with my story because it is my story."

"When I read your manuscript, I kept thinking that it was too realistic," Fanny said. "Do you remember my idea of the sprite? Why don't you try it that way, instead of portraying the mysterious woman on the train as an escapee from a mental ward?"

Katharine's knife paused midcut. "No, I don't think so. It's not the sort of story I write."

"Then let me try my hand at it," Fanny said. "We can collaborate on it."

Katharine glanced at Henley, then down at her lap. "I'm not like the rest of you," she muttered. "I don't believe I would be very good at collaborating."

"Are you going to work on it some more?"

"I hadn't planned to."

"Well, then, why don't I give it a go?" Fanny said. "The spirit-world angle would change the whole gist of it."

Katharine bit her lip, considering. "All right. I suppose if you want to try . . ." Her eyes went to Henley's again.

Fanny knew what they all were thinking: that she wasn't any more fit to get the story published than Louis's cousin. What a pleasure it would be if she could prove them wrong.

"I don't know why you want to bother with that," Louis said when they were in bed. "I don't think it's a good idea."

"Why not?"

"It's not your story now." Louis yawned.

"But she consented," Fanny said.

"With her lips, yes."

"It will be different, more of a fable when I'm done. Much better. Anyway, I suggested the nixie idea to her before she wrote her version. Haven't we all thrown ideas around, shared them? As I recall, 'The Suicide Club' was Bob's idea."

Louis was silent. When his breath came regularly, Fanny rose from bed and tiptoed to the desk where Katharine's manuscript lay. It was so clear what was wrong with the thing. No one wanted to read such a dreary, depressing story. Fanny thought she would keep the young man on the train as a character who is going out into the country. She would load him down with gear and high hopes for a quiet day of fishing in a stream. At first he would be annoyed by the waiflike creature he meets on the train; but she would not be insane. She would be a water sprite trying to find her way back to the river out of which she'd been fished. As the two leave the train, headed for the river, the young man could become smitten by her simple wisdom and free spirit. But the untamed creature he is growing to love—after a lovely playful interlude—will disappear into the water, as if in a dream.

Henley would hate that sort of mystical little tie-up, but Fanny loved the twist. It wouldn't take that much work to make the piece into a story someone would publish. She would call it "The Nixie."

CHAPTER 51

"Bogue went out fighting. There is a note of rightness in that," Louis said.

Lloyd was digging a hole in the garden for the dog's body, while Fanny, weeping, painted a rock with his name.

"Why now?" Lloyd asked Louis. "How many times did he bark at that spaniel when it walked by the house?"

"One time too many." Louis sat in a chair on the lawn, watching mother and son prepare the grave.

There had been nothing sweet about the public Bogue. Privately, he was a cuddle. In the morning Bogue burrowed his way beneath the sheet and counterpane until he found Louis's feet, then draped his hairy body over them and snored, starting every once in a while— chasing a rabbit in his dreams, Louis supposed. Often, before Louis began writing, Bogue had already put in a good day's work, announcing through the hedge with fierce barks that the crowing rooster next door should not strut too confidently, that the moment of judgment might appear as suddenly as a new opening in the shrubs. Before breakfast scraps arrived in his bowl, Bogue had already chased some hound down the road, striking a blow for all small dogs in a big dog's world. Occasionally, he left the intruders with wounds.

"Why did he have to do that? Chase every dog he ever saw?" Lloyd's voice cracked with anger at the needlessness of Bogue's death.

"Simply his nature," Louis said. "He probably was the last of his litter to get at his mother's teat, or some such injustice. Made him feisty."

"He would just throw his body into the fray," Lloyd said. "It was never an even fight."

"Maybe he knew that *life* is not an even fight," Louis mused. "Given the odds, it's the stand one takes that matters."

. . .

THE TROUBLES IN Ireland weighed heavily on Louis's mind of late. In reading about a particular Irish family caught up in the violence, he began to see his own fate tied in to theirs. Two years earlier, in 1885, an Irish Catholic farmer in Kerry named Curtin had been murdered when he resisted a robbery by Irish nationalists who wanted his firearms and ammunition for their cause. Curtin's children, including two of the older girls, fought off and killed one of the intruders. When the Curtins gave police the names of their father's murderers, the family was boycotted. No food or supplies could reach them, ostracism being the price for their betrayal. Anyone who violated the boycott to assist the family would risk murder.

As they sat by the fire after dinner, Louis lit a cigarette and explained the strategy that had been shaping itself in his head all day. "Just imagine, for one moment," he said, "how significant it would be if a well-known person—a famous writer—went to the Curtins' farm and brought the world's attention to that beleaguered family."

Fanny looked askance at him as if he had lost his mind. "What are you saying?"

"I am saying that I am willing to go to that place, that farm, after telling the press what I am doing. Don't you see? It could bring an end to this absurd boycott."

"Or you could end up like that farmer. Dead," Fanny said. "When did this cause become so close to your heart? Yesterday? Don't you hear what you are saying? You want to commit suicide."

"Well, and why not?" Louis got up and kicked a basket full of kindling wood. "I'd rather use up what time I have left as a spendthrift than die daily in the sickroom. In the end, what matters is the stand one takes against the inevitable."

"Oh, Louis, for God's sake."

A few days later, when he spoke again of going to Ireland, they were eating breakfast. Fanny eyed him calmly. "You haven't touched your eggs or sausage. When you are well, I will go with you. But for today," she went on in her low, singsong way, "we must simply get you outside. The sun is shining." She rose from the table before he could protest.

Fanny was humoring him now, but he knew if he got himself to Ireland, there would be no use trying to discourage her. She would go, for better or worse, and stand with him.

Louis allowed Valentine to dress him in layers of knitted and boiled wools. It was May, and catkins on the big beech tree had begun to open. They had been in Bournemouth for three years, but he felt as if he'd been a householder there for forty. He was a weevil in a biscuit. His body was growing more useless by the day. If he could get himself to Ireland, he could hurl his ruined carcass into the fight in one wild, final, noble act. How much better that would be than to slowly disintegrate further.

It was with these thoughts that he turned the brass knob of the front door to find a red-cheeked delivery boy coming up the walk with a telegram from Edinburgh. Louis opened it quickly and found it was from his mother.

Come as soon as possible. Your father is dying.

CHAPTER 52

Thomas Stevenson, on first look, appeared to be napping. When Louis found him in his bedroom, he was sitting upright in a chair, wearing his broadcloth suit, and holding a pipe in his hand.

"Father," Louis said, leaning over so Thomas could see him. He patted the old man's knee, and the pipe, which had been propped loosely in his fist, fell to the floor.

Thomas's glazed eyes blinked toward his son's face, then closed again.

"He doesn't even know who I am."

Standing behind Louis, Maggie Stevenson quaked with sobs. "Nor does he know me." She turned to Fanny and drew her into the family circle, placing an arm around her waist. "He would have wanted it this way. He always said that any man who respected himself would not die in bed. He wants to spend his last day fully dressed, having smoked his pipe."

"But is he comfortable?" Fanny asked.

"No, he can't be," Maggie said. "But this is what he always said he wanted."

"Did he actually smoke a pipe today?" Fanny asked.

"Yes."

"Well, then." Fanny knelt before her father-in-law. "Master Tommy," she whispered. "Would you like to lie on the bed for a bit?"

The old man looked blankly at her. He had slid down and to the side of the wing chair, where his fragile body was folded like a rag doll. His eyelids fluttered.

When they managed to get him lying flat, still wearing the suit, Fanny took Louis aside in a corner of the bedroom. "You must tell him it is all right if he leaves us now. Tell him how good a father he has been. Tell him his work is finished and he has done a fine job."

Left alone in the room with his father, Louis saw Fanny's wisdom. Thomas Stevenson had waited to leave them until his boy got home. Now he needed to be released. Louis knelt beside the bed and put his mouth near his father's ear.

In a few hours, the old man was gone.

RAIN FELL IN slanted sheets the day of the funeral. Despite having a cold, Louis greeted guests to the house but took his leave after a half hour when he felt too exhausted to continue. Uncle George Balfour followed him upstairs to his bedroom.

"I cannot in good conscience allow you to attend the burial, Lou," he said. "You are a very sick man. If this cold goes into your lungs, it could kill you. And I don't intend to let that happen on my watch. It's all up to you. You have a fibroidal lung disease that can't be cured. It *can* be managed, and if you take care of yourself properly, you can avoid the hemorrhages." Louis's uncle produced a respirator mask shaped like a pig's snout from the medical bag he carried with him wherever he went. "Strap this on your mouth and nostrils. There's pinewood oil in there. The vapors will do you good."

Now Louis stood in his robe at the window of his bedroom. Outside, a river of black umbrellas and carriages filled Heriot Row. Fanny and his mother filed out in black veils, followed by his cousin Bob, who would stand in for him during the service at the cemetery. Louis watched Bob help Maggie into the carriage and then Fanny. How changed Bob looked. He wore his world-weary demeanor not nearly so handsomely as he had when he was twenty-five. He was a professor of fine arts in Liverpool and looked like every middle-aged don Louis had ever known—wise and disappointed. How quickly the wild boy had dissolved.

Alone in the house, Louis cast about, seeking he knew not what. Some sense of sorrow on this funeral day? He didn't feel it. He was glad that his father was no longer suffering, that the old man's spirit was happily released. Thank God he and his father had made their peace or he would be feeling very different.

Louis wandered into his parents' bedroom. It had always served as their sanctuary; he hadn't been in the room much since he was a small boy running in and out. He climbed onto the bed on his father's side and felt the indentation in the mattress where he had lain every night for so many years. Louis examined the white marble fireplace mantel in front of him, where his mother had placed mementos from his childhood: a silver baby rattle and a photograph of Louis when he was three. He was a round-faced child with blond ringlets, attired as boys were at that age, in a white dress with a tartan silk sash around his middle. His father probably had gone to bed and awakened every morning to that picture for the past thirty years. It was how he would have preferred to think of his son, for those earliest years were the most comfortable times for his father as a father. He had read lovingly to Louis when he was small, taken him on outings, showered him with attention. It was when Louis started to form his own opinions that his father had found him impossible to understand. Poor man. What a hopeless cause Thomas Stevenson had faced, trying to shape his odd and puzzling offspring.

Louis took up a pen and paper to write out an obituary. He began listing a few of his father's feats: harbor engineer; legend in the world of lighthouse builders. Perfected the revolving holophotal sea light. Together with his brothers, Alan and David, carried on the tradition of their father, building lighthouses that guided sailors to safety and saved untold lives. A humble man who took no patents on his inventions; regarded his work as a duty to the nation.

How to capture the real man in a newspaper obituary? It couldn't be done. How could he say that his father was a morbid man, preoccupied with sin and death, almost paralyzed when he contemplated the terrors of hell? That he lost too much time to slinking about in childish snits? That he bore a thousand prejudices and yet provided moral guidance to his friends and acquaintances who regarded him as something of a holy man. That, despite being a fierce Christian and Conservative, he insisted any woman who wanted a divorce should be free to have it, and that no man who asked the same should be granted it. That he loved sunflowers and antique furniture the way some people loved the works of Michelangelo, and that he made the drollest remarks at family gatherings. That he kept only a few books near him, mostly Latin texts, and a copy of *The Parent's Assistant,* a book of little moral tales he had read to Louis as a child. That, religious as he was, he had succumbed to the sin of pride when he installed the grandest bathroom on Heriot Row.

Someday I will write a real account of you, Louis thought, *something beyond these facts of your life embalmed for a half column of newsprint. I will write you a book.*

Louis wrote down the phrase *My dear, wild, noble father.*

He was struck immediately by the words. A week earlier he had been longing to end his own life in a wild and noble way. Somewhere in the unfolding events of the last two days, a sea change had come over him. He wanted to live. Desperately. Louis strapped on the hated pig snout and breathed deeply.

A FEW DAYS after the funeral, the reading of the will took place in Thomas's study. The document called for Louis to get three thousand pounds, his minimum entitlement from his mother's marriage settlement. His mother would get 2,000 pounds and then live on the rent from the twenty-six-thousand-pound estate. When she died, Louis would inherit. And in the event of Louis's death, Thomas Stevenson specified that Fanny would inherit it all, then Lloyd.

Louis noticed Fanny nodding solemnly, clearly honored by his father's recognition. How like his father, Louis thought, to protect her.

"One other thing," the lawyer added, browsing the legal document over his gold-rimmed glasses. "Your father's will asks that you take care of the children of his brother Alan, if they need help."

It made sense. Uncle Alan had been a key member of the family business before his breakdown and eventual death. A proper, equitable distribution of funds from the three brothers' family business might never materialize, and Louis's understanding of the company's earnings and value were murky.

Bob and Katharine would need help, if not soon then sometime; of that, Louis was fairly certain. Luckily, he was making money from his writing, for his three thousand pounds wouldn't last long. He knew there were people who would think he'd become a rich man on the death of his father. They would be wrong. He would arrange an annual stipend of some sort for Bob and Katharine—not too little, certainly not too much, as he didn't have it.

. . .

"WHY DON'T YOU come back with us to Skerryvore for a while?" Louis said. He was helping his mother respond to a pile of notes. "I don't like leaving you here alone."

When Margaret Stevenson looked up, her pained eyes softened. "I would like that," she said. "Very much."

"I must tell you, we may not be in England all that long. Uncle George says Colorado is not a bad idea for the winter. What would you think of that?"

"Oh." Maggie Stevenson sighed gratefully. "I think I should enjoy seeing America." Her cheeks, pink from a blanket of tiny blood vessels spread upon them, flushed red. "I have some money coming out of your father's business. I believe there is enough of it to cover a winter in Colorado for all of us."

After the funeral, Lloyd returned to Bournemouth for the summer. "I don't want to go back to school in the fall," he announced to Fanny and Louis, "and not just because you're talking of going to Colorado. I want to be a professional writer." He shifted from foot to foot, glanced at Louis, then looked down. "Maybe apprentice with you?"

"But you've only finished two years of university," Fanny said.

Louis looked at Lloyd. He was six feet tall, sober and studious in his thick glasses. In a deep voice accented by his years in English schools, Lloyd put forth his case. "I have been writing since I was eleven, when you gave me the printing press. I've gotten much better, and it is what I want to do more than anything else I can think of. Why should I stay at Edinburgh when I could learn more from you about writing than any old professor can teach me, and we would be traveling, and I could . . ."

Louis thought he heard real passion. Passion was the easy part; the proof would be on the page. The boy had written some clever little stories over the years. Well, and how could he say no?

Louis elevated his eyebrows in Fanny's direction. She returned a nod. "It will be a peripatetic sort of education," he said. "But sometimes those are the best."

Beaming, Lloyd shook Louis's hand and then shook it again.

In a twinkling, Louis realized afterward, their household circle had expanded by two full-time members and their lives changed dramatically. Fanny found renters willing to take Skerryvore for half a year, booked passage for five, including Valentine, on a steamer to New York, gave away jars of preserves to neighbors, and put Adelaide Boodle in charge of feeding the wild cats in the chine. They departed Skerryvore with sleeves sticking out of trunks and tempers frayed but dressed respectably, at least.

In London, their old friends trooped to Armfield's Hotel to see them, from Henley and Henry James to Katharine and even Cummy. It was a sweet farewell but for Henley, who couldn't resist firing a parting shot. "It's a pity you must go," he told Louis. "You won't be understood in America."

A day later, when they arrived at the docks to board the ship, they found Colvin there to see them off, with a bag of books for Louis and a bouquet of pink carnations for Fanny. In their cabin, they found a case of champagne sent by Henry James.

Drink for seasickness and general merriment, his note read. *Bon voyage, dear ones. I await the stories.*

CHAPTER 53

At Le Havre, where the *Ludgate Hill* stopped to pick up more passengers, Fanny managed to go up on deck to enjoy the stillness of the boat in port. It was late afternoon and the light of the day was beginning to fade. Stacks of hogshead barrels on the quay shone golden brown in the sun. Fanny heard a chorus of neighing. She squinted and saw a herd of something coming aboard—horses, it looked like.

"They *are* horses," she said to her mother-in-law. "A lot of them."

They watched as masses of animals boarded. "Ninety-one, ninety-two . . ." Maggie Stevenson counted. "There must be over a hundred," she gasped.

"Is it a circus?" Fanny asked.

"No, my dear." Maggie pointed to a herd of cows coming on behind the horses. "We are on a livestock boat. I'm quite sure of it."

Louis had gone down to have a closer view of "the pageant," as he called it, and Fanny could see him on the side of the ramp, watching. She spied several cages, obviously for large animals, rolling onto the ship. Through the bars of one of them, a long hairy arm extended out toward Louis, as if in greeting. Fanny saw her husband reach out his own arm, missing by a foot the touch of the ape's fingers.

"No wonder this passage was a bargain," Fanny muttered when Louis returned to their cabin. "Not a word was mentioned of animals when I bought the tickets."

"Think of it as an adventure, Fan," Louis said. "How often does a man get to chat with one of his simian cousins? The baboons are such beauties! I'm told they're headed for zoos in America. The palms of their hands! The eyes! I'd swear some of them were saying hello to me." He pulled her up from her berth. "Come up to the deck. It will help your stomach."

Louis grabbed two bottles of champagne from their supply. As the ship departed Le Havre, Fanny followed him as he went about dispensing cups of it to the pale, queasy souls lying on steamer chairs, shivering in blankets.

"Will you have some Henry James?" Louis asked a pallid woman. "Champagne, madam," he explained when she looked confused. She took the cup of wine gratefully and drank it down.

LOUIS GREW STRONGER with every passing day on board the steamer. The sea breezes nourished him in a way that no city or country air had ever done. Watching him, Fanny thought he was more like the man she'd met in Grez than he had been at any time since. He walked—*sprang*—miles at a time around the deck, talked to everyone he encountered, studied fishing boats that passed by, seagulls, rope knotting. He reveled in standing in the wheelhouse with the captain, bandying about nautical terms. Word spread quickly among the odd assortment of fellow travelers that he was an author of some reputation, and soon enough crew and passengers and animal keepers were his best friends.

"Those stallions are worth twenty thousand pounds," Louis told Fanny when they were dining in the saloon. "The owner says he paid first-class passage for them." After dinner, Louis took Fanny's hand and led her to the lower deck to see the caged apes he'd befriended—some thirty of them.

"Pity they are going into zoos, where they will be cooped up for good," Louis said. "Those are mating pairs. I can attest to that—they don't mind who's watching. But the funny part is how they . . . court. I'd call it courting. They have lovers' quarrels and little intimacies. These two over here? The keeper had them both in hats the other day, and they were trading. Trying on the other one's cap."

"You did that when we were at Silverado," she said.

Louis led her over to another cage. "And this fellow?" He opened the cage door; a middle-size baboon climbed into his arms as nonchalantly as if it were Louis's own child. "His name is Jacko," he said.

With no one else around, Fanny allowed herself to simply stare at the long member of the baboon. "I don't think I've ever seen such an overtly . . . sexual animal."

"And the poor fellow's all alone in his cage, I don't know why. It's not easy being a captive ape. Doesn't seem right to deny him his rare pleasures." Louis stroked the top of the animal's head. "At least you're not a human, Jacko. You'd have ideals and convictions to bother with." He eased the ape back into his cage.

"You're having the time of your life, aren't you, Mr. Darwin?"

"I believe I could be happy simply living at sea," he said grinningly, and in a blink, his countenance changed. "I was caged in Bournemouth, Fan. It wasn't a life."

As the voyage progressed, the seas grew wilder. The boat creaked as furious waves tossed it back and forth, up and down, through one whole night. "Terrifying," Louis admitted when he crawled from his berth after the raging tempest had passed.

Fanny lay in her bed with a bucket at hand. It was no longer news in the family that she had no sea legs, and Louis did. Valentine and Lloyd were mostly of Fanny's constitution, but the real surprise was Louis's mother. Maggie Stevenson showed more pluck than any of them knew she possessed. She strode the pitching deck as if it were a city sidewalk, the white veil of her widow's cap whipping behind her in the wind. She accompanied Louis on his walks with Jacko and ate her supper heartily in the saloon, where horses eyeballed the diners through the portholes.

On the fourth evening out, the high winds turned nightmarish. Cups and saucers began to fly during dinner hour, and people left behind their ox tongue and mutton chops to retreat to their cabins. "The waves are curling right over the decks," Louis said when he crept back to their stateroom. He and Fanny clung to the sides of their berths and watched as fittings from their cabin shook loose, then slid back and forth across the floor. Outside, bells clanged crazily as the ship bucked and rolled. The turmoil lasted for hours, and once, when the door of the cabin flew open, she heard the screams of the monkeys and the clomping hooves of terrified horses.

"Tea and biscuits?" Louis called out to her in the noise.

"No," she groaned.

"Henry James?"

"Yes, yes, right away," she shouted back, and took the whole bottle to her lips.

By the end, they had been on board nearly two weeks. Fanny and Louis, watching from the deck, were ecstatic when they saw a small boat appear to lead the steamer into New York. A young sailor on the *Ludgate Hill* stopped his work to watch. "See that pilot boat, Mr. Stevenson? I worked on it for about a month right before I come on this one. The captain's a tough master, he is." He laughed. "Do you know what we called him? Mr. Hyde."

Fanny shot a startled glance at Louis, who shrugged. "The book has been selling well over here, they say. Too bad it has mostly been pirated. We might have gotten rich." He looked down at her. "Are you feeling up to going to the play premiere when we get there?"

"I wouldn't miss it," she said.

When the *Ludgate* pulled into New York, it was a few passengers short. A number of the baby monkeys, sickened by the voyage, had died and been tossed overboard. Everyone looked shaken. Everyone but Louis, who appeared to be glowing with youth and vigor. The only evidence of the harrowing passage was the condition of his coat, which had been mauled to pieces by Jacko during the storms.

Fanny blessed the earth when they walked down the ramp and onto terra firma. She had traveled by ship often enough to know that her body would be swaying for a good couple of days. They climbed into a carriage and proceeded to their hotel, talking gaily the whole way of beds and baths and hotel food. From the side of the carriage, she looked out at the dresses on the street. Seven years, and how the clothing had changed! The women of New York were wearing bustles again.

In the hotel lobby crowded with men, Will Low stood waiting to see them, looking highly respectable in a suit—not at all the bohemian painter they had known and loved ten years earlier in Grez. "Louis!" he shouted when he spotted his old friend, whereupon the entire lobby full of men turned at once.

"Mr. Stevenson! Mr. Stevenson!" they called out as they closed in on Louis. "*New York Herald* here!" someone hollered. Notebooks appeared, arms waved above heads as they hurled questions at Louis, who looked mortified. Amid the shouts, Fanny heard two names shouted again and again: Jekyll and Hyde.

CHAPTER 54

<Saranac, New York   February 1888>

Saranac, New York   February 1888

My dear Fanny Sitwell,

I am thinking of the Robert Burns line that Louis is so fond of quoting: The best-laid schemes of mice and men so often go askew. Our lives are living proof of it, as they have been for some time. When last I wrote, we were on a ship with a load of apes destined for American zoos. We are now settled for the winter not in Colorado, as planned, but an outpost in upper New York, near the Canadian border. Louis caught a cold at the end of our journey and a doctor warned him against a train trip across America. So we decided to stay in Saranac and to take a cottage—a hunting cabin, they call it here—in a colony for tuberculosis patients that is similar to the one in Davos. Except that it is much colder here. Temperatures are well below zero, and the morning trip to the privy behind the house is painful indeed.

Louis thrives in this place. He is even fattening up on mare's milk, which was prescribed by the doctor. Mrs. Stevenson is stoic in these daunting circumstances, as is Lloyd. I am the least charmed by this punishing cold, and I curse my puckered scalp every morning. I recently went to Montreal—took Valentine with me to translate—and we returned with five enormous buffalo coats, which have improved everyone's mood.

Louis has begun a new novel that he is calling The Master of Ballantrae, *a story about the 1745 Scottish uprising, with which he is obsessed. As it turns out, Louis is an enormous sensation over here, and in New York the press won't leave him alone. One publishing fellow named McClure offered him $10,000 a year to write a weekly column for one of his newspapers,* The *New York*

World. *Louis was appalled and told him the amount was too much. He took another offer instead that better suits his temperament: For $3,500 he will write a year's worth of articles for* Scribner's *about whatever he fancies. But McClure, who resists taking no for an answer, will serialize* The Black Arrow *over here.*

I cannot describe well enough the profound change in Louis's health while he was on board that ship. We all understand now that sea air is the best medicine, even more than cold air in a high altitude. We have entertained many possible destinations, including Japan, but lately the talk is of a cruise in the South Seas. Mrs. Stevenson is enthusiastic and has offered to underwrite a monthlong voyage. One day when Louis and Lloyd were poring over a map of the islands, we had another visit from the persistent Mr. McClure. When he got wind of a possible voyage among the Gilbert Islands, he made an offer to Louis on the spot. He said he would pay him a handsome sum to write a series of letters for his newspaper syndicate (the New York Sun *and others) about his travels among the islands in that area of the world. Now we are all aflutter with the idea of a cruise. I am heading off to San Francisco via Indianapolis (for a visit with my family). I will look into possibly hiring a boat of some sort when I get to California.*

One other bit of good news: The March issue of Scribner's *will contain not only a story by Louis but also my story, "The Nixie." My third published piece!*

I carry you with me in my heart, Fanny Sitwell. The steadiness of your friendship warms me in this cold place. As I know more, I will keep you apprised. Please give our love to Sidney, and to Henry James, whose champagne saved me.

Fondly, Fanny

CHAPTER 55

⁓

The ink was frozen, as it had been every morning since December. Louis grabbed the bottle from his desk and went to the woodstove in the sitting room to warm the black chunk inside. He found his mother bundled up in her buffalo coat and mittens.

"How are your ears this morning, dear?" Maggie Stevenson asked her son.

"Did you go through the window again?"

Maggie Stevenson grinned sheepishly, her face a little white wafer above an enormous fur ruff at her neck. "I'm none the worse for it."

Since their arrival in Saranac, his mother had been climbing in and out of her bedroom window and walking around the outside of the house to get to the sitting room, rather than cut through Louis and Fanny's bedroom, where Louis worked. It was but one of the inconveniences she endured cheerily.

Fanny had a wood fire going, but the room was frigid. The five of them would stay together there so as to keep warm. Louis would work in the morning with a hat pulled over his ears, as would Lloyd, who pounded away with gloved fingers at his typewriter. The two men would ice-skate on the pond nearby in the afternoon, or Louis would walk through the snowy hills by himself, carefully avoiding the other tubercular inhabitants, who bore a startling resemblance to those at Davos. Pink-cheeked in the ten-below weather, they flew by him on horse-drawn sleighs, calling out giddy pleasantries.

As soon as the ink melted, he would pen a letter of introduction for his new friend McClure, who was headed to London on a foray into the English publishing world, seeking talented writers for his publications. Louis had suggested that Henley act as his agent in London. He would write notes to Henley, Colvin, and Baxter, alerting them that an American newpaper syndicator would be soon knocking on their doors.

"The neighbors offered to take me into town on the buckboard to-morrow," Maggie said. "I'll get groceries and go to the post office."

"I can make that trip," Louis said. "You don't have to."

"No, you work. I rather enjoy the cold air."

Louis hardly recognized the delicate matron of 17 Heriot Row. He wondered if a part of his mother had been buried all those years while living with the powerful and protective Thomas Stevenson, for she seemed to have blossomed since his father's death.

The words came quickly in the morning, and despite the sounds of boots on wood, the clang of pans, and the repeated fussing at the fire-place as Fanny and Valentine heated up soapstones to put under their feet, Louis lost himself in his novel about the Scottish uprising. He couldn't seem to get away from that pivotal moment in history when the Scots rose up against the English and were defeated. Louis wanted the book to have sweep, to possess an emotional depth that would satisfy Henry James, and to have a female character who would earn Fanny's approval. He wanted a tragedy: brother against brother. He wanted no less than the fall of a great house caused by the father's sin of duplicity.

"DID YOU FINISH your chapter?" Fanny asked later that afternoon. Standing at the stove, dressed in a petticoat with thick wool stockings pulled up to her knees, a heavy pair of boots, and a coat, she was frying a slab of ham in a skillet. Through the window just beyond her, snow fell softly, erasing the rabbit and deer prints that threaded over the white drifts.

"I did."

"Are we to have a reading tonight, then?" Maggie asked, looking up above her reading spectacles at her son. She was seated by the hearth, her feet propped on a fat log to avoid the freezing drafts of air that shot across the floor.

"I'd prefer to hear a little of Melville," Louis said. "He has just come among cannibals in the Marquesas Islands."

Lloyd lifted his head. He was studying a world map spread out on a table in front of him. "I cast my vote for *Typee*," he said.

After dinner, they gathered around the battered map. Lloyd's finger traced the route of Melville's journey in the South Pacific.

"If we could get a boat in San Francisco, we might sail to the Marquesas," Lloyd said, placing a forefinger on the map. "Here is the island of Nuka Hiva where Melville first encountered cannibals."

"Are they still eating people there?" Maggie asked cautiously.

"*Cannibales!*" Valentine gasped.

"Former cannibals," Louis said. "The directory says the missionaries have reformed them."

"Oh, think of the warmth," Fanny said.

"Palm trees . . ." Lloyd added.

". . . the air full of the smell of coconut." Maggie sighed.

"McClure would pay me in installments for those South Seas letters."

They turned in unison toward him.

"We could afford to do this?" Lloyd asked.

"If I accept his offer? Quite." Louis grinned. "What is wealth good for, anyway? Just two things, as I see it—a yacht and a string quartet."

"CAN YOU BEAR another sea journey?" Louis asked her when they were alone in bed. "You've hardly recovered from the *Ludgate Hill.*"

Fanny was quiet. "We would be out how long?" she said after a while. "A month before we saw land again?"

"It depends on where we sail *to.* If we leave from San Francisco, my guess is that it would be three or four weeks before we reach the Marquesas."

Her fingers played over her lips. "I could do it," she said, "I could do it. I want to go see my mother. I could continue on to San Francisco . . . look into hiring a boat."

It would not be easy on her, he knew. But cold air and altitude were not easy on her, either. He was healthiest in places that laid her flat from dizziness or nausea or melancholy. Only in Hyères had they found a place that worked its spell on both of them.

Louis glanced at her face. He could tell she was mentally packing her trunk.

CHAPTER 56

"Letters from home!" Maggie Stevenson called out when she returned from her errands in Saranac. Louis helped his mother out of her heavy coat and boots. He heaped them in the corner, where they commenced to steam.

Fanny had a letter from Indianapolis; Louis's was from Henley in London. The words "Private and Confidential" were printed in the left-hand corner. *Odd,* he thought. Perhaps Henley was in rough financial straits and did not want Fanny to see a plea for a loan.

Louis went to his room and sat down on his bed to read the letter.

> *March 9, 1888*
> *Dear Boy . . . I am out of key today. The spring, sir, is not what*
> *it used to be. . . . I've work in hand; I owe not more than a*
> *hundred pounds; I am beginning to make a reputation; my verse is*
> *printing, and promises well enough; other joys are in store, I*
> *believe; and I'd give the whole lot ten times over for—*enfin! *Life is*
> *uncommon like rot . . . If it weren't that I am a sort of centre of*
> *strength for a number of feebler folk than myself, I think I'd be*
> *shut of it damn soon . . .*

So, he is down in the dumps again, Louis thought. He pictured his friend as he'd seen him many times, with his big, sad face in his hands.

> *I read "The Nixie" with considerable amazement. It's*
> *Katharine's; surely it's Katharine's? The situation, the environment,*
> *the principal figure—*voyons! *There are even reminiscences of*
> *phrase and imagery, parallel incidents—*que sais-je? *It is all better*
> *focused, no doubt; but I think it has lost as much (at least) as it*

*has gained; and why there wasn't a double signature, is what I've
not been able to understand . . .*

*I wish you were nearer. Why the devil do you go and bury
yourself in that bloody country of dollars and spew? . . . Lord, you
are 4,000 miles from your friends! C'est vraiment trop fort.
However, I suppose you must be forgiven, for you have loved me
much. Let us go on so till the end. You and I and Charles . . .
'Twas a blessed hour for all of us, that day thirteen years syne,
when old Stephen brought you into my back kitchen, wasn't it?
Enfin—! We have lived, we have loved, we have suffered; and the
end is the best of all. Life is uncommon like rot; but it has been
uncommon like something else, and that it will be so again . . . is
certain. Forgive this babble, and take care of yourself, and burn
this letter.*

Your friend, W.E.H.

Louis reread the letter and then read it again. It wasn't the first time
Henley had poured out his misery to Louis in desperate agitation. But
the paragraph about Fanny's story was a sudden, vicious punch administered between endearments and self-pitying complaints. Rage blossomed in Louis's chest when he read the letter a fourth time. It wasn't
his imagination. Henley was accusing Fanny of plagiarism.

"What is it?" Fanny asked. She had come into the room without his
notice and was standing behind him. Louis froze. How could he keep
the letter from her? He turned slowly, caught her puzzled look, and
knew in that moment it was no use trying to hide it. He handed her the
letter and watched her face blanch when she came to the paragraph
about her story.

"But this is ridiculous . . . it's a lie! Katharine told me I could use the
story line. She said she wasn't so interested in the thing anymore and
that my idea would change its meaning." She put a hand to her chest,
her fingers spread wide. "I don't understand. You know me, Louis. You
know I would never—"

"Calm yourself, Fanny. I will take care of this."

Louis threw on his coat and boots and went out into the snow. He
trudged through the fields around the house, playing over in his mind
what he could recall of the evening at the Henleys' in London when

Katharine told everyone of her story idea. Louis remembered her resistance to Fanny's suggestions and her refusal to collaborate. But there had been another dinner a year later, at Bournemouth, when Henley admitted he'd had no luck selling the finished piece. Louis couldn't remember Katharine's story very well, except that it was a paltry, miserable little thing. Fanny had wheedled her again for a chance at it, and Katharine had been hesitant again. Having known her from childhood, Louis saw the wariness in his cousin's features, heard it in her voice. Yet she had given verbal permission, albeit reluctantly, for Fanny to take it and adapt it. Fanny's version was better, though Louis didn't know how close they were in phrase. Louis hadn't lingered on it. He'd written a cover letter to the editor of *Scribner's* and sent in Fanny's story along with his own assignment for the magazine. And they had bought it. Both pieces had appeared in the March issue.

Louis inhaled deeply. It was nearly April and bitterly cold; the freezing air stung his lungs. He would have to write to Katharine to insist that she set straight Henley's memory before the whole thing became a colossal scandal. It occurred to him then that he couldn't do so, for Henley had marked his letter *Private and Confidential. How dare Henley insult my wife and then leave me no recourse to appeal to the memories of the others who were present at that dinner!*

Louis walked sullenly back to the house. When he found Fanny in the bedroom, she was heaving the quilt off their bed to shake it. "I've never stolen a thing in my life. Never!" She swung the quilt around and knocked over a pile of books on the bedside table. "How dare he accuse me of such a thing?"

Louis sank down at his desk chair, still wearing the heavy fur coat. "I don't remember Katharine's goddamn story."

"I changed it. How is this different from what you and all the others have done for years? How is it different from the dozens of ideas I've given to you? I offered Katharine a double signature, and she didn't want it. Don't you see? This nonsense does not concern my story. It concerns the fact that Henley *hates* me because I 'stole' you away from him. He has always hinted that I am inferior because I am an American. That business about America being the bloody land of dollars and spew? That is an insult aimed directly at me. How would you feel if he said that about Scotland? Admit it! He's insanely jealous of you. He can't bear your success. Now he's gotten wind you're famous in America, and it's the final straw."

Louis took up his pen and ruined six pieces of paper before he managed to compose a reply to Henley.

March 22, 1888

My dear Henley,

I write with indescribable difficulty; and if not with perfect temper, you are to remember how very rarely a husband is expected to receive such accusations against his wife. I can only direct you to apply to Katharine and ask her to remind you of that part of the business which took place in your presence and which you seem to have forgotten . . .

When you have refreshed your mind to the facts, you will, I know, withdraw what you have said to me; but I must go further and remind you, if you have spoken of this to others, a proper explanation and retraction of what you shall have said or implied to any person so addressed, will be necessary.

From the bottom of my soul, I believe what you wrote to have been merely reckless words written in forgetfulness and with no clear appreciation of their meaning; but it is hard to think that any one—and least of all, my friend—should have been so careless of dealing agony. To have inflicted more distress than you have done would have been difficult . . .

You will pardon me if I can find no form of signature; I pray God such a blank will not be of long endurance.

Robert Louis Stevenson

THEY LAY AWAKE through most of that night, talking into the dark.

"It's unbearable to think that Katharine and Bob are somehow entangled in this treachery," Louis muttered. "But I can't see that Henley would have had the nerve to send such an accusation if he hadn't spoken to them first about their memory of the facts."

"Katharine is Bob's sister. Blood is thicker than water. As for Henley, he's in love with Katharine. He makes a perfect fool of himself around her. He is making a big show of defending her honor." Fanny blew her nose furiously. "I hate them all."

She finally slept, but he could not. "Heavyhearted" didn't begin to describe the elephant pressing down on his chest. It had long been a joke among them that Henley had the tact of a pachyderm. "I reserve the right to insult my friends," Henley used to say when they confronted him.

He'd come into Louis's life when he was in full rebellion against his father. Henley, Bob, and Baxter had become his new family. They swore allegiance to one another a thousand times in taverns, and on deadlines for *London,* in letters, through serious illnesses and love affairs gone bad. They had hauled one another out of pubs when they were too drunk to get home by themselves, out of debts and blue funks. They had leveled their true opinions at one another's work and foibles even when it was painful, because they'd sworn their fealty to Truth. What kind of friend would not give another friend the truth?

That was the card Henley was playing in his letter. As if his friendship superseded Louis's marriage.

There had been so much give-and-take over the years between friends; Louis never had kept a scorecard. Henley had worked as Louis's unpaid agent during the early years, when they were all near broke. But Louis had shown his own kindnesses to Henley, giving him money, or loaning it when he got married, contributing stories to *London* for no pay in order to keep Henley's magazine alive.

When he examined it now, he saw other ways he had repaid Henley. The plays, for instance. All those hours Louis had spent propping up his old friend by collaborating on plays were hours lost for his own work. He had known it at the time and done it anyway, because he loved Henley despite all his flaws. He would have risked his life for the man. He could not bear the thought of putting his old friend to the door. But this was not the first rift his friend had caused.

Fanny was right when she said that Henley was jealous of her because she'd "stolen" Louis. "He is a man who wants to run the show. He has lost his power over you," she'd said, "and he cannot stand it."

But it was more than that. Henley carried a deep sense within him about the essential unfairness of life. Though they were sworn brothers, he nursed a grudge against his best friend. He could not bear that a man like Louis, born into such comfort, could meet with success as an artist so readily. Henley believed he possessed the same talent as Louis but had been dealt a far more difficult hand. He bore other scars besides the stump and crutch; he was irrevocably marked by the poverty and loneliness he'd known in childhood.

Part of his struggle was that he was a poet, and poetry was not as marketable as fiction. He'd had to turn to being an editor. What a bitter pill for him, after all those years of idealizing Art as his life's purpose. But Henley had made a solid reputation for himself as an editor, and his poetry was being recognized as important. A volume of his work had just been published, for God's sake. Yet it wasn't satisfying enough that he was succeeding at last as an artist. It seemed he wanted Louis to suffer.

By four a.m., Louis despaired of ever sleeping. He got up from the bed and wrote a cordial letter to Katharine, asking her to set straight the facts of the matter. In a letter to Baxter, he poured out the anguish and rage swirling inside him.

I fear I have come to an end with Henley . . .

CHAPTER 57

Louis waited. He imagined the ten-day voyage of his letters on a steamship. The fastest he would hear from Henley or Katharine would be twenty-some days. Since Henley's malign letter arrived, his work had been at a standstill. Louis mostly stayed inside his bedroom, buried under the heavy bedcovers, unsure he could conceal his turmoil in front of his mother and Lloyd. His stomach roiling, his gloved fingers quivering with fury, he wrote one letter after another to Baxter, his only confidant about the matter. *How I wish I had died at Hyères, while all was well with me.*

When a letter came, it was from Katharine and proved to be a masterpiece of equivocation. Henley's letter had been written without her consent, she claimed, though he had a perfect right to be astonished. If Fanny believed she had a right to the story idea, well, far be it from Katharine to disagree. As for her own feelings, she wouldn't discuss the matter a syllable further. At the end of the note, she wrote, *It is of course very unfortunate that my story was written first and read by people and if they express their astonishment it is a natural consequence and no fault of mine . . . I trust this matter is not making you feel as ill as all of us. Yours affectionately, Katharine de Mattos.*

It was the last words of the last sentence that stayed with Louis. *All of us.* That meant Katharine, and Henley, and Bob. Louis could imagine the three of them sitting together, the two men assisting Katharine in choosing just the right words to appease Louis without giving an inch.

He found himself wondering if he had misunderstood something, if he had made a mistake in remembering the conversation about "The Nixie." He wondered if Fanny deserved the blame Henley was hurling against her. Even if it were true that Fanny had made an error of judgment on that stupid little story, was it right that Henley attack her with such impunity? Were Louis's loyalty and kindness nothing to him?

Again and again he thought, *What good is a man if he will not defend the honor of the woman he loves?*

And what did it matter, even if Fanny *had* overstepped propriety? They all knew Fanny well enough to know she sometimes steamed ahead and thought about a thing later. Surely they knew it wasn't her intent to plagiarize the story.

They were her friends, supposedly. Fanny had cared for Bob when he was depressed and broken. She had helped Katharine with her pitiful stories in the past, had put up with Henley's remarks because he was Louis's good friend. Wouldn't a true friend let the matter pass? If Henley's wife, Anna, had been accused of such a thing, even if she had been guilty of it, Louis would not have spoken of it to her husband. In fact, he would have tried to keep the information *from* Henley.

SICK. SICK. SICK. Sick with regret that he had not spoken in Fanny's defense against Henley's rudeness to her before now. Sick that he hadn't insisted she give up the idea of redoing Katharine's idea. For nights on end he could not sleep, until he resorted to codeia. When he rose from bed, he was rested but tearful. For days he ached with regret, and then he grew vexed. He tromped through the woods for hours at a time, mentally shouting the truth at his wife.

You love an adversary, don't you, Fanny? How powerful you must feel in your holy indignation! You enter the fray cocksure and fists flying. Who'd guess that a woman with your backbone would crack so easily for a few crumbs of praise?

He was angry at himself that he had not told her frankly what he knew. *You are trying to find recognition in the wrong place. Give it up!*

He stopped and watched his breath send clouds out in front of him. How galling it was to think of Fanny in California, apparently not suffering the way he was, if her letters were any indication. She had been having a wonderful time visiting with her sister Nellie and her old friends. *I shall write an apology or something,* she had said almost lightheartedly, among many tidbits of news about dining with Rearden and Dora and looking about to procure a schooner for a Pacific cruise. Was she covering her real pain? Was she wounded to the quick to have her moral character questioned? He didn't know.

That was the thing about Fanny. Her temper would flash like quicksilver and then disappear. Meanwhile, here he sat stewing, regretting that he had indulged her by sending her story to his editor at *Scribner's*.

Ambition. That was at the root of Fanny's foolishness. He had seen ambition often enough in a man who took leave of his moral compass in a fit of mad enthusiasm. He'd seen such ambition in women, though rarely so naked, which made it all the more unseemly.

IN LATE APRIL, when Henley's response arrived in Saranac, it trumped Katharine's for insincerity. His original letter was not meant as an affront, he wrote, but merely as a "reminder." He did not respond to Louis's request for a retraction but offered instead a tepid apology, if he had offended their old "kinship."

Louis held the letter in his hands while new tears spilled from his eyes. *How cruel a twist that I am called upon to give up my dearest friends for the sake of his wife's honor.* And yet that was what he understood must happen. "I'm finished with you," Louis said to the letter. "I'm finished with Katharine. I hope to God I am not finished with Bob."

Outside the bedroom where he was holed up, he saw a crocus shooting through the snow. He thought of his mother and Lloyd sitting by the fire, imagining their improbable cruise, unaware of his true misery. They believed he was in here writing. During the agony of the past month, he had hardly paid attention to his real kinships.

"What do you say we go down to New York for a while?" he asked them that evening over dinner. "I can call on my editor at *Scribner's*. And McClure will be back from England with stories, I hope. And then on to see Will Low, perhaps?"

AFTER NEW YORK CITY, they did visit Will Low in New Jersey. It was May. They stayed at a hotel in Manasquan and amused themselves by sailing around in catboats. It was there that McClure, freshly returned from Europe, tracked him down. He and Louis talked for hours on the porch about the differences between the state of publishing in England and in America.

At one point during their discussion, Louis left briefly. As he approached the porch again, he overheard McClure speaking quietly: "Do you know these people, this Henley and his literary circle?" he asked Low. Out of sight, Louis stood perfectly still, riveted. "Stevenson sent me to these people. I can hardly believe they are his friends. They diminish him so! They all say how dear a friend he is to each of them, and then they say, 'Oh, but Bob is the real genius of the family.' Or 'Louis's talent is overrated.' Or 'He's wasting his gifts.' On what, I'm not sure. An American audience? On his choice of subject matter?

"And I get the distinct impression that they can't bear his wife. Henley said she was . . . what was the word? Primitive. Said the woman was *primitive*! Now, tell me, who needs enemies with friends like that?"

Standing in the shadows just beyond the door, Louis trembled. Who else besides Henley did McClure mean by "his literary circle"? Gosse? Surely not Colvin. *This bloody nightmare will not cease.*

One afternoon, while he was dining outside with Will Low, a telegram arrived for Louis. He saw it was from Fanny and opened it, a little afraid something had gone wrong. She'd had to go into the hospital to have a lump removed from her throat, but the growth had turned out to be benign. Or had it? He glanced quickly at the message and then, laughing, handed it to Lloyd to read out loud.

Can secure splendid seagoing schooner yacht Casco *for seven hundred and fifty a month with most comfortable accommodation for six aft and six forward. Can be ready for sea in ten days. Reply immediately.*
Fanny

Louis took out his notepad and scribbled a sentence for the messenger to return.

Blessed girl, take the yacht and expect us in ten days.

CHAPTER 58

The front door of the Taylor Street apartment building was open when Fanny found the address. A pigtailed girl sat at the bottom of the heavy door, holding it ajar with her back. Fanny went into the hallway and looked at the mailboxes. *Strong, 3rd Flr.* She lifted her hem above muddy boots discarded on the steps. Going up, she smelled the ammonia odor of cat urine in the second-floor hallway. On the landing of the third floor, she leaned against a wall to calm her heart, which was racing like a hummingbird's. There were four different apartments on one floor in this cheap-looking place. Which was Belle's? And if Fanny could figure out the correct door, would her daughter even open it? Eight years it had been. Fanny heard a child's chattering through one of the doors. She drew herself up and knocked on it.

Belle's mouth fell open. "Mother," she gasped when she saw Fanny's face. "I didn't know you were coming. You didn't write . . ."

I gave up trying, Fanny thought. "I'm in San Francisco for a couple of weeks. I wanted to see you."

They stood apart and silent for a few moments. Belle studied her mother's face and the feathered hat on her head. Fanny took in her daughter's weary eyes and her upper arms, which were plump as sausages underneath her print dress.

Belle glanced over her shoulder into the apartment, then turned back to Fanny. "Come in," she said.

In the threadbare parlor, a boy sat on the floor cutting paper with a scissors.

"Austin, this is your grandmother." The boy looked up, momentarily puzzled, then smiled openly.

Fanny gazed into the eager, homely little face. He'd apparently just had a bath, for his hair was wet and combed back. It was blond, and the few strands that were dry were straight and fine as cornsilk. She longed to hug the boy but feared frightening him. He didn't know her, after all. Seven years the child had been her grandson, and they didn't know each other.

"Nice to meet you, Austin," she said. "I have a little something for you." She fished around in her bag and pulled out a cloth sack filled with tin horses. "I brought them all the way from London. Each one is a little different."

"Thank you," the boy said, looking almost alarmed by his good fortune. "Thank you!"

Fanny felt her knees go weak and buckle to the floor. "Come to me," she said, stretching her hands out to him. "Will you come to your grandma?" The boy stepped gingerly over the toys on the floor and came close. She swept him into her arms and nuzzled her cheek against his damp hair. "Mmmm," she said, "I love the smell of clean boy. There's nothing better."

Austin laughed and wriggled away. Fanny stared in wonder as the boy's hands set the horses gamboling around the floor.

"Joe is not here," Belle said. "He sent us over when there was talk of a revolution in Hawaii."

"I heard that," Fanny said, pulling her eyes away from the boy. "Dora told me."

Belle appeared to summon her dignity and gestured with one arm around the tawdry apartment. "We're going back as soon as possible. This is only temporary."

"Why don't I take you both to lunch?"

"The lady across the hall is having a birthday party for her daughter, who is Austin's best friend. Mrs. Grady will keep him until I return." Belle looked down at her worn dress. "Give me a minute to change clothes."

"The boat is called the *Casco*," Fanny explained. They were sitting at a table by the front window of a sunlit café. "It belongs to a doctor named Merritt who lives in Oakland. He has agreed to lease it to us for a six-month cruise, complete with captain and crew."

"Where will you take it?" Belle asked.

"The South Seas—the Marquesas Islands first. After that, the low islands of the Paumotus and then Tahiti. Eventually, we will make our way to Hawaii. We've discovered Louis thrives when he is at sea."

Belle looked at her cautiously. "But *you* don't. Six months?"

"Ah, well. How bad can it be?" Fanny leaned back in her chair and felt her daughter's presence wash over her like warm milk. "I've missed you so much," she said.

Belle dropped her head and began to cry. Fanny bent forward and wrapped her arms around her daughter. "The past is past," she said. "I want you in my life. I want to be a proper grandmother to Austin."

"Where is Sammy?" Belle asked, blotting her face with a handkerchief.

"It's Lloyd now, remember? He's here in town, helping me provision the boat. We've been running around like crazy people, laying in supplies. He wants to see you, but I needed to see you alone first."

"Is he going with you?"

Fanny nodded. "So is Louis's mother. And a French-Swiss girl who works for us. Valentine."

The corners of Belle's mouth fell, as if she were crushed not to hear her own name in the passenger list.

"How is Joe doing?"

Belle hesitated. "He had a lot of commissions from wealthy people when we arrived in Honolulu five years ago. A big sugar baron hired him to paint landscapes of Hawaii. The king put him to work, too. We became quite friendly with the Hawaiian royal family, as you may have heard."

"Dora wrote to me about that."

"I'm planning to go back soon. Joe is respected there . . ." Belle's brave voice trailed off. She looked out the window. "His work is very spotty now," she said softly. She pressed her fist into her cheek. "Some days I don't know how we are going to get through."

Fanny breathed in, waited.

"Do you remember at Grez how Bob Stevenson taught us to squint when we were painting a landscape?" Belle asked. "He said that if you squint, you can get the essence of a scene without being distracted by a lot of details. It helps you see exactly where the light is."

"I remember," Fanny said.

"I wish I could just squint at my life and see the light. I have tried so many ways to make things better. But I don't know what to do anymore."

"Is Joe sick?"

Belle nodded, choosing her words. "You never got to know Joe, really. When he is well, he is one of the kindest men on earth."

"So he's drinking." Fanny didn't mention the opium smoking.

Belle drew in a deep breath. "Last I saw him, yes. Ultimatums don't work. Back home in Honolulu, he's gone all night and sleeps all day. It's an affliction."

"Sometimes the only thing to do is go away."

Belle met her mother's gaze. "I *am* away at the moment, and that's not the answer." Her voice was cool now. "We have a child. Austin adores his father."

They fell silent. Fanny glanced at the table next to them, where four women were having lunch. They leaned forward as they spoke, sharing confidences, laughing at once. She'd never had much of that—lunches with women friends. It struck her that she and her daughter had served as each other's best friend for many years. Why had she let the estrangement from Belle go on so long? Pride? Distance? How absurd it seemed now. All the demands on Belle's part for money, and the withholding of it on Fanny's part, seemed to be much less about dollars and much more about a desire for love and respect.

"You poor little soul," Fanny said, stroking her girl's hand. "Come down to the *Casco,* Belle, what do you say? Lloyd so wants to see you."

BELLE'S BREATHLESS ENTHUSIASM, the girlish prattle she fell into when she was excited, returned the minute they reached the dock. "It's practically new! Ninety-five feet? It looks even bigger. And the brightwork!" On deck, Belle reached out to touch one of the freshly varnished spars that gleamed amber in the afternoon sun. Inside the cabin, she ran her palm along the brass fittings, the velvet curtains and cushions.

Fanny introduced her daughter to the crew working on deck. It was thrilling to watch them polishing and scrubbing and scrambling around the magnificent two-masted schooner.

"It's too nice to be taking out on the ocean," Belle observed.

"Don't be misled by the trappings," Fanny said. "Louis is gambling every nickel he has on this trip. He believes it's his last hope to avoid the undertaker. He has been deathly ill for—"

"Belle?" Lloyd's deep voice came from behind them. "Is it really you? Because it looks like you from the back."

Fanny watched as her daughter turned and jumped at the sight of her twenty-year-old brother. Belle flung her arms around Lloyd, who lifted her up off her feet. "You're such a big thing now," she said, sobbing again. "And you talk British."

After a while, they sat together at the table in the cabin and studied a map. Lloyd showed Belle the route to the Marquesas. "June twenty-sixth we depart. If all goes as planned, it will be four weeks before we see land again."

"You're going to Hawaii?"

"At some point," Lloyd said.

"I should be back there by the time you arrive in Honolulu. You'll need different clothes, Mother," Belle said. "It's blazing hot in the islands. I know a tailor."

"BELLE HAS NEXT to nothing." Fanny lay with her head on Louis's shoulder. She had gone up by train to Sacramento the day before to meet him and his mother and Valentine. They were all ensconced in the Occidental Hotel, waiting for the moment when they would depart.

"You expected that."

"I stocked her kitchen while I was provisioning the boat. How long will that last, two weeks? She should stay in California and divorce him, but I can tell she's not going to. She's too proud."

"Did you give her money?"

"A little." Fanny sighed. "Although it just sustains the disastrous marriage, I'm afraid. But I can't bear to see her so down."

Outside, a trolley car squealed past the hotel.

"I gave money to someone else, too," she said.

"Who?"

"Paulie, Sam's wife. She came by the hotel a week ago. She's almost stone deaf and poor as a church mouse. He left her with nothing when he disappeared."

"Is he dead or just gone?"

"Who really knows? But do you know what she said to me? 'You were right about that man, and I was wrong.' I couldn't help feeling sorry for her, and I kept thinking, *If it weren't for Louis, I would be in her shoes right now.*" Fanny lifted her face to look at his. "I love you, Louis Stevenson. Even if you forget wedding anniversaries."

He rolled over on his side and propped his head on his hand. "I know a man is supposed to remember his wedding date. I remembered, and then I forgot again." He ran a finger along the ridge of her nose. "The truth is, other days stick better in my mind. Such as the day I looked through the window at the Chevillon and saw you sitting there. That was the day I nailed my colors to the mast. It was *twelve* years ago. Shouldn't that be the real anniversary day?"

She slid her leg over him. Their lovemaking had a rhythm and a history, a flow of whispers and cues. It brought them together even in the worst of times. It was where they started after they had shouted cruelties at each other, when no words could fix a rift. There were no whispered intimacies at those times, just bodies moving in tandem and serving as proof that they could still connect.

In the past when they had been away from each other, as they had been for two months, their reunions were sexual frenzies followed by gentle togetherness. Now, though, Fanny sensed a reticence in Louis. Was he still angry at her over the fight with Henley? Was he withholding his trust? Or was she only imagining a coolness in him?

"THEY'RE CALLED *holoku*s," Belle said. "You wear a little chemise with a ruffled hem under it. That's called a *muumuu*."

Fanny, Aunt Maggie, and Valentine were standing with Belle in the Chinatown shop of a tailor named Yee Lee. He was holding up tropical dresses for the women to try on. The loose lawn dresses were gathered above the bosom and flowed out in folds from the yoke.

"'Mother Hubbards' is what we used to call them," Fanny said. "Good Lord, they're like altar-boy vestments."

"Certainly appear just as chaste," Belle said when Valentine tried on a *holoku*. The French girl groaned at her reflection.

"I must say," Aunt Maggie remarked, turning left, and then right in front of the mirror, "I am one queer-looking customer."

"Goodbye, corsets!" Fanny shouted gleefully.

The women moved on through the narrow streets of Chinatown, past the stands displaying pickled foodstuffs that were unrecognizable to Fanny. She had already bought kegs of dried beef, sides of bacon, tinned fruit and vegetables, flour, lard—vast amounts of essentials for the ship's pantry. Now she sought out pawnshops, where she gathered an assortment of old gold wedding bands for trading with natives.

"I SHOULD HAVE written," Belle said. "Joe told me not to write." She and Fanny stood together on the sea wall. Nearby, a party celebrating the *Casco's* departure was in progress on the boat. Friends and crew members mingled with newspaper reporters.

No man could ever keep me from writing to my mother, Fanny wanted to say, but she managed to hold her tongue. She could imagine the suffering that lay behind and ahead of her girl. Shame ran through her once again when she remembered the stupid, cruel things she had said long ago about Belle having a baby.

"I have my own regrets," Fanny said. "I wanted for you things I didn't have. You always used to say that I lead with my temper. I have a pent-up volcano inside me that has to erupt sometimes." She chewed the insides of her cheeks. "When the anger builds like that, it seems I'm not myself until I've made the world around me black with smoke and ashes. But oh, Belle, the remorse that follows. No one knows how I pay with regret."

"Oh, I know, Mama. Your children know. So does Louis."

Of course they knew. What was she thinking? They had all seen her suffer for things that flew out of her mouth. They'd seen her near paralyzed while she went over and over some falling-out with a loved one. "You make people out to be perfect saints," Louis had chided her. "And when they fall off the pedestal, then you turn on 'em." It was an ugly truth about her nature that she hadn't wanted to hear.

Belle was blood; Fanny loved her fiercely, however separated they had become. And she would love Austin as utterly.

"Will you go back to Bournemouth after the trip?" Belle had asked during lunch.

"Perhaps," Fanny lied. She never wanted to set foot in England again. Henley and the others had made sure of that. By now word of her supposed plagiarism was surely making the rounds in London's literary salons. Henley hated her enough to spread such calumny. A return to Skerryvore was unthinkable, at least for now. *They took my home right out from under me,* she wanted to tell Belle. But she didn't.

There were many things that went unsaid. Such as the fact that Fanny had been in town for weeks before contacting Belle. When she arrived in San Francisco and visited her old doctor, she'd learned she had a throat tumor and had undergone an operation. Until she knew the tumor was benign, she believed she might be dying. When writing to Louis back in Saranac, Fanny pretended she was quite recovered from the hurt of Henley's insult, so as not to worry her husband any further. In fact, the mere thought of it sent her into a torment. *How can I even defend myself?* To write about the matter to Fanny Sitwell or Sidney Colvin would be to exacerbate the situation. Surely they knew of the mess.

She had lain in a San Francisco hospital bed, feeling desperately alone and devastated by the cruelty of the London liars. It was all she could do to keep from reaching for the bottles of arsenic and morphine that stood on her bedside table and ending the agony with a couple of swallows.

Louis had a sense of loyalty to old friends that bordered on the ridiculous. These monsters were the very people he had named as heirs in his will! Would he change it now that he'd been betrayed? Not likely. When she began to heal, her rage had grown. She wrote an angry letter to Baxter about her will, cursing Henley and Katharine as slanderers and murderers, knowing full well that he was a friend to them, as Louis had been. *While they eat their bread from my hand—and oh, they will do that—I shall smile and wish it were poison that might wither their bodies as they have my heart.*

She had exploded righteously and, when she cooled off, sent a calmer second letter to Baxter. But she was done with the London crowd. Whom would she miss among those people? Only Fanny Sitwell and Sidney Colvin. And Henry James, God bless him. A note had arrived this very morning that made her love him all the more. *I wish I could make you homesick and somehow persuade you to return,* he'd written to them.

Fanny thought about what lay ahead. She hated and feared the sea.

She would never say so to Louis, of course. She had secured the schooner knowing full well she would be sick and terrified every day of the voyage. They were betting much of their money on the chance that a six-month cruise might save his life. Now there was nothing to do but wait and let the hand reveal itself.

At five a.m. on June 26, a tug pulled the *Casco* out through the Golden Gate to open sea. "See you in Honolulu!" Belle shouted from the dock.

Fanny waved and waved at the figures of her daughter and grandson until they disappeared in the foggy morning. Then she turned her back to the shore and faced the wide ocean.

Part Three

"Aw-haw-haw!" Louis shouted into the roar of the waves. The *Casco,* sleek as a giant marlin, was slicing through the Pacific waters at an almighty speed, the world ahead of it a vast blue-gray where sky melded into sea. In the next moment, though, the yacht was heeling so near the ocean's skin that Louis feared he might topple over the bulwark. In front of him, the blue expanse had disappeared behind the starboard side of the boat. Salt water sprayed his face.

"She's runnin' with a bone in her teeth!" he called out jubilantly to Lloyd, who was clinging to his spectacles with one hand and a shroud with the other. "Do you know how many miles this wild vessel has covered in the past twenty-four hours? Two hundred fifty-six!"

"Woo-hoo!" the boy called back. "That's better than a steamer!" When the boat righted itself, they clambered below.

"I'm mortal hungry," Louis said to Fanny. "Any dainties down here?"

She padded away to the galley. Louis pulled off his wet shirt and laughed. Above the pallid skin protected by his trousers, he saw his arms and chest were already turning brown from a week in the sun. By God, dare he say it out loud? *I feel wonderful.*

The first couple of days at sea, he had kept to his cabin, as had everyone in the family, including Valentine. Even Captain Otis, who acted the part of the salty sea dog, had been unable to come to meals for the first two days. Only Maggie Stevenson possessed unassailable sea legs. She ate like a sailor and walked the decks as if she'd been born on a boat. Her single concession to nausea was to decline a breakfast of red herring and mutton chops on the first day. She had been sitting up top ever since, happily knitting Lloyd a pair of socks as the schooner raced southwest.

Fanny suffered the worst. For three days, she was too seasick to partake of anything but sips of water and a rare ship biscuit. On the fourth day of the voyage, she shakily crept from her bunk, barefoot and dressed in one of her new *holokus*. What Otis and the crew thought of her, Louis could only guess. She had worn her hair cut just above shoulder length for some time, and though he was used to it, she was the only woman he knew who wore it in that fashion. When he saw her sitting on the deck with that mop of curls shaking furiously in the wind as she smoked and stared fixedly at the horizon to steady her stomach, even Louis could see that his wife made quite an unconventional picture. He suspected her manner disconcerted Otis, who steered clear of her.

"He has us pegged as wealthy eccentrics," Fanny said when they discussed the captain's cool attitude.

"Well, any customer who can spend two thousand pounds on a six-month cruise must seem rich indeed to him," Louis said.

"Little does he know it's most of your inheritance."

This morning Fanny had started the day badly with Otis by striking up a conversation with his helmsman while he was seated at the wheel, which was located in the cockpit where they all gathered. She had peppered the Russian with a dozen questions when Otis instructed her not to talk to the man while he was steering. Louis could tell the captain preferred Fanny out of sight, in her berth. He probably preferred all of them in their berths. Even Maggie had incited Otis's ire when she walked along a narrow part of the deck too close to the rail.

"What would you do if my mother-in-law fell overboard?" Fanny asked provocatively after the captain chastised the sprightly woman.

Otis stared ahead impassively. "Note it in the log," he said.

The voyage, so far, had been easy and was beginning to take on a rhythm. Louis was the first passenger out of his berth at dawn. He helped raise the American flag that the vessel had come equipped with, then hoisted the Union Jack that he'd provided. As the sun rose and the smell of coffee floated through the open companionway door, Louis breathed deep the salty air and blessed the sun, blessed the four pilot birds that had followed them since they left San Francisco, blessed the flying fish that glided above the blue-green waters with their fins out-spread. If there were a finer way to begin a day, he couldn't conceive it. After a while, he forced himself to go below, where he would lie in his bed and write intently. He felt a supreme urgency to get down on paper the things he was seeing, the comments of the sailors, the laconic remarks of Otis, whom he knew he would transmute into a fictional character someday.

Without a cabin boy, a position Otis had failed to fill before departure, Valentine took on the morning job of folding up the bunks so the area could become a sitting room. Lloyd's job was official photographer, documenting the cruise with pictures that might be used in the South Seas book. Fanny was chief consultant regarding food and injuries. She remained queasy, but her seasickness did not keep the cook from coming to her regularly for instructions, or the injured mate, who tumbled during a storm and had to have his head sewn up.

The doctoring kept her mind focused during some of the terrifying weather of the cruise. A squall would descend upon the *Casco* in the midst of calm weather and throw the inhabitants around like rag dolls. After three days of squalls, with the lee rail dipping below the foaming sea and the wood of the boat groaning as if to break under the punching waves, even Louis quailed. He crawled to the berths, where the women had taken refuge, and called out, "I never should have subjected you all to this!"

Fanny stuck her greenish face out of the bed curtain. "The timber remembers it used to be an oak trunk," she said bravely. "It wouldn't dare split."

When the weather calmed, she went back into the galley to teach the cook how to season his bland meat dishes. One afternoon while she was going through a storage cabinet in the pantry, she called to Louis: "What is a sail doing in here?" Louis reached back into the corner cabinet where some pans were stacked. He tugged at the canvas, which felt heavy. When he got it out on the floor, he saw it was wrapped around two iron weights. Also tucked inside was a small flag—American.

"It's nothing," Louis said, "just overflow." But he knew perfectly well what it was. Otis had packed away the necessities for a burial at sea. In that moment he understood how the captain viewed Louis's frail self: food for the fish.

That evening, when the dour Otis bit into the chicken on his plate, he looked up in wonder. "What's this?" he asked.

"A Mexican sauce I used to make in Monterey. It's called salsa," Fanny said. "A little hot, but tasty, don't you think?"

"Yes," he said, with new respect. "Yes."

After dinner, everyone assembled for the big event of the day—the viewing of the sunset—then adjourned to the cockpit "drawing room," where they gathered around the table, studying the chart.

"I haven't been to Polynesia," Captain Otis said when they pinpointed the island of Nuka Hiva, their first destination, "but the directory says there are two distinct sharp peaks."

"Oh," Maggie said. "I thought you had already traveled to the Marquesas."

"I know a number of men who have," he said.

"Did they speak of cannibals?" Valentine asked.

"Yes," he replied, "but these were old sailors. They sailed there some time ago."

Louis didn't say it out loud, but the directory of which the captain spoke—*A Directory for the Navigation of the South Seas*—also made reference to the morals of Marquesan women. Back in Saranac, when they were poring over the thick book one frigid evening, Lloyd had read aloud a paragraph to Louis and Maggie that caused them all to sit up straight: "'The one great feature which distinguishes these natives in the eyes of Europeans is their unbounded licentiousness. The women . . . appear to have not the slightest idea of chastity or delicacy.'"

Sitting in his buffalo coat by the fire, Louis had raised his brows and said slyly, "Nuka Hiva was Melville's first stop on his voyage.'"

"'Their whole conduct, gesture, and motive appear directed to one end,'" Lloyd had continued reading from the directory that night back in Saranac, despite the deep sighs coming from Maggie Stevenson. "'Their character has been often portrayed, and must be familiar to all readers of the Pacific voyages. It is a point, too, which ought to weigh much with the commander who would bring his ship here.'"

Maggie had changed the subject back then as she did now, by taking out a deck of cards. She teamed with the captain in a game of whist and roundly defeated the others.

Sensing that the ice was finally thawing between the taciturn captain and his passengers, Louis ventured an observation that he'd been wanting to explore. "I realize this is not your boat. But don't you think the *Casco* is overrigged and oversparred? I wonder if a racing boat, glorious as it is, is suited for this kind of cruise."

Louis immediately regretted the question, as the captain didn't answer but merely withdrew to his own quarters. *Just when I was making headway with the man!* Louis chastised himself.

Maggie Stevenson, oblivious to any turmoil, started another hand of whist. When Otis emerged from his cabin, he was carrying a bottle of brandy. "Oh, good," Maggie cried. "I will deal you in." Otis poured small glasses of brandy all around.

"How nice," Maggie cooed. "May I propose a toast?" She raised her glass to the captain, the Russian at the wheel and another sailor standing by, Valentine, and her family members one by one. *"To the Cascos!"*

There were cheers all around.

"Now, tell me," Maggie said to the captain when she'd quaffed her brandy, "have you ever read *Treasure Island*?"

Louis flinched. How like his mother to embarrass him. She asked almost everyone she met this question. Louis waited for the usual "I liked it" that people offered, especially those who hadn't read it.

Otis drew on his pipe, smiled slightly, then lifted his glass and clinked it to Maggie's. "Yo ho ho," the captain said.

CHAPTER 60

"Land!"

Fanny heard Louis's shout as if in a dream. She lifted her head off the pillow, shook it, then slid down from her bed. Maggie was already standing there in her robe. The lantern in her hand lit the soles of Valentine's feet, which were coming down at them from her berth overhead. The women hurried along the hallway and up the ladder to the deck, where they found Louis and the captain staring through binoculars into the near darkness. Louis handed the glasses to Fanny. A long low shadow spread itself wide across the distance. "Morning comes on fast here," the captain said. But this morning was spreading lazily, to reveal a thick patch of clouds sitting atop the water.

Otis ordered the crew to cruise along the northern shore of Nuku Hiva island with Anaho Bay as their goal. The cook came up with coffee and passed around cups as they watched the dawn give way to day. "There are the two peaks!" someone shouted. Within the hour, the captain had sailed into the bay and dropped anchor.

Bright light illuminated the bank of fog lying on the water between the *Casco* and Nuku Hiva. The block of white covered their view of the beach, but above and behind the cloud layer, they saw brilliant green peaks rise up to points in the blue sky. Through the white mass, a black form appeared. Lloyd was the first to spot it. "Canoe!" he shouted. Paddles projected from either side. As the form grew larger in the distance, they saw a figure stand up and sit down. Two men came into focus, dressed in proper linen pants and coats. Fanny, Maggie, and Valentine hurried below to dress. When they came back up, the men in the canoe were bobbing alongside the schooner.

"Permission to come aboard?" the white man called.

"Permission granted," Otis replied.

A ladder was thrown over the side, and the men climbed into the

Casco. "Regler," the white man introduced himself with a German accent. "And this is Chief Taipi-Kikino." The chief, a good six feet tall, had two parallel blue bands tattooed across his nose and cheeks; he was a smiling man with excellent white teeth and bronze skin that gleamed with fragrant coconut oil. He shook their hands, then shook them again. In the distance, Fanny spotted two more canoes emerging from the low-hanging cloud.

"Valentine, go below quick and prepare tea. More visitors," she said, nodding in the direction of the canoes.

In the time it took Regler to explain that he was a trader living on Nuka Hiva, a dozen native men had climbed up the ladder—giant men in loincloths with tattooed thighs and arms, knives at their waists, and handsome, glowering faces. They brought with them an assortment of items—plaited straw hats, oranges, coconuts, bananas—and held them out for sale.

The turn toward commerce took Fanny by surprise. Apart from the Stevenson party's greetings, no cordialities had passed among them. An odd period of staring ensued.

"All right. Tell them I will buy the bananas," Fanny said.

"The man wants a dollar," Regler said rather apologetically.

"For a bunch of bananas? Tell him twenty-five cents. And that's too much."

The native men snorted their disgust when Regler translated. One of them swept his arm about to take in the schooner and its fine trappings. "You no rich?" he said ironically. A round of taunting laughter went up.

Before Fanny knew what was happening, the men were swarming the boat, with Louis in anxious pursuit.

"Dear heavens," Maggie whispered. "We're at their mercy."

Fanny went below so Valentine wouldn't be frightened. She found the girl quaking in the galley; the cook was nowhere in sight. Fanny stood at the entrance of the kitchen and waved away the men when they poked their heads through the door.

WHEN THE NATIVES had departed, everyone on board stared at one another in wonder.

"How extraordinary," Louis said.

"It's not really how they are," Regler said. The trader had a clean-shaven chin and preposterously long and curly hair growing from his cheeks, like sheepskin saddlebags. "What you saw just now was a bit of posturing. When you befriend them, you will find they won't accept money for food. With these folks, food isn't something you own. They give it as a gift, and they know eventually they'll be reimbursed, so to speak. There is a lot of back and forth with the gift-giving. Sometimes it wears a man out." He laughed. "Why don't you come with me to the island, Captain Otis? I will find you chickens and coconut milk and coffee—whatever supplies you need. And the chief has offered to take your letters over to the next bay."

Maggie jumped at the news of a mail steamer. They all promptly retrieved their letters. Regler turned to Lloyd, who had stood dumb-founded on deck during the visit. "Young fellow, you come, too. We will need extra hands."

While the men were gone, yet another canoe arrived, this time with fourteen men and boys led by the chief of chiefs, Ko'oamua. The chief might have been wearing a suit of clothes, so thoroughly was his body tattooed with blue arabesques. Maggie didn't flinch at the sight of his nakedness. He came bearing gifts of welcome and showed every sign that he was a fine gentleman. He and his men followed Louis in single file on a tour through the fore and after cabins and up the forecastle companion. They all settled on the floor of the cockpit and stared at Lloyd's typewriter, which was set up on the table. By way of entertain-ment, Louis asked their names and typed each phonetically, handing out the individual strips of paper. Ko'oamua took over the typewriter at that point and punched out the names of each of his family members.

"The man knows some English but not enough. And God knows, we haven't a syllable of theirs. It's bloody frustrating not to be able to talk to them," Louis said to Fanny. "We might as well be from different planets." He was thumbing madly through a book about Polynesian languages.

Fanny shrugged. She went to the supply of gifts she had brought from San Francisco and handed around some cheap cigars. The men burst into smiles and left peacefully.

· · ·

"THERE AREN'T THAT many of them left, not compared to their old numbers," Regler said that evening over dinner on the boat. "They've had sickness of all kinds—cholera, smallpox, syphilis. Taipi-Kikino is a chief, but the big chief is Ko'oamua, whom you also met today. He's been converted by the missionaries. It wasn't that long ago, though, you could see him striding proudly along the beach right there." Regler pointed to the stretch of sand opposite the *Casco*. "He was wearing a tapa cloth around him. And out from its folds, what did he pull? A human arm that he chewed bites out of. I suppose it belonged to one of his enemies—former, that is. They call human flesh 'long pig.' The man appeared to enjoy it, all right."

"Long pig. How picturesque," Fanny muttered.

Between courses, Regler raked his fingers thoughtfully through his whiskers. "The days of long pig are over with now. So will be the tattooing, if the French have their way. They're against it. Too much a reminder of the old savage days. The fact is, the natives won't stop with their tattoos. Some things you can't take away from people," he mused. "Get a look at Queen Vaekehu's tattoos if you go visit her, which you should. She's gone missionary, but at one time her legs were the main attraction for visitors to the island."

In the morning, they all went ashore. As their canoe approached the beach, the people of Anaho stopped to get a good look at them. There were women among the men, most of them half-clad and damp. It appeared they were returning home from a morning bath. When Fanny, in a *holoku,* and Maggie, in a proper dress and veil, stepped onshore, the women came forward and startled them by calling out, "Hello! Hello!" Another in the crowd—a man who had come aboard the *Casco* yesterday—gestured toward Louis with his eyes and said to the gathered, *"Ona."* A round of nodding followed.

"What does that mean?" Louis asked Frère Michel, a portly young French priest who had joined the greeting party.

"'Owner,'" he responded. "It is a word of respect. It means you are *très riche, monsieur.*"

Fanny watched Louis—so pale and slender a specimen compared to these strapping men—fairly beam with pleasure at his new notoriety.

"Some of them speak pidgin English," the priest said, "but do not assume they comprehend everything you say. Would you like a tour?"

Fanny, Louis, Maggie, and Lloyd followed Frère Michel, who was joined by Taipi-Kikino and Regler. Fanny guessed which of the locals had "gone missionary" by what they were wearing. A few men wore European-style trousers; some women wore *holokus*.

They visited a large oblong building with an open gallery set on a platform of stones. Several people—a family, it appeared—promptly emerged from the thatched-roof house to stare back at the "Cascos," as they now called themselves. In a matter of moments, Fanny and her family were welcome guests sitting on the floor in the house's central open room on woven mats.

"Look closely at the mat upon which you are sitting," Frère Michel said. "It is made of tree bark and has probably taken the woman of the house a year to make. It is the islander's greatest wealth, these *tapas*. Some of them have been in families for decades." The priest nodded toward a man preparing a drink. "And that is *kava*. You will drink it often here."

Fanny watched the man prepare the drink. He chewed on a plant root until it was in shreds, then added water and mixed it in a wooden bowl, which was passed around to them. Maggie shot a horrified glance at Fanny as she sipped the liquid, but took the bowl in her turn and made a show, at least, of sipping. Next they were served roasted pig on banana leaves and mashed breadfruit covered in coconut cream.

"Would you ask the hostess if she will share her recipe?" Fanny requested. Soon the priest was translating the simple instructions.

"I want to give them something," Fanny said to her family as they prepared to depart. "Have you anything at all?" Louis and Lloyd searched their pockets while Maggie held the tip of her widow's veil, as if she feared Fanny might snatch it off her head. In her pocket, Fanny felt her tobacco pouch and papers.

Having instructed the men at the table to roll cigarettes, she rose with the others and went outside, where dancers had gathered to entertain the visitors. A fellow pounded a barrel as five men leaped about, escalating their jig into gymnastics as they climbed upon each other's shoulders and jumped off. Some of the native people milling about were nearly naked, wearing only a rolled-up piece of fabric around their waists. Others had on *lavalavas*, large handkerchiefs tied at the waist that covered the private parts. The men sported extraordinary tattoos on their flanks and thighs that so completely covered their skin, they appeared to be wearing tight pants down to their knees. Yet others mixed European-style clothing with native garb. A few of the men had white lime caked in their hair. It seemed that everyone wore a sprig of nature: a flower behind the ear, a wreath around the neck, tendrils of vines wrapping the midsection. The fragrance of the flowers mixed with the smells of ginger, coconut oil, and the dung of fat black pigs moving among the audience with the kind of freedom she'd heard cows enjoyed in India.

Fanny began to laugh. *What a strange turn life has taken!*

When the dancing finished, an elderly man burst into song. "What is he saying?" she asked Regler when the song had gone on for some time.

"It is a story about your visit. A rich man and his wife have arrived in a silver ship to this island. He is composing it as he goes. That is what the people do here."

Next came a tour of a girls' school run by nuns, and then the church, where Frère Michel took them into his little office to make a pot of coffee. Fanny could see the caution on Louis's face. He was entering the camp of the enemy: a missionary, and a Catholic one, at that. She watched him walk over to the bookcase to scan the titles and take the man's measure.

"It is not the coffee you are accustomed to," the priest warned. He shrugged. "One adapts."

"I am trying to adjust to their manners." Louis laughed. "Yesterday we were ridiculed for not buying their coconuts, and today they opened their homes and *served* us coconuts."

The priest folded his hands in his lap. "Yesterday's display reflects how these people are treated by traders. They expect to be cheated, and they were perhaps trying to establish their power in the bargaining. It was a performance, in a way. Today is far more sincere. They have a rather complex sense of etiquette."

"Yes?"

"It has evolved over time, I think. They haven't anything like a court system. No legal structure to speak of," the priest said. "No mechanism for appealing wrongs. In the absence of laws, it's rather useful to have strict rules of etiquette, don't you think? They tell everyone how to behave. There are rules for all sorts of things. One doesn't just wake up a chief in the morning by shaking his shoulder, for example. You must tickle his feet. Their *tapus* are their laws. There are *tapus* for fish, for women . . ."

"Yes?"

"If they find there are fewer fish in an area, they will declare a *tapu* for that place until the fish come back."

"And the ones for women?" Fanny asked.

"Ah, women can do very little. They marry young and have many restrictions. On some islands, the women are not permitted to eat meat. So the men form clubs and cook and eat together. On this island, the chief recently removed the *tapu* against women using roads that men have built, which is all the roads. Up to now, they had to walk through fields. If they wanted to cross the road, they had to wade through a stream. They cannot use a man's saddle for their horses— that's another *tapu,* though I don't know the origin of it. Some chief became annoyed with his wife borrowing his equipment too often, I suppose. But the women are clever. They have figured a way around it. It seems they are permitted to use the saddle of someone who is not a native. My saddle is borrowed quite a lot, as is Mr. Regler's. And so it goes."

"I want to invite the women to come to the boat tomorrow," Fanny said. "I don't know if you can arrange it."

The priest smiled. "I shall see what I can do."

When the group arrived the next morning, Fanny had jam and hard ship biscuits waiting. Dressed in *holokus* and fragrant with fresh flowers in their hair, the women hardly noticed the tray of food on the table, for they were caught up in their multiple reflections set off by the mirrors lining the walls of the saloon. They were not strangers to mirrors, but many at one time were an oddity, and wildly entertaining. The women lifted their hems to examine the backs of their legs, tilted their heads to admire their faces. In time, their attention turned to the lush velvet on the cushions around the table. One woman hoisted her dress and, exposing legs and buttocks tattooed in spiral patterns, rubbed her bottom on the crimson cushion. Valentine, who was serving tea, pressed her lips tight in quiet horror. But Fanny's mind filled with a picture of herself some ten years ago in Fanny Sitwell's elegant drawing room, lying on a chaise with her foot in a cast while her hosts stared at her as if she had just leaped out of a gulch in the wild and woolly American West. Fanny remembered vividly the one odd longing in her mind that day: to bury her face in the luxury of Mrs. Sitwell's velvet curtains and thereby confirm everyone's worst instincts about her class and character.

Fanny took the woman's hand and placed it on the velvet curtains of the ship windows. Then she put her own face against the fabric to demonstrate, and encouraged the woman to do the same. When the native woman had given her cheeks a satisfying rub, her great brown eyes looked at Fanny seriously. She ran a finger along the tanned skin of Fanny's forearm, then touched her own arm. "All same you," she said.

CHAPTER 61

"To think we were wearing buffalo coats a few weeks ago," Maggie Stevenson remarked. She had put on her widow's veil for the priest's visit and wore shoes over her bare feet, unlike her daughter-in-law, who had stopped making such concessions some time ago.

The family, along with the priest, were all sitting on the deck of the *Casco,* feeling the soft bulge of each wave as it lifted and lowered the boat before breaking into tinsel-bright strands on the shore.

"It doesn't seem real," Fanny said. "The beauty of this place—of these people—is beyond anything I ever conceived."

"Yet there is a sadness, a kind of defeat I have sensed here and there among them," Louis said. "Or am I imagining that?"

"No, you are not imagining. They have lost much," the priest said. "To diseases, to alcohol and opium—the gifts of civilization. There are many suicides. If you chip away at their culture, people forget who they are." He looked at Louis. "I know what you are wondering. How dare I speak of such loss if I am part of the cause?"

Louis conceded the point with a nod.

"I believe we have done some good by helping to end cannibalism. As for the rest, I don't know," the priest said. "When I came here, the bishop said to me, 'You are coming into a culture that is more civilized than our own.' I have pondered that remark a great deal."

POLITE EATERS OF human flesh? Suicides in paradise? None of it added up, and Louis had no real sense whether the reported facts were correct. Yet for him, there were strands of familiarity in the stories.

"When the English defeated the Scottish, they deposed clan chiefs and stripped the people of their kilts and bagpipes," he told Fanny that night before retiring. "They weighted down their lilting Gaelic tongues with the thumping ballast of official English."

"How odd to feel sympathy for cannibals that their old ways have been taken away," Fanny said. "But there it is."

Louis shook his head. "I wonder how it is on other islands, where there has been less contact with foreigners. Are their populations declining? Are the people of other islands as depressed as the Marquesans appear to be?"

"If they have been stripped of their identities, I should think so," Fanny mused.

Louis shook his head. "I cannot help but think of the Highlanders."

"Oh, Louis, you can't compare all the world to Scotland at every turn."

"No, I suppose not. On our island, we much preferred drawing and quartering. Though the old Scots shared one decorating pleasure with these island peoples: displaying heads on pikes around the old homestead. Otherwise, I admit our savagery is entirely different."

CHAPTER 62

⁓

In the near darkness, Fanny threw a *holoku* over her head, pulled the blanket from her berth, then felt her way along the passage leading to the companionway. Her bare feet found the steps, counted them. Up on deck, she made out the figure of her husband in his striped trader's pajamas, sitting cross-legged near the railing. She sank down next to him, wrapped them both in her blanket, and rested her head on his shoulder. The only sounds were the lapping of waves against the hull and the cry of a single bird flying overhead. As first light came up on the little island of Hiva Oa, they sat there together like theatergoers, silent and watching.

"It's yet another restaging of the Creation," he whispered. "Are you weary of the same old thing?"

She laughed. "I never grow tired of it."

The island's mountains, darkly furred with foliage, formed a silhouette behind two strips of clouds. A veil of mist covering the peak loomed gray as lead. But on the water's surface, cloud wisps lit white by the hidden sun danced across the glittering waves. All parts of the picture—clouds, waves, light and dark air, even the mountains—appeared to be undulating together.

"I think I could live and die here," she said.

"You smell like coconut." His fingers stroked her neck, then sought her breasts. He groped around in the folds of fabric. "Does that thing you wear have a drawstring at the bottom as well as the top?" he asked.

"Let's go to your berth, love."

"You said you felt odd about—"

"They're not up yet."

Louis's tiny cabin had a narrow bed with a blanket and a finely woven little pillow made from pandanus leaves that a Marquesan had presented to him. Immediately beside the bed was a projecting shelf that served as a desk. The porthole in his room was open, and a cool breeze blew across her face. She heard sheep bleating hungrily on the hillside near Anaho beach, heard the chink of crockery in the galley as she felt the pulse of his heart quicken against hers.

It was Louis who broke the silence afterward. "I woke up this morning," he said softly, "and I had to convince myself yet again that this whole spectacle"—he pointed toward the window—"this morning in eternity is not a dream. Do you understand what I'm trying to say? To be here, living an adventure bigger than anything I dreamed of as a boy is one thing, but to be here and be *well,* not just well but feeling positively spruce, is beyond all—"

His voice cracked. A ray of sun shot through the window and lit tears rolling down his cheeks. She squeezed his hand to comfort him but, in the next moment, saw him smiling broadly. "Do you see what an infant I've become? Yesterday I stood in the surf and let the waves simply knock me over. I picked up shells like those children I used to watch on the beach at Bournemouth. And do you know, a little sea creature crawled out of his house to have a look at me. No child could have been more wonderstruck than I at that tiny speck of life. I have spent most of my days on this planet trying to get well. And now, to have hope of good health? It is a whole new world for me, Fanny.

"I want to write a book on the South Seas," he said as he pulled on his clothes. "There is so much here. The history of these people, their myths, the language subtleties. I will write chapters and take parts of what I write to send McClure as travel letters. Two birds with one stone. I can already see it's going to be a devil of a big book."

"I haven't seen you this well in such a long time." She embraced him. "You've never had such rich characters to write up."

Louis's strength had grown steadily from the moment the sea air hit his lungs. He pranced around the *Casco* as it heeled and heaved, surefooted as a mountain goat. He *looked* different. There was meat on his bones, though anyone seeing him for the first time would take him for a starveling. But to Fanny, who had lifted and turned his body through long, terrifying nights in Oakland and Hyères and Bournemouth, he was a new man. To see the wind billowing his shirt as he clung to a shroud, to see such wild joy in his eyes, was something she had frankly despaired of ever witnessing again. The wonder of his good health struck her as it struck him: a miracle.

It wasn't only Louis who had been altered by the trip. Maggie Stevenson had shown herself to be a woman Fanny hadn't known existed. "She's returned to the girl she was before her marriage, I think," Louis observed. "It makes me realize how heavily my father influenced her." And Lloyd—how changed *he* was. He seemed charged with excitement. He was making photographs, writing stories, participating as an adult in the gatherings they'd had with natives.

Fanny had been taking notes on an irregular basis, and she sat down now to try to capture what she was feeling.

Louis says he feels alive in an entirely new way, and I must say I share the feeling. I am freer now, to be sure. There is no house to keep and I am able to explore as I choose, so long as Louis is well. I do feel healthier, as he does. My headaches are gone. Only the seasickness remains a constant. It will never let up, I am quite certain. But the wretchedness of a sick stomach is overshadowed when I witness the happiness of my two boys.

Oh, the things we all have seen! In the two months we've been in the Marquesas, most of it was spent on the island of Nuka Hiva. When we departed, we gave a ride to Frère Michel to the island of Hiva Oa, where we are anchored now. Just yesterday Louis and he rode up the green hills on horseback, a feat that would have been unthinkable six months ago in England.

How far away Bournemouth seems, how distant the people we knew there. Henley no longer shadows me now. He grows smaller and smaller as the world gets bigger and bigger. I feel as if Louis and I have survived a terrible test of some kind. Going away on the cruise has brought us back together.

Yesterday, when I came down to my berth for a nap, I found a poem Louis wrote attached to the inside of my bed curtain.

Fanny went to the back of the box where she kept her correspondence, pulled out the note, and pinned it to the page she had just written.

Trusty, dusky, vivid, true
With eyes of gold and bramble-dew
Steel-true and blade-straight,
The great artificer
Made my mate.

Honour, anger, valour, fire;
A love that life could never tire,
Death quench or evil stir,
The mighty master
Gave to her.

Teacher, tender, comrade, wife,
A fellow-farer true through life;
Heart-whole and soul-free
The august father
Gave to me.

CHAPTER 63

In the dining room of the Royal Hawaiian Hotel, the Cascos fell upon their roast-beef dinner with near-savage gusto.

Belle laughed. "You're starving!"

"We are," Fanny admitted to her daughter, who sat at the long and groaning table with her husband and Austin. She noticed how much better Belle looked than she had in San Francisco. She had made it back to Hawaii, as they'd hoped, and it had warmed Fanny's heart to see her girl waiting on the dock in Honolulu.

"Our supplies on the boat were very nearly gone," Fanny said. "Had we run into foul weather, we would have been in real trouble. But the wind was cooperative."

"*Cooperative?*" Captain Otis laughed. "It was a gale-force squall got us here, Mrs. Stevenson."

"I saw your arrival," Belle said. "It was remarkable you didn't slam into another boat."

"To our braw captain," Louis called out to Otis. Glasses were hoisted up and down the table. "Thank you for that splendid landing."

"One of the many miracles of this voyage," Fanny said. Her eyes met the captain's at that moment, and she saw him nod solemnly. She looked down the table at Maggie, Lloyd, Valentine, and the sailors. They were all nodding.

"Tell us!" Belle said.

The stories flowed. Captain Otis, who had been a surly, monosyllabic taskmaster at the beginning of the voyage, waxed poetic as he described with animated hands the tattooed legs of Queen Vaekehu. "For sheer beauty, I would say Nuka Hiva in the Marquesas was the most magnificent," Otis said. "But the most beautiful of the Polynesian people we met were the Tahitians." Fanny had heard those very words come out of her husband's mouth a couple of days ago. It struck her that the captain had made a study of Louis's style and opinions.

"Aye." Maggie sighed. "Big, muscled men over six feet tall, with luminous brown eyes . . ."

". . . tattooed fore and aft . . ." Louis interjected.

". . . just magnificent creatures, very well set up."

"Aunt Maggie!" Lloyd lowered his head and looked at her over his spectacles. "I didn't know you were taking notice."

Maggie put her hand up to her mouth in embarrassed delight.

"I will confirm that observation," Fanny said.

Everyone laughed, and the stories continued: of the things they'd seen in six months, of treacherous coral atolls and broken masts, of Protestant missionary wives bent on covering native flesh with fabric, of Catholic priests who descended into slovenly habits and unclean appearance in the absence of wives. They talked of the Tahitian princess who saved Louis's life by feeding him fish soup when he fell ill with fever, and of Ori a Ori, her Tahitian subchief who adopted Louis as a brother, moved out of his house, and gave it over to the Stevensons, even feeding them for weeks as Louis recovered from the one real sickness he'd had since they left. They talked of the magical beauty of Hiva Oa, where the French missionaries' battle against cannibalism had been only partly successful, where the repugnant cannibal chief Moipu spoke nostalgically of the human hand as his favorite morsel.

"The Pacific," Louis mused aloud, "is a strange place indeed. It's as if—" Just then the telephone in the dining room rang, and he nearly leaped from his chair. "Dear God," he said, "would someone stop that bleating thing?"

Everyone laughed except Louis, who was genuinely irritated.

"You were saying?" Belle said.

"It's as if the nineteenth century exists here only in spots. I don't know what to make of it entirely, but I consider myself lucky to have seen it before it changes." The Cascos fell silent, as if Louis had just spoken a truth for all of them.

Now a leave-taking was imminent. Louis had told Otis that the *Casco* should return to San Francisco without them. They were out of funds and would have to stay in Hawaii until money from *Scribner's* or

McClure found its way to Honolulu. That might take another three or four months. Then they would board a steamer to Sydney and eventually travel to England. Neither Fanny nor Louis had an appetite to race through winter weather to San Francisco on the *Casco*. There were embraces all around when the dinner ended, and a teary farewell to Valentine. Loyal Valentine, the funny, sometimes petulant young woman who had attended so faithfully to Louis during the past six years, would be moving to San Francisco to start her own life.

Outside, electric streetlights illuminated a passing streetcar. Louis stopped to gaze at the stars, which he did every night wherever he was, but tonight the lights made it difficult. "Let's get a cottage at Waikiki," he said as he and Fanny walked to the guesthouse where they were staying the night. "I can't bear all this progress."

Living on the beach, they marked time at Waikiki, waiting for word from Baxter that money was back in the depleted coffers. Louis worked on his South Seas book but was growing restless in his limbo. When Belle came with Austin to visit, Louis took long walks with them, collecting shells and tossing rocks with the boy. The child provided some distraction, and the visits comforted Fanny, who was relieved to see Belle's attitude toward Louis softening. The girl had blamed him entirely for the breakup of her parents' marriage.

Once, when he was out on such a stroll, Fanny went to his desk to look at the pages he had written. What she found shocked her. Louis had divided his work into sections, including language, songs, history, and myths, even some botany. It dawned on her that he was writing a science book, not the sort of colorful travel material for which he was already known. What on earth was he thinking?

What she saw on the desk was an outline written by a layman intent upon a scholarly paper about the South Seas islands and islanders, a layman whose own brain, brilliant as it was, could not remember the names of trees and flowers for any length of time. It was simply not his strength. Even if it were, it would take twenty years of living in these islands to write such a book. Louis kept crowing that no other white people, besides Melville and a handful of missionaries, had ever experienced what they had in these islands. Perhaps. But Melville had the good sense not to turn his knowledge into a scientific treatise. Fanny grabbed a couple of sheets of paper and went to her own desk to write a letter to Colvin.

> *Louis has the most enchanting material that any one ever had in the whole world for his book, and I am afraid he is going to spoil it all. He has taken it into his Scotch Stevenson head . . . that his book must be a sort of scientific and historical impersonal thing comparing the different languages (of which he knows nothing, really) and the different peoples . . . and the whole thing to be impersonal, leaving out all he knows of the people themselves . . . I am going to ask you to throw the weight of your influence as heavily as possible in the scales with me . . . otherwise Louis will spend a good deal of time in Sydney actually reading other people's books on the islands. What a thing it is to have a "man of genius" to deal with. It is like managing an overbred horse. Why with my own feeble hand I could write a book that the whole world would jump at . . .*

Fanny hurriedly sealed the letter inside an envelope and hid it between the pages of a book before Louis returned. Tomorrow, when she went into town, she would post it.

CHAPTER 64

⌒

My dear Fanny Sitwell,

By now Louis has told Sidney that we will be delayed from returning to England. After four months in Honolulu, it is ever clearer that Louis's health fares best at sea, and truth be told, the social whirl of Honolulu has worn heavily on us. Belle's friend King Kalakaua has entertained us royally, but we have simpler needs than ever before, and we long for one more cruise, this time to the Gilbert Islands. Louis found a new trading ship, the Equator, *which will take us on and allow us to explore different islands while it's in port, conducting its trading activities. Copra is the main product the* Equator *crew wants, and it is plentiful in the South Seas. Copra, by the way, is the dried meat of the coconut that they boil in water to make coconut oil.*

The captain of the ship is a fresh-faced boy of twenty-three who wears a tam-o'-shanter and whose speech is heavily sauced with a Scots accent. Can you imagine Louis's pure joy to have a countryman at the wheel? Mrs. Stevenson will return to Scotland for a while, but Lloyd will go with us, continuing on as photographer for the South Seas book. So will Belle's husband, Joe, who will photograph also (and hopefully straighten out his life under our watch). Belle and her little boy will go on to Sydney to live for four months until we arrive there.

How we miss you! But we will never have another chance to see this part of the world in this way. And so we go.

With dearest affection, believe me,
Fanny V. de G. Stevenson

"You're about to get your wish, Mr. Stevenson," Captain Reid said. The slender young Scot, topped as usual by his tartan bonnet, took a final gulp from a tin cup before returning his attention to the ship's wheel.

"Which wish is that?"

"For a braw adventure, sir. The *Equator* shall make for Apemama."

"Apemama? The home of . . ."

"Tembinoka, aye."

Fanny saw Louis's back straighten and his eyes shoot sparks. "The Napoleon of the Gilberts?"

"The same," Reid replied.

Louis burst into a jubilant jig.

"Have you met him?" Fanny asked.

"Oh, yes. Several times. You will, too—he does all his own trading. He comes aboard and sometimes stays overnight. Eats our food, which is all for the good, because it means we have something that he wants. He has a huge appetite for new objects." Reid laughed. "He has a huge appetite."

"And he has copra . . ."

"Houses of it. That's how he sells it. By the houseful."

"Are you afraid of him?"

Reid's brows went up. "Well, I don't cross him. He has killed cold-heartedly in his day. They say he murdered one of his wives who betrayed him. Put her rotting corpse out in front of his palace as a lesson to the others. He won't let whites stay on his island but for one broken-down old fellow who is a recluse. Oh, he allowed a missionary to stay around long enough to teach him English, then booted him off. He won't even let traveling natives from other islands stay. No, Tembinoka must be the only man in charge, you see. He has a few chaps as lieutenants, but mostly, he is surrounded by his women. Has a whole harem." Reid turned to his first mate. "Smarten up the ship. We are headed into Apemama."

In a few minutes, sailors with mops and buckets were scrubbing decks and overhauling the trading room. In the distance, Fanny could see the slender strip of atoll and its interior lagoon. "So small a kingdom for so great an ogre," she mused aloud.

The *Equator* edged carefully through shoals until they dropped anchor. The sun was so glaringly bright upon the beach that the glittering white strip seemed to bore into Fanny's retinas. Onshore she saw a village smattered with high-roofed huts but no people. Apart from the sound of the waves, the scene was eerily quiet.

"Now we wait for our visitor," Reid said.

Soon enough, a handful of people appeared. A boat carrying the king and a large ladder approached the ship. "He once had a ship's ladder collapse under him," Reid explained. "Now he brings his own."

Fanny understood the need when she spied the king climbing onto the *Equator's* deck. Tembinoka's large head of black hair came up over the ship's railing, and then his great brown forearms lifted up a massive body attired in a costume that stole her breath away. It was a cardinal-red velvet uniform so braided and beribboned, she wondered if somehow the king had seen a Gilbert and Sullivan production. If his costume revealed a giddy streak, his face did not. He had a hawkish nose, piercing black eyes, and a fiercely sober mouth. *He's all business,* she thought.

After Reid introduced the king to Louis and Fanny, Tembinoka began his appraisal of the trading room's contents. Bored quickly by the bolts of fabric and appliances, he moved through the ship, poking his head into every cabin. When he got to Fanny's room, he spied a dressing case that caught his fancy.

"It is utterly worthless," she whispered to Louis, "certainly useless for a man. I keep my hair combs and such in there."

"I am afraid we can't sell it," Louis piped up.

The king looked at his face for the first time. "How much?" Tembinoka asked in his high voice, clearly having assumed that Louis was starting a round of haggling.

"Gift from a friend," Louis said, "so sorry."

The king looked at him wearily, like a man accustomed to a familiar gambit. *"Kaupoi."* He smirked. Fanny suspected the word meant "rich man" or, more cynically, "Mr. Important." Tembinoka took a bag of coins from a retainer and spread out twenty pounds in gold. Twenty pounds!

Louis said, "I don't sell anything. Please accept this as a gift."

Fanny emptied the case and Louis put it into the king's hands. They watched in horror as his features melted with shame. He was accustomed to being cheated by white men but was startled by white generosity. When he prepared to depart the boat with Fanny's case under his arm, Louis seized the moment. "Might my wife and I stay on your island for a couple of weeks while the *Equator* makes its rounds to other islands?" he blurted out.

The king dropped his head and did not respond, only descended his kingly ladder. Within a short time, a carved wooden jewel box appeared as replacement for the gift, but no answer to Louis's question came with it.

"Why do you want to stay on his island?" Fanny asked.

"Because he is a story, I can tell already," Louis said. "He is like no one else."

When Tembinoka returned early the next morning, they were seated at breakfast. Upon his approach, Fanny surmised the king was bringing one of his women, for she spied a dress in the distance. In fact, it was Tembinoka himself coming into the saloon, attired in a woman's green silk frock, a pith helmet, and blue glass spectacles. He sat across from them, and after a few syllables of greeting, proceeded to stare silently at each of them. Fanny squirmed under his inspection and made work of chasing her eggs across the plate with her fork so as not to have to look up again. Louis chatted on gaily as if it were all perfectly normal. Captain Reid interjected that Louis was a knowledgeable man whose main interest in the South Seas was to come to Apemama and report back to Queen Victoria all he'd learned. At that point, Louis's jaw dropped and he fell silent.

After what seemed an eternity of staring, the king said simply, "You good man, you no lie" and "You good woman. You come my island."

So it was that they found themselves living in Apemama. Tembinoka ordered that four houses on stilts should be moved to the spot of their choice on the beach. Lloyd and Fanny and Louis watched in amazement as many sets of legs moved together under the big upturned-basket houses they called *maniaps*. If one of the movers tarried in his work, the king aimed his Winchester just above the offender's head, and the fellow stepped livelier.

"I can only assume some locals have been displaced because we are here," Louis worried aloud. "That can't be too good for neighborly relations."

When the huts were in place, Tembinoka decreed that his subjects should observe an invisible *tapu* circle around the group of houses. The king walked the circumference himself so that no misunderstandings might occur. No native was to go inside that circle or disturb the new-comers in any way. Then he made clear his expectations of the Steven-sons. He wanted to come to their house when the spirit moved him, to enjoy what they were eating. If he did not come, they were to send a plate of their dinner to his compound. His people would work for Louis and Fanny, but only Tembinoka could give them orders. And one other thing: He liked it quiet. No noise.

The latter prohibition was stunningly evident that first night on the beach. Huddled under a mosquito net with a pot of insect powder burning nearby, Fanny and Louis listened for some sounds of life in the village but heard only the gentle lapping of waves.

In the following days, the king showed them his kingdom. He met them each day in a dazzling new costume fitted carefully to his figure, each garment bearing exaggerated dimensions of features one found in European clothing, and each made up in vibrant fabrics with decorative flourishes unlike any they'd ever seen. Tembinoka had a style distinctly his own. On the morning he was to show them his storehouses, he ap-peared in a turquoise silk morning coat with tails that fell to his heels.

"That is a lovely color," Fanny said, and she meant it. "It is the color of the sea."

Tembinoka nodded at the compliment. He led them to his palace, a collection of rustic buildings surrounded by a fence. Inside the huts, women of every age, shape, and manner of dress moved about, attend-ing to their responsibilities. Some cleaned, some nursed babies. A few slept on mats. Taking them all in with a sweep of his arm, the king said, "My family." He summoned his first wife and introduced her formally to Fanny and Louis. The oldest of the women, she seemed gracious and on perfectly good terms with the other wives in the household.

The king summoned a woman in charge of firearms, who returned with a case containing a disassembled pistol that he specifically asked for. Then Tembinoka directed a different woman—this one in charge of napery—to show Fanny recently acquired embroidered napkins.

Next he took them to a large building where a grim-faced woman in charge of its contents unlocked the door and ushered them in. Piled from floor to ceiling were the machinery and fripperies of civilization that the king had managed to lay his hands on: bolts of fabric, piles of blue eyeglasses, feathered hats, high-button shoes in every size, barrels of tin cups, jars of ointment with lids gone rusty, axes, Winchesters, cases of tobacco, spittoons, inkpots, clocks, and stoves.

After the tour, they sat on the king's terrace and drank *kava*. It soon became clear why the chief was allowing them to stay: He had his own agenda. He pressed them with questions. How many fathoms high is Windsor Castle? the palace builder wanted to know. How much did it cost to buy a schooner in Sydney? Evidently, the king's choice to preserve the islanders from the influence of other cultures meant he was in quarantine, too.

From navigation and building, his thoughts turned to medicine. The girl in charge arrived as instructed, holding a bottle of laxative syrup.

"You savvy?" he asked Fanny.

"Yes, I know it."

"Good?"

"I use this." Fanny wrote down the word *Castoria* for him.

"Betta?"

"Much better," Fanny said. "The ship carries it. We will get some for you when the *Equator* returns."

The king pulled a meerschaum pipe from his pocket. He signaled a young lady who stayed nearby with matches and tobacco. As all his subjects were required to do when they approached him, she crouched and then crawled over to him.

In his simple English, Tembinoka told the legend of his family's beginnings—the first parents being a heroic woman and a shark—about the wars his ancestors had waged, the wars he had waged, and the uncle he had to send away from the island for betraying him. He talked of his own power and how he liked things organized. Fanny's instincts about Tembinoka were confirmed as he talked on. Despite his tight-fisted approach to governing, he talked of how deeply he cared for his people. The king was a smart fellow. He was not only the ruler of some three thousand people, he was their chief poet, architect, historian, philosopher, and inventor.

In the evening, as they left the king's quarters, Fanny noticed old crones sitting intermittently along the enclosing fence. These were the palace guards, she learned later, who watched through the night for any irregularities. They communicated with one another by throwing stones.

That night Louis and Fanny stayed awake for hours under the mosquito net, scribbling madly into their diaries by the light of a lantern, intent on noting every exotic detail they had witnessed.

"Where are the men?" Fanny wondered aloud.

"They're out there, in the huts and elsewhere, but they're invisible, aren't they? Obviously, they hold inferior positions, except a few of his trusted minions. Did you notice those fellows who came in to confer with Tembinoka about doings in the village? I'm sure they were spies. They must come in every day to fill his ear."

"The king is keeping a tight lid on his strange little paradise," Fanny said.

Louis scratched his head. "I suppose Tembinoka thinks he can maintain control of his kingdom by keeping outsiders away, especially whites. You can't blame him. But his quarantine can't last. His little cache of Winchesters is nothing against the German or French or American cannons. When one of those countries decides he has something they want, he is going to topple. And along with him will go the identity of the people—their oral history, the legends, the songs. Isn't that how these things work?"

In the weeks that followed, no native people came across the *tapu* line to visit them. They named their clutch of huts Equator Town and watched as life went on around them, just beyond the line. Sometimes they saw the king walk past and out into the water with one of his retainers, where they climbed into a fishing boat—for the king liked to fish—untied the boat's rope from the anchor—which happened to be a sewing machine—and headed out to sea. When they came back, Fanny would likely be presented with a large fish, which meant the king would be joining them for dinner. She planted salad greens that flourished and, in time, delighted Tembinoka.

In the mornings, Louis wrote. In the afternoons he and Lloyd collaborated on a novel set in the Pacific. After, they fantasized about having their own copra trading boat. In the evenings, Louis walked on the beach under the stars, playing his flageolet.

Fanny couldn't forget her husband's dire predictions for the future of this little silver crescent of sand sitting out in the vast blue ocean. She had grown fond of Tembinoka. She heard in his conversation the pride of a man who had built up a society that was modern, compared to the world he had inherited from his predecessors.

The *Equator* was overdue by nearly two weeks, and Fanny expected it would come any moment. They were all ready to go, their provisions were running short, and they were sorely tired of eating wild chicken. She wanted to give the king a gift before they left. Though the man seemed to have one of everything, he lacked a flag for his kingdom. One morning she quickly sketched out a design. She envisioned a banner with three stripes—yellow, green, and red—with a black shark at its center, and below it, the words *I bite triply.*

"It's a reference to the shark's three rows of teeth," she explained to Louis.

That night a copra trading ship called the *Tiernan* was in harbor. The king threw a big party with fireworks and dancing but, strangely, did not invite them. Fanny and Louis were inside their hut when they heard a gunshot near the palace.

"Do you think someone has shot the king?"

"The thought hadn't occurred to me, but now that you say it . . ." Louis got up, loaded their pistols, and put them near at hand.

In their hut in Equator Town, they lay awake listening.

Someone shot at a dog, the king explained when he came by the hut the next morning. Fanny was glad to see Tembinoka alive, though he was, uncharacteristically, a little drunk. She showed him her design for the Apemama flag, and he beamed his approval. He didn't stay long. Louis was not there, and the king seemed like a small, tired child when he said, "I want to go home."

Louis arrived next, with urgent news. "The captain of the *Tiernan* says we can take passage with him to Samoa. No one knows what has happened to the *Equator.*"

"All right."

"We'll have to pack quickly. They depart tomorrow."

The next day, Fanny cast her gaze at their belongings, strewn around the hut, which she couldn't bring herself to pack. "Captain Reid is expecting us to be here," she said, but her shoulders sank and she admitted what was on her mind: "I have this dreadful premonition . . . I don't want to go."

"The lady has a premonition." Louis sighed. But he did not pursue his teasing and canceled their passage.

When the *Equator* arrived the following week and the Stevensons climbed aboard, Tembinoka wept on the dock.

"DID YOU GET the news about the *Tiernan?*" Reid asked them over a dinner of octopus and clams on the boat that evening.

Fanny caught her breath.

"Becalmed, they were, just bobbing around with no wind, so everyone went to sleep, I suppose, when up sprang a squall that made the boat turn turtle. It was just a day or two out of Apemama."

"I can't believe it," Louis said. "We just saw them off."

"Sixteen dead," Reid reported gravely.

They fell quiet. Fanny remembered the faces of the men they had befriended and wondered who among them had died.

In the coming days, when storms chased the *Equator* from Apemama to Samoa, Fanny settled her blankets in a narrow galley-way so she wouldn't be thrown from her bed. Waves came over the prow and poured down below, leaving her in a shallow lake. She was terrified, but she would never admit that to Louis. Instead, she lay fully dressed, with an umbrella over her head, thinking about the lost men on the *Tiernan,* who went from dreams to death in the flutter of an eye.

CHAPTER 65

1889

When Fanny first clapped eyes on their future homestead in the South Seas, she was standing on the side of a mountain, two and a half miles above the town of Apia, on the island of Upolu in Samoa. The sighting of the property lacked the thrill she'd felt on first seeing the house in Bournemouth, or the chalet in Hyères, or even the little cottage in Oakland where she had raised her children. She wasn't even looking for a place in Samoa. They had merely gotten off the *Equator* for a couple of weeks while Louis researched the history of the islands for his newspaper letters. His best source was a local trader, one Mr. Harry J. Moors, who promptly offered his home as the place they should stay during their visit. He happened to be the local land agent as well.

"Moors wants to show us some property this afternoon," Louis said after breakfast.

"He's enterprising, I'll give him that. We've been here all of three days," Fanny replied. They were taking an afternoon stroll through Apia, looking it over. On its main street, where drinking shops alternated with churches and houses, sin and salvation appeared to be tied in the contest for Apia's souls. Pouring out of tavern doorways came the deafening whine of hurdy-gurdies. Within, tawdry-looking women drank with sailors.

The town was full of whites—some four hundred, Moors had told them—mostly British, with about ninety Germans and fewer than twenty Americans. "The whites you'll see are missionaries, expatriate farmers, traders, sailors, and beachcombers who washed up in Upolu and never left," Moors said. Fanny noticed the whites had mixed enough with natives that there were plenty of "half-castes" on the streets of Apia. Moors himself had a native wife.

"Would you seriously consider living here?" she asked Louis.

He shrugged. "I wouldn't want to live in town. But you heard the doctor. If I am to remain well, I'll have to stay in this area for the bulk of my time. And you need a place to land, Fanny. I just don't know if Samoa is the right spot. We might be better off near Sydney. Bigger port, more culture."

"It can't hurt to look at it, I guess," she said.

Standing on the hill in the tropical sun that afternoon, with Mount Vaea climbing up in the distance, Fanny's eyes scanned some three hundred acres of tangled forest and undergrowth, a mess of impenetrable branches and liana vines.

"Upolu and Savii are the biggest of the islands in Samoa, but we get the most contact with the outside world here in Upolu." Mr. Moors swept a hand across the treed landscape. "Look at it! Five rivers, all of 'em full of freshwater prawns; a high waterfall and a smaller one that has a bathing pool below it. It's nigh-hand to paradise." He kicked the toe of his boot into the soil. "You can grow anything here, the year round. Oh, there's the occasional cyclone, but that's about it. You might consider a plantation of a couple of crops; people do that to help pay for the cost of the land. Locals will keep it going while you're away." The trader took off his straw hat, wiped his forehead with a sleeve. "Folks call this place Vailima, which is Samoan for 'five rivers.'" He pointed to a spot on the hillside. "Right there would be the best place for a house. That's where I'd put 'er. You'll know exactly when a mail ship comes in."

Sweating profusely, Fanny stared in wonder at Louis, who seemed excited by the land and infused with new energy now that the temperature was well into the nineties. "You are the only person I know who perks up in a heat wave," she said.

"How many mail deliveries?" Louis asked Moors.

"Four a month. You can't beat that."

As they dressed for dinner at Moors's house that evening, Fanny said, "Did you notice how filthy the beach in Apia was? What kind of town would allow animal carcasses and offal to remain there? I don't know what to think of this place." Nor did she know what to make of Mr. Moors, a brawny Michigander whose heart appeared to retain a nook of sentimentality and whose fingers were in a lot of Samoan pies.

He was mainly a trader, with a post in Apia and a string of trading posts on other islands. But he was also the person who would sell them the land on Upolu, arrange to have it cleared, build the cottage for them, and act as their banker, since he had considerable money to loan until their funds could get to the island. He was a big financial force in town. She suspected his enthusiasm for having them as neighbors had something to do with Louis's fame but more to do with his money.

What the people of Apia thought of *them* on first sight was apparent in the face of a missionary who happened to be at the harbor when the *Equator* pulled into port. She and Louis and Lloyd disembarked from the boat barefoot. Fanny wore a *holoku,* bracelets, big gold hoop earrings she had acquired in Tahiti, a straw hat on her head, and her guitar slung over her back. Lloyd wore hoop earrings, blue glasses against the sun, and carried a battered fiddle. Louis, she supposed, was strange-looking simply for the slender figure he cut, but with his somewhat seedy cotton trousers and shirt, and the flageolet in his hand, and a twenty-five-cent white cotton yachting cap on his head, he might have been a beachcomber. All of them were smoking.

The missionary man, Reverend Clarke, had looked puzzled and then hopeful when he saw them tromping along the coral-and-sand main street of Apia. He approached Louis and asked, "Are you folks minstrels?"

"After a fashion, sir," Louis replied cheerily. "Have you work for us?"

A few days running, they rode horses over the hills above Apia. Louis was vigorous in the Samoan climate, staying in the saddle for five hours and then, over long dinners and drinks, talking with the trader and his wife, Nimo, about the politics of the place, on which Moors was an expert.

Impulsively, they decided to buy the property. They authorized Moors to embark on building a cottage where they would live while a larger house was constructed. Fanny calculated that they could sail on to Sydney, get a steamer and return to England, see old friends—what friends were left—collect their possessions, and be back to Samoa in eight months, by September 1890, when the cottage would be done and the house under way.

Reverend Clarke, a decent, gentle man, appeared excited by the idea that they would be neighbors but clearly felt compelled to tell them the truth about the land. "The locals say your property only has four rivers," he said regretfully, as if the information might spoil the deal.

"Close enough," Fanny said.

Later she would wonder: *What made me think I could make this wild place a home?* Then she would remember what she saw the day they bought the land: an orchid growing on a tree limb. It was an exquisite thing, glowing white and tinged with rose and green, perfect in form, flourishing in health, a spot of beauty secretly tucked into ordinary brown bark. That was what she would make Vailima—an unexpected jewel in the Samoan forest.

CHAPTER 66

1890

Cold germs found Louis easily enough in Sydney. Soon he was coughing, and then, for the first time since he fell ill in Tahiti, he was hemorrhaging.

They had ended their cruise on the *Equator* dreaming of a return to Europe, if only for a visit. Now even that diminished plan was crushed.

"You will die if you go back to Britain," a Sydney doctor told Louis. "You cannot return for *any* length of time. It's as simple as that."

The news staggered Fanny. She watched Louis struggle bravely to put a good face on it. "There are only a few people in England and one or two in America whom I will truly, *truly* miss." After a day or two, though, he could not conceal his despair. "I heard a church bell this morning," he told her, "and I was back in Swanston, in my grandfather's country church." His eyes looked off, as if he were seeing, just behind her, the old parishioners he once knew. "It was so vivid! I wanted to be there." He shook his head. "I am going to die in exile. When I return to Scotland, it will be to a grated cell in the Calton Burial Ground."

As his fever rose, Fanny saw what had to be done. She went down to the docks, looking for a boat that might take them out to sea while they waited for the cottage to be finished. A maritime strike was under way, and boats were not leaving Sydney. Only one, a copra trading ship called the *Janet Nicoll*, had a nonunion crew and intended to sail despite the strike. When Fanny inquired about taking passage, she drew a flat no from the shipping company owner, Mr. Henderson, who communicated to her through a representative.

"I didn't get a chance to explain myself properly," Fanny told Louis when she returned from the harbor.

"Oh, I think the owner got your message clear enough. He doesn't want us, my dear. The man has his hands full just getting his ship out of port."

"I'm going back tomorrow," she said, "and I'm going to get us on that boat. You can stake your wig on it."

The following afternoon, Fanny waited outside Henderson's office for an interview. When he opened his door, he wore a scowl. "Madam," he said, "this is a working boat with fifty men. There is no place to put a woman."

"I sailed as the only woman on the *Equator,* sir," Fanny said. "I have lived the same way the men live. You would not have to make any special accommodations for me. And I can afford the fare, whatever that might be."

The man shot her a baleful look that asked, *Why my ship?*

"My husband is extremely ill. We have found that he regains his health when he's at sea. Yours is the only ship that will be leaving this harbor, and the sooner my husband gets sea air in his lungs, the better."

The owner nearly guffawed. "All the more reason why I cannot take you on, madam. The last thing I am equipped to handle is a sick man." With that, his head withdrew, and he shut the door.

Progress, she thought. The man spoke with a Scottish accent. Was there a living Scot who did not feel pride in the accomplishments of a countryman, particularly one as beloved as Louis?

The next day, she stopped at a bookstore before going again to the Henderson and McFarlane shipping company. When she went in search of Henderson, his assistant informed her he would not see her.

"Tell him I won't bother him after today."

Some thirty minutes later, Henderson's harried face peered around the half-opened door. Fanny reached into her satchel and held out to him copies of *Treasure Island* and *Jekyll and Hyde.* The man looked blankly at them.

"Do you know these books?"

"Mmm," he grunted.

"My husband, Robert Louis Stevenson, wrote them. You are Scottish, yes?"

"Yes."

"Then you know that Mr. Stevenson is a national treasure to your people. To have my husband perish here because he could not get out to sea would be an incredible loss to his countrymen. You could have a hand in saving his life."

The man chewed his tobacco furiously.

"I will not hold you responsible if he dies at sea," she said, her voice quavering. "This is his only chance. Do you understand?"

"Wait here," he said, taking the books she pressed into his hands.

She paced outside his door. When he returned, he planted himself in the doorway with his arms crossed. "This ship sails with sealed orders. Do you know what that means?"

"No."

"It means you will not be told where we intend to sail. I shall be on the ship, and I can assure you, you will have no say in where we go. We will be out for four months, and during that time, you will receive not a particle of special attention. If you get off the boat at one of our stops and are not on board when we depart, we will not look for you. We will leave you. Do you understand?"

"I do." She turned to go but stopped in her tracks. "I forgot to mention. There are three of us, not two. My son is traveling with us." She hurried away and didn't look back.

Fanny raced around Sydney buying gifts. She remembered the women she had met already, both native women and the wives of missionaries and traders. She hadn't encountered one yet who wasn't starving to have a pretty new garment or decoration. She ended up buying printed fabrics and a box full of artificial flowers to make wreaths. In a dry goods store, she came across a notebook labeled *Lett's Australasian Diary and Almanac, 1890.* She needed a proper journal. She bought the *Lett's* and wrote her name on the cover.

On this voyage, she intended to keep good notes. Memory was a fickle thing, and Louis counted on the details she pulled out of her journals. But it was more than that. Already they had been at sea for nearly two years. This would be the third and last ship voyage before they settled into the house in Samoa. It was a piece of her life she didn't want to lose.

The following morning, she wrapped Louis in blankets and walked behind as four strong sailors carried him aboard on a gurney. It might have been a funeral procession, with Fanny carrying armfuls of artificial flowers. At one point, a drunk young white man with a rose in his lapel rushed up in an attempt to assist the sailors, but lost his footing and pitched backward off the gangplank into the water, where he flailed around until someone rescued him.

Fanny opened the porthole in their cabin so Louis could gulp the sea air as the ship departed. An exile he might be, but at least he was alive.

CHAPTER 67

Fish striped in vivid hues of orange and white and black swam around his ankles. A crab dotted with brown spots scuttled past his toes. Green fingers of sea life with flesh-pink tips waved all around him.

"Why don't you come with us?" Fanny called to her husband. She held on to her straw hat with one hand and a bundle of skirt with the other as she climbed out of a canoe.

"I want to collect a piece of this coral," he answered. Louis stood calf-deep in the ocean, his pants rolled above his knees, his shirt abandoned on the sand. In the water surrounding him lay an astonishment of coral.

It was a perfect day, somewhere just south of the equator, on a slender thread of land called Arorai in the Gilbert Islands. They had been at sea in the *Janet Nicoll* some two months; he knew it was June in the year 1890, but he had lost count of the date and day of the week. He hadn't any idea of the hour; it would have been a sacrilege to consult a watch. He had hitched a ride to shore in a native's canoe and was stricken nearly blind by the violent glare of the sun on the water. As his eyes adjusted, he saw that the reef was made up of a mass of spherical shapes, each a labyrinthine miracle of squiggling grooves.

Louis went back to the ship and fetched a hatchet. With the sound of the surf pounding in his ears, he chopped at the coral. He knew no proper names for the exotic objects in this fantasy, but he wanted a piece of it. Through the clear water, he saw the rippled patterns the waves had made on the ocean floor. Was there a single straight line in all of the Pacific? Even the sand bore the mark of nature's art. Surely Darwin must have dropped his notebook in awe at the beauty of the Pacific.

As the morning heat rose, the air singed Louis's nostrils. He splashed his face to cool off, tasted the briny seawater in his mouth, longed for drinking water. But he couldn't bring himself to leave this spot.

The Big Book of the South Seas soaked his brain. Colvin had written to him in Sydney, objecting to his concept for the volume. He was singing the same tune as Fanny, that the book should be in the vein of *Travels with a Donkey*. The letter left Louis feeling uncomfortably out of tune with the two people he trusted most. Neither seemed to understand that he wasn't the same man who had written that early book.

Something had happened over the two years since he and Fanny had left Bournemouth. He wasn't entirely sure what it was, but he felt himself changed. Physically, to be sure. To function in the world as other men functioned, to no longer view himself as an invalid, was still miraculous to him. He felt more alive than he'd been in a very long time. He was hungry to learn about the world, to *be* in the world.

Louis continued hacking at the coral. He felt the muscles in his arms growing sore, yet he kept chopping, curious to see how far the new sap in his limbs would take him. After a time—how long, he wasn't certain—he saw Fanny and Lloyd returning from the village.

"What are you doing?" Fanny asked when she got close. She stood in the water next to Louis, her arms laden with necklaces of red seeds and shark's teeth. "You fool!" she exploded. "You haven't moved from where we left you this morning."

Louis held up the pieces of coral he had managed to dislodge. "Have you ever seen such extraordinary patterns?"

"How ignorant you are, Louis. That's common brain coral in your hand. Any schoolboy in San Francisco knows that and will give you specimens." Fanny was fuming. "You should see yourself—burned to the color of a brick! You're going to be blistered head to foot."

"I SAW THE letter from Colvin," she said when they were alone in their cabin. "I'm glad he agrees with me that it's a bad idea to approach this material in such an impersonal way."

"Colvin is doing what Colvin does," Louis said. "He hates an idea when I present it to him, and then, when the book is a success, he claims he knew it would be all along."

"Louis, listen to me. We have seen things that no one else has seen. And to write in an academic way about the South Seas people with only a few personal anecdotes is a terrible mistake. You should have seen what Lloyd and I saw on the island today. The people were so colorful. There were women walking around in these little doll hats they'd gotten in trade, and they'd made them into hair ornaments."

"I have no desire to cast myself as the witty narrator who tells amusing stories about the quaint characters I encounter in my rambles," Louis said. "It belittles them, and it cheapens the significance of the tragedy happening to the people here. This material is bigger than I am, and there's too much at stake. What we are witnessing is the imminent disappearance of ancient traditions. It's been passed on orally, and if their way of life continues to degenerate, their history will be lost. Not just their history but their wisdom. Somebody needs to document their languages, their rituals and beliefs, to alert the world to what is happening here."

"How can you suggest that I would want you to cheapen the material?" She bristled at the idea. The cabin was full of things she'd been collecting, and she threw a pile of rolled *tapas* aside in order to sit down. "You are the brilliant writer on this journey, and I am a poor second by comparison. But if you choose to ignore the stories of what we've experienced, *I* will tell them. This is *our* journey, Louis, not just yours."

"We are not one person!" he shouted.

"Have I no voice?"

"You are free to do as you please."

"We wouldn't even be on this ship if I had not talked our way onto it!" She raised her chin defiantly. "Henry James says I should publish my letters. Well, I assure you I will. Along with my diary from this trip, if need be."

He left the stifling compartment in a fury, desperate for fresh air. Up top, he lit a cigarette and watched the fellows working on deck. They were all black sailors, some from the New Hebrides islands, some from the Solomons, and they all spoke surprisingly fluent English. Perhaps they didn't understand one another's native tongues; he wasn't sure. One of them was named Sally Day. Fanny had come into the cabin a week ago to report that she'd overheard another sailor respectfully call him Sarah. They'd had a chuckle over it.

That was precisely the sort of tidbit she wanted him to include in the Big Book, and he didn't blame her. It was funny and sweet, but where was the room? The bigger story to tell was about what was happening to men like them from their home islands. For years, ships piloted by slavers had been "recruiting" native men and carrying them off to distant islands to work as laborers. "Blackbirding," people called it, as if it were a hunting sport. At best, the workers ended up as indentured servants; at worst, they died in captivity as slaves. "They take my uncle away," one sailor had told Louis. "Ten years, fifteen . . . no one see him again." In their three voyages, Louis and Fanny had come across laborers who had been dumped on far-flung islands after their service, with no hope of making their way home.

The bigger story was about what *commerce* was doing to the South Sea islanders. It was enough to hear Fanny mention that she noticed native women on Arorai wearing doll hats; Louis had seen the same phenomenon a hundred times. Yes, it expressed the clever way the native people took the brummagem of the trading ships and found some use for it. But it was an image that sickened him, for it showed how profoundly the influence of foreign *things* was having on the culture. He was struck by how the ships were creating an appetite among the people for more things. And while the traders collected copra to sell to manufacturers who would turn it into coconut oil and sell it to merchants in Europe and America at considerable profits, the islanders got dolls' hats.

I need to tell that story.

Sometimes he wondered what it all said about human beings. These ships hurrying port to port, this busy moving around of goods in the name of progress and industry. And religion, that must not be forgotten, for it was aboard the ships as well. The South Seas were a wilderness like any other. First came explorers and then a wave of missionaries and traders who brought their brand of enlightenment to the poor savages. *Is this what we've been evolving toward? Is this the best that the crown of creation can do with his mighty gifts? Is commerce what makes us superior to apes?*

He was too much of a realist to romanticize the South Sea islanders or demonize the whites who traded with them and lived among them. But as far as he could see, not much good had come of Europeans bringing their notions of civilization. Of the islands they'd visited, it seemed that the ones with the least contact with the outside world had fared best. And in many places, the *kanakas,* as the natives were called, had been hideously misused by the colonizers.

Fanny had no claim to be the arbiter of what he wrote and published. He had been pleased enough to see her taking notes so diligently with her journal propped on barrels, on her pillow, on the floor, whenever she had a moment to write. Her notes were useful to him, and her perceptions about the women she'd encountered on this voyage were especially interesting. But her perceptions were not identical to his. Proud as she was of her instincts, they were often flawed.

Maybe it was the money that worried her. After all, McClure was committed to ten thousand dollars for the fifty-two letters; a piece of their future was riding on that horse. Or maybe she was disappointed because he didn't want to write about their adventures in a romantic vein, the way he had written *Travels with a Donkey.* He'd been positively possessed when he wrote that book. It had been an open love letter to her. Was she worried that at fifty, she didn't look like the woman he'd fallen in love with?

Her wrinkles didn't disturb him; they were a map of her amazing life. He loved his wife, though love seemed an inadequate word to contain all the emotion that passed between married people. After fifteen years, shouldn't disagreeing with Fanny be easier? When they quarreled, he felt as if he were walking barefoot across jagged coral. Shouldn't their marriage be smooth by now, like a polished stone?

⸻

CHAPTER 68

Louis ambled through Apia on his horse, Jack. The town was alive with the afternoon noise of children, dogs, and chickens in the fenced yards adjoining the low wood houses. He had spent the past few hours sitting on Moors's verandah, drinking stiff coffee and chewing on local politics. They had a view of the harbor, where an overturned German man-of-war appeared like a political cartoon titled "Samoan Troubles." Louis knew enough about recent history to see the wrecked ship as a sad symbol for the mess created in Samoa by Germany, Britain, and the United States.

"Samoa is no different from any other little outpost," Moors had said. "Once the big powers put money in a foreign place, they insert themselves into local politics and stir up tribal rivalries for their own purposes." The trader pointed toward the ship. "Mind you, it wasn't over a year ago there were *six* men-of-war out there, all of 'em spoiling for a fight." He snorted. "A hurricane settled that tiff. Tossed those ships over like toys in a tub. Killed two hundred sailors. That's when the Powers figured out they were three big dogs fightin' over a mighty small bone. They had their Berlin conference; the Germans put their puppet, Malietoa Laupepa, in the king's seat; and they agreed to send over a 'chief justice' to settle disputes among all the parties." He put a plug of tobacco in his cheek. "It can't be done."

Moors's knowledge of tribal history and the financial interests of the Powers had been useful in Louis's letters for McClure's newspapers. Better yet was the trader's knowledge of the island's hidden wonders. He had already led Louis on afternoon rides through the bush to blue lagoons where locals bathed, and to lava caves where swiftlets swooped past them in the darkness, calling out to one another in clicks.

As Jack turned toward Vailima, Louis saw bare-breasted girls along the road, beautiful brown girls wearing flowers in their hair, bead necklaces, and scanty kilt-like *lavalavas* tied round their waists. He smiled at the notion that his eyes had grown accustomed to such naked beauty. What would Baxter or Colvin do upon encountering such females? Fall from their mounts, no doubt.

The air grew silent and the path rougher as he rode beside a high lime hedge, then ascended the hill into the bush. On either side, ropy vines wound around thick trunks, knitted themselves through branches, and hung down like fat snakes from the great canopy to the thick scrub below. Louis passed through a tiny village just below his own land where a family was drinking *kava* in their open-sided house. The lanterns were already glowing. *"Talofa!"* someone greeted him from beneath the thatched roof.

At a bend in the road was a clearing where he often stopped to look up at Vailima and down at the coastline. To the west of Apia lay a string of German settlements that continued along the coast until they reached Mulinuu, the official seat of the Samoan king. Louis could see distinctly the coconut and cacao plantations owned by the Hamburg company with a very long name that everybody called "The German Firm." "It might as well be an arm of the German government," Moors had groused.

In Apia and to the east, English and Americans populated the coast. It was a cruel irony that while the natives preferred to live along the water, whites had claimed the harbor section of Upolu's northern shoreline. Forced to live away from the town in areas where decent roads and basic amenities ended, the native people moved through Apia as foreigners. That center of commerce was run by white administrators for the white settlers and was immune to the rule of the native king. But the white kingdom was not a happy one. The town, jointly held by whites of different nationalities, was divided into bickering camps.

Louis shaded his eyes and studied the coastline. All around the island, the surf crashed up and over the coral reefs. He turned toward Vailima, where he saw a windowpane in the new house glint copper gold as it caught the sun.

They had been living on the island for three months, sheltering in the cottage. The house was a simple structure, a two-story clapboard with three main rooms on the first floor and five bedrooms upstairs. The house's size made the locals gasp. He and Fanny didn't think it was too big; they would use every square inch of it for their extended family. What made it extravagant was the fact that all the building materials had to be imported, either from the States or from Australia and New Zealand. Everything: nails, window glass, doorknobs, redwood boards. The German Firm had taken the contract and gotten the materials from the harbor to Vailima by dray horse and cart, up the treacherous, furrowed road from Apia.

Dinner will be waiting, he thought, *such as it is.* There was a provisions shortage that Moors insisted would be temporary, caused by the fact that the men-of-war hadn't come into Apia harbor for extended stays of late. With the reduction in population, suppliers were not shipping food into the town as they once did. Fanny's garden would soon be producing, but in the interim, they ate a lot of breadfruit. The night before, he and Fanny had shared one avocado for supper.

When the conch shell was blown to call in anyone out in the fields, it would be he and Fanny who gathered at the table, along with Henry and Lafaele, two Samoan members of the household. Henry Simele was a bright, strong, plain-faced fellow who oversaw the day workers and did whatever job was required. When he began working with them, he'd asked Louis to teach him how to speak more complex English, or "long expressions," as he called it, in exchange for Samoan-language instruction. The two met every evening for a mutual lesson. Henry always arrived freshly bathed, his chest decorated in fern garlands or a flower wreath. It turned out he was a chief on his own island of Savaii, but he had to work at Vailima to earn money for all the feasts he was expected to host.

Fanny was especially fond of Lafaele, a loyal fellow whom she was trying to turn into a gardener. He was a fine-looking man: muscular, with curled hair gone red from using slaked lime on it. Louis suspected the name to be a version of Raphael, so he called him "the Archangel." He *was* that—good-hearted and a great believer in the supernatural.

Both men seemed to regard Vailima as home. Louis was touched when Henry said, "*Our* house is a gentle house." At one of the early social gatherings he and Fanny attended in Apia, the wife of a diplomat advised Louis to treat his servants like family: "You'll get more work out of them." Louis had been offended by the crassness of her remark, though he'd already witnessed the nugget of truth in the statement. His familiarity with the Scottish clan system helped him make sense of Samoan life. The extended family was at the heart of both cultures. Everyone knew his role in the scheme of things, showed the proper respect for superiors and elders, and drew identity from the clan.

In a couple of months, once they were in the big house, Lloyd would return with the contents of the Bournemouth house, Louis's mother would join them, and if they could persuade Belle, she and Joe and Austin would take over the Pineapple Cottage, as they called the little place they were living in now. When it was finished, the new place would look like a barracks. It was not a Highland country house—the sort of building his countrymen might picture as the ideal home. But it would be enough for him. And the prospect of his own extended clan settling around him in Samoa was enormously comforting. He wouldn't be lonely.

"*Talofa,*" Louis called out when he saw Henry standing at the gate of the paddock.

"Hello, Tusitala," Henry said.

Tusitala. Louis smiled to himself as he rode his horse to the barn. His new native name pleased him. *Teller of Tales.*

⌒

CHAPTER 69

*F*our A.M. *and I am wide awake, thanks to a noisy honeyeater singing out in the forest. Reverend Clarke tells me the natives believe that when that bird sings in the middle of the night, it is warning that a ghost is near.*

As the hurricane season approaches, we work against the clock to get the house finished and seeds in. With Lloyd in Britain, where he is arranging the sale of Skerryvore and collecting Louis's mother, it is just Louis and me, and of course Henry and Lafaele, and a few day workers.

Of these 300 acres, we will clear only about fifteen at most. It is all we can ever manage, I think, for the jungle reclaims cleared land quickly. Louis says we should grow cacao. I think coffee and have begun a large number of cuttings in small pots to be planted out soon. I have made a plan to divert water from a mountain stream to pipe into our house as well. We are building the reservoir just now. There is plenty to worry about, but there are gifts, too. Last night when we sat outside, Louis said, "These are the real stars and moon, not the tin imitations that preside over London."

Now, when I get up in the morning, my legs do not feel like jelly, as they did on the boats. I am so grateful not to be sick to my stomach and terrified, the way I was nearly every day at sea. It's not the staying but the coming that I object to.

I could not have conceived two years ago that the solution to our search for a home where Louis could regain his health would be Samoa, of all places. But indeed, I believe we are at last on solid ground.

Fanny set aside her diary, closed her eyes, and listened to the sounds of insects and birds awakening. It was always a single triller who started the morning music, but in a minute thousands of creatures would join in, sending up swooping ribbons of coos, chirps, and clicks into the indigo morning. How they loved the sound of their own chorus! They wove their ribbons together intentionally, she was certain of it, because periodically they would all stop at once—insects and birds alike—as if on cue, as if to catch their breath before going on.

When the sun tore an orange line through the clouds and lit the hillside, the music slowed. There would be individual songs called out here and there, but she wouldn't notice a chorus again until dinnertime, when the frogs took over. They croaked so loudly that Louis complained he might be losing his hearing. A booming glee club, they were. Fanny was so enchanted by the frog song that she didn't care if she missed the end of someone's sentence.

At dawn, too alert to remain in bed, she went by lantern light to her toolshed. Fog was rolling up the hill, puffing across the clearing like pale smoke as she pulled out the things she would need for the day. Her ambitions for Vailima grew by the hour. She had three pigs—a white boar and two sows—and she wanted many more. She saw a big farm: a real, producing farm from which she could feed her family and work crew. There would be more horses and eventually a cow for milk. And more gardens, profuse with every vegetable she might crave. She saw a plantation operation with cash crops that would eventually support Vailima. Maybe she would grow both coffee and cacao and make a run at a perfume business as well, since Henry had found ylang-ylang trees on the property.

She could tell other people had lived on this land. Henry came upon evidence of a banana plantation in a soggy area of the bush. Excited, Fanny made a muddy foray into the swamp to have a look. To think she had so much of her own property to explore—three hundred mysterious acres! Never in her wildest dreaming had she considered the possibilities of such a canvas.

There had been the most basic beginnings to make: a fowl house for her Cochins, a paddock to clear, a barn and pigpens to build, and seeds to plant, starting with the buffalo grass she'd ordered from the States. The tough buffalo grass would keep out weeds once it was established. Today she would follow behind the tiller, planting grass in the morning and vegetables in the afternoon. Thinking of the seeds she'd ordered from Australia made her heart thump. Long green beans, peas, radishes, melons, corn, artichokes, eggplants, tomatoes. When a neighbor gave her six lovely pineapples, she planted their tops in hopes of having her own grove.

All the books she had ever read on botany and gardening and landscape design seemed to have been driving toward this moment in her life. She thought of the Englishwoman, Gertrude Jekyll, whose brother, Walter, used to visit them at Bournemouth. Fanny once visited her house in Surrey and nearly fainted when she saw corn stalks growing in the woman's extraordinary flower border. *And I thought I was the only gardener in England with corn between my roses.* When Walter saw Fanny's garden at Skerryvore, he said to her, "You plant in strokes, as Gertrude does. She is a painter, too."

The woman *was* an artist with plants, and Fanny had in mind a flower garden at Vailima that would equal Gertrude's. It would not be easy to imitate such an effect in the space around the house. A beautiful garden was a three-dimensional composition made up of ephemeral materials. It was far harder to make than a painting; she knew that firsthand. But what she had in mind was even harder: a vast architected landscape of flower and vegetable gardens, ponds, and plantation crops moving out into the hillside.

As Fanny began hoeing a new section, the fog thinned and the damp world around her turned silver-bright. In the field beyond, she saw the brown earth was marked with shimmering green lines where her beans had begun to quicken with life. After an hour, covered in dirt and already sore, she went back to the cottage, where Louis stood on the little porch, drinking his morning coffee.

"Good mornin', Weird Woman," he called out. It was his latest pet name for her, no doubt in reference to her recent fascination with Samoan superstitions, as well as her appearance this morning. She was wearing the wide brim of a hat—only the brim. She had separated the crown and tossed it away so that her scalp could catch the occasional cool breeze.

"Louis, do you think we are still on friendly terms with Walter Jekyll and his sister, Gertrude?"

"I suppose. Why do you ask?"

"I'm thinking about writing to Gertrude to ask for some seeds, but I don't know if I dare. I've never had a sense of how they felt about us after you borrowed their family name for the story."

Louis shrugged. "At least it wasn't *Dr. Hyde and Mr. Jekyll.*"

They stood together, contemplating the clearing near the house, where dozens of burned tree stumps poked up from the soil. Fanny envisioned a great sward where the family could play lawn tennis, but the ugly black things reminded her how far they had to go. "What would Gertrude do with those stumps, do you suppose?" Fanny wondered aloud.

"Why, set flower pots on 'em, girlie!" Louis said.

Fanny savored this part of the day, when they talked of what they intended to get done on the land. In the past, such planning would have been unthinkable, but Louis was joyfully well. For hours on end, he waged death contests with the wretched sensitive plant—green murders, he called his battles—and emerged invigorated, whooping like a warrior and shouting, "I love weeding!" He cut swaths through the bush to make paths, returning filthy and triumphant. He rode his horse back and forth to Apia at a terrifying speed, given the condition of the road. He rejoiced in the muscles growing strong in his thighs. When she massaged the back of his neck at the end of a long workday, she glimpsed lines of white skin hidden within furrows of brown. "You are turning the color of the earth," she told him.

It gave her peace to see Louis so vigorous and happy. She occasionally found him standing still in a spot, listening to birds in the forest. "Do you hear that? They're chuckling like children out there."

Fanny worked so hard some days that her arthritic knees would not come up off the ground. When Henry found her stuck between her garden rows, he would lift her by her middle and move her to the next section that had to be planted. Louis worked just as hard.

Before dinner, they went to the pool near the house that was surrounded by orange trees; there they bathed among water lilies. Standing in the waterfall that poured over a rock ledge, Louis called out, "This is a fairy story!"

A FEW DAYS earlier, while Louis was in town, he was approached by Mr. Sewell, the U.S. consul, who asked if he might bring a pair of famous Americans up to Vailima. "John LaFarge, the painter, and a historian named Henry Adams," Louis told her. "LaFarge is a friend of Will Low. But I never heard of the other one."

"Their timing couldn't be worse," Fanny protested. "What will we feed them?"

"I told the consul they should bring their own food."

"You are the best attraction Sewell has to offer on this island, I suppose. The equivalent of Queen Vaekehu's tattooed legs. 'Not to be missed!'" she teased.

Next day, Adams and LaFarge appeared in the clearing with Sewell as their guide. While Louis greeted them, Fanny ran into the cottage to wash her arms and feet and put on shoes. It was afternoon. They had spent the morning installing a stove in the outdoor cookhouse, and they were both covered with black grease. There was no time to bathe or change. Both travelers were balding fellows, slightly older than Fanny, and pinched in aspect. LaFarge was polite, but Adams could not conceal how appalled he was by the spectacle in front of him. He appeared thunderstruck as he gaped at poor Louis, who was wearing grease-streaked white linen trousers with a brown sock on one foot and a purple sock on the other. In the space of a minute, Fanny was fairly certain she loathed Henry Adams.

Louis, on the other hand, was beside himself with joy. It was almost embarrassing to see how excitedly he approached the men. He was like a puppy, eager to play, jumping around a more reserved dog who is not done sniffing, as indeed Adams was not, for his nostrils were flared from the moment he arrived, and they seemed incapable of deflating. Louis toured the men around the cleared property, talking of their plans. Later, over a simple meal on a table outside, he pitched one topic after another at Adams and LaFarge, seeking to spark the kind of brainy repartee he'd so missed since leaving his old friends in London. The painter was clearly cultivated but politely reserved. Adams was more forthcoming, promptly revealing that there were *two* American presidents in his family tree. In his Boston Brahmin accent, he expanded on his own interests, in particular how American education was producing a crop of young people ill prepared for the coming century. "Second-rate" was a phrase he used to dismiss any number of people, places, and ideas. Sewell turned the talk back to Vailima, and the herculean task of building a house when the materials had to be imported. The historian's snobbery seeped through his every remark. "One must lower one's standards in the tropics, of course." Adams sighed. "Lord knows, Henry Adams certainly has."

Fanny engaged the man's eyes. "We don't stand on too much ceremony here," she said. "A simple way of life thankfully preserves us from that burden. Someone without imagination might look at this place and see squalor, but we see possibility," She smiled sweetly. "And we are grateful to be living in Samoa, among people with truly humane manners."

If her remark had landed as she hoped, Adams gave no sign of it, as he'd turned his attention to swatting mosquitoes. But Louis's eyes had widened at her retort.

"Good riddance," Fanny muttered when the men left.

"Is the hostess feeling a bit churlish?" Louis said.

"What a ridiculous prig! Does Adams always refer to himself in the third person?"

"Louis Stevenson was wondering the same thing," Louis said.

Standing there, she looked at her husband as Henry Adams must have seen him, an emaciated figure with legs so long and thin, he resembled a stork. Her eyes followed Louis's legs to his mismatched socks, and then she began to laugh uncontrollably. He looked down at his feet, sank onto the porch step, and laughed, too.

She realized their happiest times had been just like this, when the two of them were alone with the rest of the world at bay, as they'd been at Hyères. They did best when they were making a new beginning, planning and creating together. She savored having Louis to herself, without friends or family. His jokes and thoughts were only for her. Pulled away from his writing by the physical work at hand, and miraculously healthy, Louis seemed reborn.

They had been through wretched times, and Louis had relapsed often enough that she'd learned not to trust the moments of reprieve. But she couldn't help thinking, *This feels different.*

During those first months at Vailima, an impetuous joy overtook her. She would walk out to find Louis in a field valiantly weeding, fall on her knees beside him, and declare, "Fanny Stevenson loves you madly."

CHAPTER 70

*H*enry *informs us that the workers have given us native names. I am Tamaitai, for "Madam," and sometimes Aolele, "Flying Cloud."*

Fanny looked up from her diary to find Henry standing over her. "Lafaele stepped on a nail, Tamaitai. The native doctor is out there."

"Oh, that's no use." Fanny capped the ink bottle. "I'll be right down."

When she found Lafaele, he was lying on the ground, his foot in the hands of an old man.

"What is happening?" she asked Henry, who stood nearby.

"The doctor say the devil got in him through the nail hole. Now the devil want to take over his body."

"Thank the doctor very much for coming. We will fetch him if things get worse."

She washed out the wound, treated the puncture with carbolic acid solution, wrapped the foot and fed Lafaele salicylate to dull the pain. His terrified expression remained.

"Close your eyes," she told him. She put two fingers on his eyelids. "You are going to be just fine. My devils are more powerful than his devils. Now go to your bed, and we will bring food to you."

At dinner with the family, Henry said, "Lafaele is feeling better. He says you are a great healer."

"I rather like that."

"Now if you could just persuade him to go into the bush to our banana plantation," Louis said. "He claims he has seen a devil in the form of a strange man come out of the forest."

"Vailima is overrun with ghosts, if you believe the men," Fanny said. "Lafaele says there is one in our spring. And another near the garden. I heard something like a rumbling the other day, and I must admit, it gave me pause." She took a bite of the breadfruit on her plate and thought of how tired she was of breadfruit. "And then there is the spirit whose name translates to something like 'Come to Me Thousands.' Have you heard of her?"

Louis shook his head.

"The cook says there is an evil female *aītu* who preys on women when they are alone. Appears as a crone and asks for some favor, a bit of bread, say, and if she doesn't get it, woe to the lady. Slips into her body while she is sleeping. Apparently, the poor woman possessed by her will leap up and run through the hills crazily and carouse all night."

"Sounds like a fellow's dearest fantasy," Louis muttered. He pushed his chair back from the table. "Say, Moors invited us to come down to their house for Christmas Eve dinner."

"Thank heavens!" Fanny said. "There won't be a holiday dinner at Vailima this year, I can assure you. My plants aren't near ready to be harvested."

On Christmas Eve, Louis saddled up Jack, and Fanny rode the pie-bald horse they'd bought from a traveling circus for his mother's eventual use. In spite of the rainy season, it was a fine afternoon, and they rode down to Apia in high spirits. Fanny wore a split skirt that Dora had sent her from San Francisco, which freed her from riding sidesaddle.

Moors and his wife had invited a local lawyer, three other Samoan women, plus a colorful missionary from Tonga. Mrs. Moors was a mature, graceful woman. She had spread the table with a banquet of Samoan and American foods, and Fanny did her best not to ravage a plate in two gulps. Seated next to Mr. Moors, she described the rumbling sounds coming from somewhere near the garden.

"As I recall, there's a cave in that area," Moors said. "It's possible that runaways from the German plantations are hiding there. I suspect there are plenty of labor boys living in the bush near Vailima."

"We aren't far from a plantation. During the day, I can hear them call in the workers with a conch shell." Fanny sipped her wine. "It is strange to think of runaways hiding out there. I don't know how they survive during the rainy season. Lafaele says they live on yams they dig up. Imagine how hungry they must be."

"I understand you are quite a medicine woman," Moors said, changing the subject.

"Word travels quickly."

"Oh, you have no idea. In Apia, rumors are the main form of discourse. If it has to do with spirits, all the better." He chuckled. "There is a native word for spirit. It is *aītu*—"

"I know the word," she said.

"Then you know there is always some rumor of *aītus* going around."

"What is the latest news in town about the supernatural world?"

"Some fishermen saw a war canoe with four spirit men in it coming into shore. It is said that one of the fishermen who saw them is on his mat, dying." Moors shook his head. "The natives take all this as a sign of war coming. They are hurrying around looking for ammunition."

"Doesn't that worry you?"

"The part about the ammunition? Not in the least. It is nothing new."

"I must say, Mr. Moors," Fanny remarked, "that when you showed us the property and told us about the waterfalls, and the streams, and the secret banana plantation, you forgot to mention it's common knowledge that Vailima is overrun with *aītus*."

"An oversight," he said. "But it's actually a good deal. The locals won't be tempted to steal from you if your land is regarded as haunted. So the ghosts, you might say, are a gift." Moors lifted his glass. "Happy Christmas to you, Mrs. Stevenson!"

At around eleven, Fanny and Louis took their leave. Rain began to fall as the lights of Apia disappeared behind them. In the darkness of the forest, the horses grew skittish on the path, cocking their ears at the burbling sound the wind and rain made in the trees. Flying foxes whipped past overhead. Weird whitish bars of light appeared here and there on the forest ground.

"What is it?" Fanny asked when Louis stopped to gape.

"Phosphorescent light from the dead wood," he said. "Looks like grating over hell. No wonder the natives think the nighttime is full of bogeys. Scary, ain't it?"

A great gust of wind came up the hill, knocking Fanny's hat off into the darkness and lifting high the manes of the horses.

Louis's Jack quailed. He took off uphill, and Fanny's horse hurried behind him.

CHAPTER 71

1891

Louis shortened the reins, bent forward, and pushed his weight into his boot heels to lift off the saddle. Up ahead a pig fence, one of many constructed—incredibly—right across the road by native farmers to corral their livestock; Louis dared the horse to clear it. Jack never broke his canter, sailing over the crude barrier of cocoa posts as if he were steeplechasing. "A fine beast you are!" Louis shouted to the horse, whose neck lathered whiter with each jump. Louis had counted eight pig fences on his way to Mata'afa's camp; now they repeated the jumps as they returned to Vailima.

Louis felt exhilarated, coming away from his first meeting with the rebel chief. Mata'afa was all Moors had said he would be. The chief had the bearing and vision of a great statesman when he spoke about the need for his people to take control of Samoa's destiny. Louis had looked at the chief and thought, *Here is the man who will bring this country out of chaos.*

He knew the thrill pulsing through his body was not only from the fence leaping; it came from being an actor in something real. Louis tried to remember the last time he'd engaged in the public life of any place he had lived. He'd been a sickly hermit in Bournemouth and Hyères and Davos. But he was well now and eager for the game. Louis had never felt so much a *citizen.* And if ever there were a moral obligation to behave like a citizen—for God's sake, to head off war—now was the moment.

WHEN HE RETURNED home, Louis wrapped himself in a *lavalava* and walked down to the bathing pool. It was his favorite ritual of the day, one he sometimes shared with the Samoans who worked at Vailima. Today he was alone. The spot was a vision of paradise, surrounded as it was by wild orange trees, its banks dripping with ferns and fragrant yellow jessamine. He picked two oranges, cut them, then squeezed them over his head, as the natives did, to clean their hair. All around, bright birds he had no names for hopped among the branches of shrubs he intended to identify when he got a moment. He'd never been good at remembering tree and plant names; he was doubly challenged in this place. He laughed to himself for the hundredth time at the exotic turn his life had taken.

Ahead, the day held other pleasures. Lloyd was just back from England. Having arranged the sale at Bournemouth and the shipment of Skerryvore's furniture to Vailima, the lad had escorted Maggie Stevenson to Sydney, where she waited for the right moment to come to Samoa. Soon Louis would fetch her and bring her to Vailima.

He was glad Lloyd was back. It meant they would work together on *The Wrecker,* their comical tale about a motley group of unscrupulous adventurers bent on striking it rich. During the months the boy was in Britain, they had attempted to collaborate long-distance, which had been mightily frustrating. Today they would put in two or three hours. Louis would write another column for McClure's syndicate, describing his visit to Mata'afa. He would fit in some weeding, so that when the conch shell was blown for dinner, he could tell himself he had earned his keep at Vailima. Afterward, they would all sit outside and share news from their letters; Lloyd was going into Apia today to collect the mail.

It was a miracle they got any letters at all. Four times a month, a mail steamer running between San Francisco and Sydney passed near the island, and a local boat went out to meet it. When the weather cooperated, a seaman on the ship tossed mailbags into the smaller vessel. When conditions were bad, the bags were not tossed, or worse, they disappeared into the waves.

At the house, he found that Lloyd had already passed out everyone's mail. Louis savored the sight and feel of the thick pile on his desk. He sorted the letters: Edmund Gosse and Sidney Colvin went to the top. Baxter's he would read later; it would be full of financial figures and worries.

Gosse's missive was loaded with gossip and flattery about the letters Louis had been writing recently to the editors of the *Times* of London regarding the political situation in Samoa. *Since Byron was in Greece, nothing has appealed to the literary man as so picturesque as that you should be living in the South Seas.* Louis chuckled to himself.

Colvin's letter was about business. Louis scanned it for news and stopped abruptly at one paragraph. *The* New York Sun *has run thirty-four of your letters but has backed out of publishing the remainder of them. They say the letters haven't enough incident and experiences, but appear to be merely the advance sheets of a book. And a dull book at that.*

Louis felt the wind go out of his chest. How brutal Colvin could be in his truth telling, and how kind Gosse was in his lying. Why hadn't he seen this coming? He'd not gotten much comment from his friends in London about the columns, or his letters to the *Times,* for that matter. Louis immediately started a letter to Colvin, reminding him that the articles for McClure were only meant as preliminaries to a much more important work. He put down the pen in frustration. *Lloyd has just seen all these people in London. He will know what's going on.*

Louis threw the letter from Colvin on the dining table, where Lloyd sat alone reading a book. Louis pointed to the offending paragraph. "What are you not telling me?"

Lloyd squirmed. "What do you mean?"

"You know what I mean."

Lloyd looked miserable. In the evenings since his return, the boy had filled the family with the news from Louis's old crowd; at his stepfather's request, Lloyd had gone to see all of them: Colvin, Baxter, Gosse. Louis had not named Henley, but Lloyd adored him and had visited on his own. The stories of the old friends had been riotously fun, though Louis suspected his stepson had edited the reports heavily. No doubt Lloyd had heard an earful and, out of loyalty, was withholding the negative.

At the moment, the young man's face reflected his distress; confusion gave way to a look of pure sadness. Louis had seen the look before. He'd watched the same changes in Lloyd's emotional weather when he was eight years old. It was one of the few reminders of the lad he had been. Lloyd was fully adult now, at twenty-three. Louis had watched him change from small boy to shy stripling to outspoken six-foot-tall college student to young man with continental tastes that offended some people—Moors came to mind. Lloyd was finding his style, trying on various personae. He had returned from London wearing a pince-nez and knotted cravat and saying "quite right" quite often. If, in this most recent stage, the boy mimicked too closely the dandies he'd seen in Regent Street, Louis could forgive him because he knew who Lloyd was in his heart: a witty fellow with a soft spot for the downtrodden. If Lloyd was haughty, he was also kind to every underdog he ever met. If he was sometimes cold and undemonstrative, he was calm water in a family given to dramatic swells of sentiment.

"You are my sounding board, Lloyd, and I am yours. Tell me the truth."

"No one cares about Polynesians over there," Lloyd said. "They don't care for the newspaper columns or the idea of a book about the South Seas. They want stories like your early ones." He put up his palms in resignation. "They want stories about white men."

Louis snickered. "Then they shall get their white men. A whole gallery of the species that thrive here."

Lloyd rose smiling. "I'll see you at two o'clock," he said.

"Don't worry," Louis called after him. "Disappointing my old friends doesn't sting half as bad as it used to."

IT STUNG SOME, though. Financially, it was a loss, as he would be paid perhaps a third of what he had counted on from McClure. Equally bad was the embarrassment he felt that he had failed. He wasn't accustomed to failure, at least in the literary realm. *Am I Byron in Greece or a literary has-been living out in the bush?* Louis fretted briefly, then let it go. He used to worry about his standing in London's literary circles. It occurred to him that he cared much less these days. The circles that mattered were his family, his growing clan, and these Samoans, who were becoming his people.

It wasn't only the South Seas material that Colvin objected to. Louis knew his friend regarded his collaboration with Lloyd as a colossal waste of time. Well, a man did for his family what he could. *If I can't help my own, who can I help?*

Louis's mind flashed back to the countless tavern conversations he'd had with Henley during their periods of collaboration. They'd talked endlessly about how this or that man fit into the pantheon of important English writers and thinkers, all the while stoking each other's vanity. Henley had assured him that at his best, Louis was singlehand-

edly reviving the Romantic tradition. Louis propped up Henley by saying that his poetry would be remembered in a hundred years. *That* was
colossally wasted time. Now all Louis craved was freedom from expectations. He wanted to try so many things.

After two years of sailing the South Seas and a year in Samoa, how
was it possible *not* to move beyond the Old World to engage in these
people's lives? Self-forgetfulness came more easily in this place. Bathing
in the pool this morning, he had experienced a kind of heaven: He *was*
the water, the birds, the sweet-smelling air. He wanted to have that feeling more often.

At the moment, he felt agitated and defiant. He might be done with
his reporting and commentary for McClure, but he fully intended to
finish *A Footnote to History,* protesting the absurd incompetence of
the colonial powers in Samoa. He would name names, by God. And he
would continue writing fictional stories about life in this part of the
world.

His most recent story, "The Beach at Falesa," would be as dark a
moral tale as he'd ever told. The main character was a bigoted trader
who "marries for one night" a native woman and surprises himself
when he falls in love and stays with her. When they have children, he
discovers his beloved offspring are consigned to a disturbing racial pur-
gatory because of their mixed blood. The story was entirely unromantic. It would seduce English readers not because it had white men in it
but because it was powerful, full of living, breathing characters. As far
as he knew, it was the first truly realistic South Seas fiction anybody had
done; every other writer had gotten waylaid by the romance of the
place. He picked up his pen and continued his letter to Colvin.

*Now I have got the smell and look of the thing a good deal. You will
know more about the South Seas after you have read my little tale than if
you had read a library.*

He could picture Colvin sitting in his reading chair in his apartment
at the British Museum, with the "Beach at Falesa" manuscript in his
lap, harrumphing, "What the hell is *this*?" Louis smiled. *The worm
turns, Sidney,* he said to Colvin in his mind. *Your trusty Romantic has
gone Realist.*

∽

CHAPTER 72

Fanny's days as a farmer started auspiciously enough but frequently turned discouraging. One morning she'd arranged for Lafaele to take a wagon into town and pick up a shipment of plants. "Do not lose the plant labels," she'd instructed him. So that he understood her clearly, she showed him what she meant by *label*. In the afternoon, when he returned wearing a satisfied grin, he produced a bag he'd kept close to him all the way home. Looking inside, she found that he had taken every blessed label off the plants and put them into one safe place. When she pointed out his mistake, Lafaele's face looked as though it might crack with shame.

It was hardly the first of their disastrous miscommunications. What to do about her paltry pidgin English? What to do about Lafaele? He meant well, and he was so devoted to her that he called her Mama. Recently, while they worked together out in a field, he'd felt it somehow important to confess to her that during the previous evening he had encountered a girl on the road and had sex with her, after which he informed the girl that he would have to tell his "Mama" about it.

Fanny examined a patch of wilted yellow lettuces. These were her own personal failures; she'd planted them in too sunny a spot. That problem was easily remedied, though the rats that ate the innards of her melons could not be dispensed with so handily. The farm animals bedeviled her most. Mornings, she set out with her wooden egg-collecting box, hoping to fill its soft horsehair indentations with fresh eggs. Often enough she found her chickens were on strike, or if not, the cock had pecked holes in the eggs. Every remedy she tried was useless. The cock knew perfectly well he had the upper hand and strutted by her with contempt. The unruly pigs, which were downright mean-spirited, defied her by breaking through their pen and lumbering into the forest.

Complicating the whole picture was her awful sense of guilt that sooner or later, she would be the instrument of their murder.

That night, after a day of swine chasing, she slept on the floor next to Louis, having washed only her feet and hands. The muscles in her back made a crunching sound when she lay down on the hard wood. "Three hundred acres of our own." She yawned. "What were we thinking?"

"What were *you* thinking?" he said. His eyes stayed on the page he was reading. "You were the one who wanted to be a farmer."

Fanny was quiet, considering the idea.

Louis looked over his book at her. "You have the soul of a peasant, my dear. Accept it."

She shot a puzzled look at him, unsure of his direction. "I love the soil, yes."

"That's not what I mean. It's not so much that you love working with the earth but that you know it is your *own* earth that you are delving into. If you had the soul of an artist, the stupidity of possessions would have no power over you."

Fanny fell mute. How could Louis not know that creative energy so possessed her mind and body some days she thought she might go mad from it. That sometimes it took fourteen hours of grinding work before the forces inside her had been sated and she could lay herself down to rest.

She waited for Louis's hand to reach out to hers to say, *There now, I didn't mean that.* But it didn't come. While he dozed off, she stayed awake, nursing her trodden pride. When it was clear she would not sleep, she got up and went to a makeshift desk to write in her diary.

I would as soon think of renting a child to love as a piece of land. When I plant a seed or a root, I plant a bit of my heart with it and do not feel that I have finished when I have had my exercise and amusement. But I do feel not so far removed from God when the tender leaves put forth and I know that in a manner I am a creator. My heart melts over a bed of young peas, and a blossom on my rose tree is like a poem written by my son.

A couple of weeks later, the insult was still fresh. The joy she'd felt at the beginning of her farm making seemed to have shriveled since Louis had hurled his dart. One day, when Lafaele succeeded in planting Fanny's precious supply of seed corn, she made a show of complimenting him in front of Louis. Lafaele beamed like a man made new.

"Don't all of us love a little praise sometimes?" Fanny said when Lafaele walked away.

"Love it like pie," Louis assented.

Fanny thought of all the stories she had written that had never made it into print. She had wanted only a scintilla of recognition.

"I always thought being a peasant was the happiest of lives," she said to Louis the next night when they retired. "It is a simple, noble life."

"You are what you always wanted to be, then. I personally think the peasant class is a most charming one." He rolled over to face the wall. "Admire it immensely."

"You are condescending to me," she seethed. "Why don't you just say you appreciate art, and I appreciate mud!"

"I don't know why you're offended," he muttered. "No one should be offended if it is said that he is not an artist. The only person who should be insulted by such an observation is an artist who supports his family with his work."

"Louis, do you hear yourself? You are talking like a fool. You are saying a person is not an artist if he doesn't support his family with his work. You are saying *you* are the only member of this family who is a real artist."

He put his arm up over his ear.

"Do you know what I think?" she said. "You're angry that the *New York Sun* doesn't want any more of the letters you've been sending them, and you're taking it out on me."

Louis didn't respond. She pulled his arm down so he could not pretend he didn't hear her. "I warned you that readers would find them boring. And I was right!"

Louis sat up in a huff, took his pillow, and climbed over her and out of the bed.

Sleepless in the ensuing hours, Fanny knew Louis was camped on the floor of the new house. It was three or four o'clock before she drifted off. When she woke and looked outside, she caught sight of Louis's back as he rode off on his horse.

From her window, Fanny could see the big field where the day workers had been planting coffee seedlings for a few days. Her mind's eye skipped forward: She saw the house surrounded by acres upon acres of coffee, vanilla, and cacao trees. How vivid the picture was! She imagined herself in six or seven years—*I would not be so terribly old yet*—a woman planter and the living legend behind the vast and thriving plantation called Vailima. "There were moments when I lacked faith," Louis would admit to a newspaper reporter someday, "but my wife always knew it would be a success."

She closed her eyes, savored the image for a minute longer, then moved away from the window. Dressing quickly, she collected a hard-boiled egg from the kitchen hut that she peeled and ate as she walked out to inspect the distant field where the coffee plants grew. What she found made her heart flop. The starts, unwatered, were all dead. She should have come out sooner to oversee the men, but she'd been too busy, too trusting.

"Damned tears!" she cursed aloud, wiping her eyes as she contemplated the big field for which she'd had such high hopes. "Damned plants!" When the tears stopped, she recognized in herself a perverse sense of relief and satisfaction. This week, at least, she had failed rather grandly at being a peasant.

CHAPTER 73

*L*ouis has gone off to Sydney to meet his mother and accompany her back to Samoa. It is an obligatory trip that he didn't want to make, as he was concerned about leaving me here alone in hurricane season, but I'm glad he is gone. It will get him away from the local politics, which he has taken up with too much fervor. He may have abandoned writing travel letters for McClure's syndicate, but now he writes furious letters to the editor of the Times of London about the interference of the imperial powers in the lives of native Samoans. What care the readers of the Times? It is the preacher in Louis that makes him write those letters, and then, there is the matter of his sense of right. He's disgusted that the Germans have set up Malietoa Laupepa as the puppet king. Louis says he's a good man who's not fit to run things. We both believe the rival, Mata'afa, is the far stronger leader: He understands the importance of his people claiming and using their land so outsiders can't. Germany, in particular, has much to lose if Mata'afa's influence takes hold. Britain and the U.S. have inserted themselves into the picture, and now all three countries have consuls in Apia.

And so Louis writes his letters. He has fashioned himself a diplomat and is trying to bring about some compromise between the two chiefs. He has never forgiven himself for not intervening in the Irish boycott that left those women in Kerry defenseless. The other day he said to me, "I was silent about Ireland. I won't make that mistake here."

Among the workers, rumors fly that there will be a war. I cannot think of war; I must be ready for Louis's mother. The workers seem as weary as I am, for I have driven all of us pretty hard. But we will have a sparkling room ready for her in the new house, come hell or high water.

I have hired a new cook, a native woman named Emma who cooks all right but seems frightened to be working here. She says the kitchen is full of devils. She says that a woman and a man were murdered some time ago on the site of our cottage, and their ghosts are the very spirits who follow her

home and climb into bed with her at night. That makes three dens of dev-
ils on our property: in the barn, on the land near the garden, and now in
the kitchen.

"Henry, I want you to make some sandwiches for supper. It will be just the two of us. Emma is off today, and Lafaele has arranged to court his lady." The Archangel had already left, garlanded and smelling heavenly.

Fanny went out to the garden to finish planting a couple of precious rhubarb plants given her by a missionary. She listened for the rumbling sounds she'd heard earlier, but only the wind and birdcalls disturbed the air. Possibly what she'd heard before was a volcanic rumbling, far more serious. A chemical odor like burning sulfur hung about the farm, yet she saw no fires or smoke out in the bush. The air had the green tint that the Indiana sky carried when a tornado was approaching. In the eerie light, the plants took on a spectrum of glowing hues, from chartreuse to near black.

Leaden clouds moved in quickly from the sea, and before she finished her row, drops of rain sharp as sleet stung her skin. She hurried inside.

As blasts of wind rattled the little cottage, her head began to pound, just above the hairline. She told Henry to go ahead and eat without her, and she went upstairs to bed. No position she tried would ease the pain, which was so severe, that her skull felt close to bursting. She took out the medicine box and riffled through it. The laudanum Louis had given her for rheumatism had not worked last time. She found the bottle of chlorodyne. Her eyes went down the list of ingredients. Morphine, Indian cannabis, nitroglycerin . . . She drank a capful. Not intolerable. She waited to see if the pounding quieted.

Why, oh why, was her head going wrong now? Only Henry downstairs to help. She'd not had one of these spells for a long while, and she became afraid when she contemplated what might happen.

Sleep it off, Fanny. She threw on her nightgown and fell into bed.

When she awoke in the middle of the night, her heart and neck were pounding like horse hooves. Above, a white streak lit the ceiling. She sat up, groped frantically for the matchbox on the side table. She heard the box fall and the wooden sticks splatter across the floor. She slid out of bed to her knees, took up a match, struck it against a floorboard, and lit the candle. Shadows licked the walls. Climbing under the covers, she leaned against the headboard and closed her eyes, lest she begin to see strange things. In her mind, the face of a woman appeared. Her eyes were wild, her mouth gaping in a long O. She was clasping two small children to her chest. Fanny shook her head and opened her eyes. In front of her, the woman was standing at the end of the bed, holding each baby by a foot, so that the small bodies hung from her fists like dead white birds. "Stop that!" Fanny shouted. She leaped out of bed with a pillow and threw it at the woman, then screamed again. A loud pounding at the wall sounded outside her curtained room.

"Louis?" she called out. "Is that you, Louis?"

Henry stepped through the curtain, alarmed, as Fanny's limbs went weak. Cradling her in his arms, he led her back to bed.

THE WINDOW CURTAINS were open, and the sun was high when she awakened. A tray with tea and ship biscuits sat atop the table. In a while, Henry tapped on the frame opening to her room.

"Come in," she told him. He stood at the foot of the bed, where the hideous apparition had been the night before. "Thank you for coming to help last night."

Henry affected a philosophical shrug.

"It was just a bad dream," she said.

"Yes, Tamaitai."

"Do not tell Mr. Stevenson when he returns," she said. "Do you understand?"

"Yes, Tamaitai."

CHAPTER 74

L ouis worried the inside of his cheek with his teeth. He was not suited for bookkeeping, and it boded ill for the day's writing when he started with the account books. He was a fool with figures, but even a fool could see they were bleeding money at Vailima. For the first time in his career, his income was truly respectable—four thousand pounds a year—but upkeep and outgo overshadowed it.

The property and new house had cost twelve thousand dollars, far more than the figure he had estimated with Moors when they started the project. He searched the list of itemized construction costs, trying to fathom how a simple wood house in the tropics could cost so much, when his eye fell on the word *fireplace.* Ah, hell, he had no one to blame for that but himself. It had seemed essential to have a fireplace in any house he built, even if it *was* the only one in Samoa, as he'd been told repeatedly by astounded locals. He'd been punished already for his folly on that item. The damned thing didn't even draw.

The arrival of the furniture from Skerryvore had caused an enormous sensation in Apia, all the paintings and boxes full of china and crystal had stunned the town. The sight of a piano supported on poles carried by an army of Samoans up the three miles to Vailima had awed even him.

Then there was the new wing his mother had required the moment she arrived in May. "Lloyd doesn't have a proper place to sleep," she argued. "I'll pay for half the cost—five hundred pounds." Ha! Five hundred pounds was nothing to the seventy-five hundred dollars Moors was estimating for the addition. Lloyd had chimed in, "I'll use my earnings from the *Wrecker* on it." How could Louis say no?

Naturally, a new wing would cost even more than the estimate since that was how things worked on the island. They would be sleeping in style, all right. Dear God, what next? Another ice machine to replace the one Lloyd had bought that didn't work? There had been teas and parties galore at which they'd fed half the town and the crew of any ship that happened to be in port. As for the Great Farming Experiment under way outside, he hadn't a guess as to how much that totaled to date. Asking Fanny was to invite war. He had made that mistake earlier in the week, when she'd come into his study to tell him she needed more money.

"You forget I sold Skerryvore to help pay for this place," she told him indignantly when he remarked upon the outflow of money. "I am working as hard as I can to get a plantation going. Lord knows, I would write stories and sell them to help with the expenses if I might. But you don't want me to, do you? I am Robert Louis Stevenson's wife, after all. It is regarded as a publisher's favor to have any of my stories printed at this point. Isn't that what people said when 'The Nixie' appeared?"

Though Louis had cringed at her bitter words as she stood on the other side of his desk, he had plunged on. "I gave you a budget for the planting." He kept his voice reasonable and calm. "You now say you are out of money. All I ask is an accounting—"

She bent over the desk and positioned a quivering forefinger inches from his nose. "I wonder what would become of you, Louis Stevenson, if you had to get by as a woman must." She straightened her back and pinned him with a withering look. "You would hate it, I can assure you—to have to beg and scheme to get any say over how the household money is spent, to have to regard the clothes you wear as gifts and be beholden for whatever else comes to you. I think you would be a resentful person, indeed. I suspect you would make quite a stink about it."

She'd turned on her heel and made a defiant exit. It hurt his head to remember the scene. And it did him no good. What he knew for certain was that, exhausted as he was by the tension in the house and his recent output, he needed to work. More.

Outside, he could hear Fanny's voice growing louder. "You say you got no work?" she screeched. "I give you work, you no do it. Where you go after lunch? You hide. Now you want pay? I no pay you for afternoon. No come back tomorrow."

Louis shivered at the unabated shrillness. *Her voice used to be so soft.* He watched in shame as the men, even Lafaele, who adored her, steered clear of Fanny.

It seemed every day brought another argument. There were brief intervals of normalcy, but they never lasted long. She regularly kept the family waiting while she remained in the field long after the conch had sounded for dinner. At every turn, she looked for a fight. Once, at an English friend's home, Louis impulsively toasted the queen, and Fanny took it as a direct insult to herself, as an American. "Was that necessary?" she asked on the way home. "You seem to be taking a page from Henley. Hasn't he just come out with new verses? 'Blow your Bugle for England' or some such claptrap?"

Louis's bedroom was his sanctuary now. Early on in the building of the new house, it had become clear that he had to take for himself the bedroom they'd originally planned for his mother. He set up his office in an adjoining room and most days found the quiet he craved. He was working at a frenetic pace. Some time ago, he had abandoned the big South Seas book for Fanny's peace of mind, and for his own, since she nagged him fiercely about it. Discouraged, he'd pulled together some of his letters for McClure and written *In the South Seas,* then let it go from his fingers out into the world. Nobody would buy it, he was quite sure. It was an imperfect thing, a stunted version of a giant dream.

Now he wrote realistic stories about the South Seas and wondered if they would bring in any money. At least he'd enjoyed some hilarity in collaborating with Lloyd on his first novel. *The Wrong Box* was more Lloyd's book than his own, marked by the boy's love of mix-ups and false identities. It was a fine example of how Louis's standards had slid in the cause of mentorship.

"I don't like it," Moors had the audacity to tell him recently. "*The Wrong Box,* I mean. It isn't worthy of you. Why do you bother to collaborate?"

Louis felt his ears go hot and imagined for a moment punching Moors right between his blue eyes. *What can the man possibly understand of my life?* But he was the trader's guest, sitting out the afternoon heat on Moors's balcony, drinking Moors's beer, and facing a hill that gave Louis untold pleasure to view, a slope reminiscent of Kinnoull Hill in Perth, Scotland, except for the palm trees and native girls in *lavalavas* who were passing along a path in the distance.

"I think you know the answer to that," Louis replied. "Money. And good company. Lloyd's a great mimic, you know. He can reproduce a man's style of speaking after two or three sentences, and he has a way with comic scenes. I think the one we're working on now, *The Wrecker,* will be wonderful."

"In the end, you wrote the whole thing over."

"*The Wrong Box*? I wrote the final draft, yes."

"I much prefer your own work," Moors said. He sipped his beer. "This collaboration business is a mistake, as I see it."

Louis knew that Lloyd rubbed the trader the wrong way. The boy's English accent rang false in Moors's American ears, despite the fact that Lloyd had acquired it honestly. Louis suspected that Moors thought the boy's taste for fine liquor had come too early and, by route of his mother's marriage, too easily. It made Louis cringe, too, when he observed Lloyd at a party playing the high-nosed sophisticate with a glass of fine whisky in hand. Still, he could not tolerate Moors passing judgment on matters in Louis's life that he did not comprehend.

He rose to leave.

Oblivious to any offense given, Moors patted him on the back in the overfamiliar way a lot of Americans had. "Why don't you go to Nassau Island with me sometime soon? My cabin is nearly done over there. You can work undisturbed. I won't bother you until sundown, when I come round with a bottle of rum in my hand. You need a break from those women up there, Stevenson. You're all tied up in apron strings."

They walked through the dining room of the house, where a comely girl washed windows. Her breasts bobbed naked beneath a flower wreath around her neck.

"How is it a man is expected not to respond to such a sight?" Louis mumbled when they got to the door.

Moors grinned. "A man's a fool if he lives in paradise and doesn't taste the fruit."

Louis regretted he'd ever opened himself up to Moors. Not that he had revealed himself in the same way he always had to Colvin and Baxter. But other than Reverend Clarke, Moors was the closest thing to a confidant Louis had on the island, even though he felt uneasy about some unsavory aspects he'd heard of Moors's past, relating to the labor trade.

It was *business* that had thrown him together with Moors. The fellow was bright, an astute observer of Samoan politics, and willing to help at every turn. He was kind to his wife, though there were the usual rumors that he was not immune to the charms of other island women. Truth was, Louis needed Moors, warts and all. What other English-speaking companions did he have but for Lloyd, or his mother, or Belle? Fanny hardly counted as a companion anymore, so obsessively did she work on the farm. She had become almost a stranger.

WHEN LONELINESS HAD his foot in its trap, Louis mounted Jack and rode the poor horse as fast as he could. The two of them seemed to be in need of the same thing; they soared over pig fences as if they were a pair of coupled birds.

Some days he rode out to Mata'afa's camp in Malie, where he talked for hours with the chief and his subchiefs. No longer was he simply gathering information for his letters and books; no longer was he merely observing. The native men were his friends; Louis knew their wives and children, their fortunes, misfortunes, peculiarities. They respected him, he thought, and his status among them had nothing to do with his fame as a writer. He had studied their culture and learned their language. He had tried to wade into their world without manipulating them, except for urging peace. It was disturbing, then, when he sensed that his most outstanding quality was his wealth. For the natives had witnessed the huge wooden crates coming off ships, being loaded onto carts pulled by dray horses that struggled up the hill to Vailima, a palace compared to their own homes. He was wealthy in their eyes, and there was no getting around it. He cringed when he overheard the natives say of him, *"Ona."* It occurred to him that despite his efforts to master their language and customs and history, he might always be to them, above all, a rich white man.

CHAPTER 75

∽

1892

Louis has chosen to paint his bedroom pale blue, a chilly, repellent color with which I can do nothing. His bed is made of mats, a wooden pillow, and a blanket. He chooses to have no mattress or sheets. I choose to have both. And my room will be done in the colors I love—sapphire, emerald, and ruby.

Morning. Fanny got up off her cot and looked for something clean to put on. Her native dresses were all in need of laundering. Louis had invited Mr. Moors in for a tour of the new house, and she didn't want to greet him in the battered *holoku* she wore for gardening, all blotted with muck. In between her old gowns hung bridles, horse ropes, and straps. Leather tack seemed to disintegrate in the Samoan humidity. Her room was piled high with the things that she dared not leave out lest they turn to mush or get taken. There were boxes of tobacco, and matches, and a can of kerosene. One corner held spears, a Manihiki drum, *tapa* mats. On the bureau and trunks and boxes, spread across every flat surface, lay necklaces made of sharks' and whales' teeth, shells, bird bones, red berries. Cases of Bordeaux wine rose in a stack above her head. At her feet, a bucket from a Scottish hotel in the Highlands contained her pistol and cartridges. Boxes of things from Bournemouth had started to arrive as well, and she stopped for a moment to pry the lid off one to see what it held. Books. She lifted out her father's Bible. When she opened it, the smell of cigar smoke floated up from its sepia pages as if he were in the room.

On the Chinese chest that served as her dressing table were her tools—chisels, wrenches, nails, pincers; her toothbrush, a comb, and a pouch full of pearls; and *thank God,* the bundle of laundry. She high-stepped to get to the chest, where the clean, folded *holokus* sat atop a box loaded with salves and syrups, pills and powders—medicines she'd collected over time from Louis and the doctors, plus an assortment of patent medicines she'd found useful.

Her reputation as a healer had spread widely, and now natives and non- came to her for help. With her limited supplies, she could at least treat the pain. She'd helped a man with crushed fingers by soaking them in a mix of water and crystals of iron. When a worker came to her with elephantiasis, she relieved him with Epsom salts, though she knew it was no cure; she intended to write to the *Lancet,* asking the editor to find a doctor to do a study of the disfiguring disease.

There was so much to do, and no one else to do it except her. Her mind flew through an unwritten list of projects, great and small. She needed to organize, but she had no time. Worse, she had no idea anymore what was the most important thing. Everything called out to be fixed or cured or solved. Everything felt the same weight as it pressed down. Where to begin?

With the kerosene. It did not belong in here. If it was going to be stolen from the barn, so be it. She cleared a path to the doorway and lifted the heavy can only to find Mr. Moors standing outside, gazing in with a stunned expression. Fanny quickly pulled the mat across the opening without greeting him. The woven door curtains let breezes in and kept insects out, though they didn't allow much privacy.

She lit a cigarette and sank down on the cot. She knew perfectly well what Moors was thinking: *Poor Louis, saddled with an old wife, and a dirty one at that. Well, Mr. Moors, there are some things dirtier than mud,* she said to him in her mind. *Blackbirding, for example. Everybody knows you used to be a cargo supervisor on a boat that "recruited" black boys for the plantations. And you, Louis, you should be ashamed for not confronting your entertaining friend. Where would you run off to, though, if you could not race out of here in the afternoons to go hang about Moors's store, even though the man overcharges us for every nail and bag of flour we order from him?*

Through the open window, she heard the voice of Belle and Louis's mother, laughing on the lawn below. Tears welled in her eyes. How thrilled she had been to know the whole family would be together in one place, yet here she was, avoiding them again, feeling like an outsider among them.

She couldn't remember the last time she'd had a full night's sleep.

Weeks. She snubbed out the cigarette in a coconut shell by her bed, and lay down. *Ten minutes. I will close my eyes for ten minutes.*

"FANNY?" MAGGIE STEVENSON's voice called from the doorway, behind the drawn curtain. "I hate to bother you, dear, but you said you wanted to know. Your seeds have come."

Fanny looked at the clock. Nearly eleven. She had slept for two hours. "On the way!" she called back, and leaped out of the cot. It was almost lunchtime, but she couldn't waste another minute.

Fifteen hundred cacao tree seeds. The number had thrilled her when she'd ordered them. Now it rather horrified her. She had planned to deal with two escaped pigs today and a horse that Joe was insisting had glanders. But the seeds were here, and the seed man said they ought to be planted on arrival. That meant fifteen hundred little pots had to be plaited out of cacao leaves, then filled with dirt, then put out into the field where the cacao plantation would be. It would require all of them—the hired men, Belle, Joe, Maggie, Louis, even little Austin.

Fanny raked fingers through her matted curls and went downstairs. The first person she saw was Mary, the spotless, corseted, and shoed little ninny whom Maggie had brought over from Sydney to work as their maid. She would be of no use. Wouldn't take direction from anyone but Louis's mother. Wouldn't even take care of Maggie's veils; one of Fanny's men had to do the starching and pressing. "Phhh," Fanny huffed through her teeth when she passed her. She came upon Maggie next, who was wandering around the house winding clocks, one of the ways she believed she made herself immensely useful.

"I'll do the varnishing next," Maggie called out when Fanny passed. "It's so beastly hot."

The varnishing had been Louis's job, and it was actually a necessary one; it kept mildew and cockroaches out of the books, which constituted nearly half of their house "furnishings." Even if she had no household jobs at all, Louis's mother would never in a million years consent to getting dirty on this project. She didn't know how to cook or even clean, for that matter. She'd rather be out having tea with church ladies, or leaving her calling card. Such a life seemed deadly boring to Fanny, and the feeling was mutual, she suspected. Since Maggie had come to live with them in Samoa, the two women had learned to give each other a wide berth. She would prefer not to have Louis's mother involved in the project, anyway.

Fanny went to Louis's study next, where she found her husband and Lloyd working together. She heard Louis say, "Make yourself invisible." Their faces fell when she entered, and she wondered if Louis's words were about her presence and not some bit of writing wisdom. "I need your help," she told them. "The cacao plants have arrived." She noticed Lloyd glance at Louis, seeking a sign that it was all right for him to leave. "Louis may do as he wishes," Fanny said curtly. "You, Lloyd, will go down there right this minute."

When she arrived on the verandah, she found Joe Strong sitting on a rocking chair, a *lavalava* tied above his leggings, his parrot on his shoulder in a show of style he obviously thought was island bohemian. "I'm all tuckered out," he muttered when she approached. She almost laughed out loud. Hungover, more like. She had put him in charge of feeding the chickens. One would think that was equal to building a pyramid, by the looks of him. She wouldn't get much help, but she wasn't going to let him sit there and watch while the others worked. "I will give you an easy job, then," she told him. "Stay right where you are."

"You no got work?" she called out to Faauma, Lafaele's pretty new wife, who cleaned house for them. The girl looked like a wood nymph, with fresh flowers woven into the crown of her oiled hair, a white cloth around her hips, and the tails of a red bandanna hanging between her breasts. "You bring Lafaele me," Fanny ordered.

In the cottage she and Louis had vacated, where Belle's family was now encamped, she found her daughter at the sewing machine. Belle was in charge of cleaning the lamps, among other things, but found more pleasure in making pieces of clothing for the workers. With Louis's approval, she had made *lavalavas* out of tartan plaid. The natives had given Belle the name Teuila, which meant something like "beautifier of the ugly," according to Louis. Along with Lloyd and Joe, Belle was supposed to be part of the cooking team who had replaced the terrified Emma after Fanny fired her in exasperation.

"Belle, round up the men out in the field. Everyone should gather on the verandah. The cacao seeds are here. It's all hands on deck! Wear your worst work clothes."

Belle looked disappointed to have to abandon her sewing. "Now!" Fanny shouted over her shoulder as she departed.

She knew she'd need her best men to see it through. She had Henry and Lafaele, both of whom would walk into a fire for her. They could be counted on to stay with the project to the last planted tree. She'd had a few whites working for her at the beginning, but all the laborers at Vailima were natives, and almost all Catholic, or "popies," as the locals called them. That fact rested fine with everyone except Maggie, who was in charge of Sunday prayers and didn't know what to do with the popies who lived at Vailima.

Beyond the Pineapple Cottage, Fanny saw her ten-year-old grandson playing with a worker who should have been out in the field. Arrick had clearly been lured away from his weeding by Austin's fort, and the two of them were busy constructing a roof out of branches to set upon the walls made of mud and twigs. Arrick's age was unclear; when he'd come to Vailima, he was a scrawny thing not much bigger than Austin. His chest and back were covered in welts, gotten in his boyhood when he was bled by elders trying to drain his body of poison from an enemy camp's arrows. Whether he was kidnapped from his island or had put his X on a work contract voluntarily, no one knew. What Fanny could ascertain was that he'd run away from one of the German Firm's plantations on the island and had been hiding in the bush, nearly starving. Louis was so moved by the young man's desperate appeal to be hired that he had gone down to the Firm's office and bought out the remainder of Arrick's indenture contract.

Both Louis and Fanny had been curious about how Arrick's presence would be received by the Samoans who lived and worked at Vailima. Likely they would resent the intrusion of a New Hebridee into their society. Why, the inside help even discriminated against the outside help! Sometimes they didn't invite them in to the lunch table but sent their food out to them. How would Arrick be treated? To everyone's relief, Lafaele and Henry and the others had been won over by Arrick's sunny disposition, his small stature, and his unlucky fate.

"*Fa' ape'ape'a le tū,*" Henry said sadly. "He is like a swift. Never can rest. No home."

Soon enough Arrick was everyone's favorite. They lavished him with treats, and he had begun to put on bulk, even muscle.

"Fanny-gran!" Austin called out when he saw her. "Come look at the fort!" Fanny's anger dissipated at the sound of the boy's voice. She dropped one knee down, then the other, and crawled into the fort's opening.

"My, but this is fine!" she said. "We'll camp out here together when it's done. Now, look, I have a job for a couple of strong men. Can I count on you?"

By noon, everyone on the property was elbow-deep in the tree project. Fanny sent ten workers into the barn and set them to weaving small baskets. Another four native workers were sent out to the field to dig up dirt and bring it back to the verandah, where it went to Louis, Belle, and Lloyd, who removed lumps of clay and rocks, then filled the leaf baskets making their way up from the barn. Arrick rolled the cacao seeds in ashes to kill any insects. Austin and Faauma, who had replaced her white *lavalava* with a faded old red tablecloth, carried the seeds over to Fanny, who sat on the floor of the verandah planting a seed in each basket. Joe arranged the little containers close together on the perimeter of the verandah, where they would stay until sprouts appeared and they were ready to be planted out.

As evening fell, Belle went into the kitchen and produced a vat of hot chocolate so the Samoans could taste what they were, in a sense, making. Even in the clammy ninety-degree heat, the hot drink was wildly successful in encouraging everyone.

The verandah felt as if it were the site of an Indiana barn raising, with everyone joking. The dirtier they got, the more they laughed.

Around ten o'clock, Fanny went in to the bathroom Maggie had built for Louis's birthday; she bathed and put on a clean dress and went upstairs to collapse.

She fell into a mellow drowsiness quickly, smiling to herself over all that had been accomplished. She turned to tell him she judged the day a success and then remembered: *He no longer sleeps here.*

By the next day, Louis dropped out, pleading work duties, while Belle complained of sore arms. Only Lloyd stuck to the work. Fanny oversaw the planting while urging, cajoling, and threatening the men to keep them engaged. Some walked away from the project; others grumbled bitterly. *"O le Fa ataulāitu Fafine o le Mauga,"* she heard one of the day workers say to another. Lafaele, who stood nearby, shoved the man when he heard the remark.

Fanny stepped between the men, whose fists were raised, and sent the day worker away. "What did he say?" she asked Lafaele.

"I cannot—"

"Tell me."

"Bad man," he said.

"Tell me! I am not afraid of words. What did he say?"

His sad eyes reluctantly met hers. "'Witch Woman of the Mountain.'"

CHAPTER 76

Fanny smelled the wax on the floors, felt it on the pads of her feet. The men had polished the floorboards in the "great hall" to a high, slippery shine, perfect for dancing. The varnished redwood walls—all forty by sixty feet of them—glowed as well. She could already see colorful gowns reeling around the room. Oh, it would be just the thing to christen the new wing. She would hire a fiddler, Scottish if she could find one, and a cello player. Moors would know whom.

She admired how the room had come together with the silver and crystal, with the dining table and long sideboard from Skerryvore; it occurred to her that their furniture had traveled more than most of the people she knew. The only thing missing in the new wing was the set of eighteen chairs she'd contracted to be made from Vailima wood. They were nowhere near ready, but who needed chairs for a dancing party?

She would have to break it gently to Louis that a Christmas gala was in the making. He'd moan about the expense and say, "The Mac-Richies are at it again." He had quashed her idea of a celebration for his birthday on November 13 by reminding her that he'd given away his birthday last year—bequeathed it to a young Apia girl who was born on Christmas Day, poor thing. Louis had written up a proclamation and handed over his birthday to the child. "Quite all right. I'm done with it," he'd told her.

Fanny knew very well that he would be ecstatic to have a Christmas party. That was one of the contradictions of Louis. He would swear off a thing and then embrace it. He loved his own birthday and adored seeing R.L.S. in icing on the cake, just as he adored having troops of visitors at all hours, though he complained afterward that they interrupted his work. And he did love this house. In spite of his contempt for ostentation, he couldn't help enjoying the elegant things from Skerryvore. As long as the Christmas affair included everyone—and it would, as she'd not plan it any other way—he would go along with it.

The addition, with an apartment of rooms above for Maggie, plus two extra bedrooms, made the main house look modest by comparison. Yet that part was perfectly solid and handsome. What the whole house was not was a mansion, as island gossip had it. Recently, in Apia, Fanny had met a British woman who became excited when Fanny mentioned Vailima in their conversation. "Why, it is supposed to be the showplace of the islands!" the woman had exclaimed.

At Moors's store, the town wags were hanging about, talking nonsense, as usual. "They will kill the whites first," one English fellow was saying. "That's what my boy told me." When Fanny walked toward the back of the store, she noticed that the men stopped speaking. She knew she and her husband were controversial among some of the whites of Apia. If Fanny and Louis agreed on nothing else these days, their political views still lined up. She spoke her mind at dinner parties; he gave speeches at local meetings. His fevered letters to the *Times* had won them few friends among the German population. And since the publication of *A Footnote to History,* there was talk—surely among these very gossips—that Louis would be deported for his seditious writings.

"Offhand," Moors said when Fanny asked, "the name of a Scottish fiddler doesn't come to me. You know, the *Curacoa* may be in harbor then."

The H.M.S. *Curacoa*! Fanny nearly leaped at the prospect. "But do they play only marches?" she asked.

"Who?"

"The band of the *Curacoa.*"

Moors laughed. "I'm sure the band can play anything."

"Will you invite the captain and the band for me when they get in?" She went toward the front of the store and spoke to Mrs. Moors. "You must come at Christmas, Nimo. You gave us such a memorable feast last year."

"Of course we will come," the woman said. She walked Fanny to her horse. "I have been wanting to talk to you."

"You look so sad. Is someone sick?"

"We have known something for a while that you should know, Fanny. I've struggled over how to tell you . . ." The woman inhaled deeply. "It's about Belle's Joe. He has a Samoan wife. She lives in Apia. All the local people know about it."

Fanny wavered on her feet. "How long?"

"Off and on for two years. When he came here from Hawaii on business, that's when it started. And now that he lives here . . . well, he is in Apia often."

Fanny grabbed hold of her saddle. "Is there a child?"

"No."

"Thank you for telling me."

Riding back home, she pictured the pearl-handled revolver the Shelleys had given them in Bournemouth. Louis had been assembling weapons up at the house, in case there was a war. The revolver had come out of the big safe. She could almost feel the cool, smooth handle in her palm.

By the time she reached Vailima, telling Belle was her foremost thought. Fanny had been on the receiving end of such news more than once. There was but one humane way to do it: immediately and directly.

When Fanny got into the paddock, her heart leaped to see Joe tying up his horse. "Joe!"

He looked up, startled by her sharp tone.

"I heard something about you today."

Joe's mouth pressed in upon itself. He patted his horse to calm it.

Fanny walked near to him. "I heard you have a Samoan wife. If it is not true, tell me now."

He fiddled with a stirrup. Didn't meet her eyes.

"You pathetic little cankerworm. You look at me when I speak! After all I've done for you—be glad I don't have a revolver in my hand, because if I did, I would not be responsible for my actions. How can you do that to my girl? To your own son? You go in there with what little manhood you have, and you tell your wife—your legal wife—the truth."

Fanny took a step toward him, and he moved back. "Do you hear me?" she shouted.

Joe turned and went inside.

Once it was out in the open, the stories came to her from the natives who worked at Vailima. Joe had made a copy of the key to the storeroom and had been stealing liquor for some while. He'd been feeding the chickens lime to take a cut of the money allocated for their feed. The chickens had been dying, and yet she had not seen what was happening. The natives said she had eyes in the back of her head, and she was rather pleased that they thought it. But the whole family had been duped by Joe Strong, and she was ashamed of herself. She, of all of them, should have known better.

On December 24, Fanny hurried through the household, overseeing preparations for the party. Belle was sequestered with her sewing machine, as she had been since the day Joe walked in and confessed. She had wept for days, until she learned he was going about Apia in retaliation, spreading lies that she had her own lover, among other untruths. Now Belle appeared mostly relieved to be free of Joe Strong. She soberly stitched plaid *lavalavas* for Vailima's natives to wear at Christmas.

Fanny had taken Belle down to Apia and gotten divorce papers drawn up. Some things were easier in Samoa than the States. Now Louis was a legal guardian of Austin, who had been sent back to California to live with his aunt in Monterey and attend boarding school. In a heartbeat, the world could and did change. Joe was gone, Austin was gone, and so was Henry, who had returned to his island to be among family.

She missed Henry as much as she missed her beloved grandson. Henry Simele was a real chief on his own island to his own people, yet a servant at Vailima. If that discrepancy ever disturbed him, he had never shown it. He was a man of such self-possession, he could empty the slops buckets of the sick household during an influenza outbreak, or light lanterns to please Louis, and never once lose his royal dignity.

Christmas Day arrived and the work continued. While hanging Henry James's mirror in the hall, Fanny caught a glimpse of herself. Not long ago, in San Francisco, before the *Casco* cruise, she'd crowed to her friend Dora, "Thank God I've kept my appearance." She couldn't say that anymore. She looked terrible, and there was no time to spend on primping. There was a pig on the coals to watch, and gifts to wrap.

By five, the house was ready for the feast. Guests were due in an hour, but Samoans were always early. She paused to scan the room. She might not look good, but the tree was a triumph. Anyone familiar with

Christmas trees would wonder at her cleverness, for there wasn't an appropriate tree to be had on Upolu. She'd instructed Talolo, the sweet young man they'd hired as cook, to bore holes through a post. Lafaele had collected long-needled branches of ironwood that came close to the look of a white pine. After the post was sunk in a container of hard dirt and rocks, Fanny and Lafaele stuck the branches into the holes. They rigged candles on the "tree" and decorated it with red hibiscus flowers. Voilà! Louis seemed pleased indeed.

Up in her bedroom, Fanny went through her wardrobe. Her eyes fell upon a deep blue dress she had worn . . . when? Five years ago? Not since Boston, just before they'd gone up to Saranac. It had a flattering empire waist from which tiny pleats flowed to the floor. Across the bodice were tiers of white lace, and at the elbows, too. At the neck was a satin artificial flower, crushed only a little. How she'd loved the dress! She threw it over her head now and was pleased it still fit, then remembered the hat she'd worn with it. She found it at the top of the wardrobe, battered a bit, the brim of it misshapen but still stylish. It had enormous black ostrich feathers rising above the crown and a shimmering veil off the back. She put it on, admired how it caused her to look taller, tied the velvet ribbon under her chin. The hat *made* the ensemble. How whimsical a touch for a Christmas party! *Sweet girl,* Louis would say. *You look beautiful tonight.*

Out of her trunk she took a toiletry case she hadn't used in some time. In the dim light, she spread rouge on her cheeks.

"Fanny!" Louis's look was quizzical when she appeared downstairs. "You're wearing a hat."

"Yes." She laughed, feeling giddy as a girl. "Isn't it festive?"

Lafaele and Talolo appeared in their holiday uniforms: plaid *lavalavas* and white shirts. Behind them trailed Mr. Moors and his wife.

"Light the candles, Louis!" she ordered. "The guests are here."

When Maggie came downstairs, she appeared taken aback. "Oh," she said. "You're wearing a hat, dear."

"So are you!" Fanny shot back.

Belle swooped up and took her hand. "Mama," she whispered. "Come upstairs with me for a minute. I want to fix your rouge."

"What's wrong with my rouge?"

"It's not where it is supposed to be."

They hurried upstairs. Belle looked around the room. "You need a dressing table. Come, sit on the bed." She took a washcloth and wiped Fanny's cheeks. "I can't see your face under that hat brim." Belle removed the hat and tossed it aside. "*There* you are." She took up the jar of rouge and lightly applied the rose-colored cream to her mother's cheeks and lips. "You know, you may need spectacles, Mama."

"Nonsense. It's just too dim in here."

Belle ran a comb through Fanny's hair. "That looks better. One more thing." She retrieved a pair of scissors. "I want to snip off that crumpled silk flower. It does nothing for your dress."

Fanny's hand went up and grabbed the scissors. "Quit pecking at me! There are people arriving right now!"

Coming downstairs, Fanny took in a confusing blur of faces. Talolo was lighting the candles on the tree. She waded through the crowd, losing names as she greeted people. Lloyd was standing by the Christmas tree, announcing something. Earlier he had strung into the branches little pouches containing treats, and now he began passing them out.

The scene in front of her was not what she had imagined. The H.M.S. *Curacoa*'s crew was not there; the ship never arrived in port. Most of their white missionary friends were absent, occupied by their congregations. But a smattering of white women in holiday gowns had appeared, along with a host of native women in colorful dress. A local English farmer had brought a nephew who could play piano. Even without the *Curacoa*'s band, Fanny comforted herself, there would be dancing.

How she loved to dance. Louis was not much of a dancer; because of his bed bound years, he'd never learned properly. Recently, though, Belle had taught him and Lloyd how to do the steps of a quadrille. Belle and Louis stood now at the center of the glowing room, preparing to lead as the head couple. The farmer's nephew commenced plunking out a Haydn piece as Fanny's daughter and husband joined hands at the far end of the room. Two long lines formed quickly, men on one side, women on the other.

Fanny felt a bolt of anger rip through her so abruptly that her head wobbled. She leaped up from a step on the staircase where she'd been watching the young piano player. Dashing through the crowd to where they stood, Fanny pulled their hands apart and said, "I shall dance!"

Belle moved to the end of the line and found a stray male for a partner, while Louis, surprised, took hold of Fanny's hand.

For days after the party, Fanny stayed in her room, where she took her meals. "Tired," she said when Belle came in to check on her.

"Rest is good for you, Mama. You've worked too hard."

"Leave me be."

Fanny sat at her desk with a pen in her right hand and a cigarette in her left. She felt a story stirring in her. She could hear a woman's voice telling it: *She is a dark woman, and a seer. She has not asked for her gifts; she does not practice them out of pride. Yet she understands the conversations of birds without effort. She touches horses where they suffer and cures them with her fingertips. She sees inside men and women, sees the very spot where a person is rotting. Sometimes she can do nothing, only watch. One morning she awakens, tastes the air, and knows. "Someone wants to harm me," she tells people, but no one listens. "Someone has betrayed me."*

Fanny's hand moved rapidly as she scribbled down thoughts for the beginning of the story. She wrote furiously until Lloyd came with lunch on a tray. She saw immediately that he did not want to be in the room. He was her sweet boy once, before Louis stole his soul. Now he sat every day where she once sat, laughing, listening, helping Louis with his stories.

Fanny left the food untouched.

At night she lay awake as the sound of the waves grew deafening inside her head. Come to Me Thousands, haggard and wise, appeared before her with a shawl around her bony shoulders. She sat on the edge of the mattress.

"I am alone," Fanny told her.

"*Tamo'e, si o' u afafine,*" the old crone said. *Run, daughter.*

⌒

CHAPTER 77

"Are you ready?" Belle's curly head was poking through Louis's office door.

"The amenuensis arrives," Louis greeted her, leaning back in his chair. "Yes, come in. And look at you—stockings and shoes!"

Since his scrivener's cramp worsened a few months ago, Louis had asked Belle to take his dictation. Today she was outfitted in a neat linen dress, as if reporting to work in a shop.

"Where shall we begin?" she said, her pencil poised for action.

"Another letter to *The Times*."

Belle retrieved a piece of Vailima letterhead.

"Sir, colon," Louis began. "Will you allow me to bring to the notice of your readers the Sedition, parenthesis, Samoa, end parenthesis, Regulation, comma, 1892, comma, for the Western Pacific, comma, and comma, in particular comma, the definition in section 3 question mark . . ."

Belle's pen flew as he dictated for another five minutes. "I am, sir, your obedient servant, Lord Prickle Trumble." The amenuensis smiled indulgently at his pale joke. "You will be happy to know that is all the lawyering and protesting I shall be doing today."

"Good."

"Tomorrow, when you hear the enclosure that goes with this letter, you will despise me, I am quite certain. It's very long."

"Where are we off to next?"

"Scotland. The Pentland Hills. Brutal father, hanging judge. Romantic son banished to countryside to languish over—"

"—the Kirsties."

"Correct."

Louis had risen early, his mind teeming with ideas for *Weir of Hermiston*. He'd taken notes for a steady hour. Now the words came easily as he dictated, and Belle never paused in her writing except to ask him to slow down.

He could not have guessed two years ago that they would be able to cooperate on such a project. Belle had bitterly resented him for such a long time. After her marriage to Joe Strong, her estrangement from Fanny had only deepened her contempt for Louis. When Louis saw her in San Francisco as he and Fanny prepared to depart on the *Casco*, Belle had been damned cold toward him. And when the *Casco* delivered them to Honolulu, Belle had put on a proud show as an independent woman with an artistic social circle of her own, a *royal* social circle. Louis could see how shaky her circumstances really were. Her little family was barely surviving. Joe's addictions were devouring what money he made as a painter. It was for Belle's sake that he and Fanny had agreed to take Joe with them on the *Equator*.

Later, when Louis went to meet his mother in Sydney, he invited Belle to a meeting with him alone. There had been so much bad blood between them, he wasn't certain if she'd be open to his suggestion. But he forged ahead and invited her family to come and live at Vailima.

"I never managed to have children of my own. You and Lloyd are my only family. I want you with us. And your mother needs you."

A flood of emotions and memories erupted then, and she explained how she had come to understand why her mother had left her father. "I don't know about Joe, whether he can get better," she'd said at the time. "But I cannot come to Samoa without him. He's Austin's father." Louis promptly agreed to her request.

Belle still talked about that meeting in Sydney. "'A child at Vailima!' That's what you shouted," she liked to tell Louis. "I'd never seen you so tickled. After that, I don't think you cared a fig whether I came along with Austin or not."

She had matured enormously since the days of her vitriolic letters demanding money. She'd apologized for them. "I was behaving like a spoiled brat," she admitted that day in Sydney. They had been friends ever since. They all missed Austin. Belle was glad to have some purpose now that he was gone. She showed up every day, chatty as a magpie but a great help nonetheless. In the wake of her failed marriage, Louis had tried to make her feel she had a safe place with them at Vailima.

They worked for an hour before Belle got up to go. "Louis, I really appreciate your kindness to me."

Louis embraced her. "A grit joy it is working wi ye, Belle," he said, glancing toward the clock. "Lunchtime, isn't it?"

In turning toward the clock, he glimpsed a figure standing on the verandah. Fanny's face, crazily vexed, stared in at them through the window.

"Fanny!" Louis called out. "Come in. We were just—"

She disappeared from view and in half a second was inside Louis's study.

"Youuuu!" Fanny screamed. "Both of you!" He saw a blur of blue dress, of Fanny's arms swinging, waving, and then coming down upon the desk. Her hands went for a stack of manuscript pages, and in a heartbeat she was hurling them around the room. The papers were still flying when she pitched his inkpot, splattering black streaks across the wall.

Transfixed, Louis watched glass shards fly in a shower onto the floor. "What the *hell,* Fanny?" he cried out. He reached out to stop her, but she flew past him, pushing Belle out of the way as she charged through the door.

CHAPTER 78

Fanny darted toward her horse's stall. Before she opened its gate, her eyes fell on a bush knife hanging from a nail on a post. The heavy tool leaped into her hands, and she ran with it to the cacao field beyond the barn. She gripped the handle with both fists and began swinging at the cacao saplings. Green stalks snapped. Leafy heads fell to the ground. She swung and cut and swung until her arms could not lift the scythe.

Into the sunless bush she ran, tripping and grabbing at vines as she went. Raw wails pushed up from her belly. She brushed past a tree where flying foxes hung upside down from its branches. Wings opened—*whoosh*—blackening the green forest air.

On the wet ground, she wrapped her arms around her middle and pressed her fingers into the flesh of her back. She rocked and rocked. Beside her, a giant moth with glowing red eyes watched. She heard the sky crack and Lafaele's voice. *The devils are fighting up in the sky.*

Heavy drops of water splatted on her face, rained down on her shoulders and breast. Her dress was a cold wet skin. She stood up, shaking, and began to walk.

Ferns tangled their fronds around her ankles. Red mud sucked her feet down. Above, nodding trees groaned in the tearing wind. A snow-white owl screeched her name from a stump. Then two skulls, human, appeared on the ground with bones scattered all around.

Hervey's tiny voice came next. Faint, sweet music. "Now, Mama."

WHEN SHE WOKE in her own bed, it was to Belle's voice. "Who found her?"

"Lafaele," Louis murmured. "He went out into the forest and played his clarionette. She went to him."

"Did you give her something?"

"Yes. Her feet are cut pretty badly. Lafaele bandaged her with those leaves he uses."

"Ah, Mama," Belle said, rubbing her mother's still arm. "Mama, Mama . . ."

CHAPTER 79

Louis sat in a chair by her bed. It was after midnight, and the others had gone to try to sleep. Outside, a gale was blowing, and the rain made a hellish tattoo on the sheet-iron roof. Thank God they had found her in the endless density of the bush.

They'd been taking turns watching Fanny. Her face was waxen pale, her breathing slow. *So weak,* he would think, and then she would rise up suddenly, thrashing, and in a burst of strength try to run away.

She stirred again. Louis straightened, ready to grab hold of her. As if in imitation, she sat up. "You're the cause!" she shouted when she saw him. She tried to bite his arm, and when he drew back, she scrambled off the other side of her bed and raced to the door.

"Belle!" Louis called out. "Lloyd!"

In the hall, Belle had her arms around her mother. Louis and Lloyd pulled Fanny back into the bedroom, where she fought with the strength of a man.

"We will have to tie her down," Belle said. "Otherwise she will hurt herself. Or one of us." Louis saw a streak of blood come up where Fanny's fingernail had scratched her daughter's cheek.

Belle went to get sheets while Lloyd held his mother. She tore them in thick strips and wound them around Fanny's ankles, which Louis held fast, knotting the ends onto the metal bedstead. Belle crossed the sheets over her torso and had Lloyd tie the ends with a rope beneath the mattress. Then they crisscrossed sheets to cover her shoulders.

Lafaele was standing in a corner, riveted. He didn't speak.

In the morning, while Lloyd and Lafaele kept watch, Louis and Belle walked around the lawn, speaking softly lest the natives overhear.

"There is a doctor in Sydney," Belle said. "His family befriended me when I was there."

"Yes?"

"He has worked with people who are . . . like Mama. His name is Roth. They say he's good."

"Do you know how to reach him?"

"I'm in touch with his wife."

"Then you shouldn't hesitate."

"How will we manage a two-week cruise with her in this condition?"

"Morphine. Whatever is required."

"What do the others know?" she asked.

"Lafaele found her, and he's awful at keeping secrets. So they all know now."

"I wouldn't be surprised to see the medicine man from Apia show up for an exorcism," she said with bitter humor. "That would be like Lafaele. He and Mama are devoted to each other. He will want to help."

Belle looked up at Louis and saw the tears streaming from his eyes. She patted his back tenderly. "It will be all right."

"It's so sad, now one understands." He pulled a handkerchief from his pocket and wiped his face. "It's been going on for months, over a year, when I think back. She blows up at the slightest thing. You know your mother. She's high-strung. But lately, I've been thinking, *Something ain't right.*" He dabbed his eyes. "It breaks my heart to see her tied down."

"It had to be done."

"How did you know what to do?"

"I saw it done once. In Paris."

"At a hospital?"

"At home."

"Ah, of course, Hervey was delirious—"

Belle turned her eyes to his. "No."

Louis felt a chill run across his scalp.

"A doctor came. She was seeing things, and would wander through the apartment at night. It was for her own safety."

"I knew she was depressed after Hervey's death," he said slowly, trying to remember what she'd said about that time. "Any mother would be. But I didn't realize she had . . . broken down so."

"Well, she did. Sometimes I wonder if a little piece of her never got quite right again." Belle rubbed her eyes. "Thank God Austin is back in California—"

"—and my mother in Scotland. Neither of them could bear it, I think."

That night, Louis kept watch beside Fanny's bed, where she slept fitfully. When she woke, she looked like a demented stranger; her face made tragic contortions as she whimpered. At least she was unbound. Dr. Funk had come up from Apia and given her sleeping pills. The good German doctor, called away during his cocktail hour and mildly inebriated, had put out his cigar and come inside. When he saw the state she was in, his whole attitude sobered. "I know Dr. Roth," he said simply. "Take her to him as soon as you are able. I will prepare a sack of medicines to carry with you, enough to last the voyage to Sydney."

Pacing the bedroom, sorting through memories of their years together, Louis began to see the scattered fingerprints of an unwell woman. What had Baxter said to him just before he departed for America to pursue Fanny? *Henley fears you are going to face a life of alarms and intrigues and perhaps untruths.* Louis winced at the thought that his former friend had clearer vision than he. When he reflected on individual incidents, though, he saw how easily mistaken they were for the normal expressions of Fanny's personality. She was by nature a fiery, complicated woman. He had been drawn to her because she was earthy and untamed, compared to the overrefined girls his parents admired. She showed the very qualities he'd been trained to politely suppress in himself. *I wanted what she had.* It occurred to him that those traits, over time, had bloomed into insanity. His eyes had not seen her madness coming, but he wondered now if his unconscious mind had recognized it long ago.

He thought of Jekyll and Hyde. The characters had erupted from the deepest place inside him. The story had flowed out as if it were telling itself. There were truths in that story not even he had understood entirely. Truths about what happens when a person's supressed desires fester until they turn monstrous. He shivered to remember the words he'd used to describe the connectedness of Hyde to Jekyll. *Closer than an eye, closer than a wife.*

CHAPTER 80

1893

D r. Roth ushered Louis into his private office and settled him in a chair, then went to sit behind his desk. The Sydney doctor was a trim fellow, kindly if a touch awkward. He took off his eyeglasses and rubbed the pad beneath each eye, as if buying time before delivering bad news.

"Your wife's physical health is not good. The gallstones and rheumatism," he said, replacing the spectacles. "We have a sense of her physical ailments. Her mental situation is more difficult to analyze. She tells me she has had brain fever and congestion in the past. And that your uncle George gave her chlorodyne for head pain. It's hard to make sense of what exactly is at work in her brain. You say her moods are up and down."

"I should explain a bit about my wife," Louis said. "Fanny may look like a timid little woman, but she has an intense personality. She's a violent friend and a brimstone enemy—people tend to hate her or worship her. She is capable of—no, she *does* extraordinary things. She's always been a wonderful, supportive wife to me. The fact that I am alive is due entirely to her." Louis shook his head. "She has a habit of taking on too much, though, of overreaching. There will be a period of frenzied activity and then weeks of entire hibernation when she simply shuts the door on the rest of the world. The pattern is nothing new. But I would say that for a good year now, she has been an exaggerated version of the woman I just described. She improved immensely on the voyage over here, but I must tell you, before the breakdown, she seemed possessed. She would go out into the fields and crawl around in the dirt with a spade in her hand for ten, twelve hours at a time. Like a demented beast."

The doctor's forehead creased, and Louis realized how horrifying a phrase he had just uttered to describe his own wife.

Roth fingered a gold pin on his lapel. "Doctors tend to use the latest terms when we have no certainty of what causes the symptoms. I'm reluctant to do that, since your wife's condition could be any number of things. You say a doctor in Honolulu diagnosed her with Bright's disease. Kidney failure is sometimes accompanied by delirium. That could explain her symptoms." He shrugged. "On the other hand, it may be the change of life; it's not unheard of. Perhaps she has worked herself into a state of delirious exhaustion. Or it's possible she's reacting to some medication. She seems to have dosed herself with any number of things.

"But there is a chance, I'm sorry to say, that it's a more entrenched mental illness. We know little about how to treat mental breakdowns. What we know is that she can come back and live a normal life. Or not. It varies. All I can do is give her medicine to sedate her. Only her brain can cure itself. And every brain is different, you see. Rest is essential. Healthy food. Exercise. That's the best we have right now." He handed Louis a note for the pharmacist. "This will calm her. Give it to her right away."

"So we wait and hope it's over?"

The doctor wagged his head somewhere between yes and no.

At the Oxford Hotel, where they were staying, Louis administered the new medicine to Fanny and then took his wife and stepdaughter to lunch. Belle and Louis ate oysters, while Fanny, following doctor's orders, ate something that looked like gruel and drank Maltine for her stomach. She seemed calmer already. All three of them turned buoyant with relief at being out of the doctor's office and in the normalcy of the restaurant.

"Do you remember the first time we came here?" Louis touched Fanny's knee gently.

"To the Oxford? Yes."

"You forget I was with you, too," Belle chastised him. "It was the first time I ever saw Louis Stevenson in a blue fury."

They had retold the story time and again, but it felt right to tell it here and now. Three years before, when they'd finished the *Equator* voyage and come to Sydney, he and Fanny had gone to the elegant Victoria Hotel to check in. He had dressed in a suit to enter the hotel, albeit one that had been stuffed into the corner of a trunk for the previous six months, while they sailed the South Seas. Fanny looked no better, though he recalled they had put on shoes.

"Can you blame a man?" Louis said. "I asked for a suite of rooms on the first floor. The receptionist, without a word, hands a key to a porter who takes us up to a tiny room on the fourth floor. It was terrible. As you recall, I rode the lift down and had words with the man at the desk."

"That was just the moment when I stepped out of a taxi and entered the lobby of the Victoria," Belle said. "There was Mama, rather stunned-looking, watching the scene unfold. And there you were, at the beginning of a performance I think of as 'RLS Unbound.' *Had words?* You were apoplectic, Mr. Stevenson. But the author didn't lose his tongue for long. Oh, no. It was poetic wrath that came out of your mouth. I have never in my life heard anyone lay another human being so low, and without one curse word." She shook her head, remembering. "I have a vivid image of your luggage, sitting in that lobby, and all these fine ladies in silk dresses disgruntled to have to step around it. You had a few traveling cases, but there were other pieces—those tree trunks that had lids. The insides of the trunks were stuffed with all manner of souvenirs. And you had not just tree trunks; you had straw baskets, calabash gourds, *tapas,* fish nets, spears . . ."

"We were a bit unconventional," Louis conceded. "Still, that pretentious little man behaved as if we smelled, which we most certainly did not."

"How could you tell?" Fanny asked wryly, and they began to laugh.

Perhaps it was simply the giggle coming from Fanny's mouth, or perhaps it was the gush of warmth that had been absent from her voice for so long, but her simple remark caused the three of them to fall into hysterics. They savored the laughter, prolonged it, cried from it.

"All right. Maybe the luggage smelled," Louis said.

"The best part was when the Sydney newspaper trumpeted that the famous R.L.S. was in Sydney and staying at the Oxford Hotel. And the Victoria had to send over your mail every day!"

He smiled. "That *was* satisfying."

"HOLD ME CLOSE," Fanny said to him that night.

Her whole being seemed sweet and gentled. He pulled her into his arms, where they huddled together under the sheet like children in the dark. "Are you afraid?" he asked her.

She rested her cheek on his shoulder. "I'm terrified that the thoughts will come back and it will start again."

He stroked her forehead gently. "Do you want to tell me about it?"

She didn't answer. After a minute or two, she said, "Don't leave me alone, Louis. I don't want to be this way."

Outside their room, they heard luggage cart wheels creak down the hall.

"Do you love me?"

"Yes, Fanny, yes."

"Forgive me."

"For what?" he asked.

"For the cruelties. I don't know why I strike out—I hate myself afterward. *Hate* myself. I think, somehow, the meanness comes of fear."

In the morning, he watched her face while she slept. She looked fifteen years younger. He felt a surge of tenderness course through him, and he realized how long it had been since he'd felt such protectiveness toward her. Fanny was such a strong force, no one had seen the cracks. Her terrible unhappiness had left deep lines on either side of her mouth. At the moment, he couldn't see them anymore; it was as if the night had smoothed away all the worry.

The streets of Sydney were lively when they went out. Belle was the first to notice how a few people stopped in their tracks. "Louis," she said. "You're being recognized!"

He was already aware of eyes and fingers directed at him. He'd actually heard a passing woman ask loudly of her husband, "Is that his Moroccan wife?" Soon enough someone approached him for an autograph. The man proffered a fresh copy of *Jekyll and Hyde*. "I just popped into the bookstore and bought it. Read it already, of course."

Louis hated such attention, but now it amused him, because it had been such a long time since it had happened. The whites in Apia were used to him. They talked to him about his work, but there was no adulation, thankfully. Among the native Samoans, few of them seemed aware that he was famous for being an author elsewhere in the world.

He took Fanny and Belle shopping for new dresses and had a suit of clothes made up for himself, including a new white shirt and a white tie. When they happened upon a photographer's studio, Louis impulsively had a picture taken of the three of them sitting together on a divan. Fanny slept in the afternoon, while he and Belle went to a dressmaker and had a new gown made up for Fanny using Belle's measurements. They presented the black velvet dress to her a few days later, and Louis warmed to see her fingers linger on the duchesse lace trim.

"One more surprise." He went to the bureau, where he'd hidden more presents. With his arms behind his back, he returned to Fanny and Belle, making a deep bow. He brought his hands around to the front and gave to each of them a small wrapped box. "For my pair of fairies, plump and dark," he said.

"You go first, Mama," Belle said.

Fanny peeled back the wrapping paper and opened the shiny wooden box. Nestled in a pillow of satin she found an opal ring, with *R.L.S.* engraved inside its gold band. "Oh, Louis," she said, "you know how I love blue opal."

"Your turn," he said to Belle, who pulled an identical ring from her box, also engraved with his initials. She slipped it on her finger. "Louis," she said, "thank you! It's lovely."

"I bought one for meself as well." He slipped off the opal ring on his finger to show them its inscription.

Fanny squinted at the lettering inside the band. "*F and B,*" she read aloud, as a troubled look flitted across her face.

THEY DINED IN a fine restaurant so they could wear their new clothes. In the candlelight, with the white lace glowing against her neck and wrists, Fanny was as radiantly lovely as she had ever been. He felt her old affectionate warmth as she squeezed his arm while telling a story. The simple niceties that once were ordinary came rushing back. It was as if his wife had been returned to him after a strange and terrible journey.

At the end of their three weeks in Sydney, they boarded the S.S. *Mariposa.* They would be home in Apia by the last day in March, when the cyclone season would be nearly over and the rainy days tapering off. Fanny remarked how happy she was that her pig-chasing would no longer be conducted in mud.

Later, he would think, *Of course it couldn't last.* Roth had warned him. Still, it took him by surprise when he found Fanny sitting on a deck chair, chattering to herself. "Mother just came by to talk," she said when he sat down next to her, "and Pa was with her, too."

By the time they arrived at Vailima, the swirling madness had retaken her.

CHAPTER 81

L ouis was drifting inside the blurry edge of a dream. He saw himself as a young man, standing on the deck of a boat, staring out at a starless, silent night. He knew there were people on shore, waiting to get on the boat, but he could not see them. Suddenly, a keening wail rose up out of the blackness . . .

Louis bolted upright, shuddering. The keening continued, piercing the silence as it found its way down the hallway from Fanny's room to his. With his heart thudding crazily, he realized what he'd done: woven a dream around the terrible wail. As he came fully awake, the pounding in his chest slowed, and a sickening knowledge pressed down upon him. *It is the voice of my wife.*

He saw himself from the outside, a small figure in the midst of a tropical forest, ten thousand miles from home, alone and frightened. He wondered how, of all the paths he might have taken in his life, he had come into this nightmare, in this place.

During the two weeks they had been back from Sydney, Fanny had declined further. Mercifully, she was not violent. By day she was inconsolably sad, but her nights were full of terrifying visions. He went out into the hallway, where he found Lloyd standing outside Fanny's room in his pajamas, looking pale but alert.

"Go back to bed," Louis said. "I'll relieve Belle."

"No," Lloyd replied. "I'm up now. And I know you need to work."

Thank God for Lloyd and Belle. They'd been exemplary. Louis could not have survived this without them.

In his study, Louis drank his coffee as the dream—and the memory that suggested it—came alive again in his mind. He was a young man of twenty, still an engineering student, traveling through the Inner Hebrides archipelago on his way to view firsthand the Dhu Heartach lighthouse that his father was building at the time. He had boarded a paddleboat steamer at Skye as it headed toward Erraid. One dark night, standing at the bulwark, he noticed that the vessel appeared to be moving through fjords into a loch, where it stopped.

"Have we shifted off course?" he'd asked a boatman who stood nearby, sucking on a pipe.

"Aye," the man said.

"Why?" Louis asked.

Orders, the man explained. The boat was to collect a group of people who had been moved off their land because a deer park was to be made.

"Where are you taking them?"

"Tae Glasgow."

"And then where will they go?"

"I cannae say." The boatman shrugged. "Awa'."

Louis had looked out into the blue-black night. A lantern here and there flashed upon a figure as the silent moving mass boarded the boat. Then a keening voice rose up and echoed against the cliffs. The chilling cry seemed to speak for every exile who ever was stripped of his home; it was the sound of a soul ripping apart. As the voice was joined by a chorus of others, Louis had turned to a young man next to him and said, "They're being cleared, just as the Highlanders were." The force of that realization had stayed with him all these years.

Sitting in his dim study, Louis felt a heavy inertia in his limbs. His hand did not go out to the manuscript on his desk. Fanny's cries had set off a jumble of emotions, and his brain kept turning to the Hebrides. Haunted by the keening of the displaced people, he had proceeded on to Erraid, where he was met by his father, who was eager to show his son the miracle that was under way. Thomas Stevenson took him by boat to the large black rock jutting up from the ocean that supported the foundation of the lighthouse. Dhu Heartach had long been considered impossible to build upon, but several dozen losses of vessels and lives in the area convinced marine authorities it should be tried. At the time, Louis was unimpressed by the efforts of the Stevenson engineering firm. He had no interest in building lighthouses and thought himself doomed to proceed in the career his father had chosen for him. Now, when he remembered what he'd seen at Dhu Heartach, his breath flew out of him.

The lighthouse was being built on a reef that was pounded by waves in the fairest of weather; in foul conditions, they reached ninety feet in height. Giant two-ton boulders had to be brought over from Erraid by boat and hoisted in wild seas onto the rock. At least once the boulders were knocked off the lighthouse foundation and pushed into the foaming waves. Workers risked their lives raising that light, and his father always expressed the profoundest admiration for them.

Louis stared at the *Weir of Hermiston* pages stacked at the edge of his desk, where they had rested untouched for weeks. There was little chance he could regain the trancelike state he'd been in while producing that pile of words. He felt numbed by the terrible drama churning under his roof. How to work? How to reenter the nuanced relationship of the hanging judge and his son, Archie? An old promise came to him, one he'd made to his father's memory after he died. A nonfiction history of the lighthouse-building Stevensons might be the one thing he could write at the moment.

Sitting at his desk in the following days, poring over family records and maps, he found himself visiting the landscapes of his youth. He imagined walking the beach at Bell Rock with his grandfather. He meandered through the hills of the Isle of Lewis as his uncle Alan talked about the Arnish Point light; he watched those immense waves crash against the lifeless piece of rock called Dhu Heartach.

The brick-and-mortar feats of his brilliant relatives awed him as never before and made him wonder: *Why did I ever take up a pen? Why didn't I apprentice myself to a baker? Or build lighthouses* and *write books?* His collection of finished works appeared puny compared to his father's accomplishments.

When he looked back on his own career, he thought the only real genius he possessed as a writer was pure doggedness. He had written propped up in bed, lying down, with scorching fevers and shivering chills, between coughs and hemorrhages, through bouts of scrivener's cramp that rendered his right hand a useless red claw.

If craggy coastlines treacherous with submerged rocks had been the ground where his ancestors proved their valor, the sickbed had been his battlefield. Any honor he'd won had been earned there. Yet what good had it been?

All these years he'd believed that every time he began a story, it was going to be a journey toward some core of truth. That if he passed the world as he saw it through his soul, somebody, at least he, would be better for it. But what did he know now? Only that his soul was cracked wide open, not a fit vessel for filtering anything.

How he longed for Scotland! The other day, in a letter to Colvin, he'd spilled his frustration. *Singular that I should fulfill the Scots destiny throughout, and live a voluntary exile, and have my head filled with the blessed beastly place all the time.* How bitterly ironic to be surrounded by palm trees, flying foxes, sweet-smelling gardenias, red and yellow fruit doves. *And what do I see at every turn? My gray-pigeoned homeland.*

Memories filled his head of himself at seventeen, with his ten-shilling allowance jingling in his pocket as he and Bob walked through the Old Town's narrow closes into moldy courtyards behind cramped tenements where ragged redheaded children and friendly drunks throve like lovely mushrooms. He longed to ramble again through Edinburgh as his cousin railed against some "bleating idiot," or waxed flowery about a Velázquez painting. How he would love to go once more to Rutherford's pub to drink until his money was gone, then happily stagger through the snow back to Heriot Row.

Pacing around his office, he pulled volumes of his early writings from the bookcase and began paging through them, running his finger under lines that sounded foreign now.

By all means begin your folio; even if the doctor does not give you a year, even if he hesitates about a month, make one brave push and see what can be accomplished in a week.

The true realism, always and everywhere, is that of the poets: to find out where joy resides, and give it a voice far beyond singing . . . For to miss the joy is to miss all.

What an optimist I was. How utterly self-serious. Once identity was the most important thing. He'd written with such conviction about "the real knot of our identity" and the "central metropolis of self."

He hardly knew what he meant by those words anymore. What he felt now about identity was simple: *All that was me is gone. The Great Exhilarator is dead. Puck is dead.* The Atheist had been dead ever since he'd taken to writing prayers for Vailima's Sunday services. He wrote them for the Samoans' sake, and for his mother's sake, and he guessed for his own sake. Now the Worker seemed to be in his last throes. Louis could not seem to write anything besides the little piece about his lighthouse-building family. His imagination had dried up.

UNABLE TO WORK, he rode into Apia, where he collected the mail and called on Moors.

"You look terrible, Stevenson," the trader remarked, "and I'm not talking about the clothes you put on this morning."

Louis had been so eager to escape the house that he hadn't bothered to change out of the battered old linen trousers and shirt. "I'm feeling old and fagged, to tell you the truth."

"Does Lloyd do a lick of work up there?" Moors asked indignantly.

Louis did not respond, feigning absorption in the arrival of a schooner into harbor. More than once the trader had hinted that Lloyd and Belle were ticks on Louis's hide. He called them "the Osbournes," as if they were a type of affliction or a natural disaster. Truth was, Louis had been feeling guilt about Lloyd, whose apprenticeship had begun well enough. His storytelling was rather rude but entertaining; he could grow into a novelist in a couple of years' time with serious discipline. But Louis suspected that Lloyd wanted the life of the writer more than the art. He would have been better off to have attended classes at Cambridge, as he'd wanted to do before the expenses at Vailima precluded that plan. Lately, Louis had begun to fear that Lloyd might be one of several casualties caused by his selfish desire to gather a clan around him.

"Go to my place on Nassau," Moors was saying. "You can relax in a hammock for a month."

"Six months."

"Then lie in a hammock for six months."

"Two years," Louis said. "I think it would actually take two years."

"I know you are making a joke, but I'm not," Moors said, studying his face. "I will speak frankly to you, Stevenson. Your family drains you. They ask too much of you.

"I have spoken to any number of the Brits and Americans in this town who admire you immensely and who agree with me that you are ruining your reputation by collaborating with members of your family.

You need to get away from them to do serious work, like *Kidnapped* or *Jekyll and Hyde*."

Before, when Moors was bold enough to criticize his work, Louis wanted to pummel him. Now he looked at the man and thought, *He sees what I have been blind to.*

"When might you be able to get away?" Louis asked. He knew Moors was traveling soon to the Chicago Exposition to help mount the Samoan exhibit.

"Not for a couple of months. But you don't need me to accompany you. I've told you all along, the place on Nassau Island is yours to use as you wish. I'm having some clearing done over there. You see that steamer?" The trader pointed to a ship being loaded with supplies in the harbor. "It's headed to the Cook Islands, set to depart tomorrow. Just go, for Chrissake."

"It's not a good time."

Moors looked at him in a way that suggested he might know about the troubles up at Vailima. "Is there ever a good time? If you're worried about the women up there, you can put Lloyd in charge. He needs some grown-up responsibility. Dr. Funk is around if somebody gets sick. As for all the war rumors, they're nonsense. Anyway, Talolo can manage any situation."

Louis allowed the idea to play in his mind. A few months on Nassau Island would be enough to restore him or blissfully kill him. Either outcome would do.

"I will go," he told his friend. "Soon."

Louis left Moors. Sodden with dread at the thought of returning home, he walked the beach, stepping around parties of two or three men camped along the shore. He sat down on the sand, not far from a beachcomber who had built himself a little fire and was cooking something on a stick. The fellow was white, but his face had the sunbaked look of brown clay. He wore a kerchief around his neck and a straw hat on his head.

The man hailed Louis to come over to the fire and offered up his bottle. Louis looked down at his own clothing. He remembered the time he was staying at the Savile Club in London and had dressed up in rags to experience being a beggar. Now he wanted to laugh out loud. *At last I am taken for a proper tramp, without the least bit of effort.* He moved closer to the beachcomber and took a swig from the bottle. Gin.

"Been here long?" the man asked.

"A while," Louis said.

"Stayin'?"

"I don't know. I may travel." Louis took out a pouch of tobacco, rolled two cigarettes, and handed one to his new acquaintance. When he looked up from the rolling papers, the steamer headed for the Cook Islands filled his eye. God, how he wanted to leave! He could go right now, get money from Moors, and take passage. He would go unencumbered, the way he'd traveled with Bob long ago, without so much as a comb in his pocket.

Louis smiled to himself at the thought. *Fantasy—what a healthful quirk of the brain.* Just imagining freedom made his mood lighter.

"Where you thinkin' about?" the beachcomber asked.

"Nassau Island. Heard of it?"

"Um-hum." The man drew on his cigarette with visible pleasure. "Not much there, is it?"

"Enough. And that boat could take me."

The fellow looked out at the trading ship. "Friendly enough here," he said, pulling a sausage off the stick. "I'm thinkin' to settle down, set up a trading post, maybe find me a local girl."

Black flies buzzed at the bare shoulders and back of the beachcomber, who was dividing up his meat with a small knife in order to share it with Louis. He was probably thirty or so but looked to be a decade older. An American sailor who had deserted, probably. A decent enough fellow turned profligate by the bottle, which he offered to Louis repeatedly. "You can go over to the mission, get a square meal," he said as he handed over a piece of the sausage. "Looks like you could use it."

Louis ate and drank. "You've been traveling for a while?"

The man paused before answering, as if he heard judgment in the question. He sat up, proud. "Nobody tells me when to get up, where to go to work, or what to wear. Nobody yappin' in my ear." The man sized up Louis, who leaned on an elbow in the sand. "It's a good life, ain't it? Fellas like us got nothin' to lose."

Evening fell in Apia. The Pacific Ocean stretched out flat and blue, like an invitation.

Louis stood up, breathed deep the salty harbor air, and felt a kind of joy rush into his limbs. *I'm getting on that boat.*

CHAPTER 82

L ouis paused on his way home from Apia. He had ridden slowly up the mountain with dread pressing upon him like a wood yoke. He dismounted to collect himself and, in the gloaming, noticed birds at the edge of the bush eating fat nutmeg fruits fallen from trees. He gathered some as he listened to the roar of insects coming from the dark, damp forest.

Pushing on, he caught sight in the distance of yellow lights shining through Vailima's windows. He had explained to Talolo what "home fires" meant to a Scotsman and how it pleased him to see the radiant windows when he rode from town, especially on a night when there was little moonlight. No Samoan needed an explanation of home fires, least of all Talolo. But after their conversation, Louis could count on lantern glow to pierce the darkness of the hillside and cheer him home.

The sight of the glowing windows eased his dismay only slightly. He had been away for two days. He'd awakened this morning in Moors's house with the trader standing over him and a searing pain in his temples. "Do I have an arrow through my head?" Louis had groaned.

"Must have been quite a party you found last night." Moors grinned. "I've got hot water in the tub for you, and there's a clean set of clothes on the chair."

When the trader left the room, Louis tried to recollect the events of last night. He recalled hanging lanterns and singing. He'd made it onto the boat, or maybe he'd made it only into a bar. There had been a switch to whisky; he could still taste it in his mouth. A fuzzy image came to him of being escorted out of someplace with his elbows secured by strangers.

"How did I end up here?" he asked Moors over breakfast.

"A gentleman from the beach accompanied you to my door."

Louis began to apologize, but his friend waved him off before he could finish. "You have suffered enough in your life, old man. God knows you deserve a little pleasure. Stay as long as you wish. I sent my boy up to Vailima this morning to let them know where you are."

"Thank you."

"We have dinner guests this evening. A crowd you would like—"

"No, no. I'll do something useful with my visit to town—go talk to the English and American consuls again about Mata'afa. It will be futile. And then I shall go back."

Moors looked over his spectacles. "Nassau," he said. "It would be so easy."

"Yes," Louis muttered. "Yes."

WHEN LOUIS CAME through the paddock gate, he found Talolo holding a lantern. "Love," the man greeted Louis. "Did you eat in Apia?"

"Enough." He tipped his hat to Talolo.

"Manuia lau tōfāga," Talolo said. *May you sleep like a noble.*

When Louis entered the house, he found Belle at the dining room table, where she'd just finished eating. "How is she?" he asked.

"Louis. You're back." Belle stood up. "There's plenty of food here. Sit down and eat," she said in a pleasant enough voice. If she wondered about his absence, she gave no sign. "Mama has quieted down considerably. The medicine has left her in a stupor."

"Go rest. I'll take over." He collected a leg off the roasted chicken sitting on a platter and gathered up the abandoned *Weir* manuscript from his study so he could review it while he kept watch. In Fanny's bedroom, he found her dozing, looking peaceful. He was struck by how her hands, small as a child's, were still lovely, even after the battering they'd taken over the years.

He walked around the perimeter of the room, observing Fanny's things, orderly now. There was a worktable along one wall, on which her most recent preoccupations were displayed. Pressed leaves and flowers shared a corner with poetry and plant identification books; feathers and bird sketches with notes claimed another corner. A lantern, lit faithfully by Lafaele to frighten lingering spirits, illuminated an arrangement of turtle shell fishhooks suspended from strips of woven cloth. Next to it lay her silver medal from art school and a carefully preserved lock of Hervey's blond hair.

Fanny's mind was like her room, a cabinet of curiosities. He had fallen in love with the treasures he found in that exotic interior. Glancing around, he noticed her diary sitting on the dresser. He retrieved it and read quickly, looking for clues in the past six months that might shed some light on why her mind had broken.

The diary was all ordinary talk about the garden, the natives, influenza. He smelled a whiff of resentment toward his mother in one part. A good deal of bitterness toward Joe Strong. Mostly, it was a record of Fanny's daily life at Vailima. She talked about trying out scent making and planting India rubber as a crop to sell. There were lists: remedies she had used on a parade of sick people; things she needed, such as hurricane shutters, horse shoes, new bridles to replace the rotted and broken ones, and a saddle she wanted to buy for Belle. She wrote about seeds and harvests, from tree onions to watermelons.

She mentioned one wild Irishman on the island as a "delicious creature." My God, did she notice such things? She never said so aloud. She wrote of the animals. And she quoted him. "Louis says I have the 'soul of a peasant.'" Weeks later, she talked of it again.

I am feeling depressed, for my vanity, like a newly felled tree, lies prone and bleeding. Louis tells me that I am not an artist but a born, natural peasant. I have often thought that the happiest life, and not one for criticism. I feel most embittered when I am assured that I am really what I had wished to be. I have been brooding on my feelings and holding my head before the glass and now I am ashamed. I so hate being a peasant that I feel a positive pleasure when I fail in peasant occupations.

Louis remembered their conversation. Why on earth had he said such a despicable thing? He breathed deep at the memory. He had spat out the bitter remark because she'd interfered in his work again. He'd buckled under her haranguing but carried deep resentment. When he struck back with the peasant business, though, he attacked her very soul. Always, since he'd first known her, she had wanted to live a creative life.

Did all women married to well-known men struggle for recognition? It occurred to him that his friends thought her greatest achievement was keeping him alive. They didn't care about her other qualities. It was a sad truth that while his illness had conferred on him an air of heroism, it had marked Fanny, his nurse, as a menial. He'd always held to the idea that she didn't give a damn what people thought of her. She seemed bull-strong. He had learned rather late in the game that Fanny was the kind of woman who needed building up. But then everybody needed praise. The question was: *Can a person go mad from want of it?*

A muted cry rose from Fanny while she slept. It shook Louis nearly as much as the first time her wailing had jolted loose his memory of those anguished exiles he'd witnessed in the Hebrides. Back then, the keening of a distraught woman made clear to him the anguish of the displaced, in particular the banished Highlanders. He had been writing about that period of Scottish history ever since. Now Fanny's cry stirred uncomfortable questions. All this time, had he pitied the downtrodden, ancient Highlanders more than he'd thought about his own wife's suffering? Had Fanny gone mad from being uprooted so often? Time and again, the sweet nests she made had been pulled out from under her as she endured one more leavetaking. She was an earthbound person, seasick from the moment she set foot on a boat. Was it any wonder she had cracked after two years of cruising the Pacific? He recalled the phrase Henry had used to describe poor Arrick: *Fa'ape'ape'a e lē tu. He is like a swiftlet. He can never rest, for he has no home.* Fanny uttered no complaint, but in staying by his side, by pursuing health for him— their holy grail—she had made herself every inch the exile he was.

Louis felt his face go hot with shame. *Dear God, what an ass I am.*

He noticed her stirring. She sat up in bed, looked at him, and said, "How nice you look in that shirt, Louis." It startled him. It was as if the woman he'd known in 1876 had come to call.

"Why, thank you. It belongs to Moors. How are you feeling?"

She blinked but didn't answer, only stared impassively into space.

Louis sighed. It wasn't going to be simple. He didn't know from whence her troubles came. What mattered was to get her well. To sift through memories seeking proof of his wife's madness would be to forget her well of wisdom, compassion, and courage.

He sat next to the bed. "I am in your chair, Fan, and here I sit on my hands," he said. "After all the doctoring and solace you have given me, I don't know what to do to make you better." He lifted his satchel and put it on his lap. "I brought you something. Seeds from the nutmeg trees in the forest." He placed the fruits on the bedside trunk, where a plate of untouched food rested. Then he pulled from the bag the manuscript. "I have begun a new novel, called *Weir of Hermiston.* Would you like to hear a bit of it?"

Fanny showed no sign that she heard him. Her pupils were constricted black dots in gold-streaked pools.

"I'm sorry I've hurt you," he said. "I'm sorry we hurt each other. I don't suppose we're different from most married people. You try to run me like a perambulator, and I treat you—I have at times treated you so unkindly. We're better than that."

Louis climbed into her bed and sat on the opposite end, facing her. "It is only a beginning, Fan, but I need your thoughts on it." He lifted the first page of the manuscript and began to read. "'In the wild end of a moorland parish, far out of the sight of any house, there stands a cairn among the heather . . .'"

⌒

CHAPTER 83

In the weeks that followed, the household held its breath as it watched and waited.

"She's better, she really is," Louis said one day. "She was so sweet last evening. We talked about real things, about her sister Nellie. She's perfectly sensible again."

"Louis, she's not," Belle insisted. "She didn't eat breakfast or lunch today. Doesn't even smoke. Just sits and stares."

"I'm going to take her out for a walk in the garden. Where is she now?"

"Sitting on the verandah with Lloyd."

Louis collected Fanny and walked with her out into her vegetable plots. The sun blazed on him as he followed behind the small barefoot figure who carried an umbrella over her head. He watched her examine the rows of plants as if she were Napoleon inspecting troops.

"I think you are much better," he said.

"The eggplants are looking poorly. But see Lafaele's cabbages? They're getting nice and fat."

"Fanny. Love. Stop for a moment, talk to me. Help me understand."

She looked up at him and shaded her eyes with her hand.

"Did you have hallucinations before?" he asked.

"A couple of times."

"Why did you never tell me?"

"Those visions came after terrible events. I never expected they would happen again."

"Do you remember the story you told me about when you were a little girl?" he asked. "You used to swing on the screen door, holding tight to the doorknob. You thought the reason people died was that they let go of their hold on things, and the trick to staying alive was hanging on to something. You thought you could fend off death through pure force of will. I think you have pushed your way through hard times with your amazing will. But there are things in life that can't be brought to heel."

She pressed her lips together and turned her face toward the field.

"You blame yourself for Hervey, don't you? Even now."

Her features collapsed. "I wasn't paying enough attention. I relaxed, and then he was gone. If I had—"

He took her hand and held it. "You did the best you could, Fan. Lay it down now."

They walked on through the rows until she stopped and turned to him once more. "What am I to do?" she said, her eyes overflowing with tears. "I see bad things coming, and I want to warn off people."

"Everyone must make mistakes. It's how we learn."

"I never felt I was allowed them. For so long, with your health, there was no room for a mistake."

"Fanny Van de Grift Stevenson," he said, "you've kept me breathing against the odds, and I owe you my life. Look at me. Am I not the very picture of health? Now it's time to rest and make yourself well."

She dropped the umbrella and put her arms around his waist.

"Fanny, Fanny," he murmured, patting her back. "How is it you can be so fearless in the face of real danger, and yet at other times be afraid of mere possibilities?"

During the next few days, Fanny turned further inward, staying in her room, getting up from her chair or bed only to look through the window. He knew that she could not be quickly pulled from the dark place she had entered. But he had seen her eyes brighten a few times in response to his little attentions.

He hadn't any idea how one was supposed to help a loved one find her way out of such darkness. *What have I to fight against so unpitying an enemy? Only kindness.* Perhaps with unbridled, importunate, violent kindness, he could woo Fanny back from this hell.

He stayed with her each afternoon and read what he had written during the morning. Some days he pinned a poem to her bed curtain, where she would discover it upon waking. Once when he found her standing at the window, head bent in concentration, he knew she was reading his latest offering.

I will make you brooches and toys for your delight
Of bird-song at morning and star-shine at night.
I will make a palace fit for you and me,
Of green days in forest and blue days at sea . . .
And this shall be for music when no one else is near,
The fine song for singing, the rare song to hear,
That only I remember, that only you admire,
Of the broad road that stretches and the roadside fire.

Louis watched from the doorway as Fanny read the lines slowly, then lifted her mattress and slipped the poem under it.

CHAPTER 84

On a heavenly morning in early July, one of the workers appeared in the yard with black paint on his nose and stripes across his cheekbones. War was at hand.

For the past two months, heated talk had only grown hotter. The consuls of the Three Powers were united behind Malietoa Laupepa and eager to put down any attempt by Mata'afa at a takeover. Every trip into Apia turned up more hysterical gossip. Recently, Louis and Belle had ridden down to one of the balls that the Europeans and Americans put on to amuse themselves. A normally sensible Englishwoman told Louis that he and his family were marked for murder by Laupepa's soldiers the moment the fighting began.

He had come back that night and taken stock of their armory. There were eight revolvers, a half-dozen Colt rifles, and a variety of old swords hanging on walls. He made a drawing of the house and its vulnerabilities. And then he set about cleaning weapons. From that night on, they heard war drums pounding in the distance.

"Poor Lafaele begged to stay here. I told him yes, of course," Fanny said one morning at breakfast. "Whether they support Laupepa or Mata'afa, nearly all the men want to stay out of the fighting."

"I don't know what more I can do," Louis said. His recent attempts to intercede had come to naught. "It will be any day now, I think," he said. "I fear for Mata'afa."

"I will have Lafaele butcher the big pig," Fanny said. "Our people should eat it instead of some party of foragers."

THE WAR WOULD last nine days. It was briefly colorful, as Moors said it would be. And then it was bloody.

"Do you remember what Clarke told us about Samoans choosing

sides in a war?" Louis asked. "He said, 'You will know where they stand when the first shot is fired, and not before.'"

"Apparently, a shot has been fired somewhere," Fanny said sadly.

They were on the verandah, watching a group of their workers talking intently in a huddle on the lawn. Several of the young men had come to her and asked that their wages be held back until the fighting was over.

"Lafaele says that those who go will not support Mata'afa, even though he is a Catholic," she said. "He says they will fight as Malietoa Laupepa's soldiers."

Louis shrugged. "I have no influence over that. I'm going to ride down to town to get the lay of the land. I will speak to Lloyd and Talolo and Lafaele before I go. You'll be safe here."

"I'm going as well."

"Absolutely not."

"Louis . . ."

"I won't go, then."

Fanny looked up at his eyes. "Louis, you are a chivalrous man. But I have never been very good at staying in the back room while the action is out front. I've been in tough situations, and I have always kept my head. If you're afraid that I'm not recovered enough, I can assure you I haven't seen any ghosts today." She patted his arm. "Really, I am tip-top. And I want to see Reverend Clarke. I heard he is setting up an infirmary in the mission house. If this truly is war, they will need me."

He sighed. "Very well."

Is it every former madwoman's worst nightmare to be thought crazy when she isn't? Fanny felt that each conversation with Louis required clear proof of her sanity. Lately, she noticed people's eyes linger a little too long on her, as if weighing the soundness of her remarks. Did they think she was a danger to herself or, worse, to them? She drew in a deep breath. *One foot in front of the other, Fanny.*

In town, they found the streets full of warriors, some of them mere children, with black-painted faces and red bandannas tied around their foreheads, signifying their status as Laupepa's troops. All of them were in a high state of excitement, even the women, who carried food to the front and sometimes followed the men into battle to feed them ammunition. Along the main street, some Samoans were trying to sell their belongings. Old cherished *tapa* mats were being sold for a pittance so the families could get out of town. In the harbor, boatloads of men were coming from other islands to join in the fight.

They went into the general store and talked to the fellow standing in for Moors, who had gone with his wife and a handful of Samoans to Chicago for the Exposition.

"Rich, ain't it?" said the stand-in. "Moors is up in Chicago giving *kava*-making demonstrations, and here I stand, trying to find more ammunition and red kerchiefs and wondering if I got enough bullets to hold down my own fort."

At the mission house, they found Reverend Clarke, who confirmed that war was under way. "Three dead came in," he said, "and several wounded. There is a doctor from the German man-of-war in the other room, doing surgery. I heard eleven heads were taken to the camp of Laupepa. One of the heads belonged to a girl."

"Dear God, how can that be?" Louis said.

"She was probably mistaken for a man," Clarke said. "Her hair was cut short."

Louis went into the surgery room and came back looking peaked. "Two men in there are dying."

WITHIN DAYS, MATA'AFA was thoroughly routed and taken as a prisoner of war to the Marshall Islands, while twenty-three of his subchiefs were jailed in Apia. The war stories flowed into Vailima. Villages burned. Many dead. Mata'afa's son was killed in battle, along with his wife, who refused to stay behind. Fanny and Louis knew them both.

"Never," Lafaele assured Fanny. Never before had women's heads been taken. One warrior was said to have carried a man's head triumphantly to Laupepa, only to discover upon washing off the black war paint that it was the head of his brother.

Mata'afa's men did not take heads, the Vailima men insisted. Fanny didn't know what to believe.

CHAPTER 85

Talolo had laid out Louis's formal clothes—his best white linen suit and his boots polished to a high shine. Dressed and combed, Louis went to Fanny's room and found her at her desk.

"What are you doing?"

"Writing to Kew Gardens," she said. "I want to get this into the mail."

"Hurry now. It's time."

They went out together into the paddock, where their horses were waiting to take Belle, Lloyd, Fanny, and himself to the Apia jail. All of them had taken turns over the past few months, riding down by horseback with food or gifts for the twenty-three chiefs, followers of Mata'afa who'd landed in jail after their defeat. But today would be different. They were to be guests at a feast hosted by the imprisoned chiefs.

The jail was a dreary little building consisting of one room and six cells. It had been absolutely filthy at the beginning of their incarceration, but Louis now paid a man to clean it regularly. Any fool could break out of the jail, but these men stayed of their own accord. It was the responsibility of the prisoners to provide their own support; their people showed up every day with food.

When Louis and his family arrived, they found an almost festive scene outside, with relatives of the prisoners milling about. Entering the building, they were led single-file through a hallway toward the courtyard behind, surrounded by a corrugated metal fence. Fanny stopped in the hallway and looked into a cell. Inside, an old chief they knew named Poe lay on a mat, moaning in pain.

"He wasn't ill when I was here last time," she said, turning to a younger chief. "Do you know what his sickness is?"

"No."

In the outdoor courtyard stood a row of makeshift huts put up by the jailer to alleviate the crowding in the fetid jail. Following their guide to the largest hut, Louis detected the smells of roasted pork, or-anges, cocoa, and rice. Inside, a gathering of eighteen high chiefs awaited them, along with the jailer, who looked nervous indeed. The main chief, named Auilua, was a magnificent-looking creature, tall and muscled, with a square head and massive shoulders that were shiny with oil. Around his thick neck, he wore a large *ula*—a wreath of dried fruit pods painted brilliant red that Samoans wore on special occasions. Auilua arranged the guests alternately among the chiefs. Fanny was served *kava* first, as the wife of himself, the high dignitary of the day. Auilua began to speak, and the interpreter said over and over a particu-lar phrase as he translated: "Tusitala, our only friend."

At the end of the meal, the chiefs approached Fanny and Belle. The men removed their own crimson *ulas* and put them over the women's heads, and then Louis's and Lloyd's. As they emerged from the hut one by one, it dawned on Louis that there was some surprise in the offing, for they were being led to another hut. Inside, they discovered more chiefs and a pile of gifts. Once again, Auilua was master of the cere-mony, speaking of the objects arrayed in front of them as the handi-work of the enslaved chiefs and their families. Exquisite *tapas*, baskets, fans, and a *kava* cup were presented to Tusitala with much fanfare.

Then came a promise. When and if the chiefs are released, Auilua announced, they would build a road to Vailima from the main road to show their gratitude for Louis's unending support.

"Their words are sincere," the jailer assured him as they prepared to depart. "The chiefs told me this giving of gifts to you has never been done for any other white man by Samoan chiefs."

"Sir," Fanny interjected, "I am going to need your help. I want to get Poe out of here so he can be doctored properly. He looks very, very ill. I trust you will perhaps be engaged in some distraction when I come by tomorrow and take him? I'll arrange to have him carried up to Vailima."

The jailer, a softhearted Austrian named Wurmbrand, looked miser-able at the idea but agreed to let her spring the old chief from jail on the morrow. Louis smiled in wonder at the turn of events. He knew it shouldn't surprise him; no matter how storm-tossed his own life had been over the years, Fanny had always found a way to get him to safe ground.

•   •   •

IN THE DAYS that followed, Louis watched Fanny as she tended Poe in Maggie's old bedroom. Though she had done the same thing for Louis a thousand times—brewing broths, putting cold cloths on his forehead—he'd not studied the operation from the outside. He was struck by how competently she brought the old man back in stages, until he could stand on his own feet and walk.

He would regret to his dying day that he'd called her a peasant. *It's a grave mistake to identify a person as one thing, especially one's wife.* The woman he saw was kind, skilled, and generous—his wife of old, but so much more than a tender of others; she was every bit the adventurer he fancied himself to be. She *could* write a book of her own about her life in the South Seas. Courage was her greatest strength, and it had gotten her into places no other whites had been.

Some days she was an explosive engine, but to tamper with her inner workings seemed futile and rather dangerous. She was not his to muck with, anyway. He did not doubt her love or devotion. For the past fifteen years, she'd spent her lavish valor on him. And all the while he'd pined for Scotland, she had wanted only to be by his side.

He meant to explain to her soon something he'd come to understand. She really was an artist, but her art was not something that would be viewed in a museum or contained between the covers of a book. Fanny's art was in how she had lived her own extraordinary life. *She* was her best creation.

In trying to nurse Fanny back from her netherworld, he'd rediscovered something within himself. It had done him good to know an essential decency still resided there. That much had not changed. *In the end, what really matters? Only kindness. Only making somebody a little happier for your presence.*

〜

CHAPTER 86

"A letter from Colvin," Louis remarked when he came out onto the porch, where Fanny and Maggie sat doing needlework. "He starts with just a few tidbits of news, and then— Listen to this."

> *Do these things interest you at all; or do any of our white affairs? I could remark in passing that for three letters or more you have not uttered a single word about anything but your beloved blacks—or chocolates—confound them; beloved no doubt to you; to us detested, as shutting out your thoughts, or so it often seems from the main currents of human affairs, and oh so much less interesting than any dog, cat, mouse, house or jenny-wren of our own hereditary associations, loves and latitudes . . . Please let us have a letter or two with something besides native politics, prisons, kava feasts, and such things as our Cockney stomachs can ill assimilate.*

"Ah, Sidney," Maggie groaned. "Why doesn't he write about the weather?"

"How can such a cultivated man be so appallingly narrow?" Louis asked.

"It appears to be ignorance, and it is, to a degree," Maggie said. "But I just saw Sidney a few months ago, and he adores you, Lou."

"I know that. But with Colvin, it's as if I've betrayed him. He feels I have repudiated my homeland by planting myself here. He forgets it was my *lungs* that rebelled against his precious literary air."

"If I know Sidney," Fanny said, "you will get an apology in the next mail."

Maggie put down her sewing. "Sidney may be tired of Samoan

news, but Henry James laps it up like a kitten. He told me so when I was in London. He follows everything you write about it."

"Colvin thinks I'll lose my powers as a writer by separating myself from my roots. It's the old refrain."

"He's wrong," Maggie said. "You've said yourself that your South Seas stories are some of your best."

"Ignore Sidney's grousing. That's the thinking of a man who lives in the British Museum, after all," Fanny said. "And it's normal for those left behind to feel abandoned when someone they love moves far away. It's a sign of his loyalty."

Louis would write back to tell Colvin that he was still devoted to him but that he could not report any news without mentioning his "blacks and chocolates," because the Samoans were the people among whom he now passed his days. He loved many of them as friends and a handful of them as members of his family. To not discuss them would be to cut off Colvin from his whole life.

No scolding was necessary to remind him how much he missed his friends back in Britain. Maybe it was impossible to stay attached to people when you were separated by ten thousand miles. So much life had occurred for everyone since he was in England. Henley and his wife had had a daughter and lost her, all in the space of five years. Baxter's wife had just died. Symonds had finally succumbed to consumption in Davos. Even Colvin, whose life seemed to have settled into permanent bachelorhood with Fanny Sitwell, had sent news of a change: Fanny's wretched old husband, the vicar, had died. Maybe she and Colvin would finally marry.

Last week's mail had brought news that made Louis feel exceedingly removed from his former life. Adelaide Boodle was going off to be a missionary. Louis had responded with a fatherly letter offering up good wishes, but he was unable to restrain himself from dispensing advice. *Forget wholly and forever all small pruderies, and remember that you cannot change ancestral feelings of right and wrong without what is practically soul-murder.*

How would Adelaide receive such advice? She might well take his words to be those of a world-weary old man. Maybe he was just such a man, for he thought almost every day about death. He couldn't say so to his family, only to Colvin. But he could go at this moment and be glad of the event. *My God, I am nearly forty-four.* Never had he imagined he'd live so long. He had no taste for getting old if he was sickly; he could think of nothing worse than a wasting, prolonged deterioration followed by a tardy death. Healthier now than he had been in many years, he still suffered a host of degrading ailments, even on his best days.

There is much to be thankful for. His mother, energetic and cheerful, had come back from Scotland, and the evening circle on the verandah had grown merrier for her presence. He'd had a long letter from Bob and felt their old bond regenerating in his cousin's friendly words. Money worries had lessened, thanks to Baxter's brilliant idea: a handsomely bound release of Louis's collected works in a set to be called *The Edinburgh Edition.* Best of all, Baxter had promised to come to Samoa with a set of proofs. When that letter arrived, Louis had leaped to his feet and crowed the news to his startled family. "Baxter is coming! Baxter is really coming to Vailima!"

The prospect of his old friend joining them all on the verandah was almost more excitement than he could bear. He had told Baxter about Fanny's troubles, but his friend would not see her as she'd been. Miraculously, in small steps, Fanny had returned very nearly to herself. They were both tender, though, and spoke cautiously to each other. There were sore places that only time might heal.

The next day, bent on exercise, Louis set out to reach the top of Mount Vaea. He had wanted to climb it since they bought their land, so he packed a lunch and threw it into a knapsack.

"A blessing on your journey," Talolo saluted Louis as he departed.

"A blessing on the house," Louis replied in Samoan.

He stepped over branches and vines in the heavy bush, pushing his way upward. It was a sunny morning of crystalline air, dewdrops on shiny leaves, and joyous birdsong. Along the way, he saw majestic banyan trees and an astonishing array of multicolored birds flitting through the forest. The last part of the climb went straight up to a small plateau—the burial place of an ancient chief, Henry Simele once told him.

Sweating profusely when he reached the top, Louis shouted, *"Talofa lava!"* The magnificent prospect fit the requirements for a regal resting place, but there was no sign of humans anywhere.

He sat on the ground eating his sandwich with considerable satisfaction. How quiet it was in this place. How vivid and lovely the birdcalls. He lay on his back to soak up the sun and was flooded with another memory of Scotland.

He used to walk up to Arthur's Seat in Edinburgh, an ancient volcano similar to this place. To climb to that peak was worth it any time of year, but especially in winter, when he could look down and see the frozen ice of Duddingston Loch covered with skaters. He remembered vividly how he'd stayed through a winter sunset to watch one skater spark another's torch until dots of twinkling light flitted across the dark ice.

The sun soaked him through with a peaceful feeling he'd not felt in all too long a time. Sated, he stood and broke up the remains of his bread into crumbs, then scattered them around the mountaintop. Below him he could see white sand beaches, the buildings of Apia, the red roof of Vailima.

It came clear to him as he stood at the top of Mount Vaea. *This is where I shall be buried.*

CHAPTER 87

Louis knocked on the frame of Fanny's bedroom door. "May I come in?"

She looked up from the book she was reading. "Of course."

"Do you want to hear a bit more of *Weir of Hermiston*?"

"Yes," she said.

He sat down on a chair opposite her, but before he started, he blurted out, "I have been downhearted."

"I know. You tend to get down in the dumps just before you write something wonderful."

He shifted in his seat. "What do you say we bury the hatchet?"

"For what?"

"For everything that hasn't been good in the past year," he said. "For all of it. It's not helpful for either of us to carry around the bad old feelings. I would like to return to what we used to have."

"It's that simple?" She shot him an ironic smile.

"Ah, Fanny. I know this life you've had with me hasn't been easy. You've given over a whole chunk of your life to being a nurse. You've had to pick up and move so many times. It occurred to me that I don't ask what *you* long for. You never talk about missing California."

She tipped her head thoughtfully. "Since the day we married, you were my home. I never longed to go back to America. And I never felt lonely until the past year or two."

"You've been lonely?"

Fanny laughed. "How could I not be? You don't come to me when you are thinking something through, or to tell me about your day, as you used to. We have drifted pretty far afield from each other, wouldn't you say?"

"I've made mistakes. I have said things I regret, Fanny." He sighed deeply. "Sooner or later, we all sit down to a banquet of consequences."

"It's my fault, too. I know that. Maybe I've wanted too much of you. But lately, it seems you don't care to know what is inside here." She put her palm to her breast.

"I can see how you might have felt that, but it changed when you broke down. Truly." Louis reached over and picked up his manuscript from the floor. "I want you to listen to this. You remember where we left off, don't you? Archie is at odds with his terrifying father, the lord justice clerk. Archie has denounced his father publicly for hanging a man, and as a result he's been banished to the family's country estate. That's where he meets a woman named Kirstie."

"There are two Kirsties, as I recall."

"Aye. The first one we meet is the aunt, who's handsome, passionate—she's the housekeeper at Hermiston. She spends evenings talking deeply with Archie, ranging over many subjects, and becomes a bit sweet on him, though he's much younger. Later, she introduces him to her niece, Kirstie, a pretty, coquettish girl, and Archie falls in love with her."

Louis read to Fanny for nearly an hour. He stood as he read, and swayed as he felt the rhythm of the sentences in his body. Near the end, he came to a part he'd written about the aunt.

Kirstie had many causes of distress. More and more as we grow old—and yet more and more as we grow old and are women, frozen by the fear of age—we come to rely on the voice as the single outlet of the soul . . . Talk is the last link, the last relation. But with the end of the conversation, when the voice stops and the bright face of the listener is turned away, solitude falls again on the bruised heart. Kirstie had lost her "cannie hour at e'en"; she could no more wander with Archie, a ghost if you will, but a happy ghost, in fields Elysian. And to her it was as if the whole world had fallen silent; to him, but an unremarkable change of amusements. And she raged to know it. The effervescency of her passionate and irritable nature rose within her at times to bursting point.

When Louis glanced up, he saw that Fanny looked troubled. "So I am the elder Kirstie," she said.

"Well, a man's wife gets into his fiction. You are in her to be sure. But there is much Fanny Stevenson in the young Kirstie, too."

He read on, and when he finished, he sought out her eyes.

"It's startlingly good," she said. "Your language is cleaner. Simpler."

"You noticed."

"And the Kirsties—both aunt and niece—are flesh-and-blood women."

"Thank you," he said rather formally. "It's a love story. And there are always problems with a love story."

"I know," she said.

"For instance, I'd prefer to write the sex part of it frankly, the way I write the rest of it," he went on, "but no publisher would allow it to see the light of day." Louis felt Fanny warm to him. He sat down on the bed and rubbed her feet as he used to.

"Does it have a tragic ending?" she asked.

"I don't know. I suppose it should. The funny thing is that I suspect it will have a happy ending. We shall see. This time, when I picked it up again, the words just flowed. I hope it continues at this pace, but I am not going to rush. If I take my time, it may turn out to be the best thing I've ever done." He laughed. "My God, they should put up a plaque at Rutherford's bar as a nudge to all those miserable Scottish lads who long to be writers. I can't tell you how often I hung about that bar pitying myself, despairing of ever writing a full book, let alone ever having a wife."

"Look at you now," she said.

"And what a fine, fine wife I have." He got up and began to pace around the room, his hands fluttering as he talked. "I've been thinking lately, we need to have *fun*. A cotillion is in order, wouldn't you say? I want to see you again in that velvet dress."

"Oh, we've had so many people up."

"Dancing, wonderful food. It *is* one of the things we do well together."

"Throw parties?"

"Some of the best."

"What do you say?"

She looked at him skeptically, and he stopped pacing.

"It's a *normal* thing to do, Fan, a happy thing. That's all."

"All right," she said. "I'm game."

On the afternoon of Louis's birthday, November 13, a hundred people came up the main road and took the new cutoff to the house. Recently completed by the chiefs after their release from jail in August, the new section bore the name they had given it: the Road of the Loving Heart. Friends of every stripe came: British, Samoans, Germans, Americans. The captain of the H.M.S. *Curacoa* brought sixteen of his men. The jailer, Wurmbrand—who'd lost his job for allowing Fanny to sneak old Poe out of the jail—stayed until the end. Grudges were set aside all around as people danced and changed partners.

How strange it was that the hundreds of turns in Louis's life had brought him to the spectacle playing out just now. Never could his bounteous imagination have conjured such a picture when he stood on the North Bridge in a whipping wind, watching the trains leaving Edinburgh and longing, longing to be on one. Around him, the native members of the Vailima clan wore the Scottish plaid *lavalava*s Belle had sewn for them. The seamstress herself, who was flirting with every sailor on the premises, wore a sash in the same plaid.

Louis studied Fanny as she talked to guests, sparkling. She was wearing every diamond in the establishment, from her own earrings to Maggie's necklace and brooch. She looked lovely in her black velvet gown, and he felt a flush of longing for her in the old way. If he could go back to that day on the North Bridge and alter the years that had intervened, he would change a few things. But not this woman.

CHAPTER 88

"Something bad is going to happen today," Fanny fretted at breakfast. "Someone is in danger."

"Well, out with it," Louis humored her. "Who is it?"

"It's not you or me."

"Lucky us!"

She focused her gaze out the window to the lawn, where Austin played tennis with a neighbor boy. "It's somebody else in the family, that much I know. Somebody we love."

"Hmmm. I just saw Lloyd, and he was fit as a fiddle—actually pecking on his typewriter. Unless the ceiling falls in, I think he is quite safe. Belle is under my command this morning until lunchtime. I will only allow her one trip to the privy, and that is all. Austin is . . . well, Austin. We'll have to put Arrick on duty." Louis turned to Maggie. "Mother?" he said. "Health report."

Maggie looked up from a newspaper she was reading with a magnifying glass. "Steady as she goes. No need for Arrick to watch Austin. I'll keep an eye on him."

"Everyone is accounted for, then. Come, let's get you out to your pea patch."

"I don't know, Louis," Fanny said, shaking her head.

"Now, look, Fan. The sun is shining. Christmas is three weeks away. You haven't grown a mustache. Belle is cooking your favorite roast for dinner. Your husband loves you. Tell me, could life be better?"

She smiled grudgingly. "And you are a canary bird."

Louis laughed. It once was one of her cruelest names for him, because of his incessant, chirpy cheerfulness. Now he found it mild. "You haven't brought that one out in a while."

He walked her out into the garden, where Lafaele was hoeing. "Mr.

Archangel," Louis said to him, "would you kindly watch out for Tamai-tai this morning? Don't let her fall in a ditch or some such."

Lafaele assented.

"Do you know what I am dreaming of?" Louis said to her. "A big bowl of salad greens with dinner. Do we still have lettuces?"

"Have you ever known me not to have lettuces?"

"Will you make a nice mayonnaise dressing today?" He kissed her on top of her head.

"Yes."

"Good. I'll help."

A quicksilver change. Last night she had been laughing on the verandah, telling stories about their voyage on the *Janet Nicoll*. Now she seemed hardly fit to stand up in the garden. He walked back to the house and went to his study, where Belle was stationed at the writing desk. "Your mother is having a hard day . . ."

"I know. I noticed it immediately this morning." Belle sighed. "I hope it is not the beginning of a bout, what with Mr. Baxter coming in a couple of weeks."

"If Fanny is depressed, we won't have to pretend around Charles. He's a man for all seasons."

The thought of Baxter lightened his own mood immeasurably. He was already on his way, carrying the proofs of *The Edinburgh Edition*. No one, aside from Colvin or Henry James, could brighten Louis's life in the same way.

"Why don't you go to your mother now and come back in an hour. I'm not quite ready to dictate."

"All right. When she's finished in the garden, I'll get her started on some Christmas decorations."

"Good girl."

Alone, he assessed what he needed for the next chapter of *Weir*. In front of him were papers with phrases penned in his pained scrawl, as well as a history of Lord Braxfield, the lord justice clerk upon whom the coarse character of the father was based. He looked at his simple outline of the plot, waiting for some door to open into the chapter. *This is how it always is. I must sit on my eggs like a hen.*

He understood enough about his working method to know he

would have to be patient; there was no point in forcing words onto paper. What came from his unconscious was the only thing worth writing down for the big moments in his book. And today he was working on a big moment, the instant when Archie must understand that his beloved young Kirstie is more complicated than he realized. That *women* are more complicated than he realized.

Louis sank back in his chair, closed his eyes, and let himself fall into a half-sleep. He saw in his mind's eye the pretty redheaded young lady who used to distract him in church; he heard in his ears the Scottish voices of a half-dozen girls he had known as a youth on the streets of Edinburgh, and in the Pentland Hills when he went to Swanston Cottage on holiday. The Kirsties already had strong Border accents, but he wanted more. He would put old Scots words into their mouths—*bairns* for children, *howl* for hovel, *toon* for town—knowing full well some of his readers would rebel against the strange vocabulary. He would pull them along with enough straight English to make the reading bearable for an Englishman or American.

The voice that next came to him was Thomas Stevenson's. *I would ten times sooner see you lying in your grave than that you should be shaking the faith of other young men and bringing ruin on other houses as you have brought it upon this.* How vividly he remembered his father's enraged outpouring. Those words were precisely the burning vitriol Judge Hermiston would have hurled at his son, Archie. *God knows, they still hurt to remember them.* Somehow he would have to weave in the part about bringing ruin upon the house.

Daydreaming, he heard his own voice, the narrator's voice, and it was more confident than it had ever been. It was telling the story of a young man coming to understand the world. It was the voice of an older Louis speaking of the young Louis through the character of Archie—the sweet poetry-writing soul he once was, in all his joyful, poignant, silly innocence.

Louis sat up straight, grabbed his pen, and began a scene in which Archie arrived late for church because he'd tarried to smell the first blossoms of spring. The first person he must see would be the lovely young Kirstie in another pew. Louis was fairly cackling as he fired off two paragraphs, then stopped to admire his prose.

The lip was lifted from her little teeth. He saw the red blood work vividly under her tawny skin. Her eye, which was great as a stag's, struck and held his gaze.

Ah, young love. There it was. Embarrassing to read? Aye, but only as embarrassing and sweet as it was to experience young love. Anybody who had fallen hard at sixteen or seventeen would feel that moment of recognition. With his cramped hand, he scrawled more sentences and notes before he set down the pen, and laughed out loud. Just then a little knock came on his door.

"Avast, mate!" Louis cried when he saw Austin. "State your business."

"It's time for my lesson. Did you forget?"

"Only for a minute."

The boy came into the room and looked around. "Who were you laughing with?"

"Meself, laddie. I just had a fine visit with the Brownies."

Austin nodded matter-of-factly. He knew about the Brownies.

"And I was thinking that when I'm old and gone, schoolboys like you will someday say, 'There were three Rrrrobbies: Robbie Burns, Robbie Fergusson, and Robbie Stevenson!'"

Austin grinned. "How do you do that?"

Louis opened the boy's mouth and looked inside. "You've got all the parts you need. Roll your tongue around to loosen it up."

The boy wagged his tongue all around.

"Now put your tongue up flat against your palate and blow air out, so your tongue vibrates."

Austin produced a windy flutter.

"Now make the sound of R as you do it. Say 'Rrrrobbie.'"

"Rrrrrrrobbie!"

"Hooray!" Louis shouted.

Austin set down a deck of cards on Louis's desk.

"Ach, my boy. We need to work on a recitation for Christmas dinner."

Austin's face fell.

"We must show your mother and grandmother *something* after all these lessons," Louis said. "They'll think we haven't been working."

They hadn't been. The French lessons often dissolved into games.

"What shall I recite, Uncle Louis?"

"Oh, some welcoming remarks. *Joyeux Noel,* along those lines, but a whole paragraph. I'll make up something."

"When shall I recite it?"

"Before we set doon ta roastit bubbly-jock, laddie."

Austin blinked repeatedly, trying to translate.

" 'Turkey,' you'd say in California. Recite your little speech after the prayer and just before the turkey is served."

"All right," Austin said disconsolately.

"Here now." Louis handed him a few scrawled French sentences. "If you master it quickly enough, we will play a game of cards before we have to eat."

At lunch, Fanny, sitting quietly at the table, was silently suffering. When she caught him staring at her, she said, "I know what you're thinking, that I am a coward for all my worrying. But I'm not. For a woman, I am brave."

Louis went around to his wife's side of the table and put his hands on her shoulders. "There is no question of your mettle, my love. You are the bravest person I know." He pecked her cheek. "After lunch, why don't you and Lloyd have a tour of the cacao field? I noticed a lot of new growth when I was out there yesterday."

Standing on the verandah outside his study, Louis watched the tall son walking beside his wee mother out into the fields. The sweep of Vailima—its lawn, garden rows, fields, and forests rising up toward Mount Vaea—filled his eyes with its grandeur. Suddenly, tears filled them, for he was transported to the foothills of the Highlands near Callander. His mind's eye saw little stone houses, tweedy old men wet from rain entering a low door into a pub. He saw lakes, and smoking chimneys and children in the street. He could swear he smelled peat burning.

Fanny was still miserable at five when he went downstairs. He played a game of solitaire while she watched, so as to cheer her, and then persuaded her to begin the salad. He went to the cellar to fetch a bottle of wine. As he poked around the wine shelf, a line from a Yeats poem repeated itself for the hundredth time in his head: *For always, night and day, I hear lake water lapping with low sounds by the shore.* He'd been drunk on that line for a week. *Damn, it's good.* He wished he'd written it himself. Louis spotted an old burgundy he had been saving. *This will cheer us.*

It was a hot evening. He mixed up a whisky and soda, drank it down, then stood on the verandah next to Fanny, dripping oil slowly into the egg yolk she stirred in a small bowl. Talolo leaned on the porch railing nearby. In the distance, they saw Lloyd returning from a dip in the pool.

"A touch more oil?" Louis asked her, raising the bottle. In that moment, his knees wobbled.

"No, I think—"

"Ahhhh!" he cried out. Fire exploded behind his eyes. "What a pain!" He grabbed his head with both hands. Fanny blurred before him. Reeling, he gasped, "Do I look strange?"

Fanny lurched forward to catch him as he fell to the floor.

"Show me where the pain is," she cried. "Show me."

A gray fog fell around him. He heard wind . . . footsteps . . . there, a beam of light . . .

Fanny watched Louis touch his head. The hand fell, and his eyes closed.

"Lloyd!" she screamed. "Lloyd!" She saw him running toward her. "Go down and get the doctor from the *Wallaroo*. As fast as you can! And get Dr. Funk, too!"

Lloyd galloped wildly out of the paddock on his horse as Talolo lifted Louis's limp body and carried him inside to a chair in the great hall.

The tips of his fingers were cold. Now Maggie was in the room. Fanny rolled up Louis's sleeves, and the two women frantically rubbed his arms with brandy, trying to make the blood flow. Fanny saw how labored his breathing was, and she breathed in time with him until she couldn't take in air that slowly anymore. Lafaele came in, untied the laces of his boots, and pulled them off. Belle brought hot water and rubbed his feet vigorously, while Lafaele laid a cool cloth on his forehead.

The room fell dark as they waited. Some of the natives lit torches outside so the doctors could find their way to the house. Nearly all the Vailima men and women, having heard the word, came into the great room. Some fanned him; others crouched along the walls. Austin sat among them, watching and weeping. The ship surgeon, Dr. Anderson, arrived first. He lifted Louis's eyelids, felt his pulse.

"A cerebral hemorrhage, I'm certain," he told Fanny. He turned to Lloyd. "Can we get some air in here?" Lloyd threw open the windows. The smell of gardenias flooded the room.

Funk, who had treated Louis in the past, arrived from Apia and ordered a bed be brought into the great room so Louis might lie flat. He conferred with Anderson, and the two men worked on Louis for nearly two hours. Dr. Funk finally shook his head sadly and said, "I'm sorry, Mrs. Stevenson. There is nothing anyone can do for him."

When the doctors moved away, Lloyd put his arm under Louis and embraced him.

Fanny watched Louis's chest rise, shudder, and fall as the last ounce of life ebbed from him. She placed her cheek over his chest. His body was warm, but no beat came from his great heart.

"No!" she cried. "No, Louis! Please, no." She raised her head to look at his eyes. "I beg of you. Don't leave me!"

His lids were closed and still. Everything about him was still. He was gone.

CHAPTER 89

Talolo brought down the black dress trousers Louis had made in Sydney, and a white linen shirt. He helped Lloyd and Belle dress him. Lafaele took his hands and laced his fingers together. Belle fetched the British flag that had flown over the *Casco* and laid it across his chest.

Throughout the night, their closest friends came, feeling their way up the road under a sliver of moon. Reverend Clarke knelt with Maggie to pray. The chiefs brought their precious heirloom *tapas* to place over and around him, so that Louis might lie in state like a Samoan high chief. Someone hung a garland of flowers over the headboard. In the flickering candlelight, they kissed his hands. An old chief whispered, "The stones and the earth weep, Tusitala."

One man asked Fanny if the Catholics among them might say their prayers for the dead, and soon *"requiescat in pace"* echoed against the shiny redwood walls.

"He should be buried by tomorrow afternoon," Funk said to Fanny. "This heat . . ."

She was stunned and tried to understand what he was saying. "He wants to be buried on Mount Vaea," she replied.

"It's near impossible to get up there," Lloyd said.

Talolo stood nearby, as if guarding Louis. "It will be done," he said.

At dawn, Fanny woke to the sound of axes cracking into tree trunks and bush knives swooshing through thick viney undergrowth in the distance. She saw she was dressed in her clothes from the day before. For a few seconds, she had no memory of it, and then a bolt of agony ripped through her. She put a pillow over her head and sobbed.

In time, Belle came into the room. She wiped Fanny's face with a cool washcloth and helped her change clothes. "One of the chiefs has made a casket," she said. "Lloyd says about forty natives are out there making a path to the top."

"What shoes," Fanny muttered.

"You can't climb up there, Mama. Nor can Aunt Maggie. Please, don't try. Louis would never want you to."

"Reverend Clarke?"

"He says he is going."

"He will say the church prayers." Fanny went to her bookcase and took out a volume. She opened it and marked the page she wanted. "Are you climbing up?"

"Yes."

"Take this with you. Read aloud these three lines."

Belle read the verse Louis had begun on the emigrant train when he came to America, seeking to marry Fanny.

> Here he lies where he longed to be;
> Home is the sailor, home from sea,
> And the hunter home from the hill.

"All right, Mama, I'll read it."

By afternoon, sixty Samoans and nineteen whites appeared at the house. Several strong chiefs lifted the flag-draped casket and carried it along the Road of the Loving Heart. Fanny walked behind the casket until the road met the steep new trail. Standing near the bathing pool, Fanny watched the strong Samoan chiefs, young and old, heave the box up the track. Teams of men positioned themselves along the trail. One party of sweating and exhausted pallbearers got the coffin to a waiting party of men who took it on the next leg up the mountain. At the front of the procession, a high chief carrying a staff called out the terrible news: *"Tusitala is dead!"* Over and over, his outcries were followed by wails.

Fanny saw Belle go up the path slowly, aided by two Samoan men and followed by Austin, who climbed like a monkey through the bush, gripping thick roots to pull himself up through the mud. When the crowd of mourners disappeared, Fanny turned back and walked to the house. The heaviness in her heart was so great, she thought she might fall over. Her hand went to her chest, and in that gesture, she felt the lump inside her dress. She stopped and pulled the container of ergotin from the little pocket. For most of the eighteen years she had known Louis, she'd carried a vial. *What a useless talisman in the end.*

In the cavernous great room, she found Maggie sitting alone, heaving with grief. Fanny sat down beside her and took her hand. They did not speak. The room grew dim, and then dimmer, as the evening sounds began.

~

CHAPTER 90

1904

Fanny stood on her balcony, gazing toward the bay. The afternoon fog was rolling in and up the hill. Soon the green trees below would be wrapped in its gauze, and the whole house—banisters, door handles, glass—would be dewy moist.

She went inside to the study, where spears and *tapa* cloths hung on the walls, and opened the desk drawer. Her hand found what she was seeking. She took out the slim volume of *Weir of Hermiston,* and for the thousandth time, she read the dedication page.

To My Wife

I saw rain falling and the rainbow drawn
On Lammermuir. Hearkening I heard again
In my precipitous city beaten bells
Winnow the keen sea air. And here afar,
Intent on my own race and place, I wrote.

Take thou the writing. Thine it is. For who
Burnished the sword, blew on the drowsy coal,
Held still the target higher, chary of praise
And prodigal of counsel—who but thou?
So now, in the end, if this the least be good
If any deed be done, if any fire
Burn in the imperfect page, the praise be thine.

The first time she'd seen the verse, it was pinned to her bed curtain in Vailima during the period she'd come to think of as their second courtship. Louis had pulled her out of the darkness with love poems.

Her eyes fell on the letter Henry James had sent to her after Louis's death. She knew the first and last parts by heart. *We have been sitting in darkness for nearly a fortnight, but what is our darkness to the extinction of your magnificent light? He lighted up one whole side of the globe, and was in himself a whole province of one's imagination. We are smaller fry and meaner people without him.*

Henry James had understood her better than any of Louis's other friends, better than Colvin or Baxter. She could still see the look on poor Charles Baxter's face when he found her desolate at Vailima. By the time he arrived, Maggie had returned to Scotland, Lloyd was away, and their beloved family had been dispersed, except for the three Samoans they could afford to pay. It was just Fanny and Belle he found there. Baxter had presented her with the first two volumes of *The Edinburgh Edition* and watched her sob when she held the books in her own hands. The poor man had looked frightened, as if she might be going off her head.

But she had not gone mad. To her surprise, she kept on functioning.

The surly forest ate at the edges of her careful fields and slowly took them back. She applied herself to placing a monument at the top of Mount Vaea where he lay. One side of the stone bore a plaque with Louis's "Home is the sailor" poem. On the other, an Old Testament quotation from Naomi's speech to Ruth: *Whither thou goest, I will go; and where thou lodgest, I will lodge; thy people shall be my people, and thy God my God.*

Fanny had not seen the grave; she would never make it up Mount Vaea until the day others would carry her bones there. Having prepared her resting place next to his made it easier to leave him.

Sometimes during those long, fragrant evenings of his last year, they had sat on the verandah and fantasized about where they would go if they ever left Samoa. He would talk of Scotland, she of San Francisco. "The top of Russian Hill," she told him.

Ten years gone. Would his heart have broken to know she'd given up Vailima, and for so little? She and Belle had stayed on for a couple of years, trying to keep it going, until Fanny couldn't bear it anymore. What was Vailima without Louis? After moving to San Francisco, she lived day to day with a singleminded determination: to get a proper biography of her husband published before she died. It had taken time, but it was done, and not by her own hand, as Louis had instructed if she so chose. Nobody could tell his story better than she, but Fanny couldn't bring herself to do it. She'd known there would be plenty of work for her to do without writing the whole thing herself. There would be judgments to make as she pulled together the thousands of pieces that made up his life. She would gather those pieces and make sure they were correct.

In the end, it was a beloved cousin of Louis's who wrote the *Life of Robert Louis Stevenson*. But Fanny had helped shape it.

"For a man who spent a good part of his life expecting death to appear around the next corner, he was astoundingly cheerful," she told the cousin, who stayed at Vailima as he prepared the book.

"It was one of his finest qualities," the young man said.

"When we lived in Davos, I hated the cold weather. *Hated* it. We would drink coffee in the morning and look out the window at twin mountain peaks in the distance. He asked me one sunny day, 'What do you see?' I shivered and said, 'A lot of ice and two frozen peaks. What do you see?'

" 'I see the blue space between them,' he told me. 'I see a cup full of sky.' "

Fanny's eyes had spilled over when she told that memory. "It's sad that I didn't fully understand at the time what a gift his cheerfulness was. He gave that to me every day I knew him. It's one of the things I miss most."

SHE WONDERED IF Louis would approve of the house she had built to suit herself. Was it extravagantly self-indulgent to have a grand staircase made of step risers shorter than customary, just to suit her short legs? One night, he told her in a dream that it was just fine. But with the cable car rattling below, clanging its bell, with the electric streetlight outside the windows, she knew he could not have abided it here himself.

Fanny got up and went down the curving stairs toward the first floor. The light outside had dimmed, though it still lit the stained-glass window depicting the *Hispaniola* from *Treasure Island*.

It amused Fanny to have an elegant home with such a window. Sometimes she would walk to the Portsmouth Square area where Louis had rented a room while waiting for her divorce to come through. During that time, he had eaten on seventy cents a day. It pained her to think of it. How she wished he might be here to enjoy the fruits of his work.

She had made a life in San Francisco. Lloyd's family lived in an adjoining wing of the house. Dora Williams had a place nearby. Fanny's maid, Mary, was a constant presence. Recently, she'd taken on a wonderful young man, the son of an old friend, as her companion. She was not alone.

Occasionally, she was stopped on the street by someone who wanted to talk about Louis and his work. She knew she was something of a public figure, easily recognized in her loose velvet gowns and lace veils, her arms ringed with bracelets, her neck circled with jewelry, her feet adorned with red dancing slippers. They would look at her and think of the South Seas, perhaps, or *Dr. Jekyll and Mr. Hyde,* or Long John Silver. Well, there were worse things than being known as the eccentric wife of a great man.

If her heart felt empty at times, the rooms of the house on Russian Hill did not. All around her were reminders: the plaster cast of Rodin's entwined lovers; photographs of Louis on the *Casco,* his hair whipping in the wind; Henry James's mirror; *kava* bowls, chunks of coral, a salmon-colored moth the size of a starling, pinned behind glass. And everywhere were Louis's books. His *words.* The conversation continued.

When the city made her tired, she traveled down the peninsula to her ranch. There, on clear nights, she camped in a tent surrounded by the soft brown-shouldered foothills of the Santa Cruz Mountains. She lay with her head out the flap and gazed at the stars—the same ones that coursed over Silverado. Over Hyères, Vailima, Grez. The same stars that glittered above sails and spars at sea.

POSTSCRIPT

Fanny Stevenson devoted the remainder of her life to promoting her husband's literary legacy. She developed a close relationship with her secretary and constant companion, Ned Field, who was forty years her junior. Ignoring gossip, they lived and traveled together. Fanny built a house near Santa Barbara, California, where she died in 1914 at the age of 73.

At the time of her death, Fanny Stevenson had just completed work for the publication of her book, *The Cruise of the "Janet Nichol,"* based on her diary written during that voyage. (Fanny misspelled the actual name of the ship, the *Janet Nicoll*.) Today the book provides valuable insight into the lives of South Seas islanders and nonnatives living there during the end of the nineteenth century.

Belle Strong, Fanny's daughter, married Ned Field in 1914, six months after her mother's death. Together, the Fields took Fanny Stevenson's ashes to Samoa, where they buried them on Mount Vaea, next to Robert Louis Stevenson's remains. Etched into a bronze plaque on the tomb Fanny shares with her husband is her Samoan name, Aolele, as well as the tribute he wrote to her:

> Teacher, tender, comrade, wife,
> A fellow-farer true through life,
> Heart-whole and soul free
> The august father gave to me.

AFTERWORD

Under the Wide and Starry Sky is a novel inspired by actual events in the lives of Robert Louis Stevenson and Fanny Van de Grift Stevenson. R.L.S. was a prolific letter writer whose witty and candid correspondence documents his life before Fanny, and later with her, in a relationship that ranged over an eighteen-year period and vast stretches of the globe. Fanny, too, was an avid writer, a colorful correspondent and diary keeper. Their letters and published works, along with those of their families and friends, provided the main sources for this book. In attempting to bring to life these extraordinary characters, I have occasionally put into their mouths their own written words, and have included a few excerpts from Fanny's diaries and real letters, such as the correspondence between R.L.S. and W. E. Henley regarding "The Nixie." That said, numerous letters and diary entries are invented.

Most useful to me was the eight-volume collection *The Letters of Robert Louis Stevenson*, edited by Bradford A. Booth and Ernest Mehew (Yale University Press, 1994), which serves as a record of Stevenson's voice and personality. Fanny Stevenson's unpublished letters to her friends Timothy Rearden (in the Baeck family papers at the Bancroft Library at University of California, Berkeley) and Dora Williams (housed at the Beinecke Library at Yale) were particularly useful in understanding her time in Antwerp, Paris, and Grez-sur-Loing. I found fascinating the diary Fanny kept during a portion of her two years traveling through the South Seas Islands, published as *The Cruise of the "Janet Nichol"* and edited by Roslyn Jolly. Also of interest was *Our Samoan Adventure*, edited by Charles Neider, which contains the diary Fanny kept while living in Samoa from 1890–93 and Margaret Stevenson's letters, collected in *From Saranac to the Marquesas and Beyond*, and *Letters from Samoa*.

There are numerous biographies available about Robert Louis Stevenson. I found J. C. Furnas's passionate 1951 *Voyage to Windward* to be most illuminating and inspiring. *The Violent Friend,* by Margaret Mackay, a biography of Fanny Stevenson, provided useful information and insights as well. Other helpful biographies include *The Life of Mrs. Robert Louis Stevenson* by Nellie Van de Grift Sanchez; *This Life I've Loved,* by Isobel Field; *An Intimate Portrait of R. L. S.* by Lloyd Osbourne; Ian Bell's *Dreams of Exile* and Claire Harman's *Myself and the Other Fellow.* Among the many accounts written about the Stevensons by friends and acquaintances, I enjoyed *R. L. S. and His Sine Qua Non,* by Adelaide Boodle, for the light it cast on the Bournemouth years.

Stevenson's travel essays serve as personal accounts of specific time periods in his life and informed this book. These include *An Inland Voyage, Travels with a Donkey in the Cevennes, The Amateur Emigrant, Across the Plains, The Silverado Squatters,* and *In the South Seas.* Beyond the essays, novels, short stories, nonfiction books, poems, and musical compositions written by Stevenson, there were a number of other works I found useful. Selected titles include *Happier for his Presence: San Francisco and Robert Louis Stevenson,* by Anne Roller Issler; *Henry James and Robert Louis Stevenson: A Record of Friendship and Criticism,* edited by Janet Adam Smith; *RLS: Stevenson's Letters to Charles Baxter,* edited by DeLancey Ferguson and Marshall Waingrow; *Robert Louis Stevenson and His World,* by David Daiches; *Robert Louis Stevenson,* by G. K. Chesterton; *On the Trail of Stevenson,* by Clayton Hamilton; *The Lighthouse Stevensons,* by Bella Bathurst; *Robert Louis Stevenson: Interviews and Recollections,* edited by R. C. Terry; *The Colvins and Their Friends,* edited by E. V. Lucas; *With Stevenson in Samoa,* by H. J. Moors; and *Chinese Gold: The Chinese in the Monterey Bay Region,* by Sandy Lyden. Those readers who want to know more about R.L.S. and his world can visit an excellent website dedicated to scholarship on his life and works developed and edited by Richard Dury at www.robert-louis-stevenson .org.

ACKNOWLEDGMENTS

I wish to thank the institutions that provided access to the letters and papers of Robert Louis Stevenson, Fanny Van de Grift Stevenson, their family members and friends: the Beinecke Rare Book and Manuscript Library at Yale University; the National Library of Scotland in Edinburgh; the Bancroft Library at University of California, Berkeley; the Danville Public Library in Danville, Indiana; and the Stevenson House in Monterey, California. Special thanks go to the Robert Louis Stevenson Silverado Museum in St. Helena, California, where original manuscripts, first editions, letters, scrapbooks, paintings, clothing artifacts, and other memorabilia illuminated for me the lives and times of this legendary couple.

Many people were helpful during the writing of *Under the Wide and Starry Sky.* Key among them is my stellar editor, Susanna Porter, who has been both guide and fellow voyager since this book's inception. I also want to thank Libby McGuire and Kim Hovey at Ballantine, as well as my agent, Lisa Bankoff, for their enduring support. Various individuals contributed their special knowledge during the research process. I am indebted to Gabina de Paepe, at the Royal Academy of Fine Arts in Antwerp; Françoise Reynaud and Jean-Baptise Woloch at Musée Carnavalet in Paris; Marc Parent for his wonderful support and insights about Paris and French culture; Bernadette Plissart, manager of the Hôtel Chevillon in Grez-sur-Loing; Marissa Schleicher, Dorothy Mackay-Collins, and Dianne and Don Fraser at the Robert Louis Stevenson Silverado Museum; Kris Quist, curator at the Stevenson House in Monterey for the California Department of Parks and Recreation; and John and Felicitas Macfie, owners of Robert Louis Stevenson's childhood home in Edinburgh.

Special expertise came from a handful of translators. Thanks to Pauline Cairns Speitel for help with Scots, Sadat Muaiava for Samoan translations, and Chantal Vogel for French. For nineteenth-century medical information, I appreciate the assistance of James K. Gude, MD.

A loyal group of family and friends has served as readers of *Under the Wide and Starry Sky.* I am grateful to the following people for their perceptive thoughts: Colleen Berk, Sharon Berlin, Frish Brandt, Kathleen Drew, Polly Hawkins, Kathy Horan, Gretta Moorhead, Pamela Todd, and finally to Gail Tsukiyama, who not only read the manuscript but provided me with a bright writing haven during the winter months. Thanks also to Ellen Drew, whose knowledge of the Monterey area led me to this story, to John Drew for his support and help with research, and to Katie B. Ilalio Fa'aloua, Richard Frishman, Brenda Hartmann, Leslie Ladd, Linda Beeman, Dale Christensen, and Steve and Debbie Dells for their contributions. Finally, I wish to thank my sons, Harry and Ben, whose great hearts inspire me, and my husband, Kevin Horan, my constant friend and my own trusted critic on the hearth.

ABOUT THE AUTHOR

Nancy Horan is the author of *Loving Frank*. She lives and writes on an island near Seattle.

ABOUT THE TYPE

This book was set in Garamond, a typeface originally designed by the Parisian type cutter Claude Garamond (1480–1561). This version of Garamond was modeled on a 1592 specimen sheet from the Egenolff-Berner foundry, which was produced from types assumed to have been brought to Frankfurt by the punch cutter Jacques Sabon (d. 1580).

Claude Garamond's distinguished romans and italics first appeared in *Opera Ciceronis* in 1543–44. The Garamond types are clear, open, and elegant.